Collateral Security

by J. Atwood Taylor, III

Dorrance Publishing Co
585 Alpha Drive
Suite 103
Pittsburgh, PA 15238
Visit our website at *www.dorrancebookstore.com*

ISBN: 979-8-88812-241-9
eISBN: 979-8-88812-741-4

Introduction

Trey Fitzjames arrived at his office, as was his custom, at 8:45 in the morning. On this day, contrary to the office protocol promulgated and promoted by the managing partner, Fitzjames entered by the front door, not the back entrance. Generally, Fitzjames used the front door because he wished to see who might be in the firm's lobby awaiting his arrival, and he had a further interest in being seen by the receptionist. In this way, she would know that he had arrived and not needlessly search for him if a telephone call were made to him. Mark Petersen, the managing partner, chided him for the rule violation. Fitzjames ignored him and then, with a wry smile, would encourage him to promulgate other pointless regulations and thus justify his role as the managing partner of a small law firm.

Upon entering his private office, Fitzjames re-ordered the files and paperwork on the desk and then powered on the computer. For the succeeding ten minutes, he reviewed and responded to email messages and surveyed the calendar for the day and for the remainder of the week. The morning was clear, although he did have a scheduled early lunch with a client. He looked forward with some dread to the luncheon, which promised to be, he was confident, an exercise by which the client would probe him for advice for an hour and hence would receive $300.00 in legal services in exchange for a $25.00 meal. But he was pleased to have no meetings in the morning and before lunch. He could get some work finished without interruption.

Fitzjames repositioned a client's file from the corner of his desk to a place immediately in front of him and opened it. He surveyed the correspondence and a list that he had made of issues that must be addressed and resolved before the transaction could close. As he began the exercise of revising a closing document, the telephone chimed. The receptionist then spoke over the speaker.

"Mr. Fitzjames?" she asked by way of introduction.

"Yes," he replied.

"Mr. Fitzjames, a Mr. Fuller is here to see you. He says that he doesn't have an appointment but would be grateful if you'd take a few minutes to speak to him. He also says that he only requires a few minutes."

"Is there a conference room that's free that we could use?" inquired Fitzjames.

"Yes, sir, you could have the main conference room, until 10:00."

"Very good. Please get Mr. Fuller a cup of coffee, if he wants one, and seat him in that conference room; I'll be in in a moment."

Fitzjames put the uncompleted document in the file and closed it. He snatched up a canary yellow legal pad of paper off of the desk and a different pen from the one he had used a moment earlier. He exited his office, walked down the hallway and down the short flight of carpeted stairs, opened the closed doors of the main conference room, and entered. He closed the doors behind him and confirmed that they were secured.

Fuller, who had been in a seat at the conference room table, rose to his feet upon Fitzjames' entry. Fuller extended his hand in greeting. Fitzjames took it.

"Please sit, sir," responded Fitzjames.

"Bit unconventional, my arriving here at your office without advance notice and then holding myself out as a client interested in speaking to you," returned Fuller, retaking his seat.

"Yes, sir, bit unconventional. But, I'm prepared to assume that there's a reason for the unconventionality." Fitzjames too pulled out a chair and sat across the table facing Fuller.

"Yes, Captain, there is a reason," said Fuller.

"And, the unconventionality worked. I'm here to be seen, and I'm confident my receptionist believes that you're a client. How can I help, sir?" inquired Fitzjames.

"Particularly busy, at present?"

"With my practice, sir?"

"Yes. Could you break away, soon, easily?"

"Not easily, sir, but I can do it. It's my duty, after all. I made the commitment."

"I recognize that," said Fuller. "But you only just returned from the last assignment, and I appreciate that you have partners to keep happy and duties in your civilian life that aren't so easy to dismiss or ignore. I also don't want anyone here getting too interested in these calls away from work. The operations are intended to be clandestine, and we don't want to give away anything— even who you are and what you're doing."

"My partner, Mark Petersen, can be trusted and relied upon. He's discreet. He's got to be because of his practice, sir."

"What does he do?" asked Fuller.

"Family law. Divorce work, primarily, sir."

"Ah, I understand. You're correct there."

"I'll speak to Petersen and provide the customary explanation. He'll likely quiz me for more information. I'll dodge any deep inquiries. It'd be helpful, sir, if I had something to give him, as a blind."

"Tomorrow I'll arrange for a note to arrive about your Aunt Peggy's death. That should provide sufficient cover."

"My Aunty Peggy, sir?" asked Fitzjames with a smile.

"Yes, Captain. Your aunt who died today. You'll need to get away to be with family. Bereavement, you know, takes time."

"And, sir, where did my Aunt Peggy die?"

"Pittsburgh," replied Fuller.

"Really? That's somewhat unexpected. I had anticipated a death somewhere outside the country," replied Fitzjames.

Fuller unzipped and opened a thin, fine leather briefcase, which he had placed on the top of the table when he had entered the conference room. He removed a thick file and pushed it across the tabletop to Fitzjames.

"The details of the mission are set out there," said Fuller, tilting his head toward the file. "Don't open it here. Do it in the privacy of your office in a few minutes."

"Yes, sir," said Fitzjames, as he placed his left hand on the file and rested his left arm on the tabletop.

"Pittsburgh is the starting point. The details in the file will explain why. It gets bigger, as do the objects of the operation. After you've committed the contents of the file and recognition codes to memory, utilize the standard procedures for its destruction. Clear?"

"Yes, Major. Clear, sir," answered Fitzjames.

"Well, I'll leave then. You have everything," said Fuller.

"Very good, sir. Thanks for the visit. I'll show you out. I do that, of course, for clients," noted Fitzjames, who stood and waited for Major Fuller to rise.

"Good," said Fuller, who got to his feet and closed his briefcase.

Fitzjames escorted Fuller out of the conference room and beyond the receptionist's desk and to the lobby, where they again shook hands. Fuller left the office and Fitzjames, with the file tucked under his left arm, returned to his desk. He picked up the telephone receiver and pressed the extension to Mark Petersen's office.

"Yes, Trey?" asked Petersen, in lieu of an ordinary greeting. Petersen clearly had noted on the monitor of his telephone that the call was internal and had come from Fitzjames.

"Mark, I need to chat. Problem."

"Not a firm problem, I hope," said Peterson discouragingly.

"No, no, not a firm problem. Death in the family. Need to get away."

"I'm sorry, Trey. My condolences. Who was it? Not anyone close, I hope. I am sorry."

"No one terribly close. My Aunt Peggy."

"I don't recall you ever mentioning an Aunt Peggy. Mom's side or dad's?" queried Petersen.

"Neither. Close friend of the family. Called her Aunt Peggy because of how we all felt about her. She died in Pittsburgh. I'll need to get away. May I come down and see you and discuss it?" asked Fitzjames.

"Sure, come down. I've got a few minutes. We'll make it work," replied Petersen with the good-natured lilt in his voice that was so typical of him.

"Thanks. I'm on my way."

Fitzjames returned the receiver to the cradle. He paused and shook his head. The file was still under his arm, as he pressed it to his side to hold it in place. He disliked prevarication but appreciated its necessity, at intervals.

One

Fitzjames' flight from Orlando to Pittsburgh was simple and uneventful. *Southwest* flew regularly out of Orlando to the city. The flight was direct with no layover in Baltimore. Fitzjames gave the Southwest officials the credit for being wise enough in not routing passengers to Pittsburgh through its hub in Baltimore. The professional football fans of the two cities were locked in mortal combat annually for division supremacy in the NFL's AFC North Division. Very likely, the Pittsburgh fans would have found it particularly galling to be forced through Baltimore, with its sea of Ravens supporters, before arriving home.

The airplane touched down in the early evening. After the landing, Fitzjames walked through the terminal, beyond the statues of Franco Harris and George Washington, both of which prompted a smile, and collected his single suitcase at baggage claim. From there, he stepped outside into the cold and waited for a few minutes in a line for taxis. Once in the cab, the driver began making inquiries of him and about the nature of his business in Pittsburgh. Fitzjames, although friendly, was reticent. The driver, as a result, took the hint and shifted away from interrogation and moved to tour direction.

Fitzjames thus passed the twenty-five-minute ride from the airport, through the tunnel, and into the city proper under a stream of details from the driver about Pittsburgh and about its history and surroundings. The description was not unpleasant and proved informative. Fitzjames had previously visited the city and appreciated the driver's knowledge and enthusiasm. He was tipped accordingly.

Fitzjames stepped out of the taxi in front of a modest hotel in the Shadyside district of Pittsburgh. The hotel was part of a chain created by a high-end resort company. It was clean, orderly, and inexpensive. Although he was accustomed to and preferred more luxurious accommodations, he was satisfied. Also, his orders had been that he was to take a room in this particular hotel. The military had selected it because of its location adjacent to the hospital.

With his backpack over his left shoulder and his suitcase in his right hand, Fitzjames approached the front desk and was greeted warmly by the clerk, a young college-age woman. She was short, somewhat plump, but cute.

"Good evening. Are you staying with us this evening?" she asked, almost with a giggle upon seeing Fitzjames. He was handsome, and she was not accustomed to good-looking men taking rooms in the hotel. She also had a distinct Pittsburgh accent.

"I am. My name is Fitzjames. R. P. Fitzjames. You should have a reservation for me," he replied.

"Let me check, one second, sir," she said, as she reviewed a computer monitor. "Yes, Mr. Fitzjames, two nights. Is that correct?"

"Yes," he returned.

"Give me one moment, and I'll complete the paperwork. Do you need one key or two?"

"One's sufficient. Thanks."

Within a few moments, the clerk placed a single sheet of paper in front of him for signature, which he signed and returned to her. She created a plastic room key in the device intended for that purpose and presented the key to him. He observed that she had beautiful hands and expertly manicured fingernails. She also wore a ring on each finger, including on both thumbs. The manner in which she delivered the key to him, by sliding it slowly over the desktop, struck him as being intended to showcase her hands.

"Here you are," she said, tapping the key with the index finger of her right hand. "Room 310."

"Thank you. You certainly do have a lot of rings. You've also spent some time in front of a manicurist," said Fitzjames good-naturedly.

"Yes, thanks. Do you like them?"

"The rings?" he inquired, uncertain whether she referred to the jewelry or the nails.

"Yes."

"Indeed. They're lovely. Very nice."

"Thanks. Each one has special meaning and sentimental value."

"Really? All ten of them?" asked Fitzjames with a mark of incredulity.

"Yes."

"Fascinating. Well, tell you what. I'll come back by here at some point, and you can give me the details on each one, unless that's prying and too personal," he said.

"Not at all. That'd be great. I'd love to tell you about them." She paused and then added, "Well, Mr. Fitzjames, we're glad you're staying with us. I hope you'll enjoy your stay."

"I'm certain I will. You can call me Trey. 'Mr. Fitzjames' is a bit formal."

"Okay, thanks. Have a good evening, Trey."

"I'll do so. And, your name is Cindy."

"Yes, but how did you know that?" she asked.

"The name was on the paperwork I just signed—Cynthia Polanski. Am I right?"

"Yes. That's fantastic that you would see that. No one ever pays any attention to that sort of thing."

"Cindy, could you make a recommendation of a restaurant nearby? I've not had any supper, and I'm pretty hungry."

"Sure. What d'you like? How much ya wanta spend?" she asked. As she relaxed in her conversation with him, her local accent grew stronger.

"Price is not a major issue. Something American, not ethnic. Not tonight, anyway."

"I've just the place for ya. It's called *Cruet*, and it's not far away. You could walk or you could take the hotel shuttle. He'll be back in a few minutes. He's runnin' another guest to another restaurant just now. Come back down in ten minutes, and he'll be back. I'll tell him to wait."

"Terrific, thanks. I'll do that."

With another smile and a nod of his head, he picked up the suitcase, strolled toward the elevator, and pressed the button. He had a moment to study the lobby and to locate the fitness room of the hotel, the lounge, and the limited dining area. He entered the elevator, ascended to the third floor, found Room 310 without difficulty, opened the door with the plastic room key, stepped inside, and dropped the suitcase at the door. He switched on the light in the bathroom and the light on the bedside table. He put the backpack on the writing desk and removed his mobile telephone. He placed a call.

"I'm here. In the hotel," said Fitzjames.

"Good. Your contact will meet you tomorrow morning, as scheduled, at the hospital."

"Very good, thank you, sir."

After the call, he entered the bathroom, unwrapped a bar of soap, and washed his hands and face. After drying, he collected his telephone, room key, and wallet and returned to the lobby. As he approached the front desk, he was again greeted with enthusiasm by the night clerk.

"Hi, Trey. I told Gerry, the shuttle driver, to be ready for ya. He's just outside," she said.

"Thanks."

"I hope ya like the place. Cruet is really good. I sure like it, when I get to go there."

"I'm sure it'll be great. I'll see you, then, after a while," he replied.

Fitzjames greeted the shuttle driver who, in response, opened the sliding door of a Chrysler minivan without any return greeting. The driver was a young man of college age, too, like Cindy, the clerk. Fitzjames surmised aloud if all of the hotel employees were young. He did so in part to open a conversation.

"My goodness, does this hotel hire only university students?" he asked.

"No, no, sir," answered the driver quietly and somberly. "But the night shifts have more young folks because we're all tryin' to pay our way through college."

"Where do you go?" inquired Fitzjames as the minivan pulled out of the parking lot.

"Carnegie Mellon," responded the driver.

"That's not cheap. I understand why you're working. Great university. Are you studying engineering?"

"Biomedical engineering," he said.

"Well, great school, difficult major. You must be a bright boy," said Fitzjames warmly.

"Sir?" questioned the young man.

"Sorry, I meant no offense. Didn't mean to be condescending but complimentary. You're obviously very capable. Must be tough, though, to get all your studying done and also work at nights," said Fitzjames.

"Yes, sir. Very tough. But I have Cindy to keep me company. That helps," said the driver with a curious directness, if not hostility, in his voice.

"Indeed," answered Fitzjames, recognizing that Cindy's obvious interest in him may have been directly or indirectly conveyed to the young man and offended or annoyed him.

"Here we are, sir. Cruet is just there to the left on the corner. You can get out here, just be careful crossing the street. The cars come down the hill fast and through the intersection, if you don't wait for the light to change before crossing the street."

"Thanks for the hint. I'll be careful. Here's five bucks. Thanks for the ride," said Fitzjames and put the five-dollar bill on the console between the two front seats. Fitzjames opened the door to let himself out of the van.

"Sir, we can't take tips," said the driver over his right shoulder while reaching for the bill.

"Keep it. You need it for college. I'm happy to do it."

Fitzjames exited the van onto the sidewalk before any further objection to the tip could be made by the driver and closed the door behind him. The minivan passed in front of him, and he checked the traffic signal. It was green but there were no cars. Just as Fitzjames considered dashing across the road, despite the signal, a truck appeared, traveling at high speed and descending the hill to Fitzjames' left. The truck exploded through the intersection with recklessness. The driver had been correct and the advice was well taken. At the same time, while he waited a few seconds for the light to change to permit him to cross the roadway, Fitzjames speculated, with a smile, about whether the shuttle driver would not have rather seen Fitzjames eliminated than compete for Cindy's affections. He resolved to forego politely the discussion about her rings.

Fitzjames entered Cruet, which was high-end and was nearly full of customers, at 9:15 in the evening. The hostess offered a table to him, but he chose to sit at the bar. A table for one was odd and awkward. At the bar, he took one of the three empty stools. Three others were occupied, at the other end of the bar, by two overweight middle-aged men in business suits seated tightly on either side of a woman who appeared to be approximately thirty-five years old. She was slim, dressed in professional attire in a skirt and satin blouse with buttons on the front. She also wore dark stockings and high-heeled shoes that appeared to Fitzjames to be of quality, although he could not discern the maker. Her hair was shoulder-length, a very light brown. She was very attractive. The two men, one of whom was nearly bald and the other had unnaturally colored hair, spoke to the woman in elevated voices that were pointlessly loud for the restaurant. Both also laughed at every comment made by the other, none of which was at all humorous. They were drinking whiskey and had had too much. When the bartender placed a cocktail napkin on the bar top before Fitzjames and asked him what he would like to drink, one of the men called to the bartender by name.

"Johnny, another Jack Daniels," ordered the man, holding up an empty glass and shaking it. The ice cubes clicked against the side of the glass.

The bartender stepped away, thus forcing Fitzjames to wait.

"Sorry, sir," said the man to Fitzjames. "Local privilege."

Fitzjames made no reply. The bartender pulled from the shelf the black-labeled bottle, added additional ice to the man's glass, and filled it with the whiskey.

"Me too, Johnny," shouted the other man. He pushed his empty glass toward the bartender. Both men laughed. In silence, the bartender followed the same routine for the second man.

"Thanks, pal," said the second man. Both men again chuckled.

The bartender returned the bottle of Jack Daniels to its station among the other bottles of spirits and liquors above the sink in the bar. He returned to Fitzjames with an expression of discomfort on his face.

"My apologies, sir," he said under his breath.

"No problem," replied Fitzjames. "Local privilege. I understand."

"I suppose so. What can I get for you, sir?"

"Vodka martini, with Ketel One vodka and Martini and Rossi dry vermouth. One part vodka, three parts vermouth, three olives, over ice, please," said Fitzjames mechanically. He looked at the face of the bartender while giving the order, but his senses were all directed to the two men and the woman at the opposite end of the bar.

"Yes, sir, one part vodka, three parts vermouth?"

"Correct. With olives, on ice," said Fitzjames.

"Very good, sir."

The woman said something to the men that Fitzjames could not understand, although he could hear her voice between their chatter and laughter.

"You've got to go to the bathroom again?" asked the man, who was seated more closely to Fitzjames.

The woman had pushed back the barstool to rise. After a few seconds of further discussion and over an objection from the other man to another visit to the ladies' room by the woman, she extricated herself from between the men, re-ordered her skirt, and moved quickly to the restroom at the back of the restaurant. The two men now spoke in undertones to one another. When the bartender placed the martini on the napkin, Fitzjames ignored the drink and got to his feet and took the same path toward the restrooms as the woman had taken. The two men watched him and continued their discussion.

At the door to the ladies' room, Fitzjames waited. After some two minutes, the door opened and the young woman stepped out and was startled by Fitzjames' presence. She hesitated and then turned to return to the bar.

"Look, sorry to intrude. None of my business, I know, but are you okay? Everything all right?" he asked.

"What?" she responded.

"Are you okay? Are you safe? I just had a bad feeling and decided it made sense to ask."

"Well, thanks. Yes, I suppose I'm fine. They're just drunk, and I suppose think I'm easy. I'd really prefer to leave but managed to forget my purse. So, I've no money, no credit cards, no cellphone. And, they drove. So, I'm at their mercy."

"I'll have the hostess call a cab for you. I'll pay the fare. You can pay me back sometime."

"You can't do that. I don't even know you."

"I'm just visiting Pittsburgh. I'll give you my card in a moment. Now, I'm getting you a taxi. Follow me."

"This will likely cause a scene," she urged.

"Doesn't matter."

"They're not going to like it and may get belligerent," she said.

"Again, doesn't matter. I'll manage them. Couple of overweight, obnoxious middle-aged men who've had too much whiskey shouldn't be much trouble," he answered with a smile. "Don't worry yourself. Now, let's go."

The young woman followed Fitzjames from the restrooms, through the occupied tables of diners, to the front of the restaurant to the hostess station. As they emerged, the two men turned away from the bar and faced the woman and Fitzjames from across the room. Neither man rose from his respective barstool. Fitzjames instructed the hostess to telephone a taxi for the woman. The hostess picked up the receiver and nervously placed the call.

"Stacy, what are ya doing?" shouted one of the men at the woman.

"You can't leave with that guy. You're with us. We're going to take you home," yelled the second man.

"Hey, pal, who do ya think ya are?" asked the first man of Fitzjames.

Both men struggled off the barstools and on equally unsteady feet approached the hostess station. The restaurant had quieted as other patrons ended their conversations to watch and listen to the proceedings being directed by Fitzjames.

"The cab will be here in a moment," said the hostess to Fitzjames, although she was not looking at him but at the two men walking toward her.

Another woman appeared and stepped behind the hostess. Fitzjames presumed that she must be the restaurant manager.

"We'll wait outside for the taxi," said Fitzjames. "Avoid any trouble inside."

"Good idea. Thank you," responded the manger. She too studied the men, who had taken up positions behind Fitzjames and the young woman.

Fitzjames extended his left arm in invitation to the young woman to precede him out the door. He stood between her and the men. She glanced back at the men and in silence accepted the invitation. As she took the first steps toward the outside, Fitzjames moved his right hand to the middle of her back to create a barrier. The woman made no objection, but the movement incensed the two men.

"Listen, pal, ya can't do this. She came with us, and she's leavin' with us," announced the balding man.

"That's right, bud," said the other man, who put a hand on Fitzjames' left shoulder.

"Take your hand off my shoulder. I don't want any trouble. But if you don't remove your hand, I'll put you on the ground," responded Fitzjames quietly, quickly, and with a determination in his tone that prompted the man to comply.

Fitzjames and the woman walked out the door unmolested. They stood in the dark, in the cold, and in a light rain.

"Why don't we wait under the overhang, rather than in the entry to the restaurant," suggested Fitzjames. "Being out of sight from the interior might be prudent."

"Okay. That's sensible. I really do appreciate what you've done."

"It's my pleasure. I hope I haven't overcooked the thing a bit. Too dramatic. But I did have a bad feeling, and I trust my gut instincts in situations like that."

"Now that we're out here, I can tell you, I was pretty worried. Too much booze and too many roaming hands. Not good."

"Precisely. Here's the cab, now."

The taxi stopped at the entrance to Cruet. The driver opened his door to exit but closed it again when Fitzjames opened the back door on the passenger side and the woman lowered her head and quickly climbed inside the vehicle. Fitzjames closed the door behind her and opened the front passenger door. He spoke to the driver.

"Here's fifty bucks. Take here wherever she tells you. You can keep whatever is left as a tip," said Fitzjames.

"Got it," said the driver. He put the taxi in drive.

From the front of the taxi, Fitzjames passed to the woman a business card, which she accepted.

"I can't thank you enough. You've been extraordinarily kind," she said.

"It's no problem. I'm giving you the card so you'll call me to tell me you've gotten home safely. The cell number is on the card."

"Thank you again."

Fitzjames shut the door, and the taxi departed. He had not recognized that the two men had followed him outside and were standing behind him. They had said nothing while he spoke to the cab driver. He turned to find them both confronting him.

"We don't know who ya think ya are, pal. But you had no business doin' that. She was with us," said the balding man in loud, slurred speech. His accent had thickened, and he nearly expectorated the words. His companion followed.

"You some sorta self-appointed guardian angel for women, bud?" he asked with hostility and, with both hands on Fitzjames' chest, shoved him backwards.

Fitzjames held up both of his hands to both men. He took a further step in the reverse direction in order to put at least two yards between himself and the men.

"Look, fellas, I don't want any trouble. As far as I'm concerned, the matter is over. She's gone, and I'm going back inside to finish my drink and have something to eat."

In reply, the bald man cocked back his right arm, balled his fist, and lunged forward to strike Fitzjames. The man moved surprisingly quickly and ably, given his age and size and the quantity of liquor he had drunk. He was clearly accustomed to street fighting. Fitzjames darted to the left to avoid the blow. He grabbed the man's wrist and, with the arm fully extended, swung the man around and against the exterior wall of the restaurant. Fitzjames penned the man to the wall with his left forearm on the back of the man's neck and his right hand still on the man's wrist. The man's companion stood aside and made no effort to assist his friend. He recognized, apparently intuitively by the speed of Fitzjames' response, that Fitzjames would have little difficulty managing both of them.

"I want no trouble," repeated Fitzjames. "Now, I'm going back inside, and you two are leaving."

Fitzjames released the man and again stepped back to put space between him and the second man. He positioned himself for a second attack. But, the bald man, who was panting and who had an imprint of the exterior wall on his right cheek from having had his face pressed against the cold stone, addressed his companion.

"Let's go, Charlie. You can drive."

Without an immediate verbal acknowledgment, Charlie followed the suggestion and stepped down and off of the sidewalk and into the roadway in order to give Fitzjames a wide berth.

"Yeah, I'll drive," he said and began the walk to the parking lot.

The bald man adjusted his suit coat, glared for a few seconds at Fitzjames, and turned and followed his friend. Fitzjames remained in the same spot until the two men had reached their car. When he heard the engine engage, he reordered his own clothes and reentered the restaurant. He returned to the bar and retook his seat. His drink was still on the countertop with the napkin underneath the glass.

"The drinks and food are on the house," said the bartender.

"That's not necessary," said Fitzjames.

"Manager's orders. She'll probably come over and thank you personally in a minute. Would you like to see a menu?"

"Yes, thanks. I'm hungry, but I just need a salad. Bit too much activity for a heavy meal. And, it's late."

"We've got great salads," replied the bartender. "Take a look at the menu and decide what you'd like."

The bartender presented the menu to him. As he accepted it, Fitzjames' mobile telephone rang, and he answered.

"Hello."

"Mr. Fitzjames?" inquired the caller.

"Yes."

"I've reached home. Thank you again. I'll send you a check for fifty dollars. The cab driver got a huge tip. I don't live too far away. Should I make the check to the address on the card?"

"It's no problem. Don't worry about it."

"No, fifty dollars is a lot of money. I've got to reimburse you. I'll send the check to you to the address on your card. You were so kind. Well, goodnight and thank you again," she said.

"My pleasure," he replied.

He surveyed the menu, ordered a large salad of greens, tomatoes, and pine nuts, and then drank the martini. The ice had melted into the vodka and vermouth.

Two

The following morning the alarm in the hotel room awoke Fitzjames at 5:30. He rose from the bed, entered the bathroom, and washed his face and brushed his teeth. He put on running shorts, a t-shirt, running socks, and running shoes. For a moment, he stretched his legs and shoulders. He switched on the television with the remote device to determine the external temperature. It was just above freezing. He had packed cold-weather running gear, but it was dark and he did not know the streets and potential hazards sufficiently to justify a run out of doors. He powered off the television and collected the room key. He left the hotel room and traveled down the elevator to the fitness center. For thirty-five minutes, he did a tempo run on the treadmill. He disliked running on a treadmill. But on this morning, it was the only suitable alternative.

By 6:45, he had showered and dressed for the day and returned to the hotel lobby. His clothes were casual, Wrangler blue jeans, a polo short-sleeved shirt, and oxford sandy bucks. He also carried a windbreaker. He approached the front desk, and Cindy greeted him.

"Good morning, Trey," she said enthusiastically.

"Good morning, Cindy. You've certainly been on duty a long time—two shifts?"

"Yes, double duty, back to back. I covered for another girl yesterday on the B shift. I'm normally on the C shift, eleven to seven. So, I get to quit in about fifteen minutes or so. How was Cruet last night?"

"Good. Bit eventful, but good. Good food."

"Eventful?"

"Well, there was some trouble with some unruly patrons at the bar. Another patron, fortunately, sorted it out. The restaurant staff was grateful. Nice place. Thanks for the recommendation."

"You're welcome. But, I expected you back to talk about my rings. Remember?"

"Oh, yes, sorry. I was a bit worn out after dinner. A lot of traveling, I suppose. Wiped me out. Also, I got the impression from the shuttle driver that perhaps I was invading his territory," remarked Fitzjames with a smile.

"Oh, him, no, of course not. Well, maybe he wouldn't have liked it. He likes me; there's no doubt about that. We're dating, sorta, but nothing formal. No pledges."

"I understand. But I didn't want to intrude. I'm confident that I would've offended him, which would've been unnecessary. Can you tell me where I can get some good coffee?"

"Our coffee here is pretty good. It's also free. The dispensers are right behind you next to the lounge."

"I was thinking of something of a little higher quality. And, I don't mind paying for it."

"There's a Starbucks right outside and around the corner. There's also a Panera Bread down the street."

"Starbucks sounds good. Just outside?"

"Yes. Just step out and turn to the right. Ya can't miss it."

"Thanks. Thanks for your help. Have a great day, Cindy."

"Thanks, you too."

Fitzjames smiled again and nodded and strolled out the sliding glass doors of the hotel. A gust of wind greeted him, and he put on the jacket. The Starbucks was an appurtenance to the hotel. He entered, waited behind three other customers to place his order, paid for and received a tall cup of coffee, added cream, and exited. The coffee diminished the cold. He looked up at the sky, which was overcast and gray. He considered that it might remain cold throughout the day.

The walk from the Starbucks to the Oakland Northside Hospital was brief. He was due at 7:30. No recognition codes were required, and he had no obligation to conceal his identity. He entered through the main entrance of the hospital and was greeted by a middle-aged woman dressed in a nurse's uniform of white and pink. The outfit reminded him of the uniforms worn by young female hospital volunteers—Candy Stripers.

"May I help you?" she asked kindly.

"Yes, thank you. My name is Fitzjames. I'm scheduled to meet a Mr. Greenbaum at 7:30 this morning."

"I'll telephone his office to let him know that you're here. Mr. Fitzjames?"

"Yes, Fitzjames."

"Very good. Why don't you have a seat. It's not quite at the half-hour. But I'll let his office know that you've arrived."

"Thanks."

Fitzjames took a seat in the empty lobby. The receptionist made the call as promised but did not speak again to him. He presumed that an early arrival was not anticipated and that he would simply be forced to wait until 7:30. He glanced at his wristwatch, a *Breitling*, and concluded that he would have a fifteen-minute wait. He observed a stack of well-used magazines, got to his feet, selected a recent but not the most current issue of *Newsweek*, and sat down again. Before he could pass beyond the initial pages of the magazine, he was interrupted.

"Fitzjames?"

"Yes," he said to a man standing before him.

"How are ya? I'm Owen Hughes. I've been sent along to participate in your meeting with Greenbaum."

Fitzjames stood and shook Hughes' proffered hand. "Nice to meet you," said Fitzjames.

"Nice to meet you. So, how're ya enjoying our fair city? Little chilly today after the rain last night."

"Yes, cold for a Florida boy. But I like it. Change of pace. If it'd been warm, I'd have been disappointed. Great town."

"First time in Pittsburgh?"

"No. I've visited once before. I spent a week. Nearly made a Steelers fan out of me."

"That's good. Well, welcome back."

"Thanks."

"Been waiting long?"

"Only a couple of minutes."

The receptionist interrupted the men's conversation to announce that Mr. Greenbaum's assistant would be down in a moment to greet them. Hughes thanked the receptionist with great warmth and apparent familiarity. Fitzjames turned and returned the magazine to the collection from which he had taken it. When he turned back, a young woman had joined them. Her approach had been oddly indiscernible.

"Good mornin', Mary," said Hughes with the same friendliness and recognition that he had employed with the receptionist.

"Good morning, Mr. Hughes. Nice to see you again. Are you Mr. Fitzjames?" she inquired.

"Yes, I'm Trey Fitzjames. Good morning."

"Follow me, then, gentlemen. It's early, but Mr. Greenbaum is ready to see you."

Fitzjames and Hughes followed Mary through a set of double doors that swung open after Mary applied a four-digit code on a keypad adjacent to the doors. They walked slowly down a long corridor and then turned to the right to an elevator. They took the elevator to the second level. The hospital administration offices were situated immediately off the elevator. Mary led the two visitors through her office and to Greenbaum's. The wooden engraving in the center of the door to Greenbaum's office indicated that the office was occupied by the hospital's chief administrator. She knocked twice and paused.

"Come in," announced Greenbaum.

Mary opened the door and held it ajar for Fitzjames and Hughes to enter. She closed the door behind them.

"Good morning, gentlemen. Mr. Hughes I know, of course. Mr. Fitzjames?"

"Yes. It's a pleasure to meet you," responded Fitzjames and shaking the hand of Greenbaum.

"Nice to meet you. Bruce Greenbaum," he said by way of introduction. "I'm the chief administrator of the hospital. Mr. Hughes, should I begin, or do you want to provide the background? We've been actively cooperating with the FBI, and Mr. Hughes has been, throughout the investigation, our contact," continued Greenbaum to Fitzjames in a curiously awkward tone.

"For Mr. Fitzjames' benefit, I think it would make more sense for me to provide the details," said Hughes.

"Very well," said Greenbaum with resignation. "Please sit down, gentlemen."

Fitzjames and Hughes sat in two of the available three soft cushioned chairs in front of Greenbaum's desk. Greenbaum also sat, put on a pair of thick black-frame reading glasses, removed a file from a bottom desk drawer, placed the file on top of the desk, and folded his hands, in schoolboy fashion, on the file. Fitzjames perceived that he was struggling to compose himself.

"Last month, Mr. Greenbaum telephoned us at the local Pittsburgh office of the Bureau. Three men and one woman, over a forty-eight-hour period, had been admitted to the hospital with apparent drug overdoses. Drug overdoses are not terribly common in this part of the city, and this hospital sees very few of them. The patients received care and appeared to be recovering. The treating physicians expected all of them to come out of it, not perfectly, but with the usual post-event issues. Nothing life-threatening. But, then, completely unexpectedly, all of them got worse, much worse, and were dead within twenty-four hours.

"One week later, three more patients were admitted with similar symptoms, again apparent drug overdoses. The same treatment protocols were followed; they improved briefly, and then deteriorated and died. At that point, Mr. Greenbaum contacted us. His medical staff could provide no explanation. We opened a case and began an investigation of the deceased parties. All had an apparent history of casual drug use but nothing aggressive. Two weeks ago, five more patients were admitted and treated and then died. At this hospital alone, we've had twelve deaths."

"Those statistics are unheard of for this hospital," added Greenbaum disconcertedly.

"Absolutely. It's very odd. Very disturbing, not only for the hospital's reputation, but the nature of the deaths is creating real anxiety. We're trying to avoid a panic."

"Have other local hospitals reported similar occurrences?" asked Fitzjames.

"Yes. But not at the volume of Oakland Northside. Six hospitals in the metropolitan area have reported like cases, all resulting in deaths. Twenty-two other deaths have been confirmed," replied Hughes.

"Is your science team on it?" inquired Fitzjames.

"Yes. But we've made a decision to partner with Oakland Northside in the research. First, the concentration of cases has occurred here. Two, our science section has a relationship with this hospital. Third, the hospital has on staff a very able physician who also holds a Ph.D. and who is an acknowledged expert in infectious diseases and pandemics," said Hughes.

"Is that the FBI's supposition—a pandemic?"

"It's one of the angles at which we're looking. We're not certain about anything, and thus far, to my knowledge, the test results have not given us anything substantial," replied Hughes to Fitzjames' question.

"May I speak to the physician-scientist you've described?" asked Fitzjames.

"Certainly," said Greenbaum.

"Could we see him now?"

"Yes, of course. Mr. Hughes?"

"Yes, let's go. I've given you the contours of the problem."

Greenbaum rose from his seat, returned the file to the drawer from which he had removed it, and stepped around the desk to lead Hughes and Fitzjames out of the office. After Greenbaum spoke briefly to his secretary, the two men followed him to the elevator and they descended to the basement level of the hospital. To Fitzjames' surprise, the basement had been converted into a lab and research facility. More than a dozen white-coated men and women, many wearing goggles and protective masks, were engaged in handling test tubes and looking into the eyepieces of microscopes. Fitzjames could see the activity from the entrance to the lab through thick, protective, transparent glass.

"We must wait in this area. The interior is, of course, restricted. Dr. Reimer will join us in a moment. I asked my assistant to alert the doctor that we were on our way," advised Greenbaum.

From behind the three men, the elevator bell chimed. The door opened and a young woman, also in a white lab coat, stepped off and promptly greeted Greenbaum. She did not immediately take note of his companions. Although in the lab coat, which extended some sixteen inches below her waist, she was dressed in a professional sophisticated manner. She wore a gray skirt of light wool, cut as if it were intended to be worn with the lab coat because the two were the same length; a cream cotton lace top; and high heels with flesh-tone stockings. Although she wore no perfume, her make-up appeared to have been professionally applied, in particular the eyeliner and eyeshadow. She had tied her hair back in a tight bun and wore gold-frame glasses. She had an air of the intellectual seeking to quash attractiveness.

"Good morning, Bruce," she said casually. She then turned to the other two men.

"Dr. Reimer, this is Mr. Hughes from the FBI."

"Good morning, Doctor," said Hughes.

"Good morning," she said. She turned to Fitzjames.

"And, this is Mr. Fitzjames. He's also a representative of the government looking at the issues. I'm afraid, Mr. Fitzjames, that I don't know your official association," said Greenbaum apologetically.

"Intelligence is sufficient. Assistant to the FBI in this instance," responded Fitzjames. "Good morning, Dr. Reimer. Pleasure to see you again."

"And, you too," she replied quietly, while suppressing both surprise and embarrassment at being introduced to Fitzjames.

"You two have met?" asked Greenbaum, equally surprised but pleased that the interview would proceed more smoothly if the parties were acquainted.

"We met briefly last evening, at a nearby restaurant," replied Fitzjames.

“We met at Cruet. I hope you enjoyed your supper, Mr. Fitzjames. The food there is excellent,” she said.

“It was terrific. I hope the rest of your evening went well, Doctor,” returned Fitzjames.

“It did. Thanks.” She then spoke to the group collectively. “Listen, there’s no reason why we should use last names and titles. It just makes things more complicated. Call me Stacy, will you?”

“Good idea. I’m Owen,” added Hughes.

“I’m Trey,” said Fitzjames with a modest smile. “Bruce, we should probably get started in my office, would you agree?”

“Yes, good idea,” said Greenbaum. “We’ll go up to Stacy’s office to begin.”

“Follow me, then, gentlemen.”

Three

The three men followed Stacy Reimer, M.D., Ph.D., into her office on the top floor of the hospital. The door to the office bore a plaque, similar to Greenbaum's, that carried her name, advanced degrees, and two further acronyms that added gravity to her position. Greenbaum was deferential to her in the extreme, including insisting that he exit the elevator before the others in the party in order to hold open the elevator door to accommodate her. Fitzjames found the exercise in deference somewhat overdone. Fitzjames had, of course, the advantage of having met her at a point of weakness, not strength. The able physician by day had been the somewhat reckless, forgetful bar patron by night. Fitzjames presumed that Greenbaum only knew the Dr. Reimer of daylight hours.

For her part, Dr. Reimer took the events of the previous evening in stride. After she closed the door to her office behind Hughes, who was last to enter, she retrieved her purse from a bookshelf and removed her wallet. She drew out a ten- and two twenty-dollar bills and presented them to Fitzjames.

"Mr. Fitzjames rescued me last night. I didn't have my wallet, and he loaned some cash to me," she explained to Greenbaum and Hughes with a smile, while reverting to the use of surnames. "I don't let debts go unpaid."

"And, I can't accept the money. To do so would diminish the pleasure I had in being helpful. Keep your money. Perhaps you'll have a chance to reimburse me at another time in the future," said Fitzjames.

"Really, Mr. Fitzjames, that's not fair. You rescued me very gallantly, and I need to repay you, at least for the cash. I imagine the matter didn't end after I got into the cab. Please, I insist. I'll be offended otherwise. Please," she implored.

"I don't know what happened last night, but Dr. Reimer is not accustomed to being refused," added Greenbaum good-humoredly.

"Fine, okay," replied Fitzjames, accepting the money. "I don't like it, but it's two to one."

"Thank you," she said warmly. "Gentlemen, please sit down, and I'll run through our findings, to date, as quickly as I can."

The three men took seats in small, uncomfortable wooden chairs that encircled Reimer's desk. Hughes removed a pen and small notepad from the interior pocket of his blazer. Fitzjames perceived that notetaking would not be useful to him. He was confident that he could later obtain copies of Hughes' notes and any paperwork or other documents from Greenbaum.

"Over the course of last year, we've observed a spike in drug use in the city. We generally wouldn't see such a thing, but it's the nature of the drugs that resulted in increased activity at this hospital and others around the city. When the drugs are your typical Class-A drugs, like cocaine and heroin, no spiking occurs. But other drugs are on the rise, including synthetics. For example, we've seen cases involving ketamine and of diazepam and methadone. All of them and their use are worrying because we have trouble treating patients who overdose, as we don't regularly encounter these drugs. Most worrying, however, is what we've seen recently. These patients all appeared to suffer overdoses from ordinary drugs. They improved after treatment and then died. The deaths were violent and unexpected and, currently, unexplainable. I've got a team working on it, thanks to Bruce, who's been good enough to divert resources to the labor. We're trying to find, at least, some rational nexus between the drug or drugs that the patients took and their deaths. Particularly disturbing is that they all improved only then to die later. I'm also anxious because we know so little at present about the people we've been studying. A further problem is exposure to something unknown by the people here in the hospital doing the research. I don't know, for instance, if I've been exposed to something unknown. Time, I suppose, will tell," she said resignedly.

"Can you isolate the drugs that were taken? I'd presume that blood testing would reveal whether, by way of example, it was cocaine or heroin," said Fitzjames.

"That was my question as well. If we have at least that data, we can work with local law enforcement to find the sources," said Hughes.

"Yes, we've isolated that. Both cocaine and heroin. Equal distribution of both. Yet, some of the chemistry is odd. The basic components of cocaine and heroin have been identified. But, the organic chemical bonds are slightly different. Very odd. They're cocaine and heroin with a strange chemical spike," she said gravely.

"A spike?" inquired Hughes.

"That's the way I describe it. Our research reveals the spike. We don't know whether it's meaningful, as yet. But, it's there. My theory is that the spike amplifies the drug. But, for the present, it's just my theory. My colleagues disagree with me. One has urged that the difference in the chemistry is meaningless."

"A synthetic additive?" asked Fitzjames.

"Possibly. But such a thing is difficult and the science is very complex."

"In other words, producers in Columbia or Venezuela wouldn't have the knowledge or the wherewithal to add it," said Hughes, more to himself than to the others in the room.

"That I wouldn't know," she responded. "I can only confirm that the complexity of marrying the artificial to the natural is significant. It would require years of research and a lot of money. We've submitted grant proposals for similar research here at the hospital. We've had some success getting the grants, but they are invariably inadequate, ultimately, to get the research completed. At least ten projects have been started and then tabled for lack of funds. It's a big deal to do that sort of research. You would need government support, in my view."

"Well, Dr. Reimer, thanks for your time," said Hughes, rising from the chair unexpectedly and returning the pen and pad to his coat pockets. "We've gobbled up enough of your valuable time. If you don't mind, keep me posted on the progress of your research and findings. Here's my card. You can always find me at the cell number noted on the card."

Greenbaum, startled by Hughes' abrupt termination of the meeting, rose from the chair after Hughes had risen. Fitzjames was less surprised, being familiar with the course of FBI investigations. A truncated ending to a conference was not unusual. Fitzjames also got to his feet.

"Again, thanks for your time," repeated Hughes and shook hands with Dr. Reimer, who remained seated.

"Thank you, Dr. Reimer," mumbled Greenbaum.

"Nice to see you again and thanks," said Fitzjames as he stepped forward also to shake hands.

She stood and extended her hand to him. He accepted it and gently shook the delicate, soft hand.

"It's nice to see you again, Mr. Fitzjames. I hope we'll see each other again."

"Yes, I hope so," he replied.

Fitzjames followed Hughes out of the office and was in turn followed by Greenbaum. The three men, without conversation, descended in the elevator to the lobby level. As before, Hughes led and Fitzjames followed with Greenbaum in tow. Hughes turned and shook hands with Greenbaum and mumbled his appreciation. Fitzjames did likewise, only with more sincerity in his expression of thanks. Fitzjames followed Hughes outside into the cold. The sky was still gray and cloud-covered and the wind blew.

"We can't talk here, on the street. Here's one of my cards. I'll head back to my office. Take a taxi and meet me there in two hours. It's approximately fifteen minutes from here, so you'll need to busy yourself for an hour and forty-five minutes or so."

"Fine," said Fitzjames, as he deposited Hughes' card in his pants pocket. "I'll see you in a bit."

Hughes turned and walked briskly to his car. Fitzjames strolled up the street to the Panera Bread store and ordered a pair of fruit cups, bottled water, and a cup of coffee. He found a morning newspaper and, with it and the food and drink, sat down in the busy establishment. After thirty minutes of eating, drinking the coffee and water, and reading the newspaper, he studied his wristwatch. He removed an index card from his wallet and a pen and made notes from the information provided at the morning's conference. After another twenty minutes had passed, he rose, dropped the trash into the bin, and returned the newspaper to the stand from which he had found it. He walked down the street to his hotel and discovered a taxi, the driver slumped behind the steering wheel, doing nothing, and simply hoping to find a customer.

"Good morning," said Fitzjames.

"Mornin', sir," returned the driver, sitting up. "Where to?"

"Do you know the FBI office in town?" inquired Fitzjames.

"Sure. Climb in."

The cab made the journey to East Carson Street in twenty minutes. The morning traffic was still heavy, and commuters filled the roadways. The driver offered no conversation. Fitzjames surveyed the landscape.

Upon arriving at Pittsburgh's FBI field office, Fitzjames paid the driver the metered fare along with a modest tip and exited the taxi. No gratitude was expressed by the driver, who drove off almost before Fitzjames closed the door of the cab.

Fitzjames entered the three-storied white building and passed through the metal detection security station at the entrance without incident. He identified an information desk and inquired of the middle-aged woman, who sat at the deck and who resembled a librarian because of the reading glasses on a silver chain hanging from her neck, if she would advise Owen Hughes that he had arrived.

"Is Special Agent Hughes expecting you?"

"Yes, ma'am."

Fitzjames noted that the word *sir* appeared to have been intentionally omitted form the end of the woman's question of him.

"No need to use the word *ma'am* with me," she replied curtly.

"Sorry. No offense intended. I'm a southerner. We do that. It's inadvertent. To answer your next question, I'm a bit early for my appointment with Agent Hughes. But, my guess is that he'll see me. Just let him know that I'm here. My name is Fitzjames."

"What's that name again?" she asked while tilting her head as if her hearing were poor.

"Fitzjames. F-I-T-Z-J-A-M-E-S. Fitzjames."

"I've got it. You may sit down," she said with impatience and with the same lack of courtesy.

Fitzjames smiled at her. He glanced over his left shoulder and identified a makeshift waiting area, which resembled a vacant office without a door into which too many uncomfortable metal chairs had been haphazardly placed, if not discarded.

"I'll presume that I can wait there?" inquired Fitzjames, pointing to the office.

"Yes," she answered.

"Thank you, ma'am," he said and under his breath added, "charming."

Fitzjames entered the room and took a seat. He was the only visitor and only occupant. Other than the chairs, the room was empty of other furniture or extras. The FBI was either unconcerned about the comfort of its guests or federal budget cuts had been so severe as to force a cancellation of all table purchase, magazine subscriptions, and wall-hanging acquisitions.

After a few minutes and before the wait became oppressive, Hughes appeared.

"Hello, Fitzjames. Bit early."

"Sorry, yes, I am a bit early. I assumed that you'd not mind, if you were in. If you'd been out, I would've just waited here until your return."

"That would've been dull. As you can see, there's not much here to entertain guests."

"I did notice the absence of newspapers or magazines. I would've presumed it would make sense for the FBI to keep nervous visitors preoccupied with something, rather than make them wait in what closely resembles a prison cell."

"I agree. But, I'm not the one making that call," said Hughes with apparent frustration at such an administrative decision.

"I hope that the woman at the information desk isn't in charge. She'd likely handcuff your visitors," said Fitzjames with a sardonic smile.

"Oh, Miriam, yes. You're probably right there. She's tough. Sees herself as a true gatekeeper. Did she beat you up badly? She's not too warm."

"Manners are a little unrefined. But she's harmless. Didn't like my southern form of address."

"Ah, yes, that doesn't surprise me. Long-term federal employee. Nothing we can do with her, nothing we can do to her. That's another internal issue over which I've no control. It's one I would change."

"She's probably viciously loyal," suggested Fitzjames.

"That she is. She deserves credit for that, at least. Come on up to my office. We'll take the stairs, if that works for you."

"That's fine. Elevators get old."

Fitzjames and Hughes walked to the end of a hallway, entered the stairwell, and ascended two flights of stairs to the second level. They advanced down a corridor on that story only a few yards to an office occupied by another agent. Hughes and that agent shared the small room, which contained two inexpensive wooden desks, computer terminals, and files and papers that struck Fitzjames as being far too numerous for the space available.

"Have a seat in that chair. It's the only one we have, given the tightness of our quarters," said Hughes.

Fitzjames removed the files that occupied the metal chair, which was of the same variety as in the waiting room, and placed the files on the desk behind which Hughes now sat. Fitzjames then seated himself. Hughes hammered his fingers on the computer keyboard, and Fitzjames waited. After ninety seconds or so had elapsed, Hughes commenced the conversation.

"I wanted to get some data up on my computer before we chatted. I'll probably need to make reference to it."

"Fine."

"Dr. Reimer is making progress. Your question about a synthetic additive, a synthetic graft was right on target. Our own research points in that same direction," said Hughes gravely.

"Do you have your own people doing parallel research?"

"Yes. But we don't have the real quality and capacity that Dr. Reimer's team has. We do have some clever folks, and they can get us started. But the final conclusions, if there are any, must come from a team like Dr. Reimer's."

"Do you know any more?"

"Very little, except that Dr. Reimer is also correct that the costs of getting the science right are immense. It's too big of a job even for the most wealthy criminal syndicates. Only a government has those resources. That's our worry."

"Anything on that front?"

"We've had a host of strange events occur that appear to have no relationship. We've cataloged them and are investigating them. They may have a connection. Or, they may be dead ends and not linked with one another. I've tried to begin some sort of synthesis because all of them occurred, in time, close to one another. I've also got the reputation of being suspicious of everyone and everything. When the local case was assigned to me, I did what I always do. I conducted a global search, among our files and records, of all criminal activity of which we're aware in the entire country. It's relatively easy to do with our systems. I compare the data and then do a spreadsheet on the events, the dates, the known or suspected participants, and the location. It may appear to be macro-crime investigation, when I should be a micro guy here in Pittsburgh, yet I always feel I'm missing something if I don't do it. So, I'll print off the spreadsheet for you. You can then review it and draw your own conclusions."

"Thanks. That may be very useful. What about the foreign government issue?" inquired Fitzjames.

"Indeed. A foreign power tainting drugs in a country seen as the richest drug-consuming nation on the planet."

"Precisely. Very effective weapon."

Hughes printed the spreadsheet, which ran five pages, and delivered it to Fitzjames. Fitzjames gave it a cursory review.

"Study that at your leisure," said Hughes in reference to the spreadsheet. "But do so quickly."

"I will. And the foreign government?"

"Governments. All of the trouble spots are on the list: Russia, China, Mexico, Venezuela, Iran."

"You have data on all of them with respect to this matter?" asked Fitzjames, somewhat surprised.

"Yes, in one form or another. I created a file for you, as I was ordered to do. Here it is. I didn't include the spreadsheet, as that was my own work, my own suspicious research."

Fitzjames accepted the file. He gave a few seconds thought to how the contents of this file would compare to the file furnished to him by his superiors.

"Thanks for your help. Any objection if I pay another visit to Stacy Reimer's office? Our meeting ended more quickly this morning than I'd hoped it would. I've a few more questions I'd like answered."

"No objection. Are they personal questions?" suggested Hughes, grinning broadly.

"No, purely professional," replied Fitzjames without evincing any emotion.

Four

Fitzjames left the FBI office and returned to the hotel and to the hotel room. He deposited in his backpack the file that he had received from Hughes. He was concerned about its security, as it was too large to harbor in the room safe. But the likelihood that the housekeeping staff of the hotel would rummage through his backpack, he believed, was low. In another city, other than Pittsburgh, he might have approached the file's security differently.

He entered the bathroom, washed his hands and face, and brushed his teeth. He left the room and the hotel and walked again to Oakland Northside Hospital. The same woman was seated at the reception desk. She remembered him form the earlier visit and, surprisingly, recalled his name.

"Welcome back, Mr. Fitzjames. Do you wish to see Mr. Greenbaum again?" she asked in a friendly manner.

"Thank you, no. I'd like to speak to Dr. Reimer, if she could spare me a few minutes."

"I'll try her office. You may have a seat, if ya like," she said.

"Thanks. I'll just stand. Too much sitting this morning."

"I can certainly understand that. I haven't moved all morning."

The woman made a telephone call that was apparently unsuccessful. She tried another number, which was also a failure.

"I'm sorry, Mr. Fitzjames. I'm having trouble locating Dr. Reimer. It may take a few minutes. I have one other line I can call."

"That's fine. I'll be patient. I wasn't expected. If I have to come back later, I can do that too, if necessary."

"Well, let me try this additional extension and then I'll go back to the first one, which was her direct line."

The woman tried the third number and it too was unsuccessful. She repeated the process and had a positive outcome. Fitzjames, who stood only ten feet from the desk, could hear clearly the conversation.

"Dr. Reimer, this is Theresa Anne in the lobby. I've Mr. Fitzjames again. He'd like to see you, if you aren't engaged," she said and paused for a few seconds for a reply. "Yes, Doctor, I'd be happy to cancel that appointment for you. No problem. I'll do so right after I hang up. Should I send Mr. Fitzjames up to you or will you come down? Very good. I'll let him know. Thank you."

The woman replaced the telephone receiver into the cradle and smiled at Fitzjames.

"Dr. Reimer will be down in a moment."

"Thanks."

A few minutes passed and then Fitzjames observed the left side of the double doors that led into the interior of the hospital swing open. Stacy Reimer emerged with her right hand in the exterior pocket of her lab coat. As she walked briskly toward Fitzjames, he was struck by how her professional attire and demeanor enhanced her beauty. From his perspective, she was more attractive practicing medicine than she was drinking cocktails at a bar. She extracted her hand from the lab coat pocket and extended it to him as she approached.

"Mr. Fitzjames, it's nice of you to pay a second visit," she said with a light laugh, while shaking his hand.

"Sorry to come back without a scheduled meeting. But this morning's meeting ended more quickly than I would've liked. I didn't get all of my questions answered. Hughes brought things to a close too abruptly for me, although perhaps he had his reasons. I don't know what they are. I leave tomorrow and my assignment, as I see it, isn't completed. I need more information. I hope I've not intruded or disrupted your schedule."

"Not at all. I just needed to get a meeting off my book. Theresa Anne will take care of it. It's no problem. The meeting's with a man you know, in fact. He's a drug rep. You would have recognized him from a certain restaurant," she said with a note of humor in her voice.

"Ah, yes. I understand. He's likely better off not seeing me. I'm not certain which of the two men it is, but one of them gave me some pushback. I had to *encourage* him to be civil and leave, which he did."

"I see. Hopefully, I won't need to provide any medical services to any drug reps," she returned.

"No, not at all. I was persuasive without that result."

"Well, good, and thank you again. I was stupidly vulnerable and at my wit's end. I still owe you a debt of gratitude."

"Not at all; it was my pleasure," said Fitzjames.

"Out of curiosity, Mr. Fitzjames, what do you do for work, or do you do this thing you're doing here full time? And, is that business card that you gave me legitimate?"

"It is wholly legitimate, and I do have another job. It's my day job."

"You are a lawyer, then," she confirmed.

"Yes, in actuality."

"And, I suspected as much."

"Really. How's that?" he asked.

"Vocab. The way you speak and articulate your thoughts. Dead ringer for an attorney. I can spot it every time. Should I be concerned?" she queried.

"No, of course not. I'm a commercial lawyer. No medical malpractice nonsense for me," he responded.

"Good, I can relax," she added.

"I wouldn't think that you'd have much to worry about, as it is," he said.

"I'm teasing you. I'm not frightened by you at all, Mr. Fitzjames, whether professionally or personally."

"Good, and call me Trey, please."

"I will. Well, Trey, let's go up to my office, if you have more questions."

"Thanks."

She smiled again and turned, and Fitzjames followed her through the double doors out of which she had emerged. They took an elevator to her office, only in this instance it was a large medical elevator with doors on both sides in order to permit use by orderlies moving patients on wheeled hospital beds through the facility. Once seated in her office, Fitzjames began the conversation.

"I appreciate your seeing me a second time. As I said downstairs, Hughes ended the last meeting rather too suddenly and before I had finished."

"Certainly."

"I'm curious about what sort of timeframe you'd anticipate before your research showed something definitive."

"I'm not sure I understand the word *definitive*. That's not a term we use. If you're asking when I think we'll have a theory or some hypothesis from our research, I can certainly venture a guess."

"Yes, precisely. That's what I'm seeking."

"I suspect that, within ten days, I'll have enough data to where I'll be in a position to sit down with my folks here and begin formulating some theories. I'll likely get a written report completed in two to three weeks."

"The spike you described this morning, what's your current level of confidence in the notion that it's a synthetic additive?"

"Keep in mind, that's just my theory, at present. My subsequent report may reach a different conclusion entirely."

"I appreciate that. But assume for the sake of argument that it's a correct theory. What's your level of confidence that it's accurate?"

"Well, it is, after all, *my* theory. Setting aside personal bias because it is mine, I've got a high level of confidence that it's correct."

"By percentages, what level of confidence?"

"By percentages, I'd argue eighty-five to ninety percent."

"And, if accurate, my presumption is that a synthetic, non-organic additive could be very broad. That is, frighteningly, some very ugly contagions could be introduced as appendages to certain illegal drugs, for example, and then subtly spread through the population."

"Yes. It's terrifying. But that's a possibility and my fear. As I mentioned this morning, the science for such a thing is enormously complex and thus expensive."

"Might much of that complexity be in disguising the additive? Something that appears, at the outset or upon simple examination, to be innocuous but later proves to be severe and deadly."

"Well, if that were the designer's intention, then yes. Such a thing would be very complex."

Fitzjames paused for a moment and then removed from his wallet the index card on which he had made notes. He reviewed the card and made a notation and then returned it to the wallet.

"For now, at least, I think that's all I have. Thanks again for the additional time," he said.

"You're welcome."

"I leave tomorrow morning. I have a mid-morning flight out. But, I have no supper plans. Any chance you'd mind having dinner with me?"

"After last night, are you certain you're brave enough for that?" she inquired, smiling.

"I've got the courage. Perhaps, out of caution, you could bring along your car keys, wallet, and cellphone, in case there's trouble," he said, returning the smile.

"I don't anticipate any trouble."

"Indeed, no. This is a bit odd, but would you mind going back to Cruet? It's nearby, and frankly the menu and wine list both looked interesting, and I really didn't get a meal last night."

"Returning so quickly might be somewhat embarrassing. But, I'm probably responsible for the fact that you didn't eat."

"Do you think you could manage it?" he asked good-naturedly.

"Oh, I think so. That'd be great. What time?"

"Six-fifteen work?"

"Sure. Do I meet you there?"

"If you do, then you'll have your car and that'd be good, I imagine."

"Yes. But you could meet me here at six and we could walk. It's not far. I'd enjoy the walk."

"That sounds great. And, I commit to leave the topics discussed here out of the dinner conversation. Deal?"

"Deal. Then. I'll see you back here at six, Trey."

"I'll look forward to it."

Fitzjames rose from the chair and shook Stacy Reimer's, once again, extended hand. With a demure smile, he nodded to her in gratitude and turned and left her office. He followed the same route through the hospital to the elevator and then out of the lobby and back to the hotel. The external temperature had fallen, and it was very cold.

When he returned to the hotel room, he extracted from the backpack the file that he had received from Hughes. He placed it on the desk and switched on the lamp light. The lamp stood four feet in height and was positioned adjacent to the desk. He also engaged the desktop lamp in order to maximize the amount of light. He drew the curtains and powered off the heating system. The room grew cold almost instantly. He sat in the chair, which had four small wheels on the legs, pulled himself toward the desk, and opened the file.

For the succeeding two hours, Fitzjames studied the contents of the FBI file. Much of the documentation was dull and the details either expected or obvious. Where conclusions were drawn, they were general and not particularly erudite. The conferences with Stacy Reimer had been more informative and succinct. Moreover, only a single, individual name appeared in the file. He had anticipated more specificity as to individuals. But he was disappointed. The odd element, from his perspective, was that the individual identified was not in New York, which from the details received from Fuller, he had expected. Instead, the subject was in Kansas City.

Upon completing the review of the file, he stood and removed the mobile telephone from the backpack. He pressed in a ten-digit number and at the prompt pressed a further five-digit code. He waited a few seconds, and the call was answered.

"Major Fuller," said the recipient.

"Major, Fitzjames here."

"Yes, Captain. How are things?"

"Progressing, sir. However, I need to make a change and presume that I have the discretion to do so."

"Of course, you've got broad latitude."

"Well, I appreciate the breadth of my discretion outside the country. But in the U.S., I'm always reluctant to deviate from the expected course of investigation without seeking authority."

"We appreciate your deference. What change do you need to make?"

"In lieu of going to New York, sir, I believe it'd be more productive to go to Kansas City. The local office of the FBI has shared some details with me that make a visit to New York either redundant or wholly useless."

"Kansas City?"

"Yes, sir. Somewhat odd, if not totally unexpected. But, that's the trail. This thing is pretty ugly and potentially disastrous."

"Do you need assistance? Backup?"

"No, sir. It makes sense, as is the rule, for me to operate alone. The FBI is fully informed of the details and can take the needed steps to address the issues on the domestic front. The local FBI special agent, Hughes, is cooperating with a team of physicians and scientists and the communication is good. My view is that I should stay focused on the individuals and let the FBI do the big-picture work."

"Fine. I'll trust your judgment. I'll also alert the folks in New York not to expect you."

"Good. Thank you, sir."

"Do you want us to sort out the travel or will you handle that?"

"I'll take care of it, sir. I'll just reorder my plane tickets. Southwest, I'm confident, will accommodate me."

"Very well. Keep me posted. Standard protocols."

"Yes, sir. I will, sir. Thank you."

Fitzjames ended the call and then telephoned Southwest Airlines in order to alter his flight plan. As he anticipated, the change was simple and the cost to effect it minimal. At the same time, the flight to Kansas City was much earlier the following morning than was the now cancelled flight to New York City. He considered whether he should contact Stacy and suggest that they abandon the dinner plans. Yet, on reflection, that choice made little sense.

Three hours separated him from his return to Oakland Northside Hospital. As such, he elected to take a taxi to the nearest Barnes & Noble bookstore, where he had a coffee and browsed the bookshelves until 5:35. At 5:50, after some difficulty in attracting a taxi, he successfully signaled to a driver, who passed the store so quickly that Fitzjames presumed, that even with his right arm raised, the driver had not seen him. But the driver came to a sudden stop, put the cab in reverse, and backed up to Fitzjames at nearly the same forward speed. Fitzjames anticipated that he would have no trouble being on time for the appointment with Stacy Reimer.

The cab driver did not disappoint him. Despite the thick traffic and an extraordinary number of traffic signals, all of which appeared to show red when the taxi approached them, the driver delivered Fitzjames to the hospital at a minute before six o'clock. He paid and tipped the driver, who was pleased with the tip, and the driver thanked him rather excessively. Fitzjames entered the hospital lobby, as he had on two earlier occasions, and Stacy greeted him.

"Well, good evening, Mr. Fitzjames," she said, smiling broadly.

"Well, good evening, Dr. Reimer. I didn't expect that you'd be in the lobby waiting for me."

"I'm tired and hungry and feel as if I've been indoors for months. So, I'm ready to go. I hope you're hungry."

"Very. You aren't wearing walking shoes, so I hope the restaurant isn't far. Because it was dark last evening and I was tired, I didn't pay much attention to where Cruet is, actually."

"The heels won't be a problem. It isn't far at all."

"Terrific. Well, I'll follow your lead, then."

"Trey, I have a sense that you don't follow anyone's lead but your own."

"Perhaps you're right. I'll rephrase that statement. Give me some idea where we're going and then we'll go together, rather than with me in tow."

"That's better."

She smiled at him again and then marched confidently but, at the same time, delicately out of the hospital with him next to her. Ten minutes later, he held the door open for her in order to enter Cruet.

Five

The hostess, being the very same as on the previous evening, was puzzled upon seeing Stacy Reimer and Fitzjames enter the restaurant. But she recovered quickly when Fitzjames stepped forward and requested a table for two, with the preface that it was nice to see her again.

Cruet was only partially filled with patrons at the time of their arrival. Hence, the hostess had little difficulty seating them immediately. The table, for two, was deep in the interior of the restaurant and was situated against a window and, although among other tables occupied by other diners, offered a level of privacy that Fitzjames welcomed but which he found curious.

The hostess placed two menus and a wine list on the table before seating Fitzjames and Stacy. Fitzjames pulled out the chair for Stacy to sit before he took his own.

"Enjoy your meal," said the hostess, as she returned to her station.

"Thank you," said Fitzjames.

"You certainly are a southerner," offered Stacy.

"Why do you say that?" he asked.

"The formality and the manners. We're polite in Pittsburgh but not so mannerly. I don't think I've ever had someone pull a chair out for me to sit down," she said.

"Really? Now, that surprises me. I actually thought that you were going to say something about my accent."

"Your southern accent is apparent but modest. But your manners give you away."

"I hope it's not over the top—too much, I mean. Frankly, even if it were, I doubt I could change it. I was raised that way. In my home, growing up, better to have died a small child than forget your manners."

"Really. That severe?" she asked.

"Well, perhaps that's an overstatement. But, my folks drilled down on us about our manners. When I was fairly young, I once interrupted my father in a conversation he was having with another adult without first saying the words 'excuse me' and then waiting to be recognized in order to speak. He was not happy. I learned that lesson and didn't forget it."

"My goodness. In my parents' home, the rule was simply don't do anything to embarrass them. As long as you didn't do that, it was a free-for-all."

"Did you ever embarrass them?" he inquired.

"Only once. In high school. I went to an all-girls' school here in the city."

"Roman Catholic school?"

"Yes. Did you go to a parochial school too?"

"No. I'm a public school boy. So, what did you do?"

"You can imagine that there wasn't much liberality in the minds of the nuns about young males. Well, I snuck off of campus one day to meet a boyfriend."

"Shocking," he said with a smile.

"I didn't turn up for homeroom and for roll call, although everybody had seen me earlier the same day in school. The building was searched for me, in vain. So, the headmistress called my dad at work and told him that I was missing. She left him with the sense that something had happened to me. He went into a panic, left his job in the mill, and came to the school. He was an uneducated man, but he was very clever. After speaking to the headmistress, he had an idea where I might be and with whom. He went straight to a little diner nearby and found me. To his credit, he didn't get angry. He was more relieved, I think. And, he knew that the headmistress would mete out all the justice required to keep from doing that again. He just told me later that it embarrassed him at his work. I was particularly contrite at that point. But he was too good-natured to be angry long. He got over it immediately."

"That's a great story. No other incidents with boyfriends?"

"None worth telling."

"Okay, I can accept that. Did your father work in a local steel mill?"

"Yes. So did my dad's dad. My granddad came to Western Pennsylvania in the 1920s and got work in the mills."

"Did he get chased out of Germany or did he come voluntarily?"

"How'd you know he was German?"

"I just presumed so. *Reimer* is a relatively common German name."

"You're right. The story my dad told me was that he came of his own volition. But I've always presumed that he may have been pushed. He left Germany in the early 1920s."

"Weimer Republic. Rampant inflation, war reparations, no prospects for work in Germany—misery. I can understand it."

"Are you a historian, too?" she asked kindly.

"No. I just do a lot of reading. The period between the wars in Germany has always interested me. Was your grandfather from the south of Germany?"

"Yes. Now, how in the world did you guess that?"

"Most German Roman Catholics live in the south of Germany. I presumed that he was a Roman Catholic because of your school story."

"Bavaria. He was from a little village not far from the Austrian border. Kochel. In fact, I'm not entirely confident that we aren't more Austrian than German. But I've always said German, when asked."

"I suppose that in that part of Germany, in and around Munich, there's very little to distinguish a South German from a North Austrian. I don't speak German, but I've understood that you can't really distinguish the accents between the residents of those two parts of the two countries. That's why Hitler, in his rise to power, wasn't perceived in Germany by the German public at large as being a foreigner."

"Didn't he fight for Germany in World War I?" she asked.

"Yes. But he was an Austrian. The old joke is that the Austrians want the world to remember Hitler as a German and Beethoven as an Austrian," he replied.

"That is interesting."

"Would you like some wine?" he inquired.

"Sure. Do you know something about wines, as well?"

"Not too much, but a bit. I only know what I like," he responded and opened the wine list. "If you tell me what you'd like, I'll order a bottle. I'm not particular."

"Okay. I like sweeter white wines," she said.

"They sell Rieslings and a Moscato. Both are sweet. Before dinner, the Moscato might be better because it's not as sweet as the Riesling. Will that do?"

"Sure. Great."

"It's curious that no one has waited on us yet," he said, as he looked over his right shoulder at the kitchen and a congregated group of three of the wait staff.

"They've probably seen us talking and decided to wait until it appeared that we'd finished so as not to interrupt."

"I think you're right. And, they did fill the water glasses. Here he comes," he responded.

A waiter with a white cotton apron tied tightly around his thin waist approached them. He wore a light blue Oxford button-down collared dress shirt and a navy blue and green and yellow rep tie. His trousers were a dark gray.

"May I offer you something from the wine list, sir?" he asked Fitzjames.

"Yes. Thanks. We'll try a bottle of the Moscato, please."

"The *Monti*, sir?"

"Yes. That'll work."

"Very good. Would you like to hear our specials for this evening, or should I get the wine and come back?"

"No, I'd like to hear the specials," said Fitzjames.

The waiter described beef, pork, and fish dishes that included savory sauces and creative cooking styles, and all were accompanied by a variety of vegetable medleys. After providing the descriptions, the waiter returned to the kitchen. Fitzjames and Stacy continued their conversation.

When the waiter returned, he opened the bottled of wine and offered the cork to Fitzjames, which Fitzjames waved off as unnecessary. The waiter poured a bit of the wine into the glass in front of Fitzjames. Fitzjames sampled the wine, approved it, and the waiter poured a glass for Stacy. He then filled Fitzjames' glass.

Fitzjames and Stacy both ordered the beef special offered by the waiter. When it arrived, the dish, from Fitzjames' perspective, was outstanding. He was hungry and finished the meal quickly and well before Stacy.

"Goodness. You were hungry," she said, smiling.

"Yes. I'm sorry for eating like a caveman. Last meal for a month and all of that."

"It's no problem. Are you sure you got enough?"

"Oh, yeah, I'm fine. Don't rush yourself. I'm sorry. Bad habit of eating too fast. Always in a hurry, when no hurry exists. Bad habit," he repeated.

"I presume that I don't have to give you all of the medical reasons why a person shouldn't eat so fast. I'm not your physician, but I'll give you reasons, if you feel you need them."

"No, Doctor. That won't be necessary," he said quietly and drank a bit of the wine and then some of the water. "Again, I apologize."

"Don't apologize. It's delicious. I can understand why you ate it so fast. So, Trey, when do you leave Pittsburgh?" she queried.

"Tomorrow morning, very early," he replied. "If I were staying, I'd come back to Cruet and try those other two specials."

"Would you invite me to come along?"

"I would, if you'd come."

"I'd come."

"Is it because of the food or the company?" he inquired.

"The company," she said directly.

"That's nice. I'm complimented. I hope I haven't bored you."

"Bored me? I'm having a great time. Keep in mind that I'm used to medical dinners and doctors' conversation. Talk about dull. And, everybody's ego is intruding. Horrible stuff. Having a dinner with a mysterious lawyer from

Florida who, when asked, described himself as being with 'Intelligence' and comes to my hospital in tow with the FBI, what could be more interesting?" she said with a grin.

"Well, you haven't plied me with questions about my background. So, the *interesting* things about me, as you describe them, haven't surfaced. I've just been talking and was concerned that I was boring you."

"My guess was that you couldn't talk about those things, or wouldn't. So, I didn't ask. What can you tell me?"

"Very little. I'm sorry. I'm precluded from doing so."

"*Precluded.* That's a word only lawyers use."

"You're right. I can tell you something about my practice, if you're interested. It's dull, but it's not off limits."

"Tell me about it, then," she invited, again grinning.

For the next ten minutes, Fitzjames described his practice of law in a small Florida town. In lieu of adding color to an otherwise ordinary professional life, he chose to characterize the practice as it was. He was not generally inclined to aggrandize but often believed that in his descriptions of his practice, he failed to capture the importance of the work and the relevance of it to his clients. Stacy listened intently.

"Do you enjoy the job?" she asked.

"Not always. But broadly speaking, yes."

"Are you suited for it, in your opinion?"

"Yes, I think so. Sometimes, I perceive that I was preprogramed to be a lawyer. Bit frightening, if it's true."

"Not at all. I've often felt the same thing about medicine."

Both, when asked by the waiter, elected to forego dessert and coffee. Fitzjames requested the check and paid it by credit card, along with a healthy tip for the service.

"All set?" he asked of Stacy after signing the receipt.

"All set. Thank you so much. The food was great. And, this visit was so much more enjoyable than last night's," she said facetiously.

"And, more secure," he added.

They rose from their chairs, left the restaurant, and walked slowly to the hospital. At the entrance, Fitzjames thanked Stacy for having had dinner with him and again inquired whether she had enjoyed herself. She confirmed that she had.

"Goodnight, then," he said. "I hope we'll see each other again."

"I hope so."

"Do be careful on your next visit to Cruet, as I may not be there," he returned.

"Oh, I will," she said with a chuckle.

"Goodnight," he said and nodded his head. He turned to return to the hotel.

"Was this supposed to be a date, Mr. Fitzjames?" she inquired.

"I suppose so," he answered, turning back to her. "After a professional meeting, so something of a hybrid," he responded.

"Even if a hybrid, don't good manners dictate that you would kiss me goodnight?"

"Certainly."

Fitzjames kissed her delicately and placed his hand on her lower back. She pressed her lips to his in response and thus prolonged the kiss.

"Goodnight, Dr. Reimer," he said.

"Goodnight, Mr. Fitzjames."

He again turned and began the short walk to the hotel. Stacy entered the hospital but paused in the lobby. She considered a moment that she had just enjoyed a romantic dinner with a man who had not pushed himself upon her and in turn pressed himself into her bed. The thought was refreshing and intriguing. She was also not entirely confident that she, the physician whose intellect intimidated so many men, had not just fallen in love with Trey Fitzjames.

Six

Fitzjames arrived at the Pittsburgh International Airport well in advance of the flight to Kansas City. He had not slept well, and the wake-up call from the front desk at 4:30 A.M. was unnecessary; he had been awake since 4:00. Stacy Reimer had drifted in and out of his thoughts after having gotten into bed and he had had a restless night. At 4:15 he had entered the fitness room and thirty minutes later had completed a workout on the treadmill. By 5:20, he had showered and packed his clothing into the suitcase and re-ordered the contents of the backpack and made his way to the hotel lobby for the taxi that he had arranged for half-past-five.

Because he was not carrying a weapon, the passage through security at the airport was simple and uneventful. As he had on his first visit to Pittsburgh, he noted again that even the TSA employees were pleasant. In no other airport in America had he encountered anything other than either rude or simply indifferent TSA staff. Pittsburgh was the noteworthy exception.

The wait at the gate was brief. He boarded the plane as the last passenger in the final wave of passengers to board and took an unwanted center seat in the back of the airplane between two women, who appeared to be in their late forties and were similar in appearance. The woman occupying the aisle seat stood in order to allow Fitzjames to take the seat. Once he was settled, she sat down and spoke to the other woman, who was watching, out of the window, suitcases being loaded into the cargo hold of the plane.

"Well, Annie, it didn't work," she said, leaning forward to attract the attention of her companion.

"Full flight, I suppose," mumbled the other woman in reply.

"Suppose so," responded the first woman.

"Sorry, ladies," said Fitzjames in answer to the exchange. "It is a full flight and I'm afraid I was the last one on. Would you two like to sit together? I'll move to whichever of the seats you'd prefer to give up."

"No, no problem. I like the aisle and Annie likes the window."

"Fine. If you change your minds, let me know."

Fitzjames removed from the backpack a recent issue of *The Spectator*, a publication out of Britain for which he had only just procured a subscription. As he began an attempt to focus on the articles, the two ladies both leaned forward and began to converse. They were still talking when the plane taxied down the runway and ascended. For nearly the entire flight to Kansas City, the two chatted with one another over Fitzjames. They took a short break when their drinks arrived—both had ordered a Bloody Mary—and again when small packs of pretzels were offered by the flight attendants. But the interval of silence was too short for Fitzjames to read. He yielded, returned the magazine to the backpack, reclined the seat, and tried to sleep. The effort was unsuccessful, although the women's ceaseless conversation became less annoying.

In short order, the senior flight attendant announced over the public address system that they had begun their initial descent into Kansas City. He raised the seat, lifted and locked the tray table, and rechecked the seatbelt, all as suggested mechanically by the attendant. Within fifteen minutes, over the chatter of the two women, which rose in volume as the airplane touched down, he had arrived in Kansas City.

"Sorry we're so chatty," said the woman in the window seat to Fitzjames. "We're on our way to a family reunion and needed to catch up."

"No problem. I presumed that you were sisters," he said, while he and they waited for the other passengers in rows of seats in front of them to gather their carry-on bags and deplane.

"And how did you know we were sisters?"

"You both look just alike and your voices are almost identical."

"Really? No one's ever told us that," added the woman in the aisle seat. "That's really funny."

The two women laughed in unison and seemed to find immense humor in his deduction. After three minutes of additional waiting, the woman in the aisle seat got to her feet and squeezed herself into the aisle and into a line of other waiting passengers.

"Annie, I'll see you in the terminal. I can't sit in that seat anymore," she said impatiently.

"Okay. Wait for me just inside," said her companion.

Fitzjames smiled at the exchange and could not repress a slight shake of the head. He stood, put the backpack in the aisle seat, and waited. Another passenger permitted him to step into the aisle, which he did with an expression of gratitude. He turned and spoke to the woman still seated in the window seat.

"Enjoy your reunion," he said.

"Thank you; we will. Enjoy your stay or whatever you're doing in Kansas City," she replied.

"Thanks."

After a brief scare that his suitcase had failed to be loaded on the airplane, as it was delayed in being placed on the carousel in bag claim, and finding himself alone, he snatched up the bag. The other passengers had moved on to their own cars, hired cabs, Ubers, or tour buses. He had evaluated renting a car but had concluded that it would likely be an encumbrance, rather than a benefit in the city. Hence, he took a taxi. He had no hotel reservation but knew that he could get a room in the Westwood region of Kansas City, which was south of the city center. He told the cab driver to take him to the Marriott South Moreland.

The distance to the hotel was significant, inasmuch as Kansas City's international airport, MCI, was located well outside of town and to the north. The cab driver was a Somali. His ethnicity surprised Fitzjames, who made subtle inquiries about why the driver had selected Kansas City as home. Fitzjames' surprise was amplified when he learned that Kansas City had significant East African communities of Somalis, Ethiopians, and Kenyans, respectively. The driver's command of English was weak, although he talked endlessly. Fitzjames gave periodic acknowledgments that he understood or that the driver's descriptions were interesting. In fact, he could understand only a portion of what he was told.

After a forty-five-minute journey, the cab pulled under the *porte-cochere* of the Marriott. Fitzjames paid the fare, which was standardized because it was an airport-to-hotel destination, and a tip. The driver thanked him and expressed his hope that Fitzjames would enjoy his visit to Kansas City. Fitzjames thanked him in return and wished him good luck.

He entered the lobby through automatic sliding glass doors. The lobby was warm. Kansas City was colder than Pittsburgh had been, and the hotel staff had reacted to the outside freezing temperature by combining the central heating with a raging fire in a large fireplace next to the bell stand.

The bellman, attired in a traditional but anachronistic red suit and a top hat, greeted him. "Good morning, sir. May I assist with your bag?"

"No, no thanks. I need to check in, but I can manage it," replied Fitzjames.

"Good morning, sir," repeated a smartly dressed young woman behind the reception desk.

Fitzjames stepped forward toward her. She was wearing a business suit, as were her two other female coworkers. They were attired identically, all of roughly the same age, all had shoulder-length blonde hair with a light curl, and all wore similarly applied makeup. Fitzjames found their similarity somewhat comical. Had they been older and unattractive, it was uncertain whether he would not have laughed upon seeing them. They looked like triplets dressed by their mother.

"Good morning. You wouldn't have any vacancies by chance, would you?" inquired Fitzjames. "Sorry, I didn't have time yesterday to sort out a reservation."

"How many nights, sir?" asked the woman, while she surveyed a computer monitor and rested her fingertips on a keyboard.

"Two, perhaps three at the most."

"Just one guest?" she asked, now looking at him and away from the monitor.

"Yes, just me. Just one."

"No problem. We've got a room on the sixth floor, king-size bed, $255.00 per night."

"That's fine. I'll take it. Book me in for three nights, out of caution. Is the room available for three nights?"

"Sure. Just let us know tomorrow by six in the evening if you'll not be staying with us the third night."

"That'll work too. I should know my plans by that point."

"May I have your name, sir?"

"Fitzjames. R. P. Fitzjames. Here's my driver's license, which I'll presume you'll need. The address on it is correct. And, here's my credit card. I'll presume you'll need that too," said Fitzjames with a smile.

"Yes, thanks. I need both. Give me just a few seconds, and I'll wrap up the paperwork."

The receptionist completed the registration process on the computer, made two keys for Fitzjames, and then presented a single sheet of paper to him for execution. He signed the paper. She gave him room keys and returned his driver's license and credit card.

"You're in Room 628," she said. "Just take the elevator to the sixth floor, turn to the left, and it's down the hallway and then around the corner. You shouldn't have any trouble, Mr. Fitzjames."

"Wouldn't think so. Thanks," he responded, collecting the keys, license, and card.

"Long way from Florida," she added, grinning.

"Excuse me?"

"You've come a long way from Florida. Kansas City can be cold this time of year. I'll bet that it's a lot warmer in Florida."

With the mention of Florida, the two other women, who were not assisting customers, joined the receptionist assisting Fitzjames.

"You're from Florida? I hope you've got a good reason to be in this city this time of year. It's freezing here. I'm from Virginia and I can't take the cold here," offered one of the young women.

"Yes. Good reason to be here, I'm afraid. But I like the cold. I don't ever get to enjoy it. But the beauty of my situation is that I come to town, enjoy the cold for a few days, and hustle back to warm weather in Florida. I do understand that days and weeks of relentless cold can get tiresome."

"Awful," said the same woman.

"We'll let you go, Mr. Fitzjames," said the receptionist, who had assisted him, almost apologetically. "Enjoy your stay."

"I will. Thanks again."

The three women stood together and watched him walk to the elevator. He could sense their collective gaze as he waited for the elevator. He did not look back at them.

When the door of the elevator opened, he entered, ascended to the sixth floor, found Room 628, and deposited the suitcase and the backpack on the bed. He extracted the mobile telephone from the backpack and placed a call to Fuller in order to inform the major of his arrival in Kansas City. He removed from his wallet an index card on which he had written the name and contact information of a colleague of Owen Hughes' at the FBI field office in Kansas City. The data had come from the file that Hughes had furnished to Fitzjames. Hughes had cooperated with this local special agent when his own personal investigation and suspicions took him outside of Pittsburgh.

Fitzjames telephoned the Bureau's office. "Yes, hello, may I speak to Special Agent Casillas?" he asked when the call was answered.

"One moment, please."

Fitzjames waited only a few seconds and the call was answered by a woman.

"Consuela Casillas," she said, without a greeting or other introductory phrase.

Fitzjames had expected a male to reply but recovered quickly from the surprise. "Special Agent Casillas?" he inquired.

"Yes," she returned.

"My name is Fitzjames. I've just arrived in Kansas City from Pittsburgh. You may recall an Owen Hughes from the FBI field office in Pittsburgh."

"Yes, of course. I also recognize your name. Owen sent an email to me last night that I might hear from you. Of course, his email didn't include any particulars, other than your name and a strong expectation that you would move from Pittsburgh to here. Did he turn over his research to you? Is that how you got my contact information?"

"Yes, precisely."

"How can I help?"

"Could I come pay a visit?"

"I suppose so. I'm locked up this morning, but I could see you this afternoon. I've got a team meeting in ten minutes. The meeting will likely run at least to lunchtime."

"No problem, thanks. I've got the flexibility, so I'm prepared to yield to your schedule."

"But there's urgency."

"No doubt."

"No, you don't seem to understand. Yesterday, a report came to me of ten more drug overdose deaths in this city. All occurred at the same hospital. Before yesterday's numbers came in, we'd had seven deaths in four different hospitals spread over the entire metropolitan area. No one took any particular notice, until the reports trickled in from Pittsburgh. We saw a connection in the nature of the events and the ultimate deaths of the patients and began sharing data. But we didn't seem to be facing a problem of the same magnitude as Pittsburgh. Things have now changed. The press is all over the story. Treating physicians and assisting nurses have been interviewed, and the morning television news programs made it their top story. The local papers will have it tomorrow and will give it the same prominence. I'm certain. I've had four calls already this morning from the press, and someone was waiting to see me when I arrived. I turned him away, but it wasn't easy. Delicate balancing act when dealing with the media. I'm trying to avoid a citywide panic. Local law enforcement also has abrogated its responsibilities and turned the matter over to us. So, our job is even bigger than it might otherwise be."

"Then, it's fair to presume that your team meeting pertains to this matter," suggested Fitzjames.

"Yes. I've got to get out in front of this thing, if for any other reason simply to calm nerves. That means deployment of personnel; looping in local law enforcement, whether they want to be involved or not; and managing the media. I've agreed to do a brief television appearance in order to make a statement, at midday."

"You've got your hands full. Even if you could spare thirty minutes, that would help me. Also, any documentary data that you have that you could share with me would also be useful."

"That's fine. I can do both. I'm still a bit confused, though, about how you fit in," she added.

"After we meet, I'll have my superiors contact your office. Or, if absolutely necessary, I'll have them do so before our meeting."

"It can wait. Owen Hughes' alert to me was sufficient for my purposes. His reliability is unquestioned. Obviously, he would've been reluctant to provide that kind of detail in an email to me."

"Yes, of course."

"Will 1:30 this afternoon do for you?" she asked.

"Certainly."

"Can you find our office, or should I send a car to pick you up?"

"No, not necessary. I'll get to you. I don't want to add to your list of stresses or obligations."

"I appreciate that."

"I'll be in your office at 1:30, and thanks."

"I'll see you then, Mr. Fitzjames," she said, and the statement was followed by a discernible click as the call ended.

Fitzjames placed a second call to Fuller and requested that Fuller contact the Kansas City FBI Bureau Chief and clarify Fitzjames' authority to make inquiries and obtain information.

"No problem. I'll be done in the next ten minutes. Making forward progress?" Fuller inquired.

"Yes, forward progress, sir," responded Fitzjames.

"We got word this morning of the additional deaths in Kansas City. Five more were reported out of Pittsburgh. Anxiety is rising. You may need to redouble the pace of your investigations. Do you need a partner?" asked Fuller.

"At present, no, sir. I'm hoping that what I learn here will make another stop in the continental U.S. unnecessary. I'll keep you posted, sir."

"Do so, Captain. For the present, I've dispensed with the requirement that you provide written reports in order to keep you freer to act. But I will need phone updates."

"Of course, sir. Thank you."

"Keep at it," said Fuller, almost too softly for Fitzjames to hear, as the call ended.

Seven

Fitzjames glanced at the aged digital clock in the hotel room. He presumed that Consuela Casillas' televised statement would be broadcast at 12:30. He intended to watch the presentation. He thus had something more than ninety minutes to get himself settled in the hotel room, which would require little time, and perhaps a brief walk through the shops near the hotel.

After removing the toiletry kit from the suitcase, he entered the bathroom. He placed the small bottle of *Armani* cologne, razor, toothbrush, and dental floss on the basin and washed his hands and face. He brushed his teeth and thereafter corrected his hair and tucked in, anew, his shirt. After leaving the bathroom, he collected his mobile telephone and the room key and reconfirmed the amount of cash that he carried in his wallet. The cash was low; he would need to draw out more from an ATM, if he could find one nearby.

He left the hotel room and descended in the elevator to the lobby. He walked toward the front desk and was forced to wait a few minutes for the three clerks to complete the tasks they were performing for other guests. A different clerk from the one who had assisted him when he had arrived was the first of the three to have the opportunity to speak to him, which she did by name.

"Mr. Fitzjames, how can we help you?" she asked with a broad smile that revealed her perfectly white and orderly teeth.

"Gracious. I didn't expect to be remembered by name. Marriott Hotels must require a lot of its people if they're also required to know all of their guests' names," he said, returning the smile.

"They're not that hard on us. They like that we try to remember names, and our manager encourages it. But it's not a requirement. I wouldn't have been fired if I'd forgotten yours," she returned.

"That's good news."

"Yes. Job's safe and secure. But I did remember your name. So, how can I help you, Mr. Fitzjames?" she asked again, as the other two clerks joined her.

All three stood together in apparent but awkward, comical joyful expectation of providing assistance to him. They all smiled.

"Now, I think I need to ask three questions, since all three of you appear poised to render an answer to my single question," he suggested with another smile. "But all I wanted to find out is whether there's a coffee shop nearby, like a Starbucks?"

"Right down the street, really. Go out the front door and turn left. Walk up the hill to the traffic light and turn right. Go beyond the park, which will be on your right and beyond the fountains, and you'll find a Starbucks. Very close."

"Thanks."

"You're very welcome," replied the clerk.

He nodded and tapped the fingers of his right hand lightly on the desktop and smiled and glanced at all three of the young women. "Thanks for all the help," he added and turned and walked briskly outside.

The three clerks watched him with a similar intensity to that which they had employed after he had checked into the hotel and when he was strolling toward the elevator.

The directions provided were simple and accurate. Fitzjames found a Starbucks just beyond the park and within an upscale shopping area that was already showing the signs of a busy day for retailers. Although only midmorning and cold, shoppers filled the sidewalks and could be seen in stores. Fitzjames appreciated that each woman he observed, irrespective of age, height, weight, or apparent social standing, was carrying a bag or parcel evidencing a purchase. The local economy must, he assumed, be thriving.

Fitzjames entered the Starbucks, which had few tables but many customers. He found a place in a long line to order a coffee. After a wait of in excess of ten minutes, his name was called, and he picked up the cup of strongly brewed acidic coffee presented to him on an elevated circular wooden bar on which all drinks were placed. The Starbucks' method of beverage preparation had always astounded him. To his mind, it was a muddled operation for the creation of strange tea or coffee blends, all made to order. Yet, the drinks came fast and consistently came right. Complexity never appeared to affect the speed of completion or the accuracy of the labor.

Fitzjames could not find a vacant table but observed a few empty chairs. In lieu of the awkwardness of taking one of the vacant chairs and sitting at a table already occupied, he left the Starbucks and continued the walk westward on the sidewalk. He drank the coffee and surveyed the shops. At an electronics retailer, whose name he did not recognize, he opened the heavy, thick glass door and entered and passed through an unmanned metal detector.

A young male employee attired in a pastel-colored polo-style shirt and khaki slacks addressed him. "Good morning. Sir, sorry, but you can't bring that in," said the employee.

"What? I'm sorry," responded Fitzjames. "What's the problem?"

"Your coffee. Store rules. I'm sorry, but you can't have an open drink in the store," answered the young man in a labored effort to enforce the regulations, while at the same time seeking to remain respectful.

"Ah, no problem," said Fitzjames. "I can appreciate the rules. I'll drink it off and toss it out."

Fitzjames tipped the cup, drank the remaining coffee, and dropped the empty cup and cardboard sleeve into a trashcan over which the young employee appeared to superintend.

"Thank you, sir. Have a good day."

"Thanks, you too," replied Fitzjames.

Like the other stores, this one was busy with shoppers. Fitzjames walked through the aisles and examined the newest versions of cellular telephones, laptops, desktop computers, musical devices, and television sets. He had no intentions of making a purchase but found the equipment fascinating. After fifteen minutes of browsing, he wished the same young man at the entrance a good day, exited, and began the trek back to the hotel.

After walking a few yards, he noticed a bank with a prominent ATM advertised with a neon lighted sign. He altered his steps at the next intersection and advanced toward the bank. In route, he removed the credit card from his wallet and recalled to mind the personal identification number, which required a bit of mental effort because he rarely procured cash from an ATM. As he reached the bank, he was startled by the sudden piercing sounds of sirens from multiple police and emergency medical vehicles. They shocked the still-cold air and had no preclude. They were not at first audible in the distance, as is typical, only then to grow louder. Instead, the noise simply commenced, and it occurred to Fitzjames that the police and paramedics may have been lying in wait for an incident.

He completed the transaction at the ATM under the disruptive sounds of the sirens. After collecting the cash and receipt, he walked back to the central roadway from which he turned moments earlier. He paused and could see clearly at a distance of some seventy-five yards five police cars surrounding an ambulance. Three white-shirted paramedics were attending to two men who were motionless and prostrate on the sidewalk. Police officers in dark monocolored uniforms and with sidearms stood nearby; four encircled the emergency medical personnel. One officer held a rifle with the barrel pointed toward the sky. Onlookers had begun to congregate and certain of the officers sought to disperse them, only to have other curious pedestrians replace those who had complied and returned to their shopping.

As Fitzjames recommenced the return journey to the hotel, he overheard two gunshots fired in rapid succession. The first shot exploded at a distance, but the second was nearby. He instinctively dropped to one knee at the sound.

Fitzjames quickly studied the police reaction. They were dashing to gain cover behind the squad cars. Pedestrians were running in different directions for protection. Screams could be heard, along with incomprehensible shouting. Chaos erupted when the police officer with the rifle and his ostensible partner, respectively, returned fire in the direction of both shots. A gun battle on the streets of Kansas City's most refined shopping area ensued. More shots were fired by the gunmen and more fire was returned by the police. Meanwhile, shoppers scrambled to enter stores or vehicles for safety.

Fitzjames, of course, had no weapon. He also had no standing with local law enforcement. If he had had his gun, he would likely have been reluctant to use it and might very well have been gunned down in the fray by the police. As a result and because he suspected the location of the gunman nearest to him, he crouched and then scurried, with his head down and arms extended, across a side street to the corner of two adjoined perpendicular concrete exterior walls of a building. From that point, he raised himself sufficiently to see, just fifteen yards from him, a young man positioned behind a large cylindrical metal protrusion, part of a piece of modern art, which was painted red and, presumably, was intended to be cultural and evocative. Instead, at this moment, the artwork provided impenetrable cover for the gunman.

Fitzjames examined the man for a few seconds. He was young, perhaps in his mid-twenties, less than six feet in height, his arms covered in tattoos. He wore dark jeans, athletic shoes, and only a t-shirt, despite the cold. Fitzjames could not discern the type of pistol he held, but it was a large, ugly weapon. Although the man appeared to be focused on a point near the police, Fitzjames observed a young mother clutching an infant with one hand on the back of the child's head to the man's immediate right. She was penned down, unable to move, and terrified. She had clearly recognized that if she attempted to change her position or escape, the man might shoot her, out of either fear or confusion, or the police might mistake her for the gunman and fire at her.

The gunman had no view of Fitzjames, who was behind him. Fitzjames evaluated the options. The woman was in grave peril and her fear might prompt her to act foolishly and thus disastrously, for herself and the child. He too was at risk if his movements attracted attention. The police were too far away to be of any real effect, unless they maneuvered much closer and to a place where they could get a clear shot at the gunman. The barrier the gunman had selected was ideal for his own protection and for the impact of his violence. Modern sculpture was, indeed, serving the public at large.

Fitzjames recognized that the sole alternative was to act. He receded behind the wall, discarded his jacket to free himself from the restraint imposed by it, and pulled out of his pants the shirt and undershirt that he wore. He lowered himself and again peered around the corner. He waited for the bullets being fired by the police to break, in part for his own safety, and paused for the gunman to begin to return fire. With this distraction, the gunman was unable to sense Fitzjames approach from behind him. As the gunman emptied the pistol, Fitzjames darted toward him and then dove at him. Fitzjames struck the gunman with the full force of his weight and height in the form of a human missile. The man tumbled over with Fitzjames on top of him. The impact caused him to lose the grip on his gun. The pistol fell from the man's hand and snapped upon hitting the asphalt. More shots came in from the police and struck on either side of the sculpture but away from the two combatants.

Fitzjames brought down, in rapid succession, two blows to the gunman's head with the fist of his right hand. Fitzjames then jumped to his feet and the gunman, who had now partially recovered, attempted to rise. He swore in Spanish.

"*Hijo de puta*," he mumbled, which was quickly followed by "*Coma mierda*."

In reply, Fitzjames struck him a third time. This last blow dropped him to the ground on his stomach. With his left hand, Fitzjames pressed the man's head to the roadway and buried his right knee in the middle of the man's back. The police again fired shots, one of which nearly hit Fitzjames, as he was now visible with the gunman under restraint. Out of breath, Fitzjames shouted at the officers as loudly as he could manage.

"Hold your fire! Move in, quickly!"

The police did not immediately react. Fitzjames continued to hold down the gunman but he was strong, and Fitzjames struggled to keep him flat on the street. The gunman continued to spit profanities at Fitzjames, first in Spanish, followed by English.

"Hold your fire and move in!" repeated Fitzjames.

Fitzjames discerned the shuffle of feet growing closer and seconds later four officers stood over him with their pistols trained on him and the gunman.

"Handcuff him; I can't hold him or keep him in this position much longer," urged Fitzjames.

Two of the policemen holstered their weapons and stepped forward to assist Fitzjames. The first placed a knee on the gunman's legs and the second reordered the gunman's arms behind his back and locked a set of metal handcuffs on his wrists. Fitzjames rose, and the other two officers joined their colleagues and hoisted the gunman to his feet by pulling him by his arms.

"What prompted you to do that?" inquired the most senior officer of the group in a glib tone.

"Someone was going to die if I hadn't," responded Fitzjames, out of breath and annoyed by the question. "I'm just lucky I didn't get shot by you guys in the process."

"Exactly. We had the situation under control. We would've taken him out, and you're mighty fortunate that you weren't hit."

"Perhaps. But there was too much gunfire to be confident, in this crowd and in this place, that someone wouldn't be injured or killed by the time you took him down," said Fitzjames with irritation in his voice. "Who is this guy?"

"Who are you?" asked the officer.

"I'm a visitor in town. I'm staying at the Marriott, just up the street. I was on my way back there when this Old West-style gunfight broke out. My name is Fitzjames. I'll give you a full statement, but you'll need to wait for it. I've got to get moving. My jacket's over there behind the wall. I'll give you one of my cards, and you can call me on my cellphone for whatever information you'll need."

"If you're visiting, what's the rush? Can't you give us what we need now? It should only take a few minutes," said the officer, warming a bit.

"No. Sorry. Can't happen. To be candid, I've got a meeting in a short time with some folks at the local FBI field office, and I've got to get some things done beforehand."

"FBI? Really?" responded the officer incredulously.

"Yes."

"Who, by chance, are you seeing there?" queried the officer, who appeared to believe that Fitzjames was either a liar or lunatic.

"Special Agent Consuela Casillas. Do you know her? Know the name? I'm to see her at 1:30."

"I recognize the name. Never met her."

"Look, I'll give you my card, and you can call me. It's unimportant if you believe me about the FBI meeting. Irrelevant. But I suggest that you call Agent Casillas this afternoon, later, and make whatever inquiries you wish to make about me to her. She'll vouch for me. Now, who is this guy—the shooter?"

The officer hesitated a moment. On the basis of an instinctive capacity to measure veracity, sharpened by thirty years of law enforcement, he accepted Fitzjames' explanation and chose to give the details.

"Did you see those tattoos all over his arms?" the officer asked.

"Sure, yes, very elaborate," said Fitzjames. "I didn't, of course, study them."

"Of course not. Those body markings mark him out as a member of the *Pilotos de Moncova.* The gunman, I think, and we'll have to confirm it, is Julio Hernandez. Looks like Hernandez. He's a senior player in the Pilotos. It's the most violent, dangerous gang in Kansas City. Vicious and deadly."

"I can well believe it. I'll get you my card."

Fitzjames returned to the corner of the building. The officer followed him. He collected his jacket from the ground, where he had left it. He removed his wallet, extracted a business card, and delivered the card to the officer.

"My cellphone number is on the card."

"Lawyer, from Florida," said the officer, while holding the card at an arm's length distance in order to see and study it.

"Yes. And you are?"

"I'm Lieutenant Atherton, Kansas City Municipal Police."

"Very good, Lieutenant. Give me a call."

"I'll do so. And, uh, thanks again," added the lieutenant awkwardly and reluctantly and yet sincerely.

Without replying and without putting on the jacket, Fitzjames turned and returned to the hotel. The temperature had dropped and light snow had begun to fall.

Eight

Fitzjames returned to the hotel, took the elevator to the sixth floor, exited, and walked down the corridor to the room. He powered on the television set and, with the remote control, scrolled up through the stations in an effort to find a news report of a local broadcaster and, if possible, a press conference. The time was nearing one in the afternoon.

At the very instant when he perceived that he had either missed the press conference or could not find a station presenting local news, he encountered a middle-aged woman, in her late forties or early fifties, standing behind a rostrum with microphones before her. She wore bright, bold red lipstick. She wore no other makeup. She was thin and fit and attired in a masculine-styled dress shirt and dress pants. Although attired like a man and perhaps attempting to attenuate her femininity, she was an attractive woman. Fitzjames increased the volume on the television and listened.

The prepared statement had concluded, and the woman was fielding questions from the members of the press who were present. Most of the questions posed were simpleminded or outlandish. She answered each inquiry with grace, despite her growing and apparent impatience with the lack of depth or the promotion of sensationalism in the journalists. Another, less experienced agent would have been brittle. The final question ended the conference.

"Special Agent Casillas, can you speculate when the next death will occur?" queried a young man from the audience.

"No, sir, as that would make me prescient, which I'm not. I also don't have a crystal ball. No more questions, ladies and gentlemen. We'll furnish further information to the press once we've moved the investigation forward. Thank you," she replied and, over objections from the reporters, turned away from the microphones and left the room, followed by two male FBI agents and a male representative of the sheriff's department, a deputy.

Fitzjames turned off the television and entered the bathroom. He got out of his clothes and took a brief shower. After toweling off, he added gel to his hair, applied deodorant and a bit of Armani *eau de toilette*, and brushed his teeth. He dressed in clean clothes. He collected his wallet, mobile telephone, room key, and jacket. He left the room and returned to the lobby. Smiles from the three clerks again greeted him.

"Are any taxis available outside or will you need to call one for me?" he asked the first of the clerks to advance to the counter.

"Good afternoon, Mr. Fitzjames. You should find one or more cabs waiting outside. Generally, they're there, just sitting. If not, I'll call one for you."

"Thanks," he responded and walked out the lobby doors.

At a distance of approximately twenty yards, two taxis, one behind the other, waited. He raised his left arm and signaled to the first, who pulled forward slowly.

He entered the back of the taxi, took a seat, and directed the driver to take him to the FBI field office on Summit Street. The driver, who was from East Africa, specifically Kenya, offered no conversation. Fitzjames discerned his origin from the small decorative Kenyan national flag hanging from the rearview mirror. The music that he played over the radio, too loudly, was also East African.

"Could we turn the music down a bit, please?" asked Fitzjames.

"Excuse me, sir?" replied the driver, who had trouble hearing the request because of the music.

"The music. Could you turn it down? It's too loud," repeated Fitzjames.

"Okay, sure," said the driver petulantly.

"Thanks," said Fitzjames.

"You don't like African music?" inquired the driver, while looking at Fitzjames in the rearview mirror.

"No, I've no objection to it. I just don't like it, or any music, too loud and certainly not in a taxi. Also, could you turn down the car heater; it's a sweat box in here."

"Okay, okay."

The driver complied and turned off the heating system. Fitzjames lowered to mid-level the passenger-side window to allow a breeze into the cab. The driver shrugged his shoulders in silence and buttoned the two top buttons of the old tattered coat that he wore. In short order, the external air cooled the interior of the vehicle. Fitzjames, once comfortable, raised the window but did not seal it.

The driver completed the journey without speaking again to Fitzjames. He did mumble complaints in an East African tribal dialect which, of course, Fitzjames could not understand. But the tone was such that the obscenities were hardly disguised. Fitzjames shook his head and upon arrival at the destination paid the fare reflected on the meter. He added a five-dollar tip, which the driver attempted to return to him, presuming that he had inadvertently overpaid. Fitzjames told him to keep it.

"Thanks for accommodating me and turning down the heater and the music," said Fitzjames as he exited the taxi.

"You're welcome, sir. Sorry for the discomfort," replied the driver, clearly stunned by receipt of the gratuity.

"No problem."

Fitzjames entered Kansas City's FBI field office. He arrived only minutes earlier than his scheduled visit. After a short wait in the lobby, Special Agent Casillas introduced herself and welcomed him. At her direction, he followed her to her office, which was a large room on the same floor as the entrance. He took a seat upon it being offered.

"I caught the end of the press conference on the TV; I didn't see the entire presentation. I got held up. It ended with a rather ridiculous question from a reporter. Something about your predicting the future," said Fitzjames, thereby opening the dialog.

"Yes. Typical. We're expected to predict crime, stop it, and arrest the culprits. Sounds like a book of science-fiction I once read," she responded with a frown and shaking her head. "Alarmists, all of them. But they may have good cause, this time, which is terrifying."

"I understand. Hopefully, I'll be able to be part of the solution."

"How can I help you, Captain Fitzjames? What can we offer?"

"Call me Trey. I see you've gotten some background data on me. May I call you Consuela?"

"Sure. That'll be fine. Yes, we've done some probing. As I told you earlier, Owen Hughes' admonition and recommendation was sufficient. But I always ask a few more questions. We've cleared you. Still some mysteries, of course, but we've learned enough to satisfy us."

"Good. In reviewing Hughes' materials, I came upon a name that caused me to redirect my steps here, in lieu of going to New York. My expectation was that the trail would take me there. Instead, it brought me here."

"Who is it? Or should I hazard a guess?"

"It's Manuel Algorta," offered Fitzjames.

"My guess, precisely."

"Who is he, from your perspective? The data in Hughes' file was vague, but I couldn't seem to get past him. His movements, activities, and connections all caused me to focus on him."

"He's a bastard," replied Casillas coldly. "Vicious, deadly, treacherous, and violent. No limits."

"Is he in Kansas City, to your knowledge?"

"Yes and no. He has illicit business connections here. He operates a drug sales and distribution ring from Colombia and Venezuela through Mexico and then north through Texas and into Kansas City. But we believe he's effective because he's the shadow behind the gangs that do his bidding. We have a particularly troubling gang here in the city. The Pilotos. Most of their activities, whether drugs, crime, or violence are, again we suspect, orchestrated by Algorta."

"I've had, strangely, some contact with the Pilotos."

"Elsewhere?"

"No, here in Kansas City and only a short time ago. You've likely been too busy to follow the events of earlier this morning. But, there was a gun battle between some members of the Pilotos and the police not far from my hotel."

"You're right. I don't know anything about it. This morning?"

"Yes, near the intersection of Broadway and West 47th Street."

Casillas turned in the chair and typed on the keyboard of the computer situated on the corner of her desk. She paused and studied the monitor, as data streamed across its face. She picked up the telephone receiver and pressed a number and waited for the recipient of the call to respond. She asked the party on the other end of the line to come to her office. She resumed the conversation with Fitzjames.

"In a few minutes, I'll be in a position to furnish to you virtually everything we have on Manuel Algorta, including aliases, operatives, lieutenants, and known associates. Agent Sorensen will join us in a moment. I've asked her to come in. We've got an entire database devoted to Algorta."

"Excellent. Thank you," said Fitzjames.

"The Pilotos are a real menace here in the county and across the state line in Kansas. But we've stayed out of the way—unless invited in, of course—of local law enforcement. The sheriff's department, in particular, seems especially sensitive to any intrusion from us with respect to gang activity. We only step in if asked to do so or if FBI involvement is legally mandated. We're occasionally asked by the police chiefs and sheriff to furnish information and research, but little more. Curiously, the current drug problem, which is tied to the gangs and specifically to the Pilotos, and thus, for us, to Algorta, is one they don't want to touch. So, they leave it to us. It's okay, at the end of the day. I don't like partnering with police officers or deputies. They're all undereducated, pistol-carrying cowboys, drunk on their badges and uniforms. They get in the way, typically. And, they've all got a chip on the shoulder."

"Harsh appraisal," responded Fitzjames.

"Perhaps, but it's accurate," said Casillas.

"I can't say, that in my own experience, personally, that I'd disagree," added Fitzjames. "It is a curious piece of Americana that we train high school graduates for six months and then give them a badge, a uniform, and gun and hope for the best."

Special Agent Maria Sorensen entered Casillas' office as Fitzjames was concluding his statement about the young cops. Fitzjames rose from his chair.

"Agent Sorensen, this is Captain Fitzjames, U.S. Army, as I understand it."

"Yes, that'll do. Nice to meet you," said Fitzjames to Sorensen with a smile.

Sorensen, without a return smile, looked intently at Fitzjames and extended her hand. He shook it. The hand was cold and the grip oddly aggressive. She said nothing and sat in the other empty chair adjacent to Casillas' desk. Fitzjames pulled out the chair in which he had been sitting, the arms of which touched the chair now occupied by Sorensen. He repositioned the chair to put a fraction of distance between them.

As Consuela Casillas gave instructions to Maria Sorensen, Fitzjames listened and took the opportunity to survey the latter. She was approximately thirty-five years old and of obvious Nordic extraction with light, almost white, blonde hair of shoulder length. She was tall and in good physical condition. Like Casillas, she was dressed much like a man. Yet, also like Casillas, the masculine clothing could not hide her beauty. The odd notion trickled through his mind that perhaps the FBI, as a result of the rigorous physical requirements for recruits, inadvertently engaged and retained attractive women. It was a curious thought, which he put out of mind in order to remain focused.

When Casillas completed the instructions, Sorensen stood and spoke to Fitzjames.

"If you'll follow me, please," she mumbled.

As requested, Fitzjames followed Maria Sorensen out of Consuela Casillas' office. Casillas said nothing when the two left here office, although Fitzjames had thanked Casillas as he exited behind Sorensen.

Sorensen walked, almost in a jackbooted march, down the corridor to the elevator. She offered no conversation and evinced no emotion, other than indifference toward Fitzjames and his visit. They entered the elevator and in silence ascended to the top floor. Again, in silence, once off the elevator, they walked down a narrow hallway to a small office. Sorensen opened the door and then took a seat behind the small wooden desk. The desk was clear of paperwork and all other evidence of office labor, except for a computer monitor. The room was austere and cold. The walls were adorned with four wall hangings, one per wall. Two were diplomas of degrees earned from small private universities, in Minnesota and in Iowa. As Fitzjames had suspected, Ms. Sorensen was a Minnesotan, at least if her undergraduate degree revealed a point of origin. The other two walls carried prints of works by Rembrandt and Rubens. Other than the diplomas and prints, the office had no other decoration.

"You may sit," said Sorensen to Fitzjames. It was not a warm invitation.

Fitzjames thanked her, quietly, and sat in the small, armless wooden chair that he collected from the corner of the room and replaced to a position adjacent to Sorensen's desk. She paid no attention to his movements and worked at the computer. The silence continued and he waited. After five minutes of no communication, he studied the time on his Breitling wristwatch and removed the wallet from this jacket in order to review his notecards and, as necessary, make notations about the subjects covered in his brief conference with Casillas.

"There's no need to look at the time. I'll be finished here in a moment. I hope I'm not keeping you," said Sorensen cynically.

"Not at all. Take your time," he replied.

"Thank you," she said, with like sarcasm and without looking at him.

"Actually, let me reframe my answer," returned Fitzjames. "I am in a bit of a rush, as are we all, in connection with this operation and problem. So, to the extent that you can move matters along, I'd be appreciative. It'd also reduce the time that you'd be compelled to deal with me, which appears to be a burden."

"No burden, just an annoyance. My view is that Manuel Algorta is a domestic problem and a law enforcement matter, not a military matter. I'm not keen on seeing the U.S. Army tied upon in domestic law enforcement, which is what I see with you, Mr. Fitzjames. But I have my orders and my duties, and I'll follow and fulfill them, whether I like it or not," she said with a measure of condescension.

"To ease your anxieties about any unconstitutional overlap of the police and the military in connection with domestic matters, this is not a developing trend. I have my orders and they're very narrow. I work alone, except when I need information. The information either comes from the FBI if the matter is domestic or from the CIA or Interpol if the matter is international. So, you needn't worry. And, once again, the more rapidly you can furnish the data, the more rapidly I'll be on my way," he answered quietly and very directly.

"You're the edge of the wedge," she said.

"I don't think so. But I'll pass along your fears to my superiors, if that makes you feel any better," responded Fitzjames, adding a smile.

Sorensen did not reciprocate the smile but returned to her labors on the computer. The silence began anew but was broken by the activity of the printer on a small table behind Sorensen. After the passage of a few more minutes, at least thirty sheets of paper had run through the printer and rested on the receiving tray. Sorensen completed work on the keyboard, opened a drawer below the top of the desk, removed a file, collected the paperwork from the printer, two-hole punched the top of all of the sheets of paper, added the papers under the metal prongs in the interior of the file, and presented the file to Fitzjames. He accepted it with a muted expression of gratitude.

"I'll escort you out of the building," said Sorensen and rose from the chair. "We can't have you roaming the halls unaccompanied. Violates internal rules."

"Of course."

Fitzjames followed Sorensen out of the office, down the hall, down the elevator, and into the lobby. The escort was conducted without comment or commentary from Sorensen. In the lobby, Fitzjames thanked her for her time and suggested to her to have a good day.

"If you need us again, my card and Agent Casillas' card are fastened inside the folder," she replied.

"Thank you," he said and passed out of the FBI facility.

He took a taxi back to the hotel and devoted the remainder of the afternoon and a portion of the early evening to studying the file furnished to him by Agent Sorensen.

He recognized that the domestic piece of the mission had concluded. Retracing his steps to Pittsburgh would not be warranted and a visit to New York would be pointless, as it would only amplify what he already knew or suspected. Such amplification was unnecessary and would only delay him.

Fitzjames closed the file and checked the time. It had been dark for two hours. He had not noticed the sun going down and the hotel room darkening. He picked up the mobile telephone and contacted Major Fuller.

"Yes, Captain?" came the customary response.

"Sir. The work here is complete. I need to get to Caracas. Can that be arranged, quickly?" inquired Fitzjames.

"Caracas?"

"Yes, sir. Caracas. Unless I'm missing something, our target can be found there."

"Very well. We'll get it sorted out. I'll recontact you later this evening with the travel details and contacts."

"Thank you, sir."

"Also, you may interested to learn that ten more deaths have occurred in Pittsburgh. Your FBI contact there, Hughes, is providing a channel of information to us. Disturbingly, one of the deaths is of a member of a medical team in the city doing research on the contagion. A physician. She'd been deeply involved with the research with a number of patients. Worked at a Pittsburgh hospital with other scientists. Now, they're re-ordering their protocols to keep up the research but also protect the researchers. It's growing larger and more frightening."

"Indeed," responded Fitzjames with a pause. "Do you have any names, sir, of the medical team member?"

"No. But it was a woman. That's all I know. I'll get the Caracas matter organized. You'll need support there. I'll get on that as well. Expect my call later this evening. Well done."

"Thank you, sir. I'll wait for your call."

Nine

"When you arrive, a local man will offer you a private taxi. He will then, if he's your contact, employ Recognition Code 4 of the protocol. Do you recall Code 4?" asked Fuller when he telephoned Fitzjames at 8:30 later the same evening. He knew the answer to his question but posed it, mechanically, nonetheless.

"Of course, sir," responded Fitzjames.

"All, I presume, fully committed to memory?"

"Yes, of course, sir."

"Good. We have significant personnel in Venezuela, primarily to keep an eye on the Chavez regime. All local people, ordered and managed by the CIA. But very few Americans. The CIA brings in its American personnel only when essential because of the risks of discovery and thus avoiding the risk of pointlessly exposing native contacts and the native payroll. If you need assistance, I've gotten assurances that the CIA will put a team on the ground within twenty-four hours of your request. It'll be your call entirely. Until then, if at all, you're in native hands."

"English speakers?" inquired Fitzjames.

"All, should you need English. I'm surprised by the question. One, your Spanish is excellent. Two, they do work with the CIA."

"Just confirming, sir. I'm always anxious about being understood—for the operations' sake."

"I understand. Money in order?"

"Yes, sir."

"Any other concerns?"

"Airline passage has been booked?"

"Certainly, all taken care of. You'll need to report to the Southwest counter tomorrow morning at 7:45. The flight to Miami departs at 8:50. At 2:30, the flight to Caracas on American is scheduled."

"Thank you, sir."

"Anything else?"

"Only one more item. Do you have any particulars on the death of the physician in Pittsburgh?"

"No, nothing. Sorry. Professional or personal interest?"

"Both, sir. I'll do my own investigation. Once on the ground in Caracas, I'll provide periodic reports, as mandated."

"Very good. Good luck, Captain."

"Thank you, sir."

Fitzjames considered a moment whether a telephone call to Stacy Reimer was sensible. The call from him might be misinterpreted by her and seen as oddly intrusive. At the same time, good judgment dictated that he should relieve himself of the uncertainty he was feeling about her welfare before he set off for Venezuela. He thus called information and obtained the number to the hospital. He requested that the operator connect him, although it was certainly beyond the hour at which he could have had any expectation of reaching her. But, if he asked for her and if she were not in the hospital, the receptionist would give him the information he wanted, even indirectly. To his surprise and satisfaction, when he asked for Dr. Reimer, without hesitation, the call was sent along to her office. He waited while the line rang. It rang five times, with no answer, and then a voicemail system was triggered. The recorded voice of Stacy Reimer briefly suggested to the caller to leave a message. He chose not to do so.

After a few seconds of hesitation, he fought off the temptation to make further inquiries about her. He suspected that with modest effort, he could obtain a home telephone number or a cellular number. Hughes could provide it, for example. Yet the exercise and his inquiries would leave peculiar questions in the minds of those whom he contacted. If his fears were unfounded, Stacy might not appreciate his inquisitiveness. With forced, intentional mental effort, he pushed the matter out of his mind.

Fitzjames returned to the file and renewed his study of the biographical data on the subject of Manuel Algorta. The file contained five discrete sheets of paper with a photograph of Algorta on each in the upper-right-hand corner. Each paper provided details of Algorta's whereabouts, travels, homes, and business venues. The photographs varied. In two photos, Algorta wore long hair and glasses, and in one of those two he had a mustache and long beard. He had the appearance of a Bedouin or a Tuareg. In two others, he was clean-shaven, wore no glasses, and his hair was cut short and neatly combed and oiled. In these latter photographs, he had the appearance of a tenor at the opera. In the last photo, which was akin to a police mugshot, his hair was disordered and his face was unshaved but not bearded. Algorta was a man of varying identities and multiple social classes. He could pose as the junkie or as the elitist. Fitzjames committed the faces to memory, as well as the data within the paperwork. He now knew and had a picture in his mind of the target.

Fitzjames closed the file and placed it in his backpack. He entered the bathroom, used the toilet, and washed his hands and face. He snatched up the room key and his wallet and mobile telephone and left the hotel room. Before he could enter the elevator, the mobile telephone chimed. He studied its face but did not recognize the incoming number. The area code, however, he did recognize as local to Kansas City. He answered the call.

"Hello," said Fitzjames.

"Is this R. P. Fitzjames?"

"Who is this? Who's calling?"

"Is this R. P. Fitzjames?" asked the caller again in a more aggressive, demanding tone.

"Answer my question, before I give you a reply to yours. Who is this?"

"This is Lieutenant Atherton, Kansas City Municipal Police. Is this Fitzjames?"

"This is Fitzjames. How can I help you, Lieutenant, except perhaps with your manners? Do you typically make calls at this time of night on personal cellphones and not introduce yourself?"

"This is police work," he said authoritatively.

"I really don't care what it is. But I do care about common courtesy. You were glib this morning and you're disrespectful now. If you want my help, at some level, you're going to have to do a better job," replied Fitzjames, as he entered the elevator and pressed the button to descend to the lobby.

"Look, Fitzjames, this is official business. Are you not going to be helpful or are you planning, by not helping, to interfere?"

"I've already assisted you once today. You've got an odd way of expressing gratitude. I'm prepared to cooperate with you, reasonably. But, as I said, I won't do it without your employing good manners, whether you like it or not. I may sound like some overbearing aristocrat or a prig, but there it is. I don't like disrespect. If I treat you courteously, then I expect you'll do the same for me," replied Fitzjames with growing impatience.

"Okay, okay. I'll play by your rules. Could we get you down here to make a formal statement about the events of the morning?" asked Atherton.

"I don't have any transportation, and I've not had any supper. I'm on my way out now to get something to eat."

"Are you at your hotel? The Marriott, right?"

"Yes, I'm in the lobby."

"I'll send a car 'round to pick you up. The officer will be there in less than five minutes. Front of the hotel. Okay?"

"Okay. Fine. I'll be outside and down the street a bit. I'll signal to him when he arrives. I don't want the folks in the hotel to see me climb into a squad car."

"Have it your way. The car will be there in five minutes, no more."

"Fine. I'll look out for it."

Fitzjames strolled out of the hotel and to the roadway. He turned and walked along the sidewalk in a southerly direction and, at a traffic light, crossed the roadway over a pedestrian crosswalk and continued southward another fifty yards to the front of a restaurant. The door of the restaurant was open, despite the cold, the sounds of a crowded, popular, and successful eatery spilled to the outside. He studied the menu, which was posted on the window to the right of the entrance. The restaurant offered American cuisine but with creative twists. The prices were reasonable. A sandwich board advertising beer and cocktails at very low cost stood to the left of the doorway.

"Hey, are you Fitzjames?"

Fitzjames looked over his right shoulder and turned. A black and gold Kansas City Municipal Police vehicle, with flashing blue and red lights, had stopped in front of the restaurant. Two officers sat in the front seats, one behind the steering wheel and the other on the passenger side with his arm resting casually on the door with an open window. Fitzjames did not respond but approached the car.

"Are you Fitzjames?" asked the policeman a second time, only more loudly and more commanding.

Fitzjames smirked as he considered that in his experience the typical police officer mistakenly presumed that his authority was amplified by asking questions more loudly than was necessary or warranted.

The presence of the police began to draw attention. Passing motorists slowed to avoid the police care and to survey the sidewalk in front of the restaurant. Three patrons, waiting inside for a table in the busy restaurant, came outside to determine the cause of the flashing lights.

Still in silence and in order to avoid the awkwardness of being retrieved by the police, Fitzjames opened the back passenger-side door of the vehicle, climbed inside, and closed the door behind him.

"Drive on; I'm Fitzjames," he said quietly.

The driver, glancing over his shoulder, studied Fitzjames for a few seconds, while the driver's partner, who did not look behind, shook his head and raised the window. The driver peered into the side mirror and pulled out into the flow of traffic. He radioed the dispatcher that Fitzjames was with them.

In the absence of conversation, which Fitzjames did not offer, he watched through the barred windows of the back seat the growing urbanization of the landscape as the vehicle advanced through traffic toward the city center of

Kansas City. Within twenty minutes, they arrived at the headquarters of the Municipal Police.

"Do you want an escort or can you find your way to the lieutenant's office?" asked the driver as he maneuvered the squad car into the entry of the building. The entry was under an ugly, old metaled awning. "If you do, Officer Pendleton can take you up."

"I'll figure it out. Thanks for the ride," said Fitzjames. "Can you open this door for me?"

Pendleton stepped out and opened the door to release Fitzjames. Pendleton slammed shut the door behind him after he exited. Fitzjames made no comment but entered the lobby and approached the desk sergeant.

"Yes?" inquired the sergeant by way of greeting.

"My name is Fitzjames. I'm here to see Lieutenant Atherton by appointment."

"Who?"

"Atherton, Lieutenant Atherton," repeated Fitzjames.

"No, I got that. What's your name?" asked the sergeant moodily.

"Fitzjames."

"Spell it."

"F-I-T-Z-J-A-M-E-S. Fitzjames."

"Have a seat," snapped the sergeant, as he wrote Fitzjames' surname on a notepad.

Fitzjames shook his head and stepped away from the desk. He did not sit but stood and waited. He was alone in the lobby, and no one else entered the building. After fifteen minutes, he reapproached the desk sergeant, read his name from the badge the sergeant wore, and spoke to him.

"Sergeant Sutton, please call Lieutenant Atherton and tell him that I've waited long enough. He either needs to make himself available now, or I'm leaving," said Fitzjames.

"What?"

"Call Atherton again and tell him I'm not waiting any longer."

"He'll be with you when he's free," said Sutton coldly, while glaring at Fitzjames through anachronistic black horned-rimmed reading glasses.

"No. Doesn't work that way. Call him and tell him that I'm not waiting any longer. He's got three minutes to make his way down here. That's all I'm prepared to give him. I've not had any supper, and I don't like the imposition this exercise is causing."

"Who'd you think you are, anyway?" asked Sutton contemptuously.

"Just call him. He's losing valuable time."

Fitzjames turned and returned to the area in which he had been waiting. He overheard Sutton speaking on the telephone with, Fitzjames presumed, Atherton. In less than a moment, Atherton appeared in the lobby.

"Sorry for the delay," he said, somewhat insincerely, as he shook Fitzjames' hand. "Could we get you something to drink?"

"No, no, thanks. I just want to get this paperwork completed and then get going," responded Fitzjames.

Fitzjames followed Atherton up two flights of stairs to Atherton's spacious office. The interior of the police headquarters was dated and smelled of too many bodies over too much time with too little cleaning. Atherton took the chair behind a metal desk and Fitzjames sat, as well, in one of three chairs against the walls of the office, although Atherton did not offer to him an invitation to take a seat.

Atherton removed a sheet of paper from inside the top desk drawer and presented it to Fitzjames with a pen.

"If you'll just sign that, we'll get you out of here," said Atherton.

"A preprepared document?"

"Yes, well, we're just trying to make things simple because you're from out of town and in a hurry."

"That's curious. Let me study it."

"You'll find it sets out the facts," noted Atherton under his breath.

Fitzjames reviewed the document that contained a brief recapitulation of the events of the morning, which were accurate, but also contained overstatements about the involvement of the police in subduing the gunman and commentary about Fitzjames' actions being, in fact, unnecessary because the police had the situation under control with little risk to bystanders. The statement read like a newspaper story of a wild vigilante, from out of town, who foolishly disrupted a well-managed police operation.

"I'm not signing that," said Fitzjames.

"Why not? It's factual."

"It's nonsense. It's also littered with subjective inaccuracies about what actually occurred. You know as well as I do that the statement's false. Your office's handling of the events this morning was botched. It was nothing more than an Old West-style Kansas City gunfight that didn't seem to take into account the risks. The Pilotos may be a thorn in your department's side, but lots of people could've been shot because of your aggression. I only acted because it was the only viable option for me. A young mother with an infant was near me. She certainly would've been killed, either by the gang member or by your errant shooting."

"We're fighting a losing battle to this gang and others, and I can't have any more bad press. Look, Fitzjames, you're from out of town. What would it hurt to help pump up the cops a bit? Help us out."

"No. Can't do it. Not on these terms."

"You must understand. You're part of the brotherhood, aren't you? You said you knew Consuela Casillas at the FBI. And, you've obviously had some training. You couldn't have subdued the shooter without it. You did that like a real pro. Come on. What'd you say?" pleaded Atherton.

"No. If you need a statement from me, I'll dictate it to you, and I'll sign that. I won't sign this."

Reluctantly, Atherton collected the paper and pen from off his desk. He tore the sheet of paper into quarters and dropped in in the wastebasket. Thereafter, Fitzjames recited slowly, in order that Atherton could type the words on the computer keyboard, the events of the morning. Only three paragraphs were required. Atherton printed the document and, after Fitzjames examined it, he nodded his acceptance and asked for Atherton's pen. Fitzjames executed the statement and added the date and time. He pushed the single sheet back across the desktop to Atherton and asked the lieutenant to call a taxi to return him to the hotel.

Ten

The following morning at 6:15 at the front desk, Fitzjames paid for his stay at the Marriott, while a cab driver stood behind him with his suitcase in hand. After receiving a warm expression of appreciation from the clerk, Fitzjames followed the cab driver out of the hotel lobby and to the waiting taxi. Fitzjames instructed the driver to put the suitcase in the back seat, rather than in the trunk.

The drive to the airport required forty-five minutes because Kansas City's expressway traffic, even before light on a weekday, was thick. At the airport, Fitzjames checked the suitcase with a skycap outside of the terminal and thereafter passed through TSA security without incident or difficulty, despite the crowds. Once he reached the departure gate for Southwest flight number 407 to Miami, he dropped his backpack into a seat and extracted the mobile telephone. He scrolled through the calls made until he found the number for Oakland Northside Hospital in Pittsburgh. He pressed the redial feature. The call was answered and at his request transferred to Stacy Reimer's office. As had occurred the previous evening, the call was answered by voicemail. He left no message. After having niggling anxieties throughout the night about her welfare, Fitzjames had resolved earlier in the morning to attempt to telephone her upon reaching the airport. Now he had done so, with no better result. Once again, he concentrated on purging the issue from his mind.

Flight 407 to Miami proved to be rough. Although the jet stream provided a tail wind, the weather systems between Kansas City and Miami were large and aggressive. The Boeing 737-300 rumbled and shook and quivered through the turbulence. Only after having passed over Tampa Bay did the airplane fly smoothly.

After arrival in Miami, because the flight on American to Caracas was international, Fitzjames was compelled to collect his suitcase at baggage claim, recheck the suitcase, and proceed through security a second time. Miami International Airport was oddly, but not surprisingly, disorganized, there being no clarity about which queues of passengers led to which gates. For example, in line with Fitzjames were four passengers on domestic flights, who discovered after twenty minutes of waiting that they were not ticketed properly for the particular security station they had selected. Fitzjames stood at the full-body scanner; extended his arms as instructed by the Hispanic TSA operative, whose English was incomprehensible as his accent was so poor; waited the few seconds required; and proceeded to retrieve his belt, shoes, wristwatch, wallet, and backpack from the conveyor.

Before reaching the gate, Fitzjames stopped at a bookstore and purchased the current issues of *The Economist* and *The Atlantic* and the daily issue of *The Wall Street Journal.* From there, he walked slowly down the concourse because a full hour stretched between the current time and when he expected boarding would begin. At the gate, he deposited the two magazines in the backpack and stood and read the newspaper, which engaged him until the American Airlines representative announced that the rows in the rear of the plane would be filled first. Boarding began apace. Fitzjames presented his passport and boarding pass, strolled down the jetway, entered the plane, and found his numbered aisle and seat. The flight departed at the scheduled time precisely. Within three hours, the plane touched down *at Aeropuerto Internacional de Maiquetia Simon Bolivar.*

Fitzjames followed the movement of the stream of passengers through the terminal to Customs and Passport Control. He experienced no unusual scrutiny from the police manning the passport stations. At baggage claim, he identified the flight number on a computerized screen above one of the carousels and waited, with other travelers, for the suitcases to appear. They did not appear quickly. Although he was growing impatient, his fellow passengers were content to wait and indifferent about the delay. He turned his left wrist to see the face of the Breitling and thus check the time.

The carousel engaged and turned in a counterclockwise rotation. The first pieces of luggage from the flight began to appear.

"Sir, do you have transportation?" asked a man who appeared behind him. He spoke in thickly and heavily accented English.

"Excuse me?" asked Fitzjames as he turned.

"Sir, do you have transportation? I have a private car. It is much more comfortable than a taxi. Taxis are bad and have bad tires," said the man, who was only five and a half feet tall, thin, bearded with black hair, and was perhaps fifty years old.

"I prefer a private car," said Fitzjames, awaiting the employment by the man of the recognition code, if he were in fact Fitzjames' contact.

"My car is excellent. It is not American. It is Japanese. Have you traveled to Japan? It is an excellent country, but the food is poor."

"Bad food ruins a good holiday," returned Fitzjames.

"Bad food and bad wine," the man responded and then continued with a grin. "Welcome to Venezuela, Mr. Fitzjames. My name is Pedro Torres. I am your contact here in Caracas. Please identify your suitcase, and I will take it to the car."

"Excellent. Call me Trey."

"*Hablas español?*" Torres inquired.

"*Sí, claro, pero prefiero ingles en este momento*," responded Fitzjames.

"*Si, es major; creo*. We'll speak in English."

"Good. My bag is the tweed Hartmann garment bag just coming around the carousel," said Fitzjames, pointing to the luggage.

Torres moved beyond where Fitzjames stood and pulled the specified suitcase from the moving conveyor. He said nothing more to Fitzjames but walked through the multitude of travelers through double doors and outside to a cream-colored four-door Suzuki Grand Vitara. Torres unlocked the car with a remote device and popped the hatch, also remotely. He placed Fitzjames' suitcase into the trunk, closed the hatch door, and then held out his right hand in invitation to Fitzjames to take the passenger seat. Fitzjames opened the back passenger-side door, while simultaneously Torres opened the door on the driver's side. Fitzjames put this backpack on the back seat and then opened the front passenger-side door. Both men climbed into the vehicle and fastened the seatbelts with an oddly prearranged synchronicity that came from being aware of the perils of driving in Latin America.

"You have visited Venezuela. You know the risks of the roads in this country," commented Torres good-naturedly.

"Yes. But it's true of all countries, other than the U.S., Canada, and the U.K. Other countries just don't have the resources to throw at traffic management and thorough policing of traffic."

"You are correct. Very true, very true. And, Caracas has too many cars. Gasoline is not expensive, and we have too much traffic. People will take a car three blocks, when they should walk. Big problem."

"Indeed," mumbled Fitzjames.

Torres maneuvered out of the parking area and onto a roadway that led to the *Autopista Caracas-La Guairá*, a modern highway that connected the nation's capital to the airport and the coast. Torres gave the Suzuki only a few seconds to adjust from an idle to maximum acceleration. Torres turned on the air-conditioning system and partially lowered the window on the driver's side and suggested to Fitzjames to do the same with the passenger-side window, which he did. Wind, layered with the exhaust of other vehicles, including large and small trucks and a multitude of motorcycles and scooters of differing sizes and styles, poured into the Suzuki. Torres lighted a Belmont cigarette and offered one to Fitzjames.

"No thanks. I don't smoke."

"It is a bad habit and will certainly kill me. But it is my only serious vice," said Torres, smiling.

"Do you acknowledge your other, less serious vices?" asked Fitzjames, returning the smile.

"Oh, yes. I have other minor vices. I have one other rather serious vice, which I am prepared to reveal only to friends."

"Well, as we're not yet friends, I won't ask you to reveal it."

"We will be friends very soon. You will know that we are friends when I tell you of my second vice."

"Fair enough," replied Fitzjames with a light laugh.

Torres took a drag on the cigarette, which he held between the first two fingers of his left hand. He held the smoke in his lungs for a full twenty seconds and then blew the smoke toward the open window, which only had the effect of causing it to reenter the Suzuki and circulate through the interior. The tobacco odor blended with gasoline and diesel fumes from the many other vehicles on the highway.

When Torres finished the cigarette and discarded it by dropping the butt out of the window, he turned to Fitzjames. "You will need a gun, of course. You will find it and ammunition in the glove compartment. My instructions were to have the gun and ammunition for you when you arrived."

"Thank you," responded Fitzjames, as he raised the window and adjusted the air-conditioning vent to direct the air flow directly at him.

He opened the glove compartment and removed and examined the Ruger SR22 rimfire, semiautomatic pistol. Four magazines, each of ten rounds, and a silencing device were also in the compartment. Fitzjames returned the handgun to its previous location and closed the compartment.

"Excellent," said Fitzjames. "When we reach the hotel, I'll move the gun and ammunition to my backpack. I'll wait until then."

"Good. We will arrive at the *Hotel Jose Antonio Paez* in approximately ten minutes. I have selected the hotel for you. It is an old hotel but has a four-star rating. Excellent cuisine. The bar is also good. Old-fashioned. When I was a boy, my father would go to the bar in the hotel, and I would accompany him. My father would tell me that a visit to the hotel was like a visit to Europe. He had been a diplomat and hated the loss of the colonial elements of Venezuela. For him, the Hotel Paez was a symbol of all that was good in the past. He was a traditionalist and a very sentimental man."

"A good man?" asked Fitzjames.

"An outstanding man and a very warm father. I was very fortunate."

"You were fortunate. Few men can say that same thing about their fathers. Most, in my experience, complain about them and grumble about their upbringing and then blame their fathers for not providing the tools and skills to confront life."

"My experience has been the same, the very same," said Torres as he slowed the Suzuki at a traffic signal.

They had reached the urban perimeter of Caracas and began the tedious journey through the city's busy streets to the hotel. Although Caracas had been modernized, it resembled in its structures, its sounds, and its odors all other large Central and South American cities. Torres' estimation of their time of arrival was correct. Despite the congestion, they arrived within ten minutes. The Hotel Jose Antonio Paez was located on *Avenida Sucre* in the *Gato Negro* neighborhood adjacent to the *Parque del Oeste*. Fitzjames could see ahead, approximately two hundred yards, the sign for the hotel on the facade of a four-storied building.

Fitzjames reached behind him to the back seat and with his left hand clutched the strap on the top of the backpack. He picked it up and hoisted it between the two front seats and positioned it on the floor in front of him. He unzipped the internal pocket. He opened the glove compartment, removed the Ruger and magazines, and placed them delicately into the pocket of the backpack and zipped it shut.

"The envelope is also for you," said Torres.

Fitzjames reopened the glove compartment and extracted a small rectangular-shaped manila mailing envelope, somewhat larger than an ordinary business envelope. It was stuffed to overflowing and was sealed. He reopened the backpack and added the envelope to the pocket containing the handgun and ammunition.

"You'll find a mobile telephone and twenty-one thousand Bolivars, along with one thousand U.S. dollars, in the package," advised Torres.

"Has the phone been preprogrammed, preset?" inquired Fitzjames.

"Yes, certainly. The number to my cellular telephone is in the memory. You can call me by pressing the call feature. It is not necessary to contact me by number."

"Well done. I'll test it once I'm settled in the room and have some privacy."

"You may call me at any time for any reason. Do not be concerned about the hour of the day," said Torres.

"Thanks."

Torres brought the Suzuki to a halt at the entrance of the hotel. Two bellmen in old-world uniforms, which fit them poorly, approached the vehicle. Torres killed the engine, asked Fitzjames to remain seated, and stepped out before the bellmen could open Torres' door. Torres silently but confidently waved off the bellmen and in imitation of the best chauffeurs opened and held ajar the passenger-side door. Fitzjames exited and waited a few seconds for Torres to bustle to the back of the Suzuki, raise the hatch, and remove Fitzjames' suitcase. With great obsequiousness, Torres shifted to the front doors of the hotel and with the suitcase in hand held open the door for Fitzjames to enter.

Fitzjames proceeded to the reception desk and completed the registration process within a few moments. Meanwhile, Torres stood behind him deferentially. After Fitzjames affixed his signature to the required hotel document and received a room key, he presented fifty U.S. dollars to Torres and received his suitcase. Torres expressed gratitude in Spanish and walked out of the hotel. Without instruction, in the final minutes, Fitzjames had played the part of the pampered American tourist. He was confident that the secrecy of the mission had been preserved.

Eleven

The reservation at the hotel had been made for Fitzjames by the local U.S. Government operatives. He had checked in to the hotel using his actual surname. There was no need to employ a false name, and too little time had separated the recognition that Caracas was the appropriate destination after Kansas City and the decision to travel to that city to arrange for an alternate, mock passport. He did not envision that his visit to Caracas would be extended beyond the reserved stay at the hotel. He sensed little risk in his identity being exposed. The likelihood of a connection being made between him and any events that might occur in Venezuela was, in his judgment, low.

Perhaps he was reckless. Perhaps he should have delayed the journey the additional forty-eight or seventy-two hours necessary in order to have fictitious paperwork crafted. The thoughts came to him, but he set them aside. He had made the correct decision on the subject, and he so convinced himself through a momentary mental debate on the topic. Speed was the central concern. Delay could only have increased the danger at home and may even have resulted in a missed opportunity to find Manuel Algorta in Caracas. Algorta was on the move. The documentation from both FBI field offices confirmed that fact. Fitzjames appreciated that swift action in Caracas was essential.

Once settled in the hotel room, which was decorated with fine furniture and was luxurious, Fitzjames made two telephone calls. On his personal mobile telephone, he first contacted Fuller. Through a numerical code system on the telephone keypad, he typed a message to Fuller confirming his arrival in the

Venezuelan capital. Voice contact was unnecessary. On the cellular telephone provided by Torres, he communicated with him. Torres answered the call instantly.

"*Diga*," he said.

"Todo esta bien. Estoy aquí en el hotel. Sabes el número de cuarto?" inquired Fitzjames.

"*Si, por supeusto*. You may use English. The line is secure and scrambled. We will not be overheard."

"Excellent. You've done good work. You know the room number should you need it?"

"Yes, of course. You have very little time, my friend. The subject will visit the bar of the Hotel Jose Antonio Paez this evening at eight o'clock. I selected the hotel for you for that reason. You recall that I mentioned that the bar was good."

"And your father enjoyed it," added Fitzjames.

"Yes, he did. God smile upon him. Algorta also finds the bar very pleasant. When he is in Caracas, he visits the bar of the Hotel Jose Antonio Paez."

"Eight this evening?" asked Fitzjames, by way of confirmation.

"Yes. I can be at your disposal, if you wish," said Torres.

"I'll need you. Do you anticipate that Algorta will be alone or with a group?"

"His custom is to arrive in the company of at least one young woman. He will also have one, perhaps two bodyguards. He does business at the hotel and, often, his visits to the bar are more than recreational."

"Come with the Suzuki at 7:45. You should have a companion for assistance. We need to have a team of three out of caution. Linger near the bar in the lobby but don't come inside. You and your companion should be ready to move quickly to the Suzuki."

"I understand."

"Look for me and follow my lead."

"We will be with you at three quarters past seven," said Torres in acknowledgment.

"Thanks."

Fitzjames removed the toilet kit from the suitcase and entered the bathroom. After unwrapping a bar of soap, he washed his hands and brushed his teeth. He got out of his traveling clothes and placed the undershirt and underpants in a plastic garment bag. Although he did not have a thick beard, he shaved for a second time. But he ran the razor across his face and neck along the lines of the growth of the hair, as opposed to against them, in order to avoid pointless skin irritation. He then took a cool shower.

Thereafter, he dressed in light linen slacks and a white shirt with six buttons running down the front. He put on dark socks and shoes. The black-tasseled Cole-Hoan slip-on loafers matched the black belt he buckled around his waist. From the interior pocket of the suitcase, he extracted a shoulder harness and fitted it in place. He opened the backpack and removed the Ruger. He inserted a magazine and confirmed that the gun was fully loaded. He applied the silencing device to the barrel and placed the pistol, along with two magazines of additional ammunition, in the holster. He put on a navy blazer with two gold buttons and adjusted the lapel to cover the holster. With a quick study of himself in the mirror, he gathered the local mobile telephone, hotel key, wallet, and the current issue of *The Economist* and exited the room. In the elevator, he deposited the telephone and key in the pockets of his pants and the wallet in the interior right jacket pocket. He stretched his shoulders and chest in an effort to improve flexibility and adapt to the fit of the holster.

Fitzjames emerged from the elevator at the ground level and walked slowly to the hotel lounge. Upon entering, he took a seat in a comfortable cushioned chair, one of three, at a small round table to the left of the bar and away from the few other patrons. The lounge, which was designed in imitation of an English pub, contained eight round tables, identical to the one at which Fitzjames sat, each encircled by three chairs. A waiter approached him and placed a cocktail napkin on the tabletop.

"*Si, señor*," said the waiter in lieu of a direct request as to what Fitzjames might like to drink.

"*Hablas ingles*?" asked Fitzjames.

"*Si, señor*. What would you like?" inquired the waiter in slow, strained English.

"Whiskey, please. Jack Daniels, without ice and with a bottled water."

"Yes, sir," replied the waiter, who returned to the bar and mumbled the order to the bartender. In a moment, he returned to the table and placed before Fitzjames a tumbler, filled nearly to the top with Tennessee sour mash whiskey, and a chilled bottle of water.

"Your name and room number, sir?" asked the waiter.

"Fitzjames. Room 402," he responded.

The waiter made a written notation on a single sheet of paper, which he held in the palm of his opposite hand, and stepped away. Fitzjames was surprised that the waiter did not ask him to repeat his surname. Outside the United States, and at times within it, Fitzjames was compelled to spell or restate his somewhat unusual family name.

Fitzjames opened the bottle and added the water to the whiskey and filled the glass. He drank a bit of the beverage and added more of the water and thus refilled the tumbler. He opened *The Economist* to the leaders and surveyed the titles of the articles. Before beginning to read the first piece on the subject of consistent Russian opposition to America on virtually all topics before the United Nations Security Council, he checked the time on his wristwatch. He had twenty minutes to wait before Algorta's anticipated arrival.

As he returned to the magazine, he observed two men enter the lounge. They approached the bar and did not take seats at a table. Both were dressed in poorly tailored charcoal-colored business suits with cream-colored shirts and dark neckties. Both had black hair and olive skin and wore light beards and thick mustaches. At the bar, they did not attempt to speak Spanish. The more senior of the two men, in English, ordered two glasses of orange juice for himself and his companion. Their English accents were strange. Fitzjames, who heard clearly the man speak, replayed in his mind the man's accent and intonation and compared it with other like accents in his memory. He listened intently to the men's conversation, which was spoken in little more than whispers, in their own language. He did not know the language but recognized it as Indo-European. After a few more minutes of additional mental analysis, he concluded the men were speaking Farsi. They were Iranians and presumably good Shiite Muslims who did not consume alcohol, hence the fruit juice order. Fitzjames took another sip of the diluted whiskey and returned to *The Economist*. He also, almost inadvertently and casually, patted the outside of his blazer to feel the pistol in the holster.

Another man entered the lounge. He was young, tall, thin, and also dressed in a business suit. But his suit was of a European design, was light gray, and fit him perfectly. The shirt he wore was blue, as was his tie in a darker shade. The knot of the tie was broad and thick, typical of the modern, style-conscious Europeans. He had high cheekbones, deep-set eyes with heavy eyelids, and virtually no chin. His hair was blond but cut short. His receding hairline was obvious, and Fitzjames presumed within five years he would certainly be bald.

The tall man did not acknowledge the other two men but instead sat down at an empty table at the opposite side of the room from the place where Fitzjames was seated. Fitzjames could not hear the man place a drink order with the waiter but waited to observe what the bartender poured for him. At the bar, the waiter and bartender spoke, and the bartender shook his head in response to a question posted by the waiter. The waiter returned to the table, reported to the man that his first drink request could not be satisfied, and took a second, to the obvious disgust of the man. The waiter advised the bartender of the man's alternative beverage choice, and the bartender filled two shot glasses with Finlandia vodka. The waiter carried both on a small tray and positioned them, as a pair, on the table. The patron gave his name and room number to the waiter and then gulped the first vodka. He put the empty shot glass on the edge of the table and away from the other. He sipped the contents of the second glass.

Fitzjames broke off his observation of the tall man and turned the pages of the magazine. He no longer could read the articles with comprehension. He concentrated his mind on an evaluation of the three men in the lounge and questions about their nationalities, their business, their intentions, and whether they were armed. He made the presumption that they did have weapons and, while they appeared unconnected, he suspected that all three men had business with Algorta.

After five additional minutes passed, a well-groomed, well-dressed man, with a beautiful young woman in high heels and short satin cocktail dress at his side, strolled confidently into the lounge. At the same time as the waiter, with great diffidence, showed the man and the woman to a table that appeared to have been reserved for them, two heavily built men stepped through the doorway. They remained standing and did not take seats. Within a few seconds, the Iranians joined the man and the woman. Only one of the Iranians sat down. The other stood behind and over his superior's right shoulder. The junior man clasped his hands behind his back and sought to avoid looking at the young woman, whose appearance, makeup, and attire clearly distracted him.

From the photographs that he had studied, Fitzjames recognized the man with the woman as Manuel Algorta. He wore no beard or mustache and his hair was cut long and parted on the side in a typical Latin fashion. He resembled a television actor in a Hispanic soap opera. Algorta and the Iranian spoke quietly in English. Fitzjames could not hear the content of the conversation but the tone and voice inflection of the parties disclosed it as being conducted in English. The woman sat back with her right leg crossed over her left thigh. She rested her hands, with their long manicured painted nails, in her lap on the small purse she carried. She was making a forced effort to be patient.

After ten minutes of conversation, Algorta, the young woman, and the Iranian got to their feet. With a smile, Algorta offered to shake the hand of the Iranian, who awkwardly accepted it. A few more words of conversation were exchanged and the three walked together out of the lounge with the second Iranian behind them. The tall man and the two bodyguards followed them.

A few seconds after their departure, Fitzjames rose, rolled the magazine in the shape of a tube, and advised the bartender in Spanish to put the cost of the whiskey and bottled water on his room charge with an added twenty-percent tip for both him and the waiter. The bartender thanked him and wished him a good night. Fitzjames exited the lounge. He observed the bodyguards outside, through the large glass entry doors of the hotel. They opened the passenger doors of two BMW sedans. The woman, Algorta, the tall man, and the Iranians took seats inside the two cars. The bodyguards served as the drivers, respectively, of the vehicles.

Pedro Torres, who was wearing a dark suit and no longer had the appearance of an impoverished Venezuelan private taxi operator, stood in the hotel lobby, as if awaiting the arrival of a guest on a diplomatic mission. Torres had watched the Algorta party and had observed Fitzjames emerge from the lounge. He dialed a number on a mobile telephone, and when Fitzjames recognized him he tilted his head to the right to indicate to Fitzjames to follow him down a hallway off of the hotel lobby. Fitzjames did so. Torres led him to a side doorway, which Torres opened after putting a metal key into a lock. Outside, in a dark alley that smelled of stale food odors, the Suzuki was parked. Its engine was running, and a woman of approximately the same age as Torres was behind the steering wheel. Torres opened the car door and took the front passenger seat. Fitzjames climbed into the back. The woman was silent and did not turn in recognition of the arrival of either Torres or Fitzjames. Her hard gaze was trained on the roadway and the path she would take out of the alley. When both doors had closed behind Torres and Fitzjames, the car shot off toward the front of the hotel.

Twelve

The BMW sedans maneuvered aggressively and at high speeds through the narrow, dark, but busy roadways of Caracas. Both had manually installed but operative blue flashing lights on their tops to indicate official business. Other vehicles and pedestrians yielded to the two cars, without objection, and acquiesced as they crossed the dividing lines of streets, one car behind the other, and encountered oncoming traffic, which halted to allow them to pass.

The flashing, rotating blue lights assisted the woman driving the Suzuki to keep the BMWs in sight. But their pace and the confusion caused by other vehicles giving way to them and then recommencing their progress made the chase difficult. The driver of the Suzuki remained calm and silent, despite Torres' frustration and his grumbling of Spanish profanity. She also maintained a discrete distance but an accurate view of the BMWs. Fitzjames could see them ahead. They remained visible and within reach. The driver of the Suzuki had played this part in a pursuit prior to this evening's exercise.

"*Creo que se van a las fábricas del gobierno*," said Torres to the woman.

"*Creo que si*," said the woman quietly.

She gripped the steering wheel of the Suzuki and increased the speed by fifteen miles per hour.

They and the BMWs had emerged from the city center and were on an open avenue that was tree-lined and multi-laned with a concrete median strip dividing the two sides of the roadway. The traffic had diminished. All of the vehicles on the avenue were moving at high rates of speed, but none as fast as the Suzuki and the BMWs.

Fitzjames had abandoned his efforts to follow the movement of the cars in his mental map of the city. He knew Caracas and its general outline. Yet the progress through the congested urban center and its tight busy streets and then to the outskirts of the city left him confused. The chase was carrying them in an easterly direction. He at least gleaned that much from the full moon overhead.

After ten additional minutes of driving, suddenly the Suzuki turned left and abandoned the BMWs, which Fitzjames observed continued eastward. Torres made no comment and had not instructed the woman to make the unexpected turn. She did not slow the pace. They were traveling down narrow roads at the same heightened speed as had been employed on the wide avenue. The woman made three more surprisingly aggressive turns and then equally surprisingly struck the Suzuki's brakes. Fitzjames appreciated that he had buckled on the safety belt, as he otherwise might have been propelled through the windshield from the back seat by the force of stop.

"We will travel on foot from this point, my friend," said Torres over his left shoulder to Fitzjames.

"Yeah, understood," replied Fitzjames.

"*Quedate aqui. Permaneces lista. Me entiendes?*" asked Torres of the driver.

"*Si, claro,*" said she, unemotionally in response.

Torres removed a pistol and bullets from under the front passenger seat. He surveyed the handgun for a few seconds, added an ammunition clip, opened the car door, and stepped out of the Suzuki. Fitzjames also exited. Torres discarded his coat and threw it through the open window of the vehicle and into the seat he had occupied. He stuffed the pistol into the back of his pants and under his belt. Only the grip remained exposed.

Fitzjames removed the Ruger from the pocket of the holster and switched off the safety. He held the weapon in his right hand briefly and applied pressure to the grip, with his finger on the trigger, in order to effect an imprint in his mind the sensation of holding a gun with which he was unfamiliar.

"Set," said Fitzjames to Torres.

"Then, we go," responded Torres.

The two men set off at a light jog with Fitzjames two yards behind Torres. They ran down three abandoned streets and then through a long, dark alley. At the upper end of the alley, Torres stopped running and began to walk slowly. He held up his left hand to Fitzjames to alert Fitzjames to do likewise and walk. At the alley's end, Torres stopped. Torres rested his right shoulder against the cold cement wall of a building and in a position to gain a vista across a wide street into which the alley terminated. Fitzjames dropped in behind him. Torres stole a glance around the corner of the building.

After a thirty-second pause, Torres whispered to Fitzjames, "You cannot see from where you are standing. But across the street and approximately twenty meters to the south, the two sedans, with the headlights extinguished, are parked. They are outside of a factory that is operated by the government of Venezuela. At this facility, the workers construct mechanical devices for oil exploration. We have followed Algorta for some time. My sources suggested that his business this evening would begin at the Hotel Jose Antonio Paez and would conclude here at this facility of the FEEP, *la Fabrica de Equipos de Extraccion de Petroleo.* Algorta has close connections with the government. The FEEP provides cover for his drug manufacturing, transport, and sale. The regime is very happy to assist Algorta, provided his drug sales are not conducted in Venezuela and provided they are directed at the United States. The government is anxious to receive the hard currency from the United States. Its reserves of dollars are constantly diminished by its borrowing to pay the costs of projects that the president and his agents undertake to buy votes and support from the Venezuelan people. The government provides cover and local protection to Algorta. Of course, Venezuela has no extradition agreement with America. Algorta sells his drugs and the government imposes a tax on the profits. Algorta is happy to cooperate because the revenue is so great that the percentage paid to the regime still leaves him a very rich, rich man," explained Torres.

"Any details on his foreign contacts?" inquired Fitzjames under his breath.

"We have very little information on that topic. Our information and our surveillance of Algorta have been domestic, primarily in government. We have detailed files on each of his government contacts and bureaucratic accomplices," replied Torres.

"Nothing on Iran or Russia?" asked Fitzjames.

"I am not aware of any prolonged dealings between Algorta and those nations, although of late the Venezuelan government has been working very closely with Iran. Petroleum matters," said Torres.

"No drugs?" returned Fitzjames.

"By our intelligence, no. Only oil and oil-related equipment and products," said Torres.

"Currency exchanges?" asked Fitzjames.

"Possibly. But, I would not think so. The Venezuelan government would not want to part with its dollars. Yes, Iran wants dollars too, but Venezuela cannot afford to sell them or transfer them or let them leak out of the country."

"I imagine that if Algorta were doing business with the Iranians independently and if he were discovered doing so, he would be doing so at great risk," suggested Fitzjames.

"In short order, the Venezuelan government would destroy him. The regime would have him arrested, tortured, and assassinated. Only a large sum of money would induce Algorta to take such a risk," said Torres.

"Can we get closer? I want to see and hear what's happening. Are they inside the factory?"

"Yes. The two bodyguards have remained outside watching both the cars and the entrance door to the factory."

"Can you see them clearly?"

"Yes, in the moonlight, they are clearly visible."

As Fitzjames reexamined the Ruger and began to devise a tactical approach to the factory door, the sounds of the engines of advancing automobiles could be heard. They approached the factory from the east. Three cars halted suddenly immediately opposite of the BMWs and their drivers. The occupants of the arriving vehicles shouted at the bodyguards as they jumped from the cars.

Gunfire ensued. Fitzjames stepped out and beyond Torres in order to observe the events. Torres placed his left hand on Fitzjames' chest in an effort to prevent him from exposing himself. Fitzjames dropped to one knee and paused.

Algorta's bodyguards returned fire but were outmatched. Within a few moments and after an exchange of rounds of bullets, both were shot and apparently killed. The shooters, who were wearing helmets and were dressed in paramilitary uniforms, in an ordered fashion stormed the interior of the factory. Torres lowered himself to a squatting position next to Fitzjames, and the two studied the building in uncertain expectation of the outcome of the unexpected attack and raid.

Within three minutes, Algorta and his female companion and the two Iranians and the tall man marched out of the factory, one behind the other, with their fingers of both hands locked behind their heads. One soldier led the group to the outside, and the remaining five followed. The ostensible senior officer ordered the Iranians and the tall man into one of the vehicles with a swing of a submachine gun by way of emphasis of his command. Although rendered in Spanish, the Iranians and the tall man appeared to understand him and complied. Once the three men were inside a black four-door utility vehicle, another soldier entered the same vehicle and its driver departed.

The commander spoke to two of his officers who, in apparent response to an order, entered the second vehicle and followed the first in the same direction from which the soldiers had come. The commander pointed the submachine gun at Algorta and the woman. Before they could plead for mercy and with astonishment and horror reflected in their faces, the commander gunned down both of them. One of the remaining soldiers advanced toward the bodies and examined them.

"*Muertos*," he said, sufficiently loudly for both Torres and Fitzjames to hear.

"*Vamos*," said the commander, who entered the third vehicle along with is subordinates. In seconds, they were gone.

Silence followed and stillness. No movement could be heard; no voices spoke. The sounds of the city were muted. Torres stood erect, and Fitzjames also rose. Torres removed a mobile telephone form a pocket in the back of his trousers. He pressed the keys and advised the woman who had driven the Suzuki that he and Fitzjames were returning.

"*Nos vamos a volver*," he said.

Fitzjames returned the Ruger to the holster and took up a position off of Torres' right shoulder, as the latter began the walk back to the Suzuki. They walked at a brisk pace and did not speak. Once in the car and in route in return to the city center of Caracas, Torres spoke to Fitzjames.

"I will monitor all police and military activities throughout this evening in order to learn, if possible, who was responsible for this action. It is very confusing to me. I did not anticipate such occurrences."

"At this point, I'd rather see us focus on the fate of the other three men. Can you do some research in that direction? Perhaps your people could sort out their identities. Or perhaps we could learn something about when they arrived in Venezuela and how long they've been in Caracas," said Fitzjames.

"I am at your disposal. I will do as you instruct," replied Torres.

"Very good. Frankly, I'm interested in both subjects. But initially, our attention should be directed at the three men from the hotel lounge," added Fitzjames.

"Yes, very well," added Torres.

The woman drove the Suzuki to the Hotel Jose Antonio Paez at a speed consistent with the flow of ordinary traffic. Thirty minutes elapsed before the party reentered the Gato Negro neighborhood of Caracas. At a distance of five city blocks from the hotel, the driver, without any directive or instruction, pulled off of the roadway and to the curb.

"You should exit here," suggested Torres to Fitzjames. "Our return to the hotel will arouse suspicion."

"Fine. Please contact me after you've done some research. It doesn't have to be complete. When you've got anything, any lead at all, call me," said Fitzjames, as he opened the back passenger door and stepped out and onto the sidewalk.

Fitzjames walked slowly to the hotel through the throng of local residents, on foot, strolling the streets of Caracas. When he passed through the entrance of the hotel, he was greeted in English by the concierge. He proceeded toward the elevator, which was immediately beyond the hotel's lounge. As he passed the lounge, he overheard laughter and voices that rang out with familiarity. He hesitated and from the lobby surveyed the occupants of the lounge. Only three patrons were present. Fitzjames observed the two Iranians and the tall man standing at the bar in jovial conversation. The tall man made a remark with a wry smile, the Iranians laughed heartily in reply. With obvious satisfaction, the tall man drank off a small glass full of clear liquid.

Fitzjames, instinctively and inadvertently, with his right hand, lightly patted the outside of the jacket that he wore to confirm the pistol was in the holster. He knew the gun was in its place. Yet touching it amplified his confidence and his options. He crossed the threshold from the lobby to the lounge. The bartender observed him as he entered. The three men were engrossed in their conversation and did not perceive Fitzjames' arrival.

Thirteen

Before the bartender could speak to him in English and ask him for his drink order, upon his approach to the bar Fitzjames spoke to him in Spanish. He placed the same order as he had earlier in the evening, a glass of Jack Daniels and a bottle of water. Fitzjames believed that using Spanish with the bartender would not, as English likely would, unduly attract the attention of the three men. His perception proved correct; the men continued their conversation without apparent recognition of Fitzjames' presence in the lounge. He took a chair at the opposite end of the long bar.

The bartender placed the whiskey and the water on two cocktail napkins in front of Fitzjames. Before the bartender could ask him for his name and hotel room number, Fitzjames placed on the bar next to the glass four bills representing two hundred Bolivares, which he expected would be sufficient to pay for the cost of the drinks. Without comment, the bartender accepted the money, processed the purchase at an old cash register nestled between liquor bottles, and returned to Fitzjames with the change. After the bartender placed the cash on the bar, Fitzjames instantly passed it back to him as a tip.

"*Gracias, señor. Muy amable.*"

"*De nada,*" replied Fitzjames.

The tall man broke off the discussion with the Iranians and signaled to the bartender, by an ugly snap of the fingers of his right hand, to attend to him. In a loud voice, enhanced, as it struck Fitzjames, by the too-rapid consumption of alcohol, the tall man ordered more vodka. The bartender complied and added

Finlandia vodka to the two empty shot glasses stationed in front of the man. However, the bartender did not fill the glasses to overflowing. Both were nearly full, but a small amount of space remained in each glass to avoid spillage by the patron, as was customary.

The man was displeased. "I am not prepared to pay you the full price for this terrible vodka if you do not fill these glasses!" shouted the tall man in English that carried a distinct Eastern European accent.

The bartender reluctantly added additional vodka to each glass. The amount poured was sufficiently small to be hardly worth the complaint. The tall man expressed no gratitude to the bartender but instead turned to the Iranians.

"If you were drinking men," he said in English, "I would share with you real vodka, Russian vodka. After such vodka, you would no longer hold to your religious principles."

The tall man laughed at the statement, which was neither clever nor humorous. The Iranians chuckled good-naturedly in return and agreed with him, to Fitzjames' astonishment. They continued their conversation. Fitzjames could not hear all of the words exchanged. But the tall man was unable to refrain from speaking more loudly then was necessary, despite that the Iranians responded to him in more subdued tones.

"More of this orange for my friends," commanded the tall man, waving his right hand for emphasis.

The bartender again complied in silence and presented two fresh glasses of darkly colored, pulp-filled orange juice for the Iranians.

Fitzjames diluted the whiskey with the water and drank slowly from the thick-bottomed tumbler. As he concentrated on the tall man's accent and appearance, he grew certain that the man was Russian. His height and build and facial structure were typical of Russian foreign attachés and the skewed ideal of a government that could not throw off its Soviet heritage. Fitzjames considered that this man's face and thick lips and dark eyes would have appeared threatening in a communist-era black-and-white photograph, where the subject was attired in a full military uniform. The man could have been, by appearance, Vladimir Putin's distant cousin.

The Russian consumed the two glasses of vodka and ordered two more, which he dispatched with equal speed. He followed the performance by slamming his hand on the top of the bar to demand the bill for the drinks. The sound startled the bartender. Yet, he recovered quickly and presented an invoice and a pen to the Russian. With an odd flourish and pointless bravado, the Russian signed the bottom of the slip of paper and placed the pen on top of it with the same aggression with which he had requested the bill. He turned and followed the Iranians out of the bar and into the lobby. The bartender watched the three men as they left and collected the invoice and pen. He surveyed the paper an instant and shook his head in disgust.

"*Sin educación,*" he mumbled.

"*Que?*" Fitzjames inquired with an expectation of procuring from the bartender, as rapidly as possible, any available information about the three former patrons.

"*Rusos y musulmanes; no tienen nada de educación,*" he responded.

"*De donde viene estos hombres? Sabes?*" asked Fitzjames. He suspected that the bartender might know the places of origin of the men.

"*Lo más alto, de Rusia. Los cortos y oscuros, de Irán. Sucios, los tres. Extranjeros de mala calidad. Todos,*" replied the bartender.

"*Turistas? Huéspedes en el hotel?*"

"*Turistas, no. Huéspedes, sí.*"

"*Huéspedes regulares en este hotel?*" asked Fitzjames in haste.

"*Si, regulares durante este año. Antes de este año, no,*" answered the bartender.

"*Gracias, señor,*" said Fitzjames, who extracted from the cash he held in the front right pocket of his trousers a note for one hundred Bolivares and placed it on the cocktail napkin next to the tumbler of partially consumed diluted whiskey. He rose from the barstool.

"*Gracias a usted,*" returned the bartender.

Fitzjames exited the lounge in search of the three men. At the desk of the hotel's concierge, he saw the Russian shake hands with the two Iranians in turn and departed. The Iranians spoke to the concierge and walked on in the opposite direction of the Russian. Fitzjames chose to pursue the Russian.

From behind him, as he walked down a corridor toward the lobby restrooms and elevator, Fitzjames observed the Russian speaking on a mobile telephone. Fitzjames moved a bit closer to the man to attempt to catch something of the conversation. It was not long or detailed and was conducted in Russian. To Fitzjames' mind, the man provided to the recipient of the call a brief report of the events of the meeting and thereafter received further instructions. After ending the call, the man entered the hotel's public restroom. The soft closing door shut behind him. Fitzjames with his right hand removed the Ruger from the holster and advanced toward the restroom and entered.

The door from the lobby did not lead into the restroom proper but to a second door. Fitzjames passed through the outer door and with his left hand pushed open the interior door. As he did so, out of caution, he held back for an instant and then entered. The brief delay prevented the kick from the Russian with his right leg and foot from striking Fitzjames in the forehead, which was the Russian's intention. Instead, the effort was wasted. The Russian recovered quickly and tried a second attempt as Fitzjames slipped through the door. The second kick was also a failure in that it did not hit Fitzjames' head, but instead his right hand. The shoes the Russian wore were apparently steel-toed. The strike on Fitzjames' hand was rendered with such force, combined with the metal, that it nearly shattered the bones of the hand. Fitzjames dropped the pistol at the blow but managed to raise his left forearm to block a third kick. The Russian stumbled, and Fitzjames smashed the man's jaw with his left fist. The blow caused the Russian to lose his footing. As he stumbled a second time and began to fall, Fitzjames crashed his left fist into the center of the Russian's face. When he hit the ground, his now fractured nose was bleeding badly. Fitzjames followed the fall with a kick of his foot to the side of the Russian's head. Semiconscious, he tried to rise but fell back to the ground. Fitzjames collected the handgun off of the floor of the restroom. Blood from the Russian's nose and forehead dripped down the man's face and stained the white tile flooring.

"Sit up," commanded Fitzjames. "Sit up against the wall and don't move."

"*Ya ne govoryu po angliiski,*" said the Russian.

"I don't speak Russian. But I know you can speak English. Sit up against the wall. If you'd prefer that I shot you, I'll kill you right here. Move," ordered Fitzjames.

The Russian complied. He pulled himself upright without standing and leaned against the wall adjacent to the urinal. The movement helped him regain his senses and he stared blankly and viciously at Fitzjames.

"Name? Unit?" asked Fitzjames.

The Russian said nothing. Fitzjames positioned the end of the silencing device on the barrel of the Ruger in the center of the Russian's forehead and with it pushed the man's head against the wall. With his injured right hand, Fitzjames searched the interior and exterior pockets of the Russian's Burberry bonded linen peacoat. The Russian gave no resistance to the search, although he mumbled what Fitzjames presumed were Russian profanities and anti-American slurs. Fitzjames extracted a wallet, a passport, and the cellular telephone from the interior coat pockets. In the outside pockets, he found nothing, except for a loaded Korovin TZ Soviet-era semiautomatic pistol. Fitzjames stepped backwards two paces and surveyed the tall man.

"You have broken my nose, American," said the Russian derisively, as he raised a hand to touch his injured face.

"Don't move. Your nose will recover. Keep your hands on the floor, or I'll kill you," replied Fitzjames.

Fitzjames placed the wallet, passport, and telephone into the right-outer pocket of his jacket. He emptied the bullets from the Korovin TZ and placed them inside the other pocket of the jacket. He then moved laterally, with the Ruger still trained on the Russian, pushed open the stall door, and tossed the Korovin into the toilet. At the sound of the splash of the water, the Russian offered a flurry of additional expletives in his native language.

"As I said, I don't speak Russian," repeated Fitzjames, who removed the local mobile telephone and pressed the redial key to connect with Torres.

Torres answered the call after the initial ring.

"I'm in the hotel lobby's men's room. I have a Russian friend here with me who'd like to meet you. Get back here immediately and bring along a first-aid kit."

Fitzjames locked the door to the bathroom to prevent entry by any other hotel guest. During the succeeding ten minutes, he stood over the Russian with the first finger of his left hand on the trigger of the Ruger. The Russian offered no conversation, in either Russian or English, and Fitzjames asked him no additional questions. Fitzjames did remove a handful of paper towels from the dispenser at the basin and dropped them in the Russian's lap for his use in plugging and nursing his broken, bleeding nose. Fitzjames also appreciated that one hand, as a result, was kept busy with the undertaking and thus out of use for any foolish retaliatory bravado.

The mobile telephone chimed and Fitzjames answered it. Torres was just outside the locked bathroom door. Fitzjames unlocked the door and three uniformed officers of the federal Ministry of Justice, one with a handgun and two with rifles, surged into the restroom. They ignored Fitzjames and instead roughly pulled the Russian off the ground and onto his feet, wrenched his arms behind his back, and fastened metal handcuffs onto his wrists.

"*Adelantado!*" shouted the senior officer to the Russian, who moved slowly out of the restroom with the three ministry officers behind him.

In their custody, the officers marched the Russian out of the hotel and bundled him into an official police vehicle of the Ministry of Justice. Hotel guests watched as the federal officials drove away with their prisoner.

Torres had entered the restroom after the police effected their exit with the Russian. He had waited until they were outside before speaking to Fitzjames.

"He's in our hands," said Torres with a smile.

"Very good. I'll presume the officers were your men," said Fitzjames.

"Well, yes. They are on our payroll. They do work for me on occasion when I make a special request. This was special. So, I called them. It would have been difficult to remove your Russian from the hotel with our people. Too obvious. Too irregular. The fear of government is so great in Venezuela that if government officers do a job, no one asks any questions. It is terrible, but it is true. Makes sometimes difficult work much easier," explained Torres.

"I understand. Well done. My right hand needs some attention. He kicked me with metal studded boots. Can you help out with that?" inquired Fitzjames.

"Yes, of course. Follow me, please, to my car," said Torres.

"Before we go, I need to get his gun. It's in the toilet."

"Excuse me?"

"Yes, it's in the toilet. I put his pistol in the toilet to keep it away from him."

"I will retrieve it. I do not want you putting your hands into a public toilet in Caracas."

"Do you intend to do so?" asked Fitzjames.

"Yes, but I am a local man. I can wash. Nothing can hurt me, not even the bacteria in the water in a toilet in this city," replied Torres, shaking his head.

Fourteen

Outside the Hotel Jose Antonio Paez, Torres' female companion, the driver of the Suzuki of earlier in the evening, attended to Fitzjames' wounded right hand. She applied an antiseptic and wrapped it in a tight gauze bandage. The hand was both bruised and lacerated where the Russian's steel-toed shoe had struck it. Although the pain was substantial, the women confirmed that no bones had been broken. Fitzjames accepted the diagnosis as, in his judgment based upon the confidence with which she tended to the injury, she had medical training.

"*Gracias,*" he said with his accent acquired from Spain.

"*De nada. De donde viene señor?*" she asked.

"*De Florida,*" he answered.

"*Tiene acento de España,*" she commented.

"*Sí. Estudie en España. Tengo el acento de Madrid y a veces de Bilbao, en el norte de España,*" he said, thereby explaining his Spanish accent and that he had studied in Spain.

"*Si, exacto,*" she said with a demure smile.

"Do you speak English?" he asked.

"Little," she replied shyly with a strong accent.

"No problem. *Háblanos español entonces. Vale,*" he added.

"*Muy bien, gracias,*" she said.

"*No gracias a usted,*" he added, examining the wrapped hand. "*Bien hecho.*"

"*Nada,*" she said and turned to return the medical supplies to the tackle box that moments earlier she had removed from the trunk of the Suzuki.

During the time that the woman spent addressing Fitzjames' injury, Torres had made multiple calls on his mobile telephone. All of the calls involved Torres dispensing orders and directives pertaining to the treatment and disposition of the Russian. After the fourth and final telephone conversation, he approached Fitzjames, who had waited somewhat impatiently next to the Suzuki. During the wait, the woman had restarted the car's engine. She sat in the driver's seat and behind the steering wheel, much more resigned than Fitzjames to a wait for Torres.

"My friend," he said to Fitzjames. "The Russian is now in route to a Ministry of Justice facility of my selection. He will be much easier to manage there and, I am confident, will be much more cooperative. Do you wish to question him or shall I do so, or shall we both do so?"

"How long can they hold him?" asked Fitzjames.

"No more than seventy-two hours. Beyond that time, other branches of government will begin to make inquiries and documents will be required. We would want to avoid such an intrusion."

"Agreed. Also, if he's kept too long, his superiors and contacts will make their own inquiries or break off or disavow him. I can't have that."

"No."

"We need to get what information we can within twenty-four hours, no more," said Fitzjames, while in contemplation of the necessity of speed when weighed against the urgency of maximizing the collection of information from the Russian.

"So little time may present problems. He will refuse to speak unless he is persuaded to do so," noted Torres.

"If you're suggesting torturing him, I won't consent to or authorize that step. He probably deserves it. But my presumption is that he's an operative. I want his boss or bosses. He needs to be convinced that his capture has been revealed to his superiors. If so, he'll likely presume that he'll be killed upon release. Then, he may talk to us. I don't have any problem with your men making him uncomfortable. I also don't object to his being persuaded that he *will be* tortured if he doesn't cooperate. Can you sort that out?"

"I believe so."

"I don't want to be there, or at least I don't want to be present until after you've done what you can without me. I want the exercise to be Venezuelan, and the men involved to speak Spanish between themselves. Questions should be posed to him in English. I don't believe that he speaks much Spanish, but he does speak English. Also, do you have any Asians on your team, any Chinese, for example?"

"We have a Japanese descendant on our team."

"Is he fully Japanese?"

"Yes. He is from Caracas but his family came from Kyoto in Japan in the 1950s. Emilio Fushimi. He is responsible for our technology and systems. I do not ask that he do field work."

"We'll need him. Can you piece together a uniform that looks like either the Chinese or Japanese army? Mock it up?"

"We could do such a thing. Why?"

"I want Fushimi to sit in on the interrogation. I want it made clear to the Russian that you'll turn him over to the Asian if he doesn't answer your questions. Periodically, Fushimi should complain, in Spanish, that the Russian is not being sincere or forthcoming in his responses and insist that he be handed over for more aggressive interrogation."

"I do not understand."

"No Russian from the west of Russia, if I'm right about his origins, will be able to resist the threat and fear of being handed over to a Japanese or Chinese military officer. Fear of the East. The British employed the same techniques with the Germans in the Second World War. Only, they used Russians. If the Germans didn't talk, then an Englishman, posing as a Russian, in a Russian uniform, would demand that the prisoner be transferred to him. The Germans would break down out of fear of the Soviets. It's worth a try here because of a lack of time."

"We will arrange it. Very interesting tactic."

"Perhaps. But we've got to learn about who's giving him orders and quickly."

"Then I will leave you. Should I telephone you or will you contact me?"

"I'll call you. The Iranians are still loose. They need to be handled differently. I'll contact you after I've made what progress I can with respect to them. It may be a long night."

"We will not sleep," said Torres with determination. He opened the front passenger door of the Suzuki, entered the vehicle, sat himself, and slammed the door behind him.

The woman tore off as the door closed.

Fitzjames returned to the lobby of the hotel. The Iranians were not present, which did not surprise him. He evaluated posing questions to the bartender about the Iranians, as he had about the Russian. But too many pointed inquiries of the same party raised awkward inquiries. He thus approached the desk of the concierge, a smartly dressed man of perhaps forty-five.

"*Si, señor?*" asked the concierge, once Fitzjames had taken a position before him.

The man noticed the bandaged hand but returned his gaze to Fitzjames' face.

"Do you speak English?" inquired Fitzjames, although he was confident of an affirmative reply. He believed it to be arrogant and in bad taste to respond to Spanish with English, with the expectation that all people spoke not only their native languages but also spoke English.

"Of course, sir. How may I assist you?"

"I'd like some information please about certain other hotel guests. Nothing too intrusive. I'd like to see them again. I met them in the lounge earlier this evening with another gentleman. The other gentleman was Russian. These two men, the men I'm looking for are, I believe, from Iran. I'd like to get a restaurant recommendation from you and then suggest to the Iranian gentlemen that they be my guests tomorrow night for supper. Could you arrange a reservation for me?" asked Fitzjames.

"Yes, sir. Of course, sir. It would be my pleasure."

Fitzjames removed his wallet from the interior of his jacket, opened it, and extracted two American fifty-dollar bills. He pulled out from under the desk one of the two chairs and sat down. He returned the wallet to the pocket and placed the cash on the top of the desk. With his left hand, he folded the bills together in half and maneuvered them across the desk to the concierge. The concierge accepted the money.

"Thank you, sir. But the tip is too generous for a reservation for dinner for tomorrow. We will have no trouble finding a table for you and your guests with so much time," he said.

"I need more than a reservation, please. If you could give me the room number or numbers for my Iranian friends, I would very much appreciate it. I'd like to extend the invitation personally," returned Fitzjames gravely.

"Sir, you must understand. Hotel policy does not permit me to share room numbers of guests without their consent."

"Yes, I see. Well, then I will speak to your hotel manager. There is no emergency. I simply wish to be friendly. Could you call the manager, and I'll wait here while you do so," said Fitzjames, who again removed his wallet and extracted five more fifty-dollar bills in anticipation of the conversation with the manger.

As he expected, the concierge was cognizant of the sum now available in exchange for the information.

"Perhaps I can authorize, personally, an exception in these circumstances without my manager's consent. Do you have the names of your friends, sir?"

Fitzjames thanked the concierge and explained that he had no names, only descriptions. He furnished them, and in seconds the concierge was able to provide their full names and their room numbers. He wrote the information on a sheet of hotel stationery, which he delivered to Fitzjames. Fitzjames responded by folding the five bills, as he had the first two, and passing them across the desk to the concierge.

"Thank you, sir. If you will speak to me tomorrow by 3:00 in the afternoon, I will have for you a reservation for dinner. How many will be dining, sir?"

"Six," replied Fitzjames.

"Excellent. I wish you a very pleasant evening," said the concierge, rising to his feet.

Fitzjames did likewise, expressed his gratitude, and said goodbye.

Fitzjames studied the paper and the names. They meant nothing to him. He walked outside the hotel and around a corner to gain some modest degree of privacy. He telephoned Fuller.

"Update?" said Fuller before Fitzjames could speak.

Fitzjames was never certain whether Fuller's curt, single-word questions or responses to telephone calls constituted a method that the major employed with all of his subordinates or whether they were reserved for Fitzjames alone. Certainly, if Fitzjames' mobile telephone were lost or stolen and if a call were placed to Fuller by an unknown third party, such responses before the caller spoke would prevent unwanted exposure or untoward revelations from Fuller.

"All's well, sir. A complete update will have to wait until tomorrow, at the latest. The purpose of this call is to give you three names and ask that you do what research you can on them," said Fitzjames, speaking quickly and in subdued tones.

"Go ahead," replied Fuller.

"Thank you, sir. The first two are, I believe, Iranians by their speech and manner, Ali Abbas Yazdi and Ahmad Rezvani. The names may be false, as I obtained them from the hotel staff. But it's what I have."

"I've got them. No spelling required. The third one, then?" asked Fuller.

"One moment, sir," said Fitzjames, as he removed from his jacket pocket the documents that he had taken off of the Russian.

The passport was issued by the Russian government and of course in the Cyrillic alphabet, which made it impossible for Fitzjames to read. However, the Venezuelan consulate in Moscow had issued a visa. The photograph on the visa was impressed with an embossed seal, and the document was affixed to the last page of the passport.

"Sir, one moment, I'm studying a Venezuelan visa. Yes, okay. The name is Nikolai Lebedev. That name too may be false, but it too is all I have. The photos in the passport and on the visa are of the subject," added Fitzjames.

"Very good. I'll get on it. Shall I phone you back, Captain, or would you prefer to call me?"

"I'll phone you, sir. I may be tied up for some time," said Fitzjames.

"Fine. My guess is that I'll have something to tell you within the hour. The two Iranians may take a bit more time. Our data on the Russian is likely more solid."

"Understood. Thank you, sir."

Fitzjames returned to the lobby and ascended through the emergency stairwell the three flights of stairs to the hotel's third floor. When he opened the door at that level, he observed at a distance of fifteen yards the Iranians stepping into the elevator. After he heard the closing of the elevator door, he descended the same three flights at three stairs per stride. He reached the lobby level before the elevator came to rest and opened and disgorged its two occupants. The Iranians did not observe Fitzjames as they advanced in the opposite direction toward three men standing in the reception area adjacent to the hotel's front desk.

When the Iranians approached, one of the three men stepped forward, greeted them, and very politely nodded his head in something resembling a light bow. The man followed this formality with an introduction of the two other men in his party. These two shook hands, in a very wooden fashion, with the Iranians. The first man then invited the group to follow him out of the hotel.

Fitzjames pursued them at a distance and was outside within seconds. He observed all five men enter two chauffeured black Maybach '62 limousines. Each of the vehicles was adorned with four small plastic Venezuelan flags, two on the hoods and two on the trunks. As they exited the hotel parking lot, Fitzjames signaled to a waiting taxi from the row of four hopeful cab drivers, all of whom had emptied their respective cars to smoke cigarettes and chat. The operator of the first taxi took a final drag of a cigarette, tossed the butt into moving traffic, entered the vehicle, and drove forward to retrieve Fitzjames.

"Good evening, sir. Where do you go?" asked the cab driver of his passenger in labored English.

"I want to follow those two official limousines up ahead. Do you understand?" asked Fitzjames, as he opened the door to the back seat and climbed inside the taxi. Fitzjames repeated the instructions in Spanish.

"Sir. We go," said the driver with a broad grin that revealed a set of bad, disordered front teeth.

The treads of the tires on the taxi marked the entryway of the hotel as he drove off in pursuit.

Fifteen

The two Maybach limousines drove only a short distance from the Hotel Jose Antonio Paez and through Caracas before reaching their destination. The building before at which the two vehicles stopped was an old colonial stucco structure. It was unmarked and without signage and resembled a Roman Catholic church that had been confiscated by the State and put to entirely new use. It was dark and cold in appearance, and the lights of the building shone only on the ground level. The upper stories were black.

At the entrance to the building, the occupants of the limousines emerged. The two Iranians followed up three concrete steps and into the building the gentleman, who had greeted them in the hotel. The remaining members of the party entered behind the Iranians. After the door closed behind them, two security men in uniform and with submachine guns took positions on opposite sides of the door.

Fitzjames watched these proceedings from a distance of thirty yards and from the back seat of the taxi. When he had observed the Maybachs slowing, he had instructed the cab driver to pull off to the narrow shoulder of the roadway.

"Do you know this place?" inquired Fitzjames of the cab driver.

"Yes, sir. This is a facility of the Ministry of Health," he said.

"Do you pass this building often?"

"Yes, many times each day."

"Is it typical to have guards posted?"

"No, sir. I have not seen the army or police at any time."

"Has this building always been a part of the Ministry of Health?"

"No, sir. It was a church until two or three years ago. The government took the church. The government's officials claimed that the building was used by terrorists. Stupid. Ridiculous. But that is what they do. If they want something, they take it."

"On what street are we traveling?"

"Avenida Urdaneta."

"Very good. Could you come back and pick me up in twenty minutes at this place, this very place? Do you understand me?"

"Yes, sir, of course."

"Twenty minutes, no more. Understood?"

"Yes, sir. Twenty minutes. I will return."

Fitzjames paid the fare requested by the driver and added the rough equivalent of fifty American dollars in Bolivares as an incentivizing tip. Fitzjames exited the taxi and waited two or so minutes for the driver to pass off beyond the building. He strolled slowly along the sidewalk, which was congested with pedestrians despite the lateness of the hour, toward the old church. Like a curious, ill-informed tourist, he stopped in front of the building and looked at its roof line and upper levels. The security guards were distracted by his presence for an instant. However, after mumbling to one another, they ostensibly concluded that he was a visitor to the city and ignored him. He walked on and up the street another twenty yards and, under an awning, leaned against the dividing wall between two seedy shops. He studied his wristwatch for the current time and removed the local mobile telephone from his pants pocket and called Torres.

"Yes, sir," answered Torres.

"I'm on Avenida Urdaneta at a unit of the Ministry of Health. According to the cab driver, the building at one time was a church. It's an old colonial structure. Do you know it?"

"Yes, sir. It represents another example of the encroaching national government. The government forced out the diocese."

"I know you've got your hands full with the Russian. But can you break away and get over here?"

"Certainly, of course. My assistant can do the work until I return. She is very able."

"How long do you need?"

"At this hour, I can be with you in less than ten minutes."

"Excellent. Bring along some photography equipment. Something powerful but not dramatic. Follow me?"

"I understand. Ten minutes."

"You'll see me on the street in the shops just to the east of the old church."

Fitzjames returned the telephone to his pants pocket and moved westward to a place on the sidewalk out of view of the guards but sufficiently close to the entrance to preserve a clear view of the two Maybachs.

Because of his height, Fitzjames stood much taller than the ordinary citizens of Caracas walking the streets. He became alarmed that his stature would attract unwanted attention. He sensed that other pedestrians, particularly women, were looking at him with undue and unsolicited interest. He needed a distraction to busy himself and reduce his visibility.

He observed at a distance of little more than ten yards a trash bin positioned outside a storefront. It overflowed with waste, which appeared to include periodicals and newspapers. He thus approached the bin and, ignoring the stench, with speed and some care extracted a magazine that had been discarded and was only lightly soiled by other rubbish. With the magazine in hand, he returned to his previous station. He turned the pages of the magazine but continued to watch the church building carefully.

Five minutes later, Torres appeared next to him on foot. He approached Fitzjames with such alacrity and dexterity that seconds passed before Fitzjames appreciated that a man was standing next to him and that the man was Torres.

"Camera?" asked Fitzjames in a whisper.

"Here, in my coat pocket," replied Torres, as he placed his left hand over the exterior left pocket of the light windbreaker jacket that he wore.

"Wait here. Take photos of anyone who comes out of the building. I'm going to walk back by the church and to the place where I told the taxi to return. My plan is to force everyone out of the building in order for you to get a complete set of photos of all of them. As needed, shift to the other side of the street or as close as you need to get. My guess is that no one will pay any attention to you."

"Certainly, I will be very obvious."

"I don't believe so. Stand ready. I'm hoping that the diversion will create enough confusion so as to make your presence irrelevant. Do you have your cigarette lighter?"

"Of course," responded Torres, who removed the lighter from his shirt pocket and presented it to Fitzjames.

"I'll take your cigarettes as well," suggested Fitzjames.

Torres complied and delivered his recently opened packet of Belmonts to Fitzjames. Fitzjames shook the packet with a flick of his left wrist and removed one of the cigarettes with his lips. He did not light it. He returned the package to Torres.

Fitzjames walked slowly toward the designated area at which the taxi would return. The path required another pass in front of the building entrance. As he approached this second time but from the opposite direction, the security guards again took note of him. Their interest in him appeared to be greater than on the first pass. To add a veil of calm, he stopped walking and lit the cigarette. The guards surveyed him but relaxed when he blew from his mouth the smoke. Cigarette smoking not only subdued the nicotine addict but also all those nearby who watched the smoker. Fitzjames was not a smoker. He was hopeful that his feigning would not be recognized.

He continued walking. On schedule, the cab pulled along the roadside. Fitzjames raised his right hand in salute and advanced toward the waiting taxi. The driver remained seated. Fitzjames stepped into the roadway and walked in front of the taxi and through the streams of light emitted by the headlights of the vehicle. He spoke to the driver through the lowered window in a soft voice in English, very slowly.

"Thank you for returning," said Fitzjames.

"Yes, sir. You are welcome," replied the driver.

"I'd like for you to do something for me," added Fitzjames, while simultaneously removing his wallet from his jacket and presenting eight hundred Bolivares to the driver.

"Yes, sir. How can I assist?" asked the driver, as he sat upright in the seat behind the steering wheel, now alert and engaged.

"I'm prepared to pay you an additional two thousand Bolivares if you'll provide a distraction."

"A distraction? I do not understand."

"I'd like for you to pull beyond the entrance of this building at the shops just ahead and cause a distraction. Any sort of distraction is fine. Just create enough noise to draw out the two guards who are standing at the entrance. I'll only need to have their attention drawn off for a few seconds. Can you do that?"

"Yes. You want the guards to come out and look at me, for two thousand Bolivares. Very simple. No problem, no problem," he said with a smile. "What must I do after the distraction?"

"Go to the Hotel Jose Antonio Paez in one hour and you'll be paid. *Entiendes el plan, me entiendes, entonces?*" inquired Fitzjames, in Spanish, out of caution.

"*Si, claro, una distracción grande para las guardias seguridades en frente del edificio,*" repeated the driver.

"*Precisamente,*" said Fitzjames. "*Después, en una hora, al hotel.*"

"*Vamos,*" said the driver, who raised the window of the taxi and drove forward slowly.

In front of the shops at which Fitzjames had also paused, the driver parked the taxi. He did not shut off the engine but got out of the vehicle and surveyed the pedestrians who crowded the sidewalks in their movements along Avenida Urdaneta. The driver began to shout profanities. Most of the pedestrians within earshot stopped to listen. The driver began, at the top of his voice, to make an extemporaneous speech about the hardship suffered by the taxi operators of Caracas specifically and of cab drivers in Venezuela generally. Within seconds, the diatribe, laced with expletives, turned on the government. Certain members of the crowd, excited by the anti-government tone of the driver's speech, cheered in response and clapped in support. Others joined in the verbal bashing of the regime.

As Fitzjames expected, the amassing crowd and shouting prompted the two security guards to leave their posts. They descended the stairs and walked beyond the Maybach limousines to the sidewalk in order to gain an unobstructed view of the proceedings prompted by the driver. Their backs were turned to Fitzjames.

Fitzjames darted at the Maybach positioned closest to him. He stood behind it and out of sight of the guards. He put the cigarette in his mouth. He removed the Ruger from the holster and shot the two front tires of the other Maybach. The crowd noise was sufficiently great to prevent the guards from hearing the firing of the pistol through the silencing device. The deflating of the tires made only minimal noise.

Fitzjames rose, slipped around to the passenger side of the Maybach behind which he had hidden. He forced opened the gas cover, unscrewed the gas cap, and dropped in the lighted stub of the cigarette. He dashed in the opposite direction and seconds later was knocked off his feet by the reverberation of the explosion. When he recovered and at a distance examined the car, it was a raging fire contained within four charred doors.

The nonplussed security guards ran back to the entrance. They were muddled by the explosion. They entered the ministry, and in a few moments the men who had previously entered, including the two Iranians, one of whom carried a thick, black briefcase in each hand, all exited the building in confusion behind the two guards.

The senior of the Venezuelans present shouted orders to the others. They responded. Two reentered the old church, and the others took up positions next to the Iranians, in order to protect them. They presumed that bombs had been planted and that other explosions would occur, very likely within the building. Hence, supervising the Iranians outside was safer and sensible.

After four minutes elapsed, a fire brigade, local police, and other officials arrived at the facility. The firefighters began working. The police officers superintended the firefighters' work but otherwise did nothing. The officials escorted the Venezuelan government operatives and the Iranians into small Japanese cars and quickly left the scene.

Fitzjames had taken a position on the opposite side of the *Venida Urdaneta* and had observed the events with other curious local onlookers. After the Iranians departed, he migrated through the crowds toward Torres. Torres stood, smoking a *Belmont*, among a throng of natives of Caracas, who had witnessed, to their great enjoyment, an anti-government harangue from a disgruntled taxi driver, which was followed spectacularly by an explosion of a German limousine at the entrance of a building that had been co-opted from the Roman Catholic church by that very same government. The cab driver and taxi, meanwhile, had disappeared.

"We need to get back to the hotel," said Fitzjames.

"Yes, sir," said Torres, who dropped the cigarette, crushed the butt underfoot, and turned to retrace his steps to his car.

Fitzjames followed in silence.

Sixteen

Torres made the return journey to the Hotel Jose Antonio Paez in under ten minutes. The traffic had lightened because of the lateness of the hour. At the hotel lobby, Fitzjames exited the automobile while still engaged in conversation with Torres in English.

"Thanks for breaking away to assist me. Get back and get your photos together. See if you recognize any of the government men in the photos. I'll recontact you later in the night. You can then give me something on the photos and perhaps something on the Russian," said Fitzjames through the open window of the closed front door on the passenger side of the vehicle.

"Yes, sir; I understand. We will have information for you when you call," responded Torres.

Fitzjames nodded in gratitude and stood upright, as Torres drove away while at the same time placing another cigarette between his lips. A cloud of smoke more visible than exhaust fumes could be seen bellowing from the Suzuki.

Fitzjames entered the hotel, greeted the concierge and desk clerk simultaneously in reply to their coordinated welcome to him, and boarded the elevator. He ascended to the level on which his own room was located and walked briskly down the corridor. At the door to the room, he paused. He could hear voices within the room and movement. He removed the Ruger from the holster and held it just above his head in his left hand and rested his finger on the trigger. With his injured right hand, he delicately and somewhat awkwardly, because of the pain, turned the doorknob. The door was locked.

He removed the metal key from his pants pocket, applied it silently to the knob, turned it suddenly, and thrust open the door to the hotel room. He burst inside with the pistol trained on two young hotel maids. Both shrieked from surprise and terror at his entrance. But, thereafter, both stood motionless and silent. They stood together next to the bed. Each appeared to be holding her breath in an effort not to move or speak.

Fitzjames said nothing. He extended his right leg toward the door and with the outside of his right foot closed the door. He kept his eyes fixed on the two maids. He did not return the handgun to the holster. The women studied his face and looked at the pistol. He could see that the maids had overturned his suitcase and emptied the contents on top of the bed. The bedspread was covered with his pants, shirts, and undergarments. They had not yet reached the backpack, which was still positioned where he had put it before leaving the room. He spoke to the two women in Spanish.

"What are you doing here?" he asked calmly.

Both women said nothing, but their anxiety was clearly overwhelming them. He suspected that a more aggressive tone would elicit the desired information. He also perceived that the women did not expect that he could speak Spanish so fluidly.

"What are you doing here?" he repeated more loudly and harshly.

Although both women were under thirty, one was clearly older than the other. The younger woman began to cry, and the older woman began to talk.

"Sir, we are here on a night duty to arrange the room for guests, such as you," she said mechanically and mendaciously.

"That is not the truth. Give me the truth. I do not have the time or the patience for lies," he responded.

The younger woman's whimpers increased to sobs. She could not hold up her head and her shoulders quivered. The older woman also showed tears on her cheeks but refrained from speaking.

"Give me the truth, please," said Fitzjames with a direct, firm tone that both calmed the women and puzzled them. "Now, please. I will not hurt you."

He looked at both women squarely and returned the Ruger to the shoulder holster. He took off the jacket and draped it over the back of the tall chair adjacent to the writing desk.

"What are your names?" he asked.

"I am Adelina," said the older, more collected woman. "She is called Soledad."

"Adelina, again, what are you doing here?"

"We were paid money to enter this room and examine your luggage. Soledad and I are the night maids who service this floor. A man, a foreigner, was standing at your door a few minutes past and asked if we could enter this room and provide information to him. He said that he would pay to each of us one thousand Bolivares if we would do so. We enter all of the rooms each evening to clean them and to turn down the spreads on the beds for the guests. We discussed the request and agreed to do it. We need money. Now, we will lose our jobs, certainly. We are sorry, sir."

"Had you ever before seen the man who asked that you do this?" queried Fitzjames.

"Yes, sir. He has often been a visitor in the hotel. He does not take rooms but comes to hotel to meet with other guests," replied Adelina.

"He comes often," added Soledad, recovering from her tearful reaction to his earlier questions.

"He is not Venezuelan?"

"No, sir," said Adelina.

"Do you know from where he comes?"

"He comes from Europe. He speaks Spanish but with a strange accent. He may come from Poland or from Ukraine," said Adelina.

"Why do you suspect those countries?"

"Europeans from the east of Europe speak Spanish with the same accent and have the same problems when they speak," suggested Adelina.

"We have many Russians here," interjected Soledad.

"Possibly Russian?" asked Fitzjames.

"Yes, sir. It is a possibility," responded Adelina.

"Please give me a description of him," said Fitzjames.

"He is short and fat," replied Soledad.

"Yes, sir. He carries too much weight, for his age," said Adelina.

"Hair color?"

"Dark, but he has very little. It is cut very short, the way one would cut hair in the army," answered Adelina.

"Age?"

"He is forty, no less," said Soledad.

"Yes. Forty would be correct. He is neither young, nor old," said Adelina.

"Very well. Say nothing of our conversation. I will not expose you, and you will not lose your work, provided you remain silent. Do you understand me?" he asked severely.

"Yes, sir," said the two women together.

He retrieved the jacket from the back of the chair and dug out the wallet from the interior pocket. He replaced the jacket and opened the wallet. He removed two five-hundred-Bolivare notes. He closed the wallet and tossed it to the desk. He delivered the cash to Adelina.

"This money is for both of you. Say nothing, as I have said, of our meeting. Tell the man who hired you that you found only clothing and some papers that you could not understand. If he asks you to enter the room a second time, refuse to do so. I may call upon you, at some point, to identify this man. Again, do you understand me?"

"Yes, sir," both women responded.

"Do you work every night?"

"Six nights. We do not work on Sundays," responded Adelina.

"Very well. Goodnight," said Fitzjames. "You may leave."

"Sir, do you wish to have your clothes refolded and re-placed? We have made a mess of your things," said Soledad with contrition.

"No. You may go. Goodnight."

"Thank you, sir," said Adelina, advancing past Fitzjames toward the door.

Soledad followed her companion and looked at Fitzjames as she moved beyond him. "Thank you very much, sir," Soledad added to Adelina's prior expression of gratitude. "Thank you."

The women left the room, and Fitzjames pushed the bolt lock of the door to secure it. He entered the bathroom, switched on the light, and washed his hands and face and brushed his teeth. He felt soiled, and those three steps refreshed him. He wanted to shower and go to bed. He was exhausted. But work remained uncompleted. He surveyed his appearance in the mirror and re-ordered his hair. He extinguished the light in the bathroom.

He collected his suitcase off of the hotel room floor, where the maids had dumped it. He put it on the top of the bed and pieced together his clothing and other articles and returned them to the suitcase in the same order they had had before the maids' invasion. He confirmed that the backpack had not been touched. He considered a moment whether something more secure should be done with the backpack and whether he could trust the promises of the maids. On both issues, he was satisfied. The contents of the backpack did not unduly expose him or reveal any secretive data that could give any party an advantage. As for the two women, the fear of being exposed and losing their jobs was sufficient to ensure their reliability.

Fitzjames removed the pistol and added additional bullets to load it fully. He returned it to the holster and put on the jacket. He evaluated the remaining cash in his possession, both American and Venezuelan currency. With the mobile telephone in his left hand and the room key in his right, he exited the hotel room. The corridor was empty. He locked the door behind him with a shake of his head, as he considered that that exercise had previously been pointless. He walked slowly toward the elevator.

Before he reached the elevator, he observed Soledad emerging from an open doorway restricted for use by members of the housekeeping staff. She carried a handful of bath towels, which by appearances she intended to deliver to a hotel guest. As he passed her, she slowed deliberately and came to stop immediately beyond him. She turned and spoke in a whisper and in rapidly delivered Spanish.

"Sir, the man is in the laundry room speaking to Adelina. He is there. He is there with her. He is very unhappy. I must go," she said and walked on to complete her task.

Fitzjames presupposed that Soledad had been ordered out of the room by the Russian in order to give him a free hand with Adelina. He leaned his right shoulder against the same wall of the corridor off of which the room lay and slid along the wall to the open door. He extracted the Ruger from the holster with his right hand and moved it to his left hand. As was his practice, he held the pistol aloft at eye level with the barrel pointed toward the ceiling.

Inside the room, he heard a male voice asking questions in Spanish. The accent was terrible, and because of it Fitzjames could understand very little of what the man asked of the maid. Yet, his Spanish was fluent. The man was notably hostile and angry and was unable to restrain the volume of his voice. He shouted the first few words of each question and then ended it in soft threatening tones. In a hushed voice, Adelina attempted to evade his questions and struggled to frame cogent answers to inquiries from a man who was accustomed to truthful replies from the overawed.

The man repeated a question twice and received the same answer from Adelina. He asked a third time, received the same answer, and then struck her. She gasped and struggled to collect her thoughts. He followed this act of violence with a repetition of the question in soothing tones but with a further treat of violence. Adelina did not respond to the question but instead pleaded with the man not to strike here again. He did so, notwithstanding.

Fitzjames swung around the edge of the doorway and into the room as the man prepared to hit Adelina a third time. She was on the floor on her knees with her left hand covering her mouth. She was bleeding from the lower lip, caused by the blows. The man was clearly startled by Fitzjames' appearance and the pistol he carried but was obviously uncertain as to Fitzjames' identity, as the man whose room he had ordered searched. In his badly accented Spanish, he spoke to Fitzjames.

"Sir, you see, this is my girlfriend. She has been disloyal to me. This is a private matter. Please go and allow me to talk more with her. Privately, privately," he said, fabricating an explanation for his conduct.

"I see," responded Fitzjames.

"A private matter, sir, between me and my girlfriend. Please put away your gun," continued the man.

Fully expecting the man to attack him if he lowered the weapon, Fitzjames widened his stance in the opened doorway, transferred the Ruger from his left hand to his right, and returned it to the holster. As he did so, the man jumped at him. Fitzjames kept his feet planted and swung his hips to the right. The man made no contact with him, but Fitzjames brought his left fist down hard on the right cheekbone of the man's face. The man stumbled, and Fitzjames struck him again on the nose with his bandaged right hand. Fitzjames winced because of the lingering pain from the earlier injury. The man slammed to the floor with a groan.

Fitzjames struck the man a third time on the back of the skull, which so dazed him as to cause semi-unconsciousness. He lay on his stomach. He moved his shoulders from side to side but lacked the strength and cerebral capacity to rise. Fitzjames removed the pistol, squatted over the man, placed the gun against the man's temple, and spoke in loud, slow Spanish to him.

"If you move, I will kill you," snarled Fitzjames.

"I said nothing to him, sir," offered Adelina to Fitzjames in a subdued voice. "Nothing."

"Yes. I know. Thank you. Please go take care of your face. I will handle this man."

Adelina got to her feet and left the room with her hand still covering her mouth.

Fitzjames stood erect and placed the sole of his shoe on the neck and shoulders of the man. He removed the mobile telephone, pressed the recall feature, and the line rang.

"Yes, sir," answered Torres in English.

"I'm sorry to keep calling you in, sending you off, and then calling you in again. I've got another situation, another good Russian for us, underfoot at the moment. I need for you to get over here to the hotel. I'm in the laundry room, which is on the same floor of the hotel as my room and next to the elevator," said Fitzjames.

"Ten minutes, sir," said Torres.

Fitzjames increased the pressure of his foot on the back of the man's neck and thus began the ten-minute wait for Torres' arrival. He could not repress a vocalization in English of his thoughts, as he looked down at the short heavy-set man with crewcut-styled hair lying on the floor, subdued.

"Dirty Russian bastard. All violence, even toward women. No informing principles. Just appetites. You filthy, dirty bastard."

Seventeen

"Tie his hands and wrists behind his back or put any sort of restraint on him that you've got," said Fitzjames to Torres, in English, just after the latter's arrival.

"Yes, sir," replied Torres, who locked the Russian's wrists behind his back with a set of zip-tie, heavy-duty police-grade handcuffs.

Fitzjames continued to restrain the man, as Torres affixed the nylon and plastic straps after forcing his arms behind his back. In Spanish, Torres ordered the man to roll to his side and then to his knees and then to his feet. Once upright, Torres told him to keep silent or Torres would kill him. The man nodded an acknowledgment.

"Take him down the stairs of the emergency exit. Keep him out of sight. Keep your gun on the back of his skull and shoot him if he tries to break away from you," said Fitzjames.

"Yes, sir," responded Torres.

"Use the same interrogation techniques with him as with the other one, only we can keep him longer. Make certain that you finish your interrogation of the first one before beginning with this one. Also, keep them separated. I don't want them communicating or his even knowing that we've got his countryman in hand, if he doesn't already know. He's pretty well informed. He tried to pay off some maids to search my room," advised Fitzjames.

"Did he obtain any information?" asked Torres.

"Nothing, fortunately. Not much to get there. At the same time, the very fact that he knew which was my room is troubling. Do what you need to do to get what information you can," said Fitzjames.

"Do the same rules of interrogation apply to this one?" inquired Torres.

"As much as I'd like to tell you that you've got a free hand, I can't do that. Same rules. But, as I said, employ the same techniques that I suggested for the first one. I'll give you a call within the hour. Also, I haven't emptied his pockets. I'll leave that to you, too," said Fitzjames.

Torres positioned the barrel of his pistol sharply under the Russian's right cheekbone. The motion caused the Russian to tilt his head back and to the left, which nearly prompted him to lose his footing. With his left hand, Torres grabbed the Russian's right forearm and prevented the fall. Torres followed this somewhat acrobatic movement with a complete pat-down of the Russian. Torres relieved the man of a Soviet-era TT-30 handgun, his wallet, five thousand Bolivares, and two thousand American dollars. Torres repeated the order that he not speak and reminded him that if he did so he would die. Torres then commanded him to walk slowly out of the room and down the hallway and down the stairs to Torres' car.

Adelina, despite her facial injuries, along with Soledad, had carried on with her work of servicing the rooms on the same floor of the hotel. Although the two women appeared to be diligent and engaged, in fact they were distracted. The conflicting emotions of fear and curiosity made their labors almost pointless. Instead of focusing on their required tasks, as they moved from room to room, they talked to one another about the events of the evening, the mutual anxieties about the effect of their foolhardy willingness to do the bidding of the Russian, and the questions they had about how the American finally dealt with him. While still in conversation in an empty hotel room with the door ajar, the two women were interrupted.

"Adelina, I need your assistance," said Fitzjames, in Spanish, from the open doorway.

"Yes, sir," Adelina responded with temerity and obvious reluctance. She walked to the door, and Soledad followed her.

The two women stood before Fitzjames.

"You do not need to be frightened. I need for you to open the doors of two hotel rooms on the third floor. You simply open the doors and service the rooms as you are doing now. I want to see you do it. Nothing will be touched or removed. I simply wish to see the rooms," continued Fitzjames in Spanish.

"We have caused so many problems, sir," suggested Soledad. "And, we do not service the third floor."

"We will help you," said Adelina sternly and thereby overruling the objection of her younger companion. She turned to Soledad. "This American saved my life. I cannot refuse a request from him. You should be grateful. The Russian would have hurt you also. And, this American has said that he will not reveal what we did, stupidly, in his room. We would lose our work. Are you so stupid?" asked Adelina.

"No. I understand. I agree. I am sorry," said Soledad.

"Apologies and gratitude are not necessary. Again, I don't intend to touch or remove anything. I want to see inside, only," urged Fitzjames.

"When?" asked Soledad.

"Now," said Fitzjames.

"What rooms?" inquired Soledad.

"310 and 312."

Adelina resolutely left the room in which she was working. Soledad closed and locked the door behind her and followed Adelina down the corridor to the elevator. When the elevator door opened, Adelina entered and Soledad followed. Soledad held open the door for Fitzjames to enter as well.

"No. I will use the stairs," said Fitzjames.

"Give me a few minutes. I must explain to the housekeeping supervisor on the third floor what we intend to do. I do not expect a problem. I can be very persuasive," added Adelina with a smile.

Puzzled yet compliant, Soledad allowed the door of the elevator to close. The sound of it descending rung out through the hallway. Fitzjames walked briskly to the stairwell and descended to the third floor. He strolled by the laundry room adjacent to the elevator, the twin of the room on Fitzjames' room's floor of the hotel. He overheard Adelina in conversation with her colleague. The conversation was littered with Venezuelan slang and understanding it was challenging. However, its effect was clear when Adelina emerged with Soledad behind her carrying four large bath towels. Adelina cleverly brandished, for Fitzjames to see, the master key to the rooms on the hotel's third floor.

Adelina knocked on the door of Room 310. Through the closed door, she announced herself as a housekeeping staff member. No reply came. She knocked and made the announcement a second time, again to no reply. She put the key in the doorknob, turned it, opened the door, and entered. Soledad followed her inside. Fitzjames entered behind Soledad, who stepped aside to allow him to pass.

He surveyed the interior of the room. No one was present. The writing desk in the room contained an elaborate portable computer system that had been pieced together by the occupant. The system had a large hard drive, two printers, and four monitors. The room was devoid of paperwork or other documents. The only other noteworthy feature in the room was the occupant's two suitcases that had been neatly closed and stowed next to the single queen-size bed.

"Very well. Let us go to 312," mumbled Fitzjames. "Quickly."

Fitzjames paused in order to permit Adelina and Soledad to exit the room before him. At Room 312, Adelina replayed the earlier exercise, announced herself twice at the door from the hallway, received no reply, and unlocked the door and entered.

Room 312 too was, at that moment, unoccupied. But unlike Room 310, no computer system had been installed. Instead, the room contained eight large black briefcases, all essentially of the same style and color. Fitzjames examined the first briefcase in his path. It had no apparent markings to indicate its origin. The case was equipped with a combination security lock. He could not open it. He picked up the case. It was heavy and apparently filled with documents. He picked up a second and a third case in rapid succession. They were equally heavy and thus equally full. Other than the briefcases, the room was empty, except for a single piece of luggage identical to the two pieces in Room 310.

"Good. Thank you. We can go," said Fitzjames.

The three left the room, and Adelina locked the door to Room 312 behind them. Fitzjames made no additional comment to the two maids but walked to the stairwell and entered. Adelina and Soledad watched him in confusion. Adelina confirmed that the door to Room 310 was also secured. She and Soledad returned together to the laundry room and returned the master key to the senior maid on the third floor. As a pair, they took the elevator upstairs to their assigned stations.

Fitzjames, meanwhile, descended the stairs to street level and the lobby. The lobby had emptied of hotel guests and visitors because of the late hour. Only two desk clerks were on duty and a single security guard, who appeared to be drowsy, awake beyond their respective bedtimes. None of the three spoke to him.

Fitzjames left the hotel and walked to a subway station entrance less than one hundred yards up the street. The roadway was quiet with only a few cars and trucks and fewer pedestrians. He removed the American mobile telephone from the back pocket of his pants and placed a call to Major Fuller.

"Yes," said Fuller after two rings.

"Any identity data for me, sir?" inquired Fitzjames.

"Still working on the Iranians. They're proving to be a challenge. The Russian was fairly easy to sort out. For the sake of argument, I'm presuming that the name you furnished is correct and that of the very person you've got locked down," said Fuller. The last sentence was made mechanically.

"That presumption, sir, is likely correct. I've given some thought to the question of whether he would've had any reason to be sensitive about keeping his true identity confidential. I just don't see it. So, I believe Lebedev is Lebedev," said Fitzjames.

"Very good. Nikolai Lebedev has had a varied career in post-Soviet Russia. He started in the Main Department of Internal Affairs in Moscow, which is Russian for the Moscow municipal police. From there, the central government picked him up, and he did a stint as a contract soldier in the Russian Ground Forces. He began as a noncommissioned officer, but was promoted to lieutenant, in short order, after serving in Chechnya. His service record there is sketchy, which tells me that he was likely involved in war crimes or in general criminal activity. After Chechnya, there's a dark period of two years. No data. Again, very likely, he was engaged in criminal activity or quasi-criminal undertakings, assisting oligarchs and that sort of thing. He reappears as a member of the Federal Security Service, the FSB, in Moscow. We can trace him clearly from there to the Russian Federation's Ministry of Internal Affairs, the MVD. He seems to have an active international dossier. His assignments have taken him out of Russia on a regular basis. He's frequently in South America. Venezuela is the destination identified most often, specifically Caracas. But he's also been in Colombia and Peru and Ecuador. Ecuador is the venue of second choices after Venezuela," advised Fuller.

"All drug growers and producers for the American market," said Fitzjames.

"Precisely," noted Fuller.

"Any known contacts between Lebedev and Iran?"

"Nothing appears in our research, at least not with Lebedev specifically. The MVD has a conduit to Tehran, however. So, if he's with the MVD, there's no reason to rule out contact with Iran simply because we don't have data on that subject with his name on it. It may not be a certainty but it's a probability," said Fuller.

"Sir, that's all very helpful and useful. I'll try you again a bit later or tomorrow morning on the two Iranians. There's still work to be done tonight—or this morning, as the case may be," said Fitzjames.

"That's fine. None of us is getting any sleep, if that gives you any comfort," offered Fuller.

"I wish it did, sir. I'm wiped out and need to sleep, at least for a few hours. But my hotel room has been compromised, and I've tasked the local contacts with 'round-the-clock work. I can't very well take out time to rest if they're all goin' at it without respite," said Fitzjames.

"Yes, I suppose. But they haven't traveled, and you have. They also aren't working independently and don't have the strain of command that you bear. I need you to be at your best, and if that means sleep, then if I have to I'll order you to get some," said Fuller in a didactic, commanding tone of voice.

"I understand, sir. At the same time, the window of opportunity is open here, and I need to be on top of developments while that window is open and before it closes," said Fitzjames.

"The latitude is yours. Do what you need to do. But sleep before you give me your next report, Captain," suggested Fuller.

"Understood, sir. Thank you," said Fitzjames, thereby concluding the call.

Fitzjames shook his head. He had not expected a suggestion from Fuller that Fuller might order him to bed. At the same time, he appreciated the wisdom being offered. He surmised that this lack of recognition of the urgency of sleep was a function of being in need of sleep. As with alcohol consumption, the best time to decide whether you have had too many drinks is not after you have drunk too much.

He returned the mobile telephone to his pants pocket and began the short walk back to the hotel. The streets were now devoid of all vehicular traffic. As he neared the hotel, from a distance of approximately fifty yards, two young women emerged from an alcove and approached him. They were both wearing lowcut, tightly fitting short dresses with pastel-colored tights and high-heeled shoes. He could see them clearly under the street lights. They addressed him in Spanish.

"Hello," said one of the women in a slow, alluring voice.

"Can we help you?" asked the second woman with the same inflection.

"No, thank you," replied Fitzjames and intentionally refused to make eye contact with either or both of the women.

As he moved to pass them out of their path, the second woman on the right of her companion put her right hand on his chest in order to stop him. As she did so, she stepped immediately in front of him and pressed herself against him. He stopped, and the first woman stood immediately to his right side, nearly touching him too with her torso.

"Please, we can help you. Come with us. Two women for you. Come," said the woman, who stood before him staring up at his face and now placing both of her hands together on his chest.

"Yes. Not too expensive. Two women. Come," said the woman to his right.

"No, thank you. I must go," said Fitzjames, while pressing forward despite the woman's presence.

"You see, he is a foreigner," said the woman to his right to her companion.

"Are you from Spain? Your accent is from Spain?" asked her companion.

"He is an American. He is not Spanish," said the woman.

"Ladies, release me. I must go," said Fitzjames more assertively.

"He is strong," said the woman to his right.

"Very strong. Come with us," said the woman in front of him, who had now moved her right hand to his left hip.

"Enough. Release me, now," ordered Fitzjames.

The strength of this command was sufficient to compel the two prostitutes to step back and out of his way. He walked on and made no further comment.

"Son of a whore! Cheap American son of a whore!" shouted one of the women at him after he had put twenty yards between him and them.

He shook his head again and ignored the insult. Once he reentered the Hotel Jose Antonio Paez, the two women returned to the place from which they had emerged onto the sidewalk.

"Pay us," said the woman, who had pressed herself against Fitzjames' chest, to a man who stood off the sidewalk and up a step, obscured in the shadows.

"Give us the money," said her companion to the same man.

"What did he say to you?" asked the man in badly accented Spanish.

"He refused us," said the woman.

"Did that surprise you?" asked the man with a light laugh.

"Yes, of course," replied her companion. "Together, we are very successful."

"I can understand your confidence," said the man with a menacing edge to his voice. "You are both very appealing. Very appealing."

"Give us the money," repeated the woman, only without the conviction of her first entreaty.

"Was he American? This is my only interest," said the man.

"Yes. He spoke Spanish like a Spaniard. But he is American. Absolutely," said the woman.

"Very well. Here is your money. Be good whores. Give the required portion to your pimp," said the man with derision and contempt.

The man presented the equivalent of three hundred American dollars in Bolivares to the two women. The first woman snatched the money from the man's hand. He laughed again and lit a cigarette and walked off in the opposite direction of the hotel.

"Russian pig," mumbled the woman who, out of fear and a sense of vulnerability, did not wish the slur to be overheard by the man.

Eighteen

When Fitzjames entered the lobby of the Hotel Jose Antonio Paez, he found it more desolate than even moments earlier. His footfall echoed through the room as he walked across the white tiled floor to the elevator. A maid was busy mopping and another was sweeping. The hotel maintained its housekeeping staff on duty twenty-four hours each day.

At the elevator, while awaiting the doors to open at the ground-floor level, he observed from across the lobby and through the glass doors and windows of the entrance two cars arriving at the hotel. In lieu of entering the elevator, he turned and took a seat among a group of comfortable chairs and tables intended for guests and visitors lingering or waiting in the hotel's lobby. He snatched up a newspaper. He opened it and surveyed it, while awaiting the entry into the hotel of the individuals who had only just arrived.

The two Iranians strolled into the lobby. As they did so, they continued their conversation with a man who entered with them, whom Fitzjames recognized from the Ministry of Health. The three chatted for another moment and then the third man—a Venezuelan, Fitzjames presumed—very formally and awkwardly wished the men goodnight. Although Fitzjames could not hear the words spoken, it was clear to him that they had spoken in English.

The two Iranians moved to the front desk and the shorter of the pair asked in English of the clerk whether any messages had been left for them. The clerk made no reply, except to request that the men excuse him in order to inquire in the office behind the desk into which the clerk entered. The clerk did not need the men's names or room numbers. He reemerged seconds later and presented an envelope to the man who had spoken to him. No gratitude was expressed for the service, and the Iranians turned aside. The clerk wished them good evening. They said nothing in response and approached the elevator. The elevator door opened immediately, they entered, and the door closed behind them. They had not opened the envelope.

Fitzjames noted the time on his wristwatch and chose to remain where he was for ten minutes. He was sufficiently tired that he had to force himself to remain alert. The chairs were soft, and the cushions conformed to the body. With little effort, he could have closed his eyes and slept. He focused on the newspaper and passed the time.

After the ten-minute period passed, he rose and folded the newspaper and returned it to the table off of which he had taken it. He chose to take the stairs, rather than the elevator, in order to use the climb as a stimulant. He ascended the stairs to the third floor, skipping every other step and moving quickly. He opened the door from the stairwell to the third-floor corridor only partially in order to determine if any other guests were awake and roaming the hallway. None were present. He entered the corridor and walked toward Room 310 and Room 312. He walked slowly and his step was light.

Without touching the door, he leaned toward Room 310 and listened for a few seconds. The room was silent, and no motion could be detected. He moved to Room 312 and repeated the exercise. Inside, he could hear activity and of items in the bathroom being re-ordered. He moved and then leaned against the wall between the two rooms. After two to three minutes elapsed, he listened again at the door of Room 312. All was quiet. The movement had ceased. He assumed that both men had gone to bed.

Fitzjames waited an additional three to four minutes, listened again in order to recheck both rooms for activity, and confirmed utter silence within each. Convinced that the Iranians were asleep, he returned to the stairwell, ascended to the floor on which his hotel room was located, walked to the room, and unlocked the door and entered. He flipped on the light switch in the bathroom and did the same with the lamp above the bed. He took off the jacket and hung it over the back of the chair at the desk. He extracted the Ruger from the shoulder holster and placed the pistol on the bedstand. He unfastened and removed the holster and hung it on the desk chair with the jacket. He pulled the white polo-style short-sleeved shirt over his head and folded it. He dropped the folded shirt on the top of the desk. He emptied the pockets of his pants. The contents he placed on the desk with his shirt. He removed the local mobile telephone from the jacket pocket and contacted Torres.

"Yes, sir," answered Torres with the same sincere, eager responsiveness that he had employed at the first telephone communication.

"All's well?" inquired Fitzjames.

"Yes, sir. We are progressing with our two friends. I also have photographs to discuss with you. If my father were alive, he would call this a good day. It has been a busy day and that would have made it, for him, a good day. God bless his soul," said Torres.

"I'm sorry that I won't have the opportunity to meet your father," added Fitzjames, with a friendliness that seemed ill suited for the present, given the nature and gravity of the relationship with his Venezuelan contact, but which struck him as quite natural. Latin Americans have the capacity to draw a person into their lives unwittingly by their warmth and familiarity. "He must have been an interesting man."

"Fascinating man. Very wise. Very clever. He did not care for Arabs or Soviets. It was not important if they were Egyptian or Syrian or Palestinian. He did not like them. The same is true of Russians, Ukrainians, Georgians. For him, they were all Soviets, all communists, and all criminals. At the hotel, he would have told you all of these things over a glass of good Venezuelan rum and a cigarette," said Torres.

"Belmonts?" asked Fitzjames.

"Of course, yes, and Pampero dark rum in a tall, thin glass," responded Torres.

"Excellent. Well, I'm calling to let you know that I'm going to sleep for a few hours," said Fitzjames.

"Good. Rest well. And, is the hand very sore?"

"No. Thanks. Not too serious. I'm planning on removing the bandages. It's fine."

"Sleep well, sir."

"Thanks again."

Fitzjames considered a shower. But he resolved to do so in the morning. A cold shower, which he preferred, although refreshing, would defeat the drowsiness and ultimately, once he fell asleep, cause him to oversleep. Instead, he simply removed his shoes and socks and turned down the bedspread. He did not pull back the sheet.

However, before he made the decision to lie down, he recognized the need for added security at the door to the room. He had little concern about Adelina and Soledad breaching their commitments to him. But other hotel staff were corruptible. A room change was pointless and would draw unwanted attention to him. Hence, he positioned the lounge chair at an angle under the doorknob. This technique was timeworn but effective. His primary goal was not to prevent an intruder but to slow him down and make his unwanted entrance as noisy as possible. To add to obstacles, he moved his suitcase to the door, opened it concave to the door, and placed it in front of the lounge chair. In the darkness, if anyone broke in, the visitor would be forced to work his way past the lounge chair barrier then, very likely, he would stumble over the open suitcase.

After these precautionary steps were completed. Fitzjames removed from his backpack the Dalvey, which was a modern mechanism but also a facsimile of a traditional alarm clock. He set it and the Breitling to ring in four hours. He placed the Dalvey on the bedstand next to the handgun. He extinguished the light in the bathroom and did the same with the light over the bed. On top of the bedsheet, with his head on the pillow and his body turned on its left side facing the door, he fell asleep instantly.

At 5:30 A.M., after four hours passed, the Dalvey and Breitling rang virtually simultaneously. The alarms were not loud, but the repetition of sound was sufficient to arouse him. Fitzjames sat up on the bed with his feet on the floor. He turned on the light over the bed and shut off the Dalvey, which continued to sound well after the alarm on the Breitling had stopped. He collected the Dalvey in his left hand, stood, and stepped to the desk to return the alarm clock to the backpack. He walked to the bathroom, avoiding the opened suitcase and lounge chair, and turned on the light. He studied himself in the mirror for a few seconds; his whiskered face and disheveled hair needed attention. He thus shaved and brushed his teeth and then shed his pants and underwear and took a brief shower of cool water. After toweling off, after removing the bandages on his right hand, and after applying deodorant, *eau de toilette*, and hair gel, he exited the bathroom and dressed.

He had not run in the last few days and was beginning to sense the absence of exercise. He was feeling thick and awkward, which was not the way in which he felt most able and effective. He resolved to run either later in the day or the following morning. For the present, although he had showered, he dropped to the floor and did three sets of twenty-five pushups, each set separated by a three-minute rest interval. The pushups were not a substitute for a run, but they did trigger the secretion of endorphins. The hormone worked its physiological purpose and made him more alert and made him believe that he was more alert.

He appreciated that the brief bit of sleep had not been interrupted. He closed the suitcase and returned it to the place in the hotel room that it had previously occupied. Thereafter, he placed both hands, respectively, on the two arms of the lounge chair in its propped, angled position under the interior doorknob of the door to the room. As he lifted the chair to pull it away from the door, the chair back struck the knob of the door in a manner similar to the way in which an occupant of the room would have shaken the knob upon turning it to leave the room. An audible click was heard and then an explosion followed.

The blast blew a large hole in the drywall adjacent to the hotel door and shattered the door, which splintered into pieces. The resulting fire engulfed the doorjamb and spread quickly to the outer wall and into the room Fitzjames occupied and to the two rooms on either side of his. The force of the explosion had knocked him into the interior of the room, to the floor, and against the desk. Had he not had the lounge chair in his hands as a shield, he would have been seriously injured. The underside of the chair was a reinforced metal. The shrapnel spray from the bomb had hit the chair bottom and largely missed him, although he had been hit in the left shoulder and right thigh by projectiles. He was bleeding from both areas, as well as from the scratch on his forehead from striking the desk.

He got to his feet, rushed into the bathroom, turned on the water in the shower, and soaked two bath towels. With the wet towels, he patted out the flames in the room and in the doorjamb. Other hotel guests and hotel staff had joined in the effort to put out the fire. They were successful, except that an elderly hotel maid had burned her hands severely in the endeavor. Other than the maid, who was escorted off the floor by other members of the hotel's housekeeping personnel in order to address her injuries, only Fitzjames had been injured.

Two members of hotel security arrived as the last embers of the fires were extinguished. They inquired of Fitzjames if he needed medical care. He refused it. With them, he examined the outside of the hotel room, the pieces of the door, and the remaining bits of the metal casing of an apparent pipe bomb filled with nails and metal fragments. Fitzjames concluded that the device had been set to explode upon his turning of the doorknob. Of course, the mechanism had been put into place during the four hours of sound, uninterrupted sleep.

At the same time as the security men talked with other guests, Fitzjames returned to the interior of the hotel room and gathered his belongings. He repacked his toiletries and the clothes he had removed from the suitcase. Minutes later, with the backpack over his left shoulder and the suitcase in his right hand, he reentered the smoke-filled, charred corridor. In Spanish, the senior security guard addressed him.

"Sir, may we do something for you?" he asked with great deference.

"Yes. I suppose I will need to be assigned a new hotel room," replied Fitzjames.

"Yes, sir, clearly, immediately. It will be necessary for you to speak to the police.

They will arrive shortly. Would you kindly do so, sir?"

"Of course. I will wait in the lobby. You will find me there."

"Thank you, sir. Please accept the apologies of the hotel management."

Nineteen

"Yes, sir. We will arrange immediately for a new room for you," said the clerk at the front desk, in English, to Fitzjames.

The clerk spoke in an agitated, deeply deferential manner. His disconcerted manner reflected the then-current state of the Hotel Jose Antonio Paez. The hotel was in an uproar. The police had arrived before Fitzjames descended to the lobby with his belongings in hand. The event had prompted the arrival of four police vehicles and nine officers. The sirens had awoken and roused from their beds all of the hotel's guests, many of whom had come to the lobby to make inquiries about the explosion that they had heard, or believed that they had heard, or the smoke they had smelled, or could still smell. The native guests appeared to treat the event as a good reason to leave the hotel. The Venezuelan man, who stood next to Fitzjames at the front desk and argued with another clerk, believed that the event obviated his obligation to pay the cost of his stay.

Fitzjames waited impatiently for the clerk to sort out the vacancies, both current and anticipated. He watched the other guests and the hotel staff interact in the lobby, while two policemen questioned hotel security personnel. Fitzjames recognized that ultimately the police would be directed to him by the security staff.

"Do you have any preferences, sir, of floor?" asked the clerk.

"Can you find something on the third floor for me?" inquired Fitzjames.

"Yes, sir, one moment. Allow me to check," replied the clerk.

The clerk returned to his computer monitor. Two lines of hotel guests formed behind Fitzjames with the angry Venezuelan man next to him. The Venezuelan man was having little success in convincing the desk clerk, combined with a hotel manager, that the events made his continued stay too dangerous and that his time spent to date in the hotel unworthy of payment.

"We have a room, sir, on the third floor. But it is presently occupied. The guests in the room are to vacate today. They have until 12:00 to do so, and we will need time to clean the room. You understand, of course, sir," said the clerk.

"Of course. Room number?" queried Fitzjames.

"Room 305, sir."

"Fine. That works for me. Transfer me, then, from my current room to 305. Here is the key to the room, although it's probably worthless now," said Fitzjames, as he presented to the clerk the metal room key.

"Thank you, sir."

"You don't need anything more from me, do you?" asked Fitzjames.

"No, sir. Nothing more. Thank you for your patience and thank you for remaining with us. May we hold your luggage for you in the office until your new room is prepared?" suggested the clerk diffidently.

"No thanks. I'll hold on to it."

"It is no trouble, sir. We are happy to do so, if you wish."

"No. It's unnecessary. I'll hold on to it. Please do what you can to expedite the cleaning of Room 305. I want to get into the room as quickly as possible."

"Yes, yes, sir. I will ask the maids to do so."

"Thank you," said Fitzjames, who turned and walked to the waiting area where he had been seated the previous evening. He dropped the backpack into one of the chairs and put the suitcase next to it. He called Torres on the local cellular telephone.

"Good morning, sir. Did you rest well? It was not a long sleep," said Torres warmly.

"Yes. I slept well. Bit of an incident, though. I'll fill you in a bit later. Can you send one of your people around to pick me up? Immediately."

"Yes, sir. A driver will arrive at the hotel in ten minutes. I am certain you will recognize the Suzuki."

"Certainly. Thanks," said Fitzjames.

He returned the telephone to his jacket pocket. He surveyed the ongoing discussion between the police and the security guards. The official interview did not appear to him to be ending or to be moving toward him. He picked up a Venezuelan news magazine and flipped the pages to pass the time. A few moments later, a middle-aged police officer of medium height and build in uniform and with an enormous handgun in the holster on his left hip advanced toward him. Fitzjames observed his approach but ignored him and continued to read the magazine. The officer stood in front of him and waited to be acknowledged. Fitzjames said nothing. After a half of a minute of silence passed with the two men standing facing one another, the police officer spoke to Fitzjames in Spanish.

"Sir. We require a statement from you. We understand that it was in your room where the explosion occurred," said the officer.

"A statement? I will explain to you what I know. I am expecting to leave the hotel in five minutes," responded Fitzjames. He took the time from his wristwatch.

"This affair is very serious. We require your assistance," said the officer impatiently.

"Yes. It is serious. I was the victim. I suppose that I could have been killed. But I have nothing to tell you. Most of your evidence is upstairs inside and outside the hotel room," said Fitzjames.

"How long are you staying in Caracas?" asked the officer.

"Uncertain. Two to three more days," said Fitzjames.

"Business or pleasure?" inquired the officer.

"Pleasure, mixed with business," returned Fitzjames.

"May I review your passport?" asked the officer.

"Of course," said Fitzjames, extracting the passport from his jacket and delivering it to the policeman.

"Please follow me," said the officer, while thumbing through the passport and examining the photograph page and then the page containing the customs documentation, which confirmed Fitzjames' date of entry into Venezuela.

Fitzjames put the backpack on his shoulder and clutched the suitcase and walked behind the officer thirty feet to the station occupied by the security personnel of the hotel. At the station, the policeman instructed Fitzjames to wait while he made a telephone call. With Fitzjames' passport in hand, the officer placed a telephone call and spoke for three to four minutes. He hung up the telephone and returned the passport to Fitzjames.

"Do you know why this explosion occurred outside your room?" asked the policeman.

"No idea. It must have been a mistake. I must have been confused with someone else."

"Perhaps. Do you intend to remain at this hotel?"

"Yes."

"Very well. If we need more information, we will call upon you again," said the officer dismissively.

He looked sharply at Fitzjames with a demeanor of distrust and stepped away to speak to another of the policemen. Fitzjames made no comment and exited the hotel. The Suzuki had arrived, and the same female driver of the previous evening was behind the steering wheel. She offered no greeting. He opened the back passenger door and placed the backpack and suitcase on the seat. He closed the door, opened the front passenger door, and in silence took the passenger seat. The woman began to drive out of the hotel entrance before he could close the door or fasten the safety belt. Two of the police officers watched as he was driven away and noted the license plate number on the car. The policeman who had interviewed Fitzjames ordered the other officer, his subordinate, to conduct a search of the plate and identify the owner.

At extraordinary speed, the woman traced through the early morning urban confusion on the streets of Caracas. Traffic was heavy, although it was still early morning. Cars, motorcycles, scooters, and trucks sounded their horns and fought their way to their destinations in all directions. Northbound travelers were as numerous as their southbound fellows. The same was true of those moving west and east. The woman ignored the congestion and drove as hard and as fast as she could in and out of lines of vehicles and between traffic signals. After fifteen minutes, they arrived at a recently constructed modern building covered in tinted glass from the ground level to the top. The structure, from the street, appeared to be seven to eight stories in height. But the actual number of stories could not be discerned. The woman parked the Suzuki in a restricted, out-of-doors parking lot at the rear of the building.

Fitzjames, with the backpack on his shoulder and suitcase in hand, followed her inside through a securitized door at the back. She gained entry through the use of a magnetic swipe card. They walked down a short corridor to an elevator. The woman again used the swipe card, and the door of the elevator opened. The keypad in the elevator had only four buttons. For a third time, the woman used the swipe card and then pressed the first of the buttons. To Fitzjames' surprise, the elevator descended below street level. Seconds later, the elevator door opened. Torres stood at the elevator to greet him.

"Good morning, Captain," said Torres warmly.

"Good morning," Fitzjames responded as he stepped off the elevator.

"I believe that your sleep was not so restful. We have learned through our surveillance that a bomb was detonated early this morning at the Hotel Jose Antonio Paez. The police have begun their investigation. Sir, am I correct that you were the target?" asked Torres.

"I was the target. You're correct. Fortunately, a lounge chair protected me from the blast and the shrapnel. A pipe bomb, I suppose. Set to explode upon turning the door handle," explained Fitzjames. "I inadvertently set it off when I pulled out the room's lounge chair that I had propped up against the door for added security while I slept. Sturdy chair, well made, saved my life, very likely."

"Well, excellent that you are safe. Do you need some aid for the wound on your forehead?" inquired Torres.

"No, I'm fine. What can you tell me?"

"We have worked through the night. Many of these matters are growing more unified, including the police investigation of the explosion at the hotel. Did an officer speak to you?"

"Yes. I was subjected to an ordinary set of inquiries by a suspicious cop, just before your driver picked me up," responded Fitzjames.

"I suspect that policeman was Cesar Quijada. I also suspect that the investigation will be a short one. Quijada is a lieutenant in the National Bolivarian Police, the PNB, of Ruben Moreno. Moreno is the senior man, by our research, in the Ministry for Justice and Internal Affairs. Moreno is a shadowy figure, a phantom. He appears and disappears. He has ties with the Russians, criminal ties. Formal connections between him and the Russian government are less certain. But he has a confederate in the Ministry of Health, Andres Fuenmayor. Fuenmayor is also a shadow. We have tracked Fuenmayor for the past three years. He has been engaged in drug manufacturing and transport and sale. All of his personal dealings have been marginal. He is on the periphery of much of Venezuelan government's anti-narcotics practices.

"Those practices in reality promote narcotics, and the government officials take their piece of the profits. Fuenmayor and Algorta had had dealings. They may have been partners at different times in different undertakings. The curious element, now, is that both Moreno and Fuenmayor were photographed last night outside the old church. They came out of the building together and drove away with the Iranians."

"You have those photos?" asked Fitzjames.

"Yes, sir. They are easily identifiable. Very clear," said Torres.

"What more do you know about Fuenmayor and Algorta?" continued Fitzjames.

"Very interesting. They were much together last year. They were frequently seen in one another's company, particularly at official gatherings and parties of supporters of the government. Over the last six months, Algorta did not regularly appear. We observed the change but did not consider it relevant. In fact, we believed that perhaps Algorta had been told that his profile and public image were of the sort that the government could not afford to be too close, in public. We did not see a fall from favor. We certainly did not foresee that Algorta would be assassinated," said Torres.

"The central questions, as I see it, are whether Algorta was acting alone and independently, which I doubt, and who will step into his shoes and fill the void now that he's been removed," said Fitzjames.

"I agree."

"Thoughts?"

"Well, sir, I believe we should focus on both Moreno and Fuenmayor," suggested Torres.

"Very well. Tell me more of Moreno's dealings with the Russians," said Fitzjames.

"The national government has been moving away from independent regional and local autonomy. For example, the municipal police force of Caracas was federalized. Now the PNB provides policing. Moreno has been instrumental in the PNB's formation, development, and expansion. But the government needed guidance and asked for Russian assistance," explained Torres.

"Sounds like a cover and is very curious," offered Fitzjames.

"Indeed, yes. It is much like inviting the poacher of the game to be the warden of the wildlife park," said Torres. "Moreno knew the Russians from his illegal undertakings and then invited those same Russians to provide supervision and training for a new federal police force. Corrupt mentors and instructors. The Russians provide instruction and thereby gain access to all of the criminal interests in Venezuela and to the corrupted officials who aid them."

"Quite a foothold," commented Fitzjames.

"Significant. With Moreno in the background and out of the spotlight controlling the entry of the Russians, he has created a self-serving network of criminality," said Torres.

"And the focus?" asked Fitzjames.

"The usual, guns and drugs. Venezuela has become the entry point and exit point of weapons of all varieties and, of course, for narcotics. The weapons are sent around the world. The drugs to the United States. Oil is used as a cover for much of the traffic. An oil refinery here could be, in reality, a weapons assembly or storage facility or a drug-producing facility. For every Russian oil tanker that carries crude that enters a port in Venezuela, two more are carrying guns and narcotics," said Torres.

"Your data also shows Fuenmayor in the drug business?" asked Fitzjames.

"Yes. Deep involvement. No Russian ties that we are aware of. But that may change with the apparent cooperation between Fuenmayor and Moreno. The combination of two powerful figures from two powerful federal agencies is frightening. With the aid of the Russians, a complete transformation in the traffic of narcotics, in particular, could occur. The traditional sources of supply could change, along with the delivery systems. With Russian support, the Mexican cartels could either be destroyed or, much worse, made much more powerful and irresistible and violent," said Torres.

"And there is the tie to Iran. Russians cooperating with Iranians in Venezuela," said Fitzjames.

"Yes. Of course, the relationship between the government and Iran is a strong one. The anxiety that raises involves Iran's nuclear science, theocratic regime, and lack of allies for trade. Iran needs Venezuela as its South American partner. Venezuela can, of course, defy mandates coming out of Washington. Colombia and most of the other countries, including Brazil, cannot afford to do so," said Torres.

"Yes. The relationship between Russia and Iran remains undefined. Cooperation and combination, particularly if it were intended to destabilize the United States, is quite plausible," suggested Fitzjames.

"Yes. It could take many forms: economic, strategic, and nuclear. If either Russian or Iran had a desire to distract the United States Government, a domestic crisis would be an alternative," said Torres.

"And narcotics might very well be the avenue," said Fitzjames.

"Yes, sir," said Torres coldly.

"Do you have anything from the Russians in custody?" asked Fitzjames.

"They have not been cooperative, which is of no surprise. The method of questioning that you suggested, with Emilio Fushimi, has been somewhat successful. There is clearly fear. We will employ the same tactic with the second man later this morning. We have deprived them of sleep. If we were to use more aggressive methods, we would learn more," urged Torres.

"No. I object to torture. Torture may be counterproductive in the end. Are the two men separated?"

"Yes, certainly."

"Good. Continue to keep at them awake, no sleep, and hold them for the next few hours and then release them separately this afternoon. Take them blindfolded to an obscure place of your choice in the city and let them go. I'd like them tracked, both their movements and communications, particularly immediately after their release. They'll likely follow some protocol of secrecy, but something may give away their larger purpose," said Fitzjames.

"Yes, sir. Do you intend to return to the hotel? That may be very unsafe for you," said Torres.

"I took another room, Room 305. I don't intend to stay there overnight. I'll use the room as a place to keep an eye on the Iranians and perhaps to identify my unsuccessful assassin. He'll certainly find my replacement room in the same way that he found my first one. I'll need for you to find another place for me to stay," said Fitzjames.

"We will do so."

"Thank you. Can you accommodate me here in your offices? I need to make a telephone call," said Fitzjames.

"This way, sir," replied Torres.

Torres guided Fitzjames to this personal office. The room was modest. It had a metal desk, a metal desk chair, a telephone, and a computer terminal. Fitzjames would have presumed that it was a vacant office, except that it had two framed photographs on the top of the desk. The smaller frame contained a recent shot of a young woman in academic regalia. The larger photograph was old and contained an elderly man, who was seated at a bar smoking a cigarette. He appeared surprised to have been captured on film. Torres observed Fitzjames, as the latter glanced at the second photograph.

"My father, sir," commented Torres.

"I thought so. Very nice," said Fitzjames.

"A great man. A great patriot," noted Torres.

Twenty

From Torres' office and behind the closed door, Fitzjames contacted Fuller in the expectation of receiving information about the two Iranians. He was not disappointed. "We've finally pieced together the disparate data that appeared, at least initially, to be contradictory. Yet, it's not contradictory at all. It makes good sense, actually," commented Fuller with the tone of a university professor giving a lecture.

"That's good news. What can you tell me, sir?" responded Fitzjames, patiently and respectfully.

"The two men are agents of the Islamic Republic. We shouldn't doubt that. Both come from Tehran but have their origins in different cities. Yazdi was born in Garmsar in the north of Iran. Rezvani was born in Tafresh, also in the north, in the mountains. They both ostensibly operate businesses and thus frequently travel in connection with commercial activities. Those businesses and commercial ventures are likely a front for governmental action and espionage. They have both made frequent visits, together and separately, to Venezuela and, for us, to other trouble spots in South America," said Fuller.

"Do we know anything about the businesses?" inquired Fitzjames.

"Very little, except that they have a medical connection. Yazdi has biochemical training and an advanced degree, earned in France, at Aix-Marseille University, in bio-engineering. Rezvani holds a doctorate in chemistry, which he earned at the University of Bern. Both are very intelligent and well educated. The business operations are medical distribution facilities. Both function in and out of Tehran and are hugely dependent upon external, imported materials to carry on. It is not clear what degree of dependence upon imports is truly legitimate or to what degree it's fiction in order to cause these men to travel to seek out suppliers. The Iranian government could be starving the businesses of resources and making use of its own self-inflicted deprivation to claim that the country is being mistreated by other nations and to claim a fraudulent rationale for sending these two men abroad to do the government's bidding," added Fuller.

"What do you know of their politics, sir?" asked Fitzjames.

"Muslims, of course. Shiites, also, of course," said Fuller.

"Yes, as I would expect, being from Iran," noted Fitzjames.

"They are both conservative and have documented attachments to Abadgaran. Are you familiar with Abadgaran? That detail is somewhat arcane," said Fuller.

"Yes, sir. As I recall, it's an alliance or union of populist, Islamic, and right-wing political parties," said Fitzjames.

"Precisely," said Fuller.

"Any noteworthy government connections?" queried Fitzjames.

"Very little data on that subject. However, we, that is you, should presuppose that they are agents of the Islamic Republic and under the supervision and direction of operatives of Iran's Revolutionary Guards," said Fuller.

"Understood, sir. And any connection to the Russians?" asked Fitzjames.

"We have very little on that subject as well. We don't have any prior direct, confirmed nexus between Moscow and Tehran involving these individuals. We've also tried cross-checks on Lebedev, Yazdi, and Rezvani and nothing matches. What we do now know, of course, is that they're all in Caracas doing business together. So, we have our nexus there, and you're in the midst of it," offered Fuller.

"Indeed, yes, sir. Still murky. Do I have broad latitude, sir?" inquired Fitzjames.

"Absolutely. Your primary target, Algorta, has been removed. But the operation protocol permits you to use your discretion," said Fuller coldly.

"Understood, sir. Thank you. On my order, the local assets here will furnish to their superiors in McLean the results of their interrogations of the two Russians. I'll presume that you'll not require a separate report," said Fitzjames.

"No, not necessary. I'll get my hands on what's sent up. No need to duplicate effort," said Fuller.

"Can you give me any updates on the situation at home, sir?" asked Fitzjames.

"Extremely serious. The research continues apace but the deaths are mounting. The media is restless, and the public may soon begin to see this situation as more terrifying. Deaths of drug addicts don't cause panic and may be cynically seen as a social good, by some—cleaning the streets. But the death toll is rising and now has broadened to include the occasional user, not just the hardened addict. The research team has been expanded and formally recognized. Political pressure made that essential. The Department of Health and Human Services, through the CDC, has made Pittsburgh, with its extensive hospital system, the center of operations. Your contact there, Dr. Reimer, who survived a medical scare herself—apparently she got ill because of the work she was doing—is leading the team," said Fuller.

"She struck me as being very able, very sharp," offered Fitzjames, suppressing a degree of relief at learning that she was in good health.

"Yes. That's my understanding. We're all on the edge here, all departments. We've got to shut this down, or we're in for trouble. Let me say again, you have wide latitude, Captain," said Fuller. "Do what you need to do. Clear?"

"Yes, sir, quite clear. Thank you, sir," said Fitzjames and ended the call.

Fitzjames touched the outside of his jacket with his right hand in order to feel the impression and contours of the Ruger in the holster below. He checked the time on the Breitling on his left wrist and opened the door of the office and stepped outside, where Torres was waiting.

"Orders, sir?" asked Torres with a level of subordination that was both respectful and respectable.

"Give a complete report on the interrogations of the two Russians to your contacts at the CIA. Also, as we discussed, release the Russians but track them. I'll leave to you getting that sorted out. Put wires on their clothing, in their cellphones, or put people on them. It's your call. Be discreet, of course," said Fitzjames.

"Of course, sir," replied Torres.

"I need to get back to the hotel," said Fitzjames.

"Mariana Lurdes will return you. Also, we have made arrangements for your accommodations this evening and for the remainder of your stay in Caracas. Mariana Lurdes will keep you at her home," said Torres.

"I would prefer another hotel with a reservation under a fictitious name," suggested Fitzjames.

"I understand. We do not believe that you would be adequately protected. Our belief is that your identity is sufficiently public such that a public hotel would be too risky. The police know you. The PNB will have scouts at every hotel, and they are very probably compromised and corrupted. No. We have discussed the matter, and Mariana Lurdes will have you at her house," said Torres.

"That may just shift the peril to her and to her family. There's risk in that plan, too," returned Fitzjames.

"Yes, sir. We have considered that risk and believe it is minimal. Please, we have decided. Now, she will take you to the hotel," said Torres.

Marina Lurdes appeared behind Torres, almost without a sound. She had overheard the conversation and came forward in advance of a summons to do so. She said nothing, only smiled at Fitzjames. He smiled in return, nodded his head, and spoke to her.

"*Gracias. Vamos al hotel, inmediatamente. Vale.*"

"*Vamos, señor; entonces,*" she answered.

Fitzjames collected his backpack and suitcase and followed the woman out of the office to the Suzuki, in a retracing of their path of earlier in the morning. Once settled in the vehicle, Mariana Lurdes drove back to the Hotel Jose Antonio Paez with the same skill, speed, and confidence that she had previously demonstrated.

The conversation between Fitzjames and Mariana Lurdes in route to the hotel was light. She spoke very little English, and thus Fitzjames spoke to her in Spanish. He thanked her again for having bandaged his injured hand and for having agreed to host him at her home. Upon being asked, she disclosed that she had a modest house, but it was large enough to accommodate him. She had no husband and lived with her recently divorced twenty-nine-year-old daughter, along with the daughter's young son. She assured him that he would not be an imposition upon her hospitality and that he would be fed well. At this latter assurance, he smiled and repeated his gratitude.

Mariana Lurdes carried on the conversation, with no reduction in the speed or accuracy of her driving. Fitzjames appreciated her skill and was reminded of the astounding capacity of women to multitask. In his view, the female brain worked effortlessly through varied, simultaneous tasks, often involving focusing on and participating in a discussion, while doing something physical. He recalled at one time commenting that he could never have worked as a bank teller because, unlike women who held that job, he could not have processed a transaction and conversed with a customer, at the same time. A task all bank tellers perform daily on multiple occasions.

As the Suzuki approached the hotel, Fitzjames suggested to Mariana Lurdes that she turn down a side street. He preferred an exit at a location away from the front of the hotel. She did as he asked, turned left some three blocks from the Hotel Jose Antonio Paez, and pulled into a parking space.

Fitzjames removed the local mobile telephone from his jacket pocket. He gave it to Marina Lurdes and asked that she program into the device her telephone number. She did so and returned the telephone to him. He tested it to confirm that the contact was simple and direct. He advised her that, notwithstanding a call from him, she should plan to return to this very location at 4:00 in the afternoon. She acknowledged the instruction and repeated it in broken English. He too repeated it but did so in Spanish.

"*Me entiendo, señor. A las cuatro de esta tarde. Muy bien,*" she said.

"*A las cuatro. Vale,*" he said and opened the door and stepped out. He opened the back door of the vehicle and collected the backpack and suitcase and closed both doors.

Mariana Lurdes slipped out of the parking space and into the traffic flow and vanished. Fitzjames returned to the hotel.

When he entered the lobby, the air conditioning was a pleasant greeting. He had begun to perspire during the walk, as the temperature had risen significantly since the early morning, and there was no breeze from the north off of the sea. He would have preferred to discard the jacket, but the concealed shoulder holster, pistol, and magazines made that alternative impossible. Thus, with a coat on in the tropical warmth of winter, in Venezuela, he had walked the streets of Caracas and entered the hotel. He approached the front desk and was greeted by the same clerk as had assisted him before dawn that same morning.

"Welcome back, sir," said the man in excellent yet labored wooden English. He spoke slowly and sought to articulate each word to perfection to minimize his accent. "Your new room, Room 305, has been prepared for you. I have the key, here, for you. May I do anything more for you, sir?"

"No, no, thanks. Thank you for having the room cleaned up so quickly," replied Fitzjames.

"Our pleasure, sir. We were hopeful that you would stay with us again, sir. We have made special accommodation for you in Room 305, and of course the hotel management has agreed to waive all charges for your stay with us," said the clerk.

"That's not necessary but thank you. I'll go on up," said Fitzjames, as he took the metal key from the countertop.

He walked to the elevator, which opened for him when he pressed the button to engage it. He entered, pressed the keypad for the third floor, and the door closed. The elevator lumbered up sluggishly from the lobby and deposited him at the third level. He stepped out and advanced down the empty hallway beyond Room 312 and Room 310 to Room 305. Out of caution and before applying the key, he examined the lock. It appeared to be ordinary and undisturbed. He evaluated the risks for few seconds, then inserted the key and turned the knob. No explosion. He entered the room and dropped the backpack and suitcase at the door. He searched the room for unusual wiring and examined the television and other electrical elements to confirm the absence of suspicious machinery. He satisfied himself that nothing was out of order and moved the suitcase to the bed and the backpack to the writing desk. He closed the door to the room.

Fitzjames took off the jacket and draped it over the back of the chair at the desk.

He removed the Ruger and placed it delicately on the desktop. He unstrapped the shoulder holster and pulled it off over his head. He entered the bathroom and washed his hands and face. He felt a bit refreshed and more alert, but he appreciated that he needed a shower and a full night's rest. He washed his face a second time with cold water, dried himself on the hand towel, and returned to the bed. He put on the shoulder holster anew, returned the pistol to its place after a momentary survey, and thrust his arms through the sleeves of the jacket. He rolled his shoulders to get comfortable. He dropped the room key into the front pocket of his trousers, extinguished the light in the bedroom but not in the bathroom, and opened the door of the hotel room to step outside into the corridor.

As the door opened and as he stepped toward the threshold, three bullets in immediate succession smashed the molding of the doorway at eye level. The shooter had fired too soon upon the door opening and had thus missed his intended target. Still inside the room, Fitzjames fell against the opposite wall from the one where the bullets had struck and bent his knees. With his right hand, he removed the handgun, switched off the safety, and held the weapon in front of his forehead with the barrel at a ninety-degree angle to the ceiling. He held his breath, waited ten seconds, and listened. He discerned, very softly and very cautiously, footfall approaching Room 305. He extracted the room key from his pocket and tossed it into the hallway. The metal key clicked and clanked as it hit the tiled floor. The shooter, confused by the sound and distracted by the motion, fired two shots in the direction of the key. At the same time, Fitzjames swung around the corner with his arms fully extended, Ruger in hand, and discharged three shots that pierced the chest of a man leaning against the door of Room 309, ten yards from Fitzjames' position. The man fell on his back from the force of the gunshots but did not release the pistol in his left hand. Writhing, the man attempted to sit up in order to return fire. Fitzjames responded by shooting him a fourth time in the center of the forehead.

Lying dead on the cool white tiles of the third floor of the hotel, this Russian would have no further opportunity to engage prostitutes to make inquiries of Trey Fitzjames on the streets of Caracas.

Twenty-One

The hallway of the third floor was quiet, despite the gunfire. No other guests emerged from their rooms. The noise of the discharges from the pistols had been muted, as both weapons had had silencing devices. The smoke was also not a distraction because the entire hotel still carried to odor of the fire resulting from the explosion of earlier in the morning outside Fitzjames' first hotel room.

Fitzjames returned the Ruger to the shoulder holster and approached the body cautiously. He presumed that the shooter had been alone but was uncertain whether a confederate was not lurking at the far end of the corridor. He examined the man quickly and confirmed that he was dead. He paused and evaluated whether to move the man to the stairwell or to Room 305 and chose the latter. He clutched the ankles and dragged the man the ten to fifteen yards to the hotel room and positioned him, in a seated pose, just inside the doorway. The labor was arduous, as the man was overweight, thick around the stomach and chest, with heavy tree-trunk legs and calves.

Fitzjames took a bath towel, applied water to it, and returned to the hallway to clean the bloodstains from the floor. He did so quietly and quickly, returned to Room 305, threw the bloodied towel into the shower, and turned the water on to rinse it. While the shower flowed, he returned to the dead man and removed from his pockets the wallet and money that he had carried and his pistol and ammunition. The gun appeared to be a semiautomatic Yarygin, an MP-443 Grach, but Fitzjames could not be certain. The wallet contained only a

Venezuelan identity card and appeared to have been emptied of its usual contents, as the wallet was well worn. The identity card of the dead man, which included a photograph, disclosed that he was Venezuelan with a residence in Caracas. Fitzjames studied the face in the photograph and then looked at the dead man's face and physique. There was a mismatch. The subject in the photograph appeared to be Latin American and Hispanic. The dead man was no Latin American; he looked like an Eastern European. The sandy blond hair, cut short, and his round head with a long, aquiline nose made him a Russian. For Fitzjames, the handgun, of presumed Russian manufacture, confirmed the man's nationality, to the extent necessary. The Venezuelan identity card was a fraud.

Fitzjames lifted the mattress of the bed and placed underneath it the dead man's pistol, bullets, wallet, and cash. He reentered the bathroom and turned off the shower. He washed his hands, dried them, and stepped out of the room. He locked the door to Room 305. As he did so, he glanced down the corridor and observed the two Iranians also locking the doors of their respective hotel rooms. They were talking quietly to one another and did not observe Fitzjames. The two men walked to the elevator. Fitzjames unlocked the door and stood, unseen, in the partially opened doorway in order to observe the Iranians. They entered the elevator, and the door closed behind them. Fitzjames emerged, relocked the door to the room, darted to the stairwell, and dashed down the flights of stairs to the lobby.

When he opened the door separating the stairwell and the lobby, he observed the Iranians, who had arrived at the lower level before he had, in the center of the lobby in a conversation with two other men, whom Fitzjames did not recognize. They wore badly tailored business suits and had the appearance of local government operatives. They listened intently to the two Iranians. The Iranians appeared to be engaged in an unsuccessful attempt to explain to the two men some event or circumstance. Fitzjames moved to the sitting area in an effort to overhear the conversation. As he did so, the Venezuelans appeared to grow alarmed at their inability to understand the broken English of the Iranians, whose voices were growing louder as they repeated, to no avail, the matter they wished to convey. The Venezuelans understood

English as poorly as the Iranians spoke it. Once Fitzjames took a seat and grabbed a magazine, the Venezuelans ushered out the Iranians. Fitzjames waited a moment and followed the four men outside.

The taller of the two Venezuelans took the driver's seat of a large four-door black BMW sedan. His partner opened the back passenger-side door for the two Iranians to enter the vehicle. After they did so, he closed the door behind them, studied the hotel entryway and parking area suspiciously, and opened the front passenger-side door and took the seat next to the driver. They pulled forward slowly and waited at the end of the driveway to enter the traffic flow. That brief delay permitted Fitzjames to hail a waiting taxi. The driver responded to the signal instantly, and Fitzjames was inside in the back seat at the very moment the BMW departed.

"*A donde va, señor?*" asked the driver.

"*Sige el BMW, el negro, por allá. Me entiendes?*" questioned Fitzjames.

"*Sí, claro, señor,*" responded the driver. "*El grande, el grande negro carro.*"

"*Exacto, apurate,*" said Fitzjames, as the taxi also entered the racing congestion of traffic.

"*Puedo seguir muy cerca, señor,*" suggested the driver.

"*No, poca distancia,*" replied Fitzjames out of a desire to see the driver pursue the BMW at a distance, rather than closely. "*Ten cuidado.*"

Pursuant to the instructions, the driver maintained a steady, but spacious pursuit of the BMW. Fitzjames sat in the center of the back seat in order to keep the vehicle in view through the windshield of the taxi. Although the traffic was heavy, the German sedan was easily recognizable among the other, smaller, primarily Japanese and Korean cars and trucks.

The BMW traveled eastward through the city and then to the outskirts and then finally into the countryside. The traffic thinned and as a result, Fitzjames told the cab driver to put more distance between them. He also assured the driver that the rising fare was not an issue. In good faith, he removed nine hundred Bolivares from his wallet and put the bills in the center of the front seat. The driver glanced at the money, collected it with his right hand, and stuffed the cash into his front shirt pocket with a wide grin.

"Gracias, señor," he said.

"De nada. Sige, sige," responded Fitzjames, urging him to carry on the pursuit.

The BMW increased its speed and continued eastward over winding roads that passed over and around mountains and through valleys. The Caribbean Sea came into sight to the north as the highway on which they were traveling swung toward and tracked the northern coastline of the country. To Fitzjames' mind, to this point they had traveled some thirty miles outside of the metropolitan area of Caracas.

The BMW turned southward, left the coast, and proceeded inland. The driver slowed as the roadways narrowed. They entered the town of El Venado Miranda, and the taxi slowed to preserve a measured, discreet distance between the vehicles. The BMW drove through the town center and beyond toward the south. Approximately two miles below the town, the BMW approached a solitary three-story concrete block building that resembled a hospital. The building had opened jalousie windows running the full length of the structure on all three floors. It appeared to be some forty years old and to be unairconditioned, although individual window units were visible in upwards of twenty-five percent of the rooms. The building bore no markings or other designation. Three heavily armed soldiers secured the entrance. The BMW pulled into the drive leading to the entrance and stopped.

Fitzjames instructed the taxi operator to continue driving beyond the building and out of the range of visibility of anyone outside or within the facility. At a quarter-mile past, Fitzjames ordered the driver to stop and pull over to the shoulder of the roadway.

"Conoces este lugar, señor?" queried Fitzjames, curious whether the driver was familiar with the area.

"Si, señor, un pocito solamente," he answered.

"Sabes este edificio?" asked Fitzjames.

"Creo que es hospital," the driver replied.

"Bien. Espérame aquí. Espero volver en sesenta minutos. Te quedas aquí," instructed Fitzjames sternly.

"*Si, señor,*" replied the driver, with deference.

Fitzjames exited the taxi and ran at a steady but not unnecessarily fast pace from the cab to the building. He stopped his run once within sight of the structure and caught his breath. He re-ordered his clothes, which had become disheveled during the run. He also repaired his hair, which had fallen loose over his forehead. With his left hand, he forced it upward and back over his left ear. Thus assembled, he moved closer to the entrance of the facility.

From a distance of fifty yards and from behind a parked Isuzu light truck, Fitzjames surveyed the entrance. The BMW sedan, which had been emptied of passengers, was situated in a specialty parking area for dignitaries located immediately to the left of the doors leading to the interior of the building and before which the three soldiers stood. The BMW was the only vehicle accorded such treatment.

On his haunches, Fitzjames kept himself covered by the truck. He removed the mobile telephone and contacted Torres. Under his breath, he conveyed to Torres his location and the time he believed he required to act. If he did not return within that timeframe, Torres was to begin a search for him and advise Torres' superiors of the situation. Torres acknowledged his understanding of the instruction, and Fitzjames thanked him for the excellent work he was doing and concluded the call. He returned the telephone to the jacket pocket and raised himself to view again the entrance of the building and observe the movements of the soldiers.

Two of the soldiers had roving commissions. They patrolled loosely and broadly throughout the perimeter of the building. The third soldier had a fixed position at the main doorway and stood guard there. Fitzjames considered the situation, as he was reluctant to execute the soldiers in order to gain access; doing so would be untidy and possibly counterproductive to the ultimate goals of his mission. Yet, he had few options. A distraction to draw them away would either prompt panic inside or a redistribution of other soldiers from within the building or from other points on site if the three soldiers were drawn to a scene. No possibility existed of gaining entry through a ruse. He did not have the means or the support to do so. He evaluated waiting until later in the day or until the following day to attempt entry. But a delay was senseless, as the Iranians were inside and might depart or be absent in twenty-four hours. Now was the time to strike. The soldiers would have to be removed.

One of the soldiers had wandered between the parked vehicles within fifteen yards of Fitzjames. Fitzjames studied him. He carried a submachine gun, ostensibly ready to be used, if necessary, at waist level. He walked between the parked cars and trucks and leaned forward to peer inside each. He did not raise the weapon when he did so. He shuffled his booted feet and appeared bored and listless, as if he had too much to drink the previous evening.

While so engaged, the soldier was unaware that Fitzjames was moving toward him between the stationary cars and trucks. When he turned and, leaning forward, studied the interior of a small Chinese automobile with tinted windows, Fitzjames rose to a height sufficient to strike the soldier on the back of the head and neck. At the blow, the soldier struck the side of the car and dropped the weapon and fell to the ground, partially conscious. Fitzjames crashed his right fist twice again on the back of his head. He passed out and lay prostrate on the hard ground on his stomach.

Fitzjames picked up the submachine gun and tossed it out of reach. He searched the soldier for handcuffs and found a metal set connected to his belt. He detached the handcuffs and forced the soldier's arms to a position behind his back and locked his wrists. He removed the belt from his waist and used it to secure the soldier's legs at the ankles. He rummaged through the soldier's pockets and found an overused, soiled pocket handkerchief in his breast pocket. Fitzjames extracted the dirty cloth and forced it into the soldier's mouth. He then dragged the soldier behind the car and thus between the tightly parked vehicles.

Fitzjames grabbed the submachine gun, examined it in an instant, and migrated between the parked vehicles to a position closer to the second roaming soldier. The second soldier was engaged in the same exercise of surveying cars and trucks as his colleague. Fitzjames had some expectation that he would have the opportunity to take down this second soldier in the same manner as the first. However, inexplicably, the second soldier stood upright and shouted out to his partner. No reply came in reply to the call. He grew suspicious. He approached the area in which Fitzjames was concealed. Fitzjames slipped back to the spot where he had taken down the first soldier and awaited the arrival of the second.

When he did arrive, he saw his fellow soldier on the ground. He did not advance to render aid but lowered himself by bending his knees and nervously held his weapon out, shifting it in uncertainty from side to side. He was very young and obviously frightened and bemused about how to react. Fitzjames paused and allowed him to conclude that an attack was not forthcoming. The soldier relaxed and then moved toward his companion. He bent over him to determine if he were dead or simply unconscious. Fitzjames cracked the second soldier at the base of the skull with the handle of the submachine gun. He gasped and fell senseless over his partner. Fitzjames secured the wrists and ankles of the second soldier in like manner as the first but found no similar handkerchief to plug his mouth. He tore the leg of his pants and with the Microtech Halo knife that he carried he cut three strips. He stuffed one into the second soldier's open mouth. He used the other two strips to secure the oral stuffing in place in the mouths of both men by lacing the strip across each man's face, under the nose, and tying it in the back of the head.

Fitzjames caught his breath and collected his thoughts in order to analyze the question of how to remove the third soldier. He snatched up the first soldier's weapon and began migrating from one parked vehicle to another to move closer to the building entrance without being seen. He had some expectation that the third soldier would recognize the absence of his two colleagues and perhaps shift off his line and away from the building. Yet, he did not alter his position. In fact, he remained in the precise position and stance and preserved the same stoic glare that he had assumed when Fitzjames first studied him. The soldier was more of a wax figure in appearance than a heavily armed sapient guard.

Fitzjames made his way to the left of the remaining soldier's position and within fifteen yards of the main entry to the facility. As he raised himself to gain a view of the soldier through the transparent windows of an antiquated, poorly maintained Ford, the sliding doors of the building opened and two men emerged. The soldier stepped aside to allow them to pass. They were both dressed in long white lab coats and wore identification badges on the front pockets. They appeared to be either scientists or physicians by their clothing. They both wished a pleasant day to the solder and began walking toward the parking area.

Fitzjames followed their movements and observed one of the men reach his automobile before Fitzjames could get close to him. The second man's car was parked deeper in the sea of vehicles. Fitzjames pursued the latter, car to car, truck to truck, raising himself when necessary to continue to keep him in sight in order to follow. Fitzjames moved as he moved and in the same direction. When the man reached his car, he dropped his left hand into a pants pocket for the keys, removed them, and opened the door to the vehicle. As he removed his lab coat and folded it over his right forearm, before taking the seat behind the steering wheel. From behind, Fitzjames jumped toward him and clutched the upper part of the man's left arm. With his right hand on the back of the man's head, in an instant and before the man could call out or ever gasp, Fitzjames forced the man off his feet and drove him to the ground, his face pressing painfully and awkwardly into the hard surface. The lab coat rested in a bundle next to him. Fitzjames shifted the man's arm to the center of his back and secured it in that position with his knee. He replaced his right hand with his left on the back of the man's head and removed the Ruger. The man offered little resistance and, when ordered by Fitzjames in Spanish to remain still, complied. Fitzjames released the hold on the man's head but pressed the barrel of the Ruger against the man's left temple. Fitzjames advised him that if he uttered a sound, Fitzjames would kill him. The man nodded his head weakly in reply.

As he had with the two soldiers, Fitzjames removed the Microtech knife and sliced the right leg of the man's pants. Although Fitzjames had no intention of harming the man, if he followed instructions, the cutting of the man's pants further terrified him. He remained utterly motionless and compliant. Fitzjames cut four strips on this occasion. With the first one, in lieu of available handcuffs he secured the man's wrists behind his back. With the second, he made a mouth stuffing and forced it into the man's mouth, to which the man offered only modest resistance. The third he used to lock the stuffing in place and tied it tightly at the back of the man's head. He opened the back door of the man's car and ordered him to climb in without raising himself to full height. He did so and sat upright in the back seat. Fitzjames commanded him to lie on his back. Once he had complied, Fitzjames used the fourth strip of cloth to tie the man's ankles. Fitzjames closed the door to the car.

He collected the man's lab coat and car keys off of the ground. He put the keys into his pants pocket and examined the identification card affixed to the coat. The coat was the property of Claudio Arocha, *doctore de biologia cellular*. Fitzjames moved away from Arocha's vehicle and, on his knees, removed his own jacket and put on the medical coat. He removed the cellular telephone from the jacket and placed it in the back pocket of his pants. He wrapped the submachine gun with his jacket and placed the bundle under a parked Chevrolet and adjacent to the rear tire on the passenger side. With his hand gripping the Ruger, he held the concealed pistol in the right outer pocket of the lab coat. He slowly stood upright above the tops of the automobiles, placed his left hand on the left outer pocket of the coat and in a casual, but self-possessed manner, walked toward the entrance of the building.

Twenty-Two

Fitzjames clutched the Ruger in the pocket of the lab coat and positioned his finger on the trigger. He rested his left hand in the left pocket in a manner that would allow him quickly to remove it to support his right hand on the pistol. He lowered his head as he approached the soldier and assumed an air of indifference in the role of a scientist simply returning to the facility at which he did his job. He had some expectation that enough human traffic came and went from the facility that the remaining guard at the entrance would not recognize that he was not a member of a science team. Alternatively, the guard may have been tasked with addressing external threats, not confirming the identities of those who entered and exited the building.

"Buenas dias," said the soldier, as Fitzjames passed him and stepped into a shallow alcove leading to the entrance.

The greeting puzzled him, but he recovered.

"Buenas," responded Fitzjames, pronouncing the word as the soldier had, as a Venezuelan would, not as a Spaniard. Fitzjames was fortunate to have the skill of listening to foreign speech and repeating it, almost in mimicry.

The soldier said nothing more, and Fitzjames passed inside the sliding glass doors of the building. He did not relax his hold on the handle of the handgun. He was entirely uncertain whether he would encounter further security personnel or military men once inside the facility. He encountered neither. Physical security within the building seemed curiously relaxed. Technological methods were employed. As the entrance doors closed behind him, he had a choice of following one of three short and identical hallways, at the end of each of which was a large gray steel door. He chose the center course and followed it twenty feet to the doorway. Next to the door on the wall on the right at the level of his waist was a device that emitted a sharp red light from the center of the instrument within a narrow opening strip. Fitzjames presumed that the door would open with the application of a duly programmed access card. He removed the identification card, which was clipped to the upper pocket of Dr. Claudio Arocha's lab coat. Fitzjames held it toward the device with no effect. He slid the card in one direction and then the other direction within the gap, also to no effect. He turned the card and repeated the process of sliding the card. This last step was effective. The mechanical lock released and a buzzing sound could be heard. He pushed open the door with his left hand, not to its full extension, but sufficiently to prevent it from relocking. With his right hand, he reclipped the identification card on the chest pocket of the lab coat. He returned his right hand to the lower pocket of the coat and to the Ruger. He opened the door and walked into the room.

The room on the other side of the steel door was an empty space that functioned as a gallery. Four ordinary doors, two on each side of the room led into laboratories that were visible through eight large, thick, soundproof picture windows on either side of the entrances. The room was empty and quiet, but the first laboratory into which Fitzjames looked, to his left, was teaming with activity. Men and women, all of whom were dressed in lab coats similar to the one being worn by Fitzjames, attended to computer monitors, microscopes, or rows of test tubes and other scientific research devices. All appeared to be wholly absorbed in their respective tasks. At the second laboratory, to his right, he glanced inside through the window and observed a scene, which was a duplicate of the first—scientists at work. He advanced deeper into the room and peered into the third laboratory and the second on the left-hand side. Again, the interior revealed ongoing scientific research, although more of the scientists were engaged in computer work. He turned and surveyed the fourth and final laboratory. Inside, clearly visible, were the two Iranians, one of whom was studying certain documents, while another man, a Venezuelan scientist by his attire, spoke to him with another scientist in attendance, standing with his hands clasped behind his back. A group of three Venezuelan scientists escorted the other Iranian through the laboratory. The apparent leader of the group would pause, make a statement, and then the Iranian would examine a computer monitor or look into a microscope. The other scientists would then provide brief commentary.

The glass of the windows was too thick to permit Fitzjames to hear the conversation. It was clear to him, however, that the scientists and the Iranians were communicating in English, not in Spanish. It was equally clear to him that this facility, either alone or in tandem with others, provided the research and the science for the projects of the now deceased Algorta. The Iranians would have no other cause to be at the facility.

Fitzjames considered his alternatives within the context of the operation. His discretion was sufficiently broad and the contours of his instructions sufficiently narrow to permit him to forbear killing the Iranians and focus on the facility. As such, in lieu of an execution, he concentrated his mind for the moment on the destruction of the building.

An edifice of the age and construction of the facility, which had no central air-conditioning but supported all of the electrical equipment that the scientific activity required, must have an external energy source. If he considered that he was seeing only a portion of the research being conducted in the building, then a facility of this nature had to have its energy provided in a manner different from other structures built in the 1960s or 1970s in Venezuela.

Fitzjames turned and walked back to the steel door. From that position, he studied the interiors of the first and second laboratories. Along the walls at intervals and running from floor to ceiling in both rooms were metal and hard plastic pipes encased in coverings of opaque glass or light plastic. Multiple electrical outlets, most of which were in use and were connected to equipment, could be seen on electrical boxes on each set of pipes.

Fitzjames forced down the handle of the steel door and exited the gallery. He walked around the corner to his right, moved down a similar corridor to another steel door, duplicated the entry process with Dr. Arocha's identification card, and opened the steel door when the lock discharged. The room that he entered was unlike the gallery. This room contained six doors leading, presumably, to offices. Fitzjames could hear discussions in Spanish behind the doors and the sounds of administrative activities, including typing on keyboards and on old-fashioned typewriters, telephones ringing, and the singing sounds of facsimile machines. No exit to the back of the building was present. He reopened the door, exited the room, and in haste made his way to the third steel door on the opposite side of the ground floor.

Once again, Fitzjames repeated the security access exercise and entered. A gallery-style design had been employed in this room on the left-hand side where, again, two doors were separated by thick glass picture windows, which straddled each door. Through the glass, he could see, at work, scientists dressed in protective headgear, body suits, and facial masks. They moved about the room or sat at stations examining test tubes or mixing chemical compounds. Fitzjames sensed a strange acrid, unpleasant odor. On the right side, the room contained four doors, ostensibly leading to administrative offices or being utilized for storage. At the far end of the room was a further door with no markings. Fitzjames moved toward it. He turned the knob and found it loose and dated, but locked. He pressed his left ear against the exterior of the door and could hear, from the interior, the steady drone of electrical equipment and computer servers.

Fitzjames removed the Ruger, assured that the silencing device was secured, wrapped the pistol with the ends of the lab coat to muffle further the sound of the shot, and fired the gun at the knob. Except for the smoke, which quickly dissipated, the gunshot left no sensory residue and could not have been detected. The firing of the Ruger was virtually inaudible. The lock was destroyed, and Fitzjames pressed open the door and entered.

The room was overfilled with equipment and machinery, including plumbing mechanisms. Multiple computer servers reflected activity with sound and light. Twelve different electrical boxes were immediately visible, all with the same piping and covering leading from them as had appeared in the laboratories. The room was hot with the heat generated by the equipment. Fitzjames concluded that this room was the energy and information command center for the entire facility, yet the amount of energy required would be greater than what rural Venezuela could provide. A further, discrete energy-producing system must be present on the site.

Fitzjames studied the piping and other devices connected to the electrical boxes. All ran to the same general position in the back wall of the room and then to the exterior of the building at floor level. The amalgamation of pipes on the floor was protected by a plastic shield. Although difficult, given the concentration of equipment and the apparent grafting of new machinery onto and in the space of other, older mechanisms, Fitzjames migrated through the room. He discovered a doorway leading to the outside but could not reach it, through the equipment. It appeared to have been permanently sealed. He found a small window that was hidden from view by a large, antiquated IBM computer server, which appeared to be an old mainframe device. He shifted it sufficiently, despite its weight, to allow a view out of the window. Visible immediately outside was an electrical transmission and distribution operation enclosed within a six-foot-high fence with razor wire stretched across it at an angle at the top. The operation was small but certainly sufficient to provide power to the building and, if necessary, the surrounding town and countryside.

Five large tanks of propane gas were also apparent and were similarly protected within the fenced area. The tanks were stationed together, in a cluster, at the southeast corner of the grounds enclosed by the fencing. Fitzjames' assumption was that the propane was utilized to power the generators and distributors or was available in the event of emergencies if the underlying power came from another source. In either event, the tanks would be kept full. On the outside of the fence, near the tanks, Fitzjames also observed two more soldiers casually chatting with one another. They held their submachine guns with the barrels pointed toward the turf.

Fitzjames turned from the window, returned the computer server to its original position, and left the room. He retraced his steps outside to the lobby and closed the steel door. The lock clicked behind him; the door was resealed. No other person was present. He removed the Ruger from the lab coat pocket and held it at his side. He walked through the sliding glass doors of the entrance and upon encountering to his left the soldier standing guard turned and fired three shots in immediate succession. The first struck the center of the soldier's neck below the jawline and the other two the left side of his chest. The soldier collapsed and dropped his weapon. Fitzjames fired a fourth shot into the soldier's forehead and grabbed the man's gun. He returned the pistol to the shoulder holster.

He followed the same path toward Dr. Arocha's vehicle. He located the submachine gun that he had wrapped in the jacket and stowed under a late-model Chevrolet. He found Arocha as he had left him, unmoved and restrained in the back seat of Arocha's car. His wide, terrified eyes confirmed that he expected that Fitzjames would kill him. Without knowing more about Arocha's role and responsibilities, Fitzjames resolved that his execution was unwarranted. As such, he dropped the weapons and opened the rear passenger-side door. He dragged Arocha out of the car by the back of his shirt collar and deposited him on the loose gravel of the parking lot surface. Fitzjames pulled Arocha away from the vehicle and closed the back door. He collected the submachine gun, opened the front driver-side door, climbed into the automobile behind the steering wheel, and placed the soldier's weapon in the front passenger seat. He put the key in the ignition and started the car.

Fitzjames maneuvered swiftly out of the parking area and onto the circular roadway that served as a perimeter of the facility. He negotiated the turn to his left, while lowering the window. As he reached the corner of the back of the building, into view came the first of the two soldiers whom he had seen through the window. They had separated and were occupying opposite ends of the structure as sentries. Fitzjames held the steering wheel with his left hand continuing to turn, while at the same time reaching for the submachine gun on the passenger seat. He kept his focus on the soldier and rested the barrel of the gun on the top of the car door through the open window and pulled the trigger.

The semiautomatic weapon blasted at least five bullets into the unsuspecting soldier. He died instantly. The noise from the gun startled his partner and prompted him to drop to the ground, although baffled, and make an effort to understand the source of the blast. Before the soldier could resolve the confusion, Fitzjames swung the vehicle to the opposite end of the building and fired at him. The man was only able to return a single shot, which struck harmlessly the trunk of the vehicle, before dying.

Fitzjames threw the car into reverse and pulled backwards in order to position Arocha's automobile in a direct line toward the collection of propane tanks. With great haste, he tore off the lab coat and threw it at the floor on the passenger side. He took hold of his jacket and held it and the submachine gun in his right hand. He opened the car door with his left hand and allowed it to come to rest against the side of the vehicle without swinging open. He transferred his left hand to the steering wheel and pressed the accelerator to the floor. The tires cried out as they spun and burned the asphalt. Fitzjames directed the car, with as much power and speed as he could draw out of it, at the propane tanks behind the fencing. When he reached a point approximately twenty yards from the target, he shifted the vehicle in neutral, released the steering wheel, put his left shoulder into the open door, and rolled out of the racing automobile and onto the pavement, while clutching the jacket and submachine gun.

Arocha's car slammed into the fence line and drove the fencing into the propane tanks. The hood of the car crumbled as it struck the tanks and set off the airbags in the interior. Gasoline drained out of the vehicle to the ground. As Fitzjames got to his feet and began to put more distance between himself and the tanks, the vehicle exploded. The explosion triggered a simultaneous blast from the first tank, which was followed in sequence by the other four tanks. An inferno was the result. Within only a few minutes, the flames had spread to the structure and a conflagration ensued. The entire facility was ablaze.

As the personnel within the building began their escape to the outside and poured out of the few available exits, Fitzjames ran in the direction of the waiting taxi.

Twenty-Three

Fitzjames completed the half-mile run in return to the taxi in less than four minutes. In route and while running, he had emptied the submachine gun of ammunition, which he had discarded in the underbrush of the surroundings through which he ran. He had stopped for the few seconds required to do so and had also disabled the weapon by cracking it repeatedly against a large cedro tree. He discarded the machine gun, as well, in like manner.

He had stopped his run when the taxi came into sight in order to catch his breath. He had also begun to perspire heavily. The brisk walk to the cab did little to either restore his oxygen supply or cool down his body. He put on the jacket. He did not want to see the driver unduly alarmed by his return to the vehicle at a run. The explosions of the propane tanks, very likely, had already caused sufficient anxiety in the driver. Fitzjames was correct.

"*Que paso, señor?*" asked the cab driver nervously when Fitzjames entered the back seat.

"*Problemas en el edificio. Nada grave. Todo esta bien. Vamos,*" replied Fitzjames in rapid, breathless speech.

"*Me parece muy grave señor. Oi explosiones. Muchas,*" said the driver in a more disconcerted tone.

"*No, no muy grave. Todo está bien. Vamos, ahora. Apurate,*" said Fitzjames, as he removed from his wallet one thousand five hundred Bolivares and leaned forward and put the bills on the front seat next to the driver. "*Vamos, inmediatamente.*"

The driver gave no response, turned on the ignition, put the cab in gear, moved forward off of the shoulder, and returned to the roadway. In Spanish, Fitzjames instructed him to continue driving in the opposite direction of the facility and from Caracas and that Fitzjames would alert him when he could turn and begin the trek back to the capital.

Fitzjames, by use of the mobile telephone, contacted Torres. He told Torres to meet him at the hotel with at least two of Torres' men. Torres asked for more information about his whereabouts, his welfare, and his plan. But Fitzjames rebuffed him and simply gave him an estimated arrival time; he was concerned about the cab driver's ability to understand English and was reluctant to furnish even the most basic of details.

After fifteen minutes of driving in an eastward direction, Fitzjames told the driver to find the most convenient exit and then reverse course and return to Caracas. The driver did as instructed. Three minutes later, the taxi was in route westward. As they approached El Venado, they witnessed multiple police vehicles and ambulance vans rushing toward the facility. Their respective blue and red emergency lights and sirens could be seen and heard. With the exception of the official response to the inferno and an increase in the congestion on the roadways, the return trip to Caracas was uneventful.

Fitzjames instructed the driver to take him to the first metro stop. The driver did so and delivered Fitzjames to the Palo Verde subway station. Fitzjames thanked him, gave to him the metered fare, and added an additional five hundred Bolivares to the already substantial sums that he had paid. Although the driver had relaxed during the return journey, it was evident, when Fitzjames exited the taxi, that the driver simply wanted his money and wanted nothing more to do with Fitzjames.

Fitzjames paid to enter the station to take the subway to the hotel. He reviewed the subway map and found Gato Negro on the same line, Linea 1, as Palo Verde. He descended the stairs to the platform and waited five minutes. He entered the eastbound train after it came to a halt and after its automatic doors opened and after it disgorged its passengers. He was the only one of the many departing passengers who waited for the arriving passengers to leave the train. That courtesy, along with being the last to enter the subway, marked him as foreign and as American.

The subway train was crowded with commuters and two police officers. The officers took note of Fitzjames, both because he was the last person to enter the car of the train and because of his height. Fitzjames observed their interest in him and settled himself among the passengers who were standing. All of the seats were occupied roughly equally by men and women of all ages, while men and women of all ages, along with Fitzjames, stood.

The two police officers migrated through the passengers to reach Fitzjames. He sensed their approach but ignored them. When the train reached the first station beyond Palo Verde, he considered an exit. But he presumed that the officers would follow and that prospect was less appealing than remaining on the train, as they would likely call upon more policemen for assistance and would have him at a significant numerical disadvantage. Instead, he held his position, while he watched other passengers enter and leave the train at the station.

When the doors closed and the train began its advance to the next station through the dark underbelly of Caracas, the two officers stood in front of him. The smaller man asked Fitzjames in Spanish for his identification. His companion, a fat man, stood behind and said nothing and sought to appear imposing. Fitzjames asked that the officer repeat the question, which he did. Fitzjames gave no reply but removed his passport from his front pants pocket. He did so without shifting his jacket and revealing the shoulder holster and Ruger. The fat man rested one hand on his hip and the other on his pistol.

The smaller man steadied himself so as to avoid losing his balance as the train shot through the tunnel. He turned the pages of Fitzjames' passport slowly and suspiciously. After running through the entire passport, he returned to the page containing Fitzjames' name and photograph.

"Mr. Fitzjames, what is your destination?" asked the policeman in English.

"*Gato Negro; puedo hablar español,*" responded Fitzjames coldly.

"*Bien. Porque te vas a Gato Negro?*"

"*Estoy en el hotel cerca de la estación. Hay problema, señor?*" inquired Fitzjames, politely but firmly.

"No. No hay problema. Rutina de la investigación. Para la seguridad. Pasa buen día, señor."

"Gracias," said Fitzjames, as the officer returned the passport to him.

The two officers returned to the opposite end of the subway car and held a consultation. At the next station, both men left the train. Fitzjames watched them and noted that the fat man had removed his mobile telephone and had placed a call and was talking with the recipient of the call. Fitzjames studied the subway map for Linea 1, which was posted above the seats immediately adjacent to the entry doors. He made the decision to exit the train at the station Cano Amarillo, two stops prior to Gato Negro.

When the subway slowed at Cano Amarillo, the doors opened and Fitzjames left the train among the mass of other passengers and followed in the crowd as it moved up the escalator and stairs to street level. He telephoned Torres and gave him a brief summary of the police encounter and of Fitzjames' whereabouts. Torres was already at the hotel awaiting Fitzjames' return. He and his men had only just arrived. They had not yet entered the hotel.

"Survey the surroundings. Is a police presence growing?" asked Fitzjames.

"Two police cars are stationed at the entrance to the hotel. They are empty. A third car has just arrived. The policemen have stepped out of the car. They do not appear to have the intention of entering the hotel," answered Torres.

"Just three vehicles, then? Six men?" returned Fitzjames.

"Yes. That would be the number of policemen that I would anticipate. Sir, another vehicle has now arrived. Two more officers," said Torres.

"Don't enter the hotel. I'll recontact you once I'm nearby, and we'll proceed at that point. Remain in your present position," advised Fitzjames.

"Yes, sir," responded Torres.

Fitzjames walked briskly from the Cano Amarillo station toward Gato Negro and the hotel. He was among many other pedestrians strolling and pacing the city's sidewalks. The odor of exhaust from passing vehicles married the aroma of foods, both fried and grilled, being prepared in restaurants and by street vendors. Had he closed his eyes and simply inhaled, he would have known in an instant that he was in Latin America. Ocular and auricular senses were unnecessary; only the olfactory sense was required to confirm his current assignment.

With the Hotel Jose Antonio Paez in view at a distance of approximately three hundred yards, Fitzjames slowed to accept a political newspaper from an old man distributing them to all who passed him and would take them. He stopped, leaned against the wall of a shop, removed his telephone, and contacted Torres.

"I'm very close. I can see the hotel from where I'm standing, although I'm still at too great a distance to see you or evaluate what's happening there," he said.

"Sir, more policemen have arrived. I have also seen Caesar Quijada, Moreno's man. I am certain that it was he who interviewed you this morning. He is a criminal in a uniform," snarled Torres.

"It's clear that they're on site at the hotel to take me into custody, protective or otherwise. It's a sham. But we've got to get inside to get to the rooms occupied by the Iranians before they return, if they haven't already, irrespective of the police. Can you get me inside the hotel thorough an employee entrance or by some other method—a blind of some sort, perhaps?" asked Fitzjames.

"I have some ideas that may prove to be successful. But we must be together. I will meet you at the entrance of the *Museo Jacobo Borges*. Do you know it?" queried Torres.

"Yes. It's near me, in the park, on Avenida Sucre," said Fitzjames.

"I will be with you in four minutes," said Torres.

Fitzjames proceeded to the museum and arrived before Torres. He waited at the entrance and held open the political newspaper as a distraction, both to himself and to others. After a few moments, a man appeared next to him but did not immediately speak. It was Torres. The exercise of complete caution dictated that he refrain from acknowledging Fitzjames until he was certain that he had not been followed and that no police were present.

"Hello, sir," Torres said at length. "My city has its surprises and never rests."

"Indeed," mumbled Fitzjames.

"Come with me, sir," said Torres and began to walk toward the hotel.

Well before the hotel entrance, however, Torres turned down a side street, which was perpendicular to the boulevard on which the Hotel Jose Antonio Paez was situated. The two men approached a poorly maintained, aged twelve-story apartment building and entered at the ground floor. Torres sought out the stairwell, and Fitzjames followed. Torres located it, and they took eight flights of stairs to the fourth floor, Piso Cuatro, at which they exited. Torres paused in the dark, shabby corridor. To Fitzjames' mind, Torres appeared to be engaged in a series of mental arithmetical calculations. After thirty seconds of contemplation, Torres gave a signal to Fitzjames with his right hand to follow him to the third door on the right side of the corridor. All of the doors were identical, except for their numerical designations. Most of those numbers were plastic and fastened to the doors. Some were cracked and others missing. Some were absent, and the resident in occupancy had used an ink pen to scrawl the number on the door. At the third door, with the outside of his right fist, Torres knocked loudly and aggressively. The speakers inside stopped talking. All was silent.

"Do not speak, sir, please," urged Torres in a whisper.

"Understood," responded Fitzjames under his breath.

Torres knocked again at the door. Movement inside the apartment could be heard but no voices. Torres removed from under his belt in the back of his trousers a handgun. He knocked a third time with the butt of the gun. The difference in sound between the fist and the pistol on the door was easily perceived and had the intended effect upon the occupants. Subdued speech could be heard again inside. A debate arose about whether to open the door. Finally, as Torres prepared to knock a fourth time, the door cracked open.

From inside, an elderly woman in a timid voice in Spanish asked Torres, respectfully, why he knocked. Torres replied that he was an official of the Ministry of Justice, held open for the woman to see an identification card in a wallet, and demanded entry. She hesitated and consulted another unseen person within the apartment. Torres repeated his demand for entry and positioned his left foot in the doorjamb to prevent it being closed. The woman received the consent of the other parties and held open the door.

Torres burst inside while waving the pistol and his identification and while claiming to be an official with the Ministry of Justice. The old woman and the three other individuals in the room, all males under thirty, raised no resistance and posed no questions to Torres about the purpose of the visit. They stood together, as a group, in the tiny living room adjacent to a new LG flat-screen plasma television set.

Torres undertook a brief but purposefully ineffective search of the premises. The rooms, including two bedrooms and a kitchen, were filled with old, worn furniture, much of which was untidy, if not filthy. The kitchen had a putrid odor and soiled dishes, glasses, and utensils filled the sink and countertops.

Torres moved from the bedrooms to the kitchen to the sliding glass door that led to the balcony. Fitzjames followed him in the role of the dutiful subordinate. Once outside on the balcony, Torres closed the glass door behind Fitzjames. Torres stood at the concrete block wall and looked over it.

"Ah, perfection, sir," he said with satisfaction.

Fitzjames stood next to him and also looked over the balcony wall. Below at a distance of no more than eight feet was the outer perimeter of the roof of the Hotel Jose Antonio Paez.

"Well done," said Fitzjames.

"I will finish here. Please wait until I begin shouting inside, then climb over the wall and onto the roof of the hotel. I believe that you will find the door to the roof locked. But I also do not believe that you will find it to be a barrier to you," said Torres. "We will rendezvous on the hotel's third floor, in fifteen minutes, sir."

Torres returned to the interior of the apartment. Fitzjames remained on the balcony. Within seconds Fitzjames overheard Torres loudly berating the four individuals about Torres' presumption that they were using illegal drugs and that he knew, although he could not locate them by his search, that the drugs had been hidden in the apartment. Fitzjames took the cue, climbed over the balcony wall, hung from the floor at the foot of the wall on the opposite side, and dropped onto the roof of the hotel.

Twenty-Four

To his surprise, Fitzjames found the door on the rooftop of the Hotel Jose Antonio Paez to be unlocked. He thus entered the hotel through the doorway, which led to a cramped room at the top of a stairwell. He descended the narrow staircase to the third floor. He did not immediately open the connection door but listened for activity. The third floor was bustling with police.

Fitzjames turned the cold metal doorknob gently and slowly in order to crack open the door to gain a vista down the corridor. A group of four policemen congregated outside Room 305. They were speaking in elevated voices to one another in an apparent disagreement about who was the senior member of the group and whether they should enter the room in advance of Quijada's arrival. One of the officers, a swarthy, corpulent middle-aged man, whose stomach rolled over his belt at the waist, asserted that he had the authority to enter, irrespective of Quijada's presence or absence. Another officer supported the claim. A third policeman insisted that no entry be effected until Quijada was present. The fourth man supported this objection.

As the officers continued their argument, two men, one of whom was Asian, exited the elevator and walked toward Room 305. As they approached, the policemen ended their disagreement, at least for the moment, and all concentrated on the two men. The heavy man stepped forward and demanded to be told why the two men had entered the third floor. Apparently, the police had sealed it, and hotel guests were barred from the floor and from their assigned rooms. Both of two men explained that they were the occupants of

Rooms 307 and 309, respectively, and that they were unaware that they were prohibited from entering either the floor or quarters. The officer, in an ugly tone, almost expectorating the words in Spanish, repeated that the floor was closed to guests and that the two men must return to the lobby. The two men did not comply but said that they wished to access their rooms, if only briefly. Their reply infuriated the officer, who in turn screamed at the two men to return to the lobby. To add gravity to his last command, he removed a pistol from the holster on his hip. He pointed the gun at the chest of the man who had last spoken.

As the two men stepped backward with their hands outstretched to indicate their willingness to comply, Torres emerged from the stairwell at the opposite end of the corridor from Fitzjames' position. Torres' right arm was rigid and fully extended with a pistol in his hand. He fired two shots at the police officer, the first bullet hit his forearm and the second struck his upper arm at the shoulder. The officer dropped the pistol at the second wound. His three colleagues sought their own holstered weapons but were all shot and killed by the two men before anyone of the three of them could return fire. Torres walked toward the fat man, who had fallen to the ground but was not dead, mumbled his name, then told him that he was corrupted and that he was a dirty son of a whore who was destroying Venezuela. Torres then put a third bullet into his head above the bridge of his nose.

Fitzjames had entered the hallway from the opposite end and had joined Torres and his lieutenants. The Asian man confirmed the deaths of the officers and collected their handguns. The other man moved toward Room 305.

"*Esperate. Ten cuidado,*" said Fitzjames to the man as a warning not to touch or turn the door handle to the hotel room. "*Es posible que exista un artefacto explosivo conectado a la puerta.*"

"*Si, señor,*" replied the man, as he receded from the doorway.

"These are my men, Captain. This is Emilio Fushimi, whose name you know, and this is Jose Manuel Maldonado. They speak excellent English. It is not necessary for you to speak Spanish to them," advised Torres.

"Very well," responded Fitzjames. "We must act quickly. Step back."

Fitzjames stood twenty feet from the door to Room 305, aimed the Ruger at the handle, raised his left arm to cover his eyes and face, and fired the pistol. As had occurred fourteen hours earlier at a different room, a bomb exploded, at the entry of the room, intended for Fitzjames or for anyone else, including foolish Venezuelan policemen, who might have sought to enter Room 305.

"*Gracias, Señor Capitan,*" said Maldonado to Fitzjames in sincere appreciation for having prevented him from his attempt to enter.

"*De nada,*" said Fitzjames.

As the smoke cleared, Fitzjames entered the hotel room, clutched his backpack and swung it over his shoulder, grabbed his suitcase, left the room, and dropped the two items in the corridor. Torres signaled to Fushimi, by waving his index and second finger of his right hand, to move down the hallway. Fushimi complied and entered the housekeeping store room adjacent to the elevator. After a few seconds, he reemerged with a large laundry cart with sheets and towels at the bottom.

"Captain, we must get inside the rooms of the Iranians, immediately," said Torres.

"Precisely," said Fitzjames. "Get the elevator to this floor and prevent it from closing."

Torres ran to the elevator, pushed the button for it to rise to the third floor, and entered the laundry room. He instantly returned to the hallway with an upright Hoover vacuum. When the elevator door opened, Torres placed the vacuum on its side in the gap in the threshold separating the elevator from the hotel floor. In consequence, the elevator door was jammed and could not close. The elevator was prevented from moving.

Fitzjames advanced to a position in front of Room 310. He fired the Ruger twice at the doorknob. With the second shot, the door swung open. Fitzjames motioned to Maldonado to enter the room.

"Tear out the hard drive of the computer and place it in the laundry cart. Don't bother with monitors, keyboards, or any other equipment," said Fitzjames.

Fushimi followed Maldonado into the room. In less than two minutes, they had separated the hard drives from the other computer equipment and had placed the machinery in the cart. Meanwhile, Fitzjames had duplicated the exercise of destroying the door handle for Room 312 and gained entry. Torres ordered Maldonado to stand as sentry at the stairwell. Fushimi maneuvered the cart from the first room to the second. Fitzjames and Torres filled it with the briefcases from Room 312. Fushimi then covered the top with towels and an open bedsheet.

"Take the elevator to the lobby and move to the alley and wait for us there to retrieve you," said Torres, in Spanish, to Fushimi.

"Yes sir," replied Fushimi, who pushed the heavy, fully loaded cart, with some difficulty, down the corridor toward the elevator.

Fitzjames darted down the hallway and picked up his backpack and suitcase. He walked swiftly in the direction of Fushimi, reached him before the latter reached the elevator, lifted and turned back the bedsheet covering, and added the backpack and suitcase to the already swollen contents of the laundry cart. He folded the bedsheet over the top and nodded to Fushimi in gratitude. Fushimi pushed and tugged the laundry cart the few additional feet to the elevator.

As Fushimi extracted the vacuum cleaner and maneuvered the cart into the elevator, Maldonado shouted down the hallway that the police were advancing up the stairs toward the third floor.

Fitzjames was inclined to rush toward the stairwell and join Maldonado and begin firing the Ruger down the stairs at the oncoming police brigade. But Torres reacted before Fitzjames could do so. He joined Maldonado, gave him a few words of instruction, and began, with Maldonado, shooting his pistol down the stairs and stairwell at the police officers. The first two officers leading the group upward were hit. They collapsed and tumbled down the stairs. Their killing caused panic, among the other policemen, and a retreat.

Torres removed from the front pocket of his pants a device that resembled a large firecracker. He lighted the fuse and dropped it between the hand railings in the stairwell. The device fell to the ground floor and smashed on the tile. When it did so, it emitted a thick manila yellow smoke that smelled of gunpowder. Simultaneously, it crackled intermittently but continuously. With the smoke, the impression left by the device was that the police's adversaries had descended the stairs and were on the offensive. The police, in response, bewildered and fearful, vacated the stairwell.

"Now we must go," urged Torres.

Torres, despite his age, ran in the opposite direction down the corridor. Maldonado and Fitzjames followed. At the door by which Fitzjames had entered the third floor from the roof, Torres stopped, removed another device from his pocket, lit the fuse, and threw it toward Room 310 and Room 312. It exploded with the same effect of smoke and crackling as had its predecessor. Torres entered the room with Fitzjames and Maldonado behind him. He climbed the stairs to the roof. At the doorway leading to the outside, he paused for a few seconds and listened.

"We must be cautious," said Torres. "This is the only other exit, other than the internal stairwell and the elevator. Certainly, Quijada will know this and will have stationed men here."

Fitzjames pressed in front of Torres and also listened at the door. The sounds on the exterior did not reveal anything to him. He squatted on his haunches, which Torres and Maldonado imitated. Fitzjames placed his left hand on the door handle, pulled it downward, and swung open the door. He threw himself prostrate onto the surface of the roof with his arms extended and his left hand supporting the Ruger, which he gripped in his right hand. Bullets poured down on the open doorway. Fitzjames returned fire and hit two police officers situated at forty-five degrees to his left. Torres and Maldonado, still inside the room, shot and killed two to the right at a similar angle to Fitzjames.

Torres stepped outside and observed that the two men whom Fitzjames had hit were only injured. One had been wounded in the chest and the other in the thigh. Without hesitation, Torres advanced toward the two officers, replaced the spent magazine of his pistol with a full round of ammunition, and shot both men in the forehead and chest.

Fitzjames got to his feet and followed Maldonado, who stood behind Torres. Torres returned the pistol to the back of his pants under his belt. He spoke to Fitzjames.

"Corrupted police. If they work for Quijada, they are criminals. Better dead. Better for our society."

Fitzjames made no reply but ran with Torres and Maldonado toward the very balcony of the apartment that Torres and Fitzjames had entered in order to access the roof of the hotel. With the same lack of hesitation, Torres ordered Maldonado to assist him in reaching the bottom of the balcony. Maldonado locked his fingers together and propelled Torres upward after Torres had placed his left foot in Madonado's cupped hands. By employing the dexterity and flexibility of a much younger man, Torres pulled himself upward and over the balcony railing and onto the balcony proper.

Maldonado held open his hands to do the same for Fitzjames, but Fitzjames declined and insisted that he assist Maldonado.

"I'm too heavy for you. *Peso mucho*," said Fitzjames. "*Vamos, ahora.*"

"*Muy bien*," responded Maldonado with a resignation that arguing with Fitzjames would be pointless and disrespectful. Moreover, Fitzjames was in fact much taller and thus much heavier than Maldonado, who was a small man.

Maldonado, with Fitzjames' aid, duplicated Torres' agility and made his way onto the balcony.

"Sir, how can you reach us?" asked Torres of Fitzjames, over the balcony.

"Take off your belts and buckle them together. Then, secure one to the bottom of the railing and then hang the pair from the railing," instructed Fitzjames.

Torres and Maldonado complied, and the result was a double leather strap that extended sufficiently low to permit Fitzjames to clutch it. With both hands, he ascended the strap in the same manner as a rope climb. He reached the floor of the balcony, grabbed it with his left hand and then his right, and swung his left leg and foot onto the floor at the reverse end. He grabbed the balcony railings and pulled himself upward and then over the top of the railing.

Torres entered the apartment with the same fictional authority that he had utilized earlier in the afternoon. The residents were overawed, again, as had previously occurred. Only, in this instance, Torres' entry from the balcony so surprised them that they said nothing. They appeared not to take notice, furthermore, that three men had entered, not just two. Torres repeated his threats to the residents and stormed through the apartment and out the front door to the corridor. They descended the stairs to the ground level and exited the building.

Torres led the two other men at a jog to a parked Chrysler minivan, which was old and battered. Maldonado took the driver's seat, and Torres took the front passenger seat next to him. Fitzjames opened the sliding door and sat in the seat behind Torres. Maldonado drove in a direction away from the hotel. But after traveling a few blocks, he turned left, traveled a few more blocks, and again turned left. Within a hundred yards of the hotel, Maldonado turned right and immediately left and stopped in an alley. A few seconds elapsed. To Fitzjames' subdued astonishment, Fushimi appeared, pushing the laundry cart, and although its wheels rolled awkwardly over the rough asphalt of the road he negotiated the cart toward the vehicle.

Twenty-Five

"Do what you can to analyze the data on the computer hard drive and in those briefcases, but I doubt that much can be gotten here. More expertise is required and that will necessitate getting the computer and documents out of the country quickly," said Fitzjames to Torres, as they arrived at the offices occupied by Torres.

"Yes, sir. I am in agreement. We have some capability in Caracas and, in particular, Fushimi. Yet, this undertaking may exceed even his skills," responded Torres.

"Let him take a crack at it, but if he doesn't make any progress within twenty-four hours, get all of it out and off to your superiors," said Fitzjames.

"Very good," said Torres.

Fitzjames, Torres, Fushimi, and Maldonado all participated in the exercise of unloading the van of its contents and transferring them to the interior of Torres' office. Once inside, in very rapidly spoken Spanish Torres gave a brief set of instructions to Fushimi.

Fushimi nodded in affirmation and stepped away and to his workstation to begin. Torres spoke to Fitzjames.

"I believe that we may have information about the Russians," noted Torres.

Torres received from a young female assistant two sheets of paper. He studied both, individually and then simultaneously, holding up the papers side by side in order to examine them.

“Fascinating. Excellent,” mumbled Torres.

“Details?” asked Fitzjames.

“Yes, sir, of course. I am sorry. I paused only because I am surprised. I am also satisfied that our efforts have been successful.”

“Explain, please,” said Fitzjames impatiently.

Given the level of violence and destruction over the last thirty-six hours, Fitzjames sensed that his effectiveness was diminishing and the operational window was closing. Speed was essential. He no longer had anonymity. The police knew him, and therefore the Venezuelan government, honorable or dishonorable, well intentioned or ill intentioned, knew him. He was a target. The assignment had to be completed with haste.

“Yes, sir. Very well. Let us take seats in my private office,” said Torres and took the few steps required to reach that office.

Fitzjames followed.

Torres sat in one of the two chairs facing the desk, not the more comfortable one behind it. Fitzjames saw the selection of chairs as a Latin gesture of respect made by Torres. Fitzjames suppressed his impatience, in consequence, and sat in the chair next to Torres. Torres placed the two sheets of paper on the desk.

“You see, sir, this is a curious element,” remarked Torres, pointing with the forefinger of each hand at the same name on both papers. “We released the Russians and then followed them. We monitored their movements and, in particular, their mobile telephones. Although no similarity existed in their movements, they both made calls to the same party, to Alberto Jimenez.”

“Who is Alberto Jimenez?” asked Fitzjames.

“Alberto Jimenez is immediate subordinate of Ruben Moreno of the justice ministry. And, his wife, Estrella Jimenez, is the mistress of Andres Fuenmayor of the health ministry,” said Torres.

“You’re confident that the data is accurate?” inquired Fitzjames.

“Absolutely. A minimal margin of error is possible. However, I rest complete confidence in this information,” said Torres. “We have the connection.”

“Indeed, yes. What do you know of Estrella Jimenez, other than that she’s Fuenmayor’s mistress?” asked Fitzjames.

"She is called Estrella. Her true name is Patricia Ernesta. She is approximately thirty-five years of age. When she was much younger, she became Fuenmayor's mistress. After five years or so, he refused to set aside his wife to marry her, and she left him. She married Jimenez thereafter. But as Fuenmayor's career advanced and as he became more politically powerful, Estrella resumed her relationship with him. I would presume that Jimenez knows very well that his wife is sleeping with Fuenmayor. It was he who gave her the name Estrella."

"The husband is forced to be a cuckold," said Fitzjames.

"I am sorry, sir. I do not know the term," said Torres. "I do not know *cuckold*."

"Jimenez willingly accepts or is forced to accept his wife's infidelity. He either can do nothing about it or willingly accept it. Perhaps if he were to take action, his own career would be damaged or destroyed," explained Fitzjames.

"Possibly, yes. But I believe that Estrella is the victim. She has my sympathy. She was at one time very beautiful but has aged through mistreatment. Both Fuenmayor and Jimenez are brutal, uncultured men. They have very likely made an arrangement to share her. Fuenmayor maintains a string of concubines, and Jimenez is a notorious profligate and womanizer. We can be confident that when Estrella is with one, the other is actively engaged elsewhere," returned Torres, as he lit a Belmont and inhaled deeply.

"Can we get close to Jimenez? Do you know anything about his movements?" asked Fitzjames.

"Very little is known," responded Torres, blowing a dark cloud of unfiltered cigarette smoke toward the ceiling of his office. "Yet, I believe we could get something more on Estrella."

"Frankly, I'd prefer that approach. She may lead us to both men. She may also, if your assumptions are correct, be subject to being persuaded to be helpful," said Fitzjames.

"That is possible. But Venezuelan women are accustomed to being badly treated by their men. To presume that this alone will convince her to assist us, I believe, is error," offered Torres.

"I'm not going that far. Granted, this isn't America, and she's not an American woman. She very probably has a much higher tolerance for mistreatment before she turns on her man or men. At the same time, if your description is correct she may be growing weary. We may not make a confederate of her, but we may get an indifferent ally. We may just offer the liberation she's seeking," said Fitzjames.

"Sir, you may be correct," said Torres with a note of confidence.

Torres stood, leaned across the metal desk, and pressed the cigarette into the molded holding piece on a fired clay ashtray. As the cigarette burned and emitted a thin snake trail of smoke that weaved upward from its position on the desk, Torres paused and considered the issues for a few moments. Fitzjames waited in silence for him to complete his thoughts. Torres extracted the cigarette and returned it to his mouth. With the cigarette hanging loosely from his lips and in the corner of his mouth, Torres picked up the telephone receiver for the landline and pressed four numbers on the face.

"Mariana Lurdes, quiero hablar contigo, en este momento," said Torres.

Seconds later, Mariana Lurdes entered the office and stood erect in the doorway in expectation, awaiting instruction. In Spanish, Torres provided the details of the research pertaining to the Russians and their contact with Alberto Jimenez. He continued with the information about Estrella and her relationship with Jimenez and Fuenmayor. Mariana Lurdes acknowledged that she was familiar with Estrella and that Estrella's reputation was such that many people in Caracas were familiar with her, namely many married men and their vengeful wives. Mariana Lurdes added that poverty made Estrella, accompanied by the desire of an attractive woman to rise out of poverty with only her appearance as a steppingstone. Dearth and want had made Estrella's present circumstance. Torres tasked Mariana Lurdes with finding Estrella this very evening. Mariana Lurdes replied that she would do so and provide a report in less than one hour. She turned and left the office.

"One hour, sir, and we will have progress," said Torres to Fitzjames confidently.

"Fine. I can be patient for an hour. Can you give a place of privacy for twenty to thirty minutes?" asked Fitzjames, who had gotten to his feet when Mariana Lurdes had arrived.

"You may remain here, in this office, my office. I have other business to attend to outside with my people. Stay here. I will leave you," said Torres.

Torres left the office and closed the door behind him. Fitzjames retook his seat, removed his mobile telephone, and contacted Major Fuller. In ten minutes, Fitzjames informed the major of the events of the last thirty-six hours. Fuller, who was not at any time particularly loquacious, was utterly taciturn during the call. He said nothing, offered less, and evidenced no emotion, neither discontent nor enthusiasm.

"Anything more, Captain?" asked Fuller coldly.

"Nothing of events, sir. Again, I do wish to confirm the scope that I have," said Fitzjames.

"Unlimited latitude; get the job completed promptly. Those are your only orders," responded Fuller.

"Understood, sir, thank you," said Fitzjames.

"Carry on, Captain," concluded Fuller, who ended the call.

Fitzjames returned the telephone to the pocket of his jacket. He did not require incentivizing to complete the mission. He knew his job and would do his duty. His focus had not flagged. But the lack of encouragement from Fuller disturbed him. He exited Torres' office and found Torres in a discussion with Emilio Fushimi. Torres stood over Fushimi, at his back, while the latter, who was seated, studied a computer monitor. Fitzjames joined them.

"Thank you for allowing me the use of your office," said Fitzjames.

"My pleasure," said Torres warmly.

"Any success?" inquired Fitzjames.

"Emilio has advised that the computer data to which he has gained access, at this point, by breaking the security code, is scientific in nature, chemical formulas and mathematical equations. The written material is in Farsi, with some English included," said Torres.

"I cannot decipher the chemistry and the mathematics without additional technology or additional physical support. My training is in linguistics and physics. I have some grounding in the chemical sciences but too little. It is clear that the data represents a series of formulas for the production of chemical substances. Iran has provided the science, and the construction and production, presumably, is here in Venezuela. The Iranians from the hotel must be the transmitting and interpreting agents for this science," added Fushimi.

"Is there anyone in your office who could study the data and who has a chemistry background?" asked Fitzjames of Torres. "I don't want to belabor the exercise, and it's not necessary to have a complete, thorough analysis. Nonetheless, I'd like to get something more in detail, quickly, if it's possible. I also want to see the data shipped off promptly to your CIA superiors."

"I understand. We have two such individuals, Nestor Ramos and Jesus Beltran. I will assign this duty to them," replied Torres, who promptly walked away and directed his steps to the opposite end of the floor.

Within a moment, two men, in the company of Torres, approached Fitzjames and Fushimi. Both were middle-aged; had short gray hair, neatly styled; wore thick black mustaches; and were dressed in similar informal clothing that caused them to resemble golf caddies. Fitzjames repressed the temptation to smile. In Spanish, Torres explained to Ramos and to Beltran the subject matter, the issues, and the urgency. Both men acknowledged their understanding and pulled up chairs to sit next to Fushimi. Fushimi commenced a brief summary of the data for the benefit of the two men.

Torres and Fitzjames returned to Torres' personal office. After they entered and before Torres could close the door, Mariana Lurdes appeared much in advance of when she was expected. Out of breath, she reported to Torres that Estrella and Jimenez were having a late-night supper at their club, el Club de Squash y Tenis de Caracas. Without delay, Torres told Mariana Lurdes that she, he, and Fitzjames would depart immediately, along with Maldonado. Mariana Lurdes was to drive the Suzuki, as she typically was tasked to do. Torres instructed her to accompany Fitzjames to the vehicle and wait and that he and Maldonado, after collecting certain additional supplies, including weaponry, would meet them in five minutes.

Within that space of time, Torres and Maldonado joined Fitzjames and Mariana Lurdes. Maldonado opened the trunk of the Suzuki and loaded four submachine guns and explosives and timing devices. Torres took the passenger seat next to Mariana Lurdes, who was behind the steering wheel. Fitzjames and Maldonado took the back seats. Mariana Lurdes received the directive from Torres to set out, and she complied. Seconds later, she had maneuvered the Suzuki into traffic and was fighting her way through the city's congested streets toward the destination.

Twenty-Six

"We will be compelled to pass security at the entrance of the Club de Squash. I will step out of vehicle when we arrive and speak with the guards," said Torres to his companions but in particular to Fitzjames, by way of explanation.

"Very well," acknowledged Fitzjames.

"I do not anticipate difficulties, but we need to be prepared to employ force," added Torres.

Torres repeated these comments in Spanish to Mariana Lurdes and Maldonado, although both had understood the contours of the comments in English made by Torres to Fitzjames. Mariana Lurdes adjusted the pistol that was snuggly positioned to the right of the driver's seat adjacent to her hip. She pulled on the handle of the gun with her right hand, in order to raise it and thereby make it more accessible. With her left hand, she continued to hold the steering wheel. Her eyes did not leave the roadway. Maldonado also readied a Glock G27 pistol and a Micro UZI nine-millimeter submachine gun.

Moments later, the Suzuki slowed as it approached the extensive decorative and extravagant metal fencing of the *Club de Squash y Tenis de Caracas*. Mariana Lurdes drove along the boulevard, which ran parallel with the fencing, to the gate marking the entrance to the club. Two security guards stood before the locked gate. Both carried side arms in holsters on their waists. Mariana Lurdes stopped the vehicle, and Torres exited. In the distance, at approximately two hundred yards, despite the late-hour darkness, Fitzjames could see three buildings in a Mediterranean style with white stucco exterior walls and red clay barrel tiled roofs. The central building had a three-story clock tower. It dominated the combined structure. The clock tower had a heavily pitched roofline that had the effect of causing the tower to appear much taller than it was.

Torres engaged in a conversation with the security guards. The occupants of the Suzuki could not hear the substance of the discussion, as Torres spoke in undertones. He opened his wallet and flashed an identification card. Neither guard was interested in studying the card closely. Torres continued to speak and did not return his wallet to his pocket. All three laughed together at some joke or other humorous comment made by Torres. Both guards nodded their heads in response to a question posed by Torres. He posed another question, and both nodded again. Torres removed cash from his wallet and presented it to the guards. Both raised their hands in front of their chests in mock objection and shook their heads. Torres confirmed their objection by shaking each man's hand with Bolivares neatly tucked in the palm. Torres returned to the Suzuki, opened the front passenger door, and retook the front passenger seat. He suggested to Mariana Lurdes to wait a moment and the gate would be opened. He was correct. The guard opened the gate, and his companion waved the Suzuki through and onto the narrow asphalt road that led to the club.

"These private clubs for the government's officials should be more generous in paying their service providers. They believe that they can train a video camera on them and be confident of their good behavior. Such a system merely encourages disloyalty, innovative avoidance, and a lack of discipline. I am confident that the review of the closed-circuit television video conducted by the security guards' captains will reflect the two guards rejecting a bribe and my shaking hands with them. The passing of money will be invisible," said Torres to Fitzjames, and Torres continued, "Avaricious fools."

The Suzuki slowly approached the club's parking area. Mariana Lurdes queried Torres about whether he preferred to have her park the vehicle or whether she should wait near the entrance to the club. Torres instructed her to find a parking space. She did so and pulled into the narrow slip with two large luxury European touring cars on either side. Only the most limited space was available to open the Suzuki's doors to exit. Once outside, Torres spoke in Spanish to Mariana Lurdes, Maldonado, and Fitzjames.

"We will make this approach directly. Mariana Lurdes will accompany me into the dining room. Captain Fitzjames, please remain with Jose Manuel unless in your judgment you must come forward and take action."

"I will follow your plan," responded Fitzjames.

"Very well," said Torres.

The party of four walked briskly toward the entrance to the club, which was below the clock tower. Each carried a pistol, and Maldonado held the UZI awkwardly and not at all clandestinely under his jacket. He had pulled his left arm out of the jacket sleeve, held the gun with his left hand against his chest, and allowed the lapel of the jacket with an empty left sleeve to cover his arm and weapon.

A black Venezuelan porter in a white dinner jacket, black pants, white shirt, black bowtie, and white gloves opened the door for Torres and the others to enter. His dark skin was accentuated by the color of the jacket, shirt, and gloves. He clearly did not recognize the group as members of the club.

"Bienvenidos, señores," said the porter by way of greeting but without enthusiasm.

"Hola," responded Torres, equally coolly. *"Donde está el comedor formal?"*

"Que?" asked the porter, who did not understand the question which Torres had mumbled quickly and quietly.

Torres repeated the question, received his answer, and turned his step in the direction of the dining room without offering an expression of gratitude to the porter. The porter appeared unaffected and accustomed to dismissive, demeaning treatment at the hands of members and guests. The porter also appeared to ignore the UZI carried by Maldonado. Fitzjames found the exchange and the outcome curious. Torres, who was warm and broadminded in his dealings with Fitzjames and with others, had treated the Afro-Venezuelan man disrespectfully. Fitzjames presumed that like so many societies that voiced monotonous, uninterrupted criticism of America for its struggles with race relations, Torres was part of a class in a culture that treated descendants of African slaves with contempt. Thus, while they continued to malign America, within their own borders, people like Torres in Venezuela discouraged equality or opportunities for equality for blacks. Fitzjames had seen the same issue countless times. Europeans would criticize the United States, over a cup of coffee with an American, for its history of racial strife and simultaneously condemn the gypsies living in their own cities to a life not much better than that of stray dogs. Fitzjames did not think less of Torres; Fitzjames would simply remember the exchange with the porter, if Torres chose to speak to him in conversation on the subject of sociological altruism. Fitzjames found equally curious the porter's having ignored the submachine gun. Certainly, the porter had seen it.

Fitzjames and Maldonado, at a distance of a few feet, followed Torres and Mariana Lurdes. At the opened doors of the dining room, another black man in similar attire to that of the porter greeted Torres. Mariana Lurdes took Torres' extended arm as if she were his wife. Torres told the host that he and his companion were guests of Pedro Jimenez and his wife, Estrella. The host appeared confused. He studied an opened book on a music stand, turned the pages, and then returned to Torres. In Spanish, he spoke to Torres.

"Sir, the guests of Mr. and Mrs. Jimenez have already arrived. We were not expecting a second couple. They are seated at a table for four and the table is not designed to accommodate two more diners. If I may have your name, sir, I will approach Mr. Jimenez and discuss the matter with him," said the host with deference.

"They are expecting us. You need not trouble them with questions. We will greet them ourselves," responded Torres with a swagger and self-confidence that overawed the host.

"Please, sir, I must have your name. This is quite out of the ordinary," urged the host, as Torres with Mariana Lurdes at his side entered the dining room and sauntered toward the table occupied by Pedro Jimenez, Estrella, and their guests.

Fitzjames and Maldonado remained just outside the dining room. The host followed Torres and at his back issued protests against his unescorted, unwelcomed entry. Torres ignored the host and moved toward his target.

"Well, this is quaint and comfortable," snarled Torres at Jimenez in slow, clearly enunciated Spanish.

"What do you want here?" inquired Jimenez, rising to his feet.

"I did not anticipate finding both you and your chief here," replied Torres, glancing first at Estrella, who appeared confused by Torres' presence, and then studying the face of Andres Fuenmayor, who was emotionless and cold but startled.

Fuenmayor's elderly wife sat at his right; she was alarmed and speechless. All except Jimenez remained seated.

"State your business here," demanded Jimenez.

"Do you know this man?" asked Fuenmayor of Jimenez.

"Yes, his name is Torres," responded Jimenez.

"Who is he and how is it that you know him?" followed Fuenmayor.

The women said nothing.

"He is a patriot," said Jimenez derisively.

"A patriot? What sort of patriot? A fascist? An anarchist? Or, perhaps he is an anachronist?" inquired Fuenmayor, equally insultingly and with a sardonic stress on the final word.

"I believe 'anachronist' would best describe him," replied Jimenez.

"Yes, I knew that I recognized the name. Torres. Son of the great man, if I am not incorrect," offered Fuenmayor with a wry smile.

"Speak negatively of my father, and I will kill you here, as you sit at this table. I swear it to you on the grave of my father," growled Torres at Fuenmayor as he turned toward him and away from Jimenez.

"Do not threaten me. You have no power here. You are a member of a cause that is lost and will never be recovered. No one remembers your father or his good deeds or his political influence. He is lost to history, as you will be. We carry the future of Venezuela. *Chavismo* is the Venezuela of the present and is the future, not your father's democracy or your outdated political notions. You are a pawn of America, an American lapdog on a short leash," said Fuenmayor, continuing to smile broadly while speaking.

"Shut your mouth," ordered Torres.

"You are nothing. You are the past. We are the future," added Jimenez, who appeared to grow in confidence because of Fuenmayor's defiance.

Torres had not, as yet, brandished his pistol. He had threatened Fuenmayor but without demonstrating to the latter that he did, in fact, have the capacity at that instant to do the very thing that he claimed he could and would do. Torres appeared to be permitting, almost drawing, Fuenmayor and Jimenez into a position where their insults would so ignite his passions that his response would be instinctive and emotional, not thoughtful or rational.

"What will you do, our American dog?" asked Fuenmayor with an expanded grin. He showed his large, clean, white, and well-ordered teeth to Torres.

"Please tell us. We do not yet understand what business you have here at my club. Or, was your purpose merely to attempt to frighten those who are your superiors, both in relevance and in culture?" queried Jimenez, who now also smiled.

Upon hearing the word *culture* used, Mariana Lurdes stepped back and away from the table. As she anticipated, Jimenez' remark was the trigger for Torres' wrath. Torres instantly removed his weapon from the back of his pants with his right hand, swung it around to the front of his body, and with a fully extended right arm aimed the pistol at Jimenez' nose and shot three times in succession. As the dead man fell backwards in his chair, Fuenmayor's wife screamed and covered her mouth with her hands. Estrella did nothing; she did not move and remained seated and silent. Fuenmayor too remained in the chair, only he raised his hands in submission, when Torres swung 'round and trained the pistol on him after having shot Jimenez.

"Let us go," said Torres to Fuenmayor. "On your feet, now, rapidly."

"Please do not shoot me," pleaded Fuenmayor in a cowardly manner, wholly inconsistent with is earlier bombast.

"You will follow your lieutenant in death, if you do not rise and follow my lieutenant out of the building. Now," ordered Torres.

Fuenmayor rose, reluctantly and in fear. He was confused and stunned but collected himself sufficiently to comply with Torres' command. He fell in behind Mariana Lurdes, who had removed her pistol and held it next to his right ear.

"Please do not harm my husband," said Fuenmayor's wife in a whimper as her husband was led away by Torres.

Torres offered no response. Estrella did not move. She said nothing and offered nothing. She also seemed untroubled by her husband's bloodstains, which darkened the left side of her cream-colored, tightly fitted, ankle-length evening gown. She stared at her husband's killer, emotionless. Fuenmayor's fate also was of no apparent relevance to her. She was remarkably self-composed.

None of the club's employees took any action. None sought to interfere with Torres or to interpose an objection to the violence or to the treatment of Fuenmayor. The employees, from the perspective of a disinterested third party, might even have appeared to be in league with Torres and his team. Yet, in reality, their collective dislike for Jimenez and Fuenmayor was so deep from long-term, consistent maltreatment that they were ambivalent about either of the two men, whether in death or in life. At the door of the dining room, Maldonado and Fitzjames took up places behind Torres, and the group of five left the building.

Outside, Fitzjames observed that another vehicle had parked behind the Suzuki. Per Torres' prior instructions, a second team had arrived minutes after the first. When the first team approached the Suzuki with Fuenmayor, two men exited the second car, and the man who had been seated in the front passenger seat opened the back passenger-side door. Torres ordered Fuenmayor into the car. Fuenmayor obeyed, and Torres followed him. The man closed the door behind Torres, who held the pistol at the side of Fuenmayor's head and pressed the barrel into his right temple. The driver took his seat and then tore off and out of the parking lot.

Mariana Lurdes lowered her pistol to her hip. She entered the Suzuki and turned the key in the ignition. Maldonado and Fitzjames were only just in time to take their seats in the back and close the doors before she backed out of the parking space in haste and started off in pursuit. Mariana Lurdes followed the car occupied by Fuenmayor, Torres, and the second team.

Twenty-Seven

Just before midnight, the two vehicles stopped in front of a set of darkened storefronts. The area of Caracas at which they ended their brief journey was devoid of human activity. Fitzjames had yet to encounter any part of the metropolis at any time of day or night that was not teeming with pedestrians and with automobiles, trucks, motorcycles, and motor scooters. This area was the apparent exception. No sounds could be heard. The only noise was the opening and closing of car doors.

Fitzjames followed the others inside a store, which was situated at the far western end of the group of five. No one spoke. Fuenmayor remained silent but was agitated. His hair was disheveled and his clothes were disordered and the perspiration was visible on his face. Torres had forced him to remove the coat and tie. Fuenmayor wore only a white dress shirt, navy blue suit pants, a black leather belt with a gold buckle, and black wingtip laced shoes.

From the street, the store appeared ordinary. It was a retail, low-end clothing store. Both men's and women's casual shirts, trousers, dresses, and skirts hung on hangers on circular metal racks. Six such racks filled the room. In the back was a small desk with a cash register at which customers could complete their purchases. Behind the desk was a door. The party walked through the racks, beyond the desk, and through the door to another, larger room.

The second room was dimly lighted. In the center of the room, a heavy metal chair had been drawn up and placed adjacent to a small table on wheels.

A light fixture hung from a narrow chain from the high ceiling. Within the crescent-shaped ballast could be seen a large bulb. The room was empty, except for the chair, the wheeled table on which certain mechanical devices with electrical wires were visible, and a piece of mobile exercise equipment, which resembled a metal pull-up bar.

One of the two men from the second car, whom Fitzjames did not know or recognize from among the personnel at Torres' office, forced Fuenmayor into the chair. No instructions from Torres had been required. The other man flipped a switch from among five on the wall across from the chair in which Fuenmayor sat. An incandescent light overhead illuminated. It was bright and hot. Fuenmayor's face, with its lines of anxiety and sweat, could be seen clearly. The heat of the light caused additional discomfort, and Fuenmayor's perspiration increased. The man who had seated Fuenmayor fastened Fuenmayor's ankles to the legs of the chair with the straps intended for that purpose. He took Fuenmayor's left arm and secured it to the chair behind his back. The right hand remained free. However, the other man took Fuenmayor's right arm, connected certain electrical nodes to each of the fingers of the right hand, and tied the right arm to the back-right leg of the chair. No one spoke.

Torres turned to Fitzjames and broke the silence. His face wore an expression of jubilation and satisfaction. Fitzjames had not witnessed Torres in such a mood. To date, their interaction had been consistent with the required protocols, and Fitzjames had been accorded the appropriate level of respect and measure of deference. At this juncture, a change had occurred. To Fitzjames' mind, Torres was losing the mission. What had begun and was to continue to be an American undertaking with Venezuelan agents on Venezuelan soil was mutating into a Venezuelan patriotic adventure.

"Sir," said Torres in English, without the typical tone of subordination, "I do not presume that you will object to our using certain methods to assist Mr. Fuenmayor in providing answers to questions." He lit a cigarette while making the statement.

"Explain," responded Fitzjames.

"We intend to employ certain methods that will make Mr. Fuenmayor very uncomfortable. If he does not provide complete, detailed, and prompt answers to my questions, then his discomfort will increase," said Torres.

"Details—general details, please," replied Fitzjames.

"We will use physical force and then electricity to extract the responses," offered Torres with a cold smirk.

"I wish to speak to you privately. Let's step back into the outer room," said Fitzjames.

Torres followed Fitzjames through the door and closed it behind him. Torres' frustration was visible. He sensed that Fitzjames would insist upon an approach to Fuenmayor different from the one envisioned by Torres.

"Torture may be unnecessary," opened Fitzjames, before Torres could speak.

"Forceful methods, sir, not torture," returned Torres.

Semantical nonsense. Torture is torture. It is possible, quite possible, in my judgment that we can get what we want from Fuenmayor without it. He's already sufficiently terrified of the prospect of being tortured that he may give us information voluntarily," said Fitzjames.

"But we cannot be certain of its truth without employing firm methods," offered Torres. "Leave to me the questions and the methods and we will have answers."

"I don't know that I agree with that, in the current situation. I'll do the questioning and do it in English. I'll presume that he speaks English," said Fitzjames.

"I believe he does, but I am not certain," answered Torres.

"Then that'll be my first question. If he's evasive or belligerent at any point during the interrogation, then I'll turn him over to you and your men for questioning. Understood?"

"Yes, sir," responded Torres, with a degree of belligerence.

The two men returned to the inner room and approached the seated prisoner under the light. One of the two men from the second car stepped behind Fuenmayor and viciously clutched the hair on Fuenmayor's head in order to hold his head erect and still. Torres growled at the man to release Fuenmayor. He did so but slowly and unwillingly.

Fitzjames stood before the prisoner. "Do you speak English?"

"Yes, I speak English," mumbled Fuenmayor.

"Speak out and speak clearly," commanded Torres in Spanish.

"I speak English," repeated Fuenmayor, nodding his head while the sweat formed on his brow and trickled into his eyes and onto his thick cheeks.

"I will be clear with you, Mr. Fuenmayor. I have very little time and little patience. I will ask you questions and will do so in clear English. You must give me complete answers, quickly. If you do not do so, I will leave my questions with these men, and they will get the answers from you. Please understand that giving me the answers will be much less painful to you than if these men must extract the answers from you. Do you understand?" asked Fitzjames.

"I understand," responded Fuenmayor in clearly enunciated English but with a heavy Spanish accent.

"Were you responsible for the death of Algorta?"

"I was under instruction from my superiors in the government to remove him."

"Why?"

"He was taking money. How do you say, in English, embezzlement? The money from the sales of drugs must, in part, be paid to the government. The percentages that Algorta was to pay were increased. Algorta claimed that the sales in the United States had decreased. Thus, he argued that he should pay less. The government's agents in the operation of Algorta confirmed that the sales were greater, not less. The instruction then came to my department, to me, to kill him."

"Is there more—as to why he was killed? Tell me," directed Fitzjames.

"More? No. He had to pay. He did not. The government needs the hard American currency. Algorta withheld the money and was killed," replied Fuenmayor nervously.

"I must remind you, Mr. Fuenmayor, I require full answers to my questions. What other reasons existed to kill Algorta?" inquired Fitzjames.

"Sir, I know of no other reason. You must believe me."

Fitzjames stepped back two paces from the prisoner. He removed the Ruger from the holster and confirmed that it was loaded. He spoke to Torres.

"You may have him. You know the questions that I would ask. When you've finished with him and before he is exhausted or dead, call me back into the room. I'll then have the pleasure of shooting him," said Fitzjames, as he returned the Ruger to the holster. He turned and walked toward the door.

Torres' man grabbed Fuenmayor's hair a second time.

"Please, sir, I understand now. I understand the question you are asking. I will answer; I will answer," pleaded Fuenmayor.

"Very well. Give me your answer," said Fitzjames in Spanish and turning again and approaching the prisoner slowly.

"May I have your promise that I will receive protection from your government in exchange for my answers?" asked Fuenmayor in English. Fear improved his command of the language.

"I can make no promise to you, except to tell you that you'll not survive this night if you don't give me the information I'm seeking," replied Fitzjames coldly.

"I must have protection. I must have a promise of protection. I will certainly be assassinated for the information that I give you," urged Fuenmayor.

"You will certainly be killed if you don't. Now, I want answers," said Fitzjames impatiently.

Fuenmayor paused to consider. He looked from Fitzjames, to Torres, to the others in the room, and back to Fitzjames. His shirt, now drenched in his perspiration, stuck to his chest, stomach, and back. He began to shake but remained silent. After a minute passed without a response, Fitzjames spoke to Torres.

"He's yours."

Torres appeared elated. He feared that Fitzjames would intervene a second time and deny him the opportunity. He barked orders at the two men, one of whom pulled back Fuenmayor's head by his hair. The other applied power to the device affixed to Fuenmayor's right hand. The odor of burned flesh was immediately recognizable over Fuenmayor's screaming. The power was cut, the screams ceased, and Fuenmayor began to sob. In English, he spoke.

"I will answer your questions," he said, as his hair was released by Torres' man.

"Why was Algorta killed?" repeated Fitzjames in English.

"He refused to participate in *la Alianza*. Yes, he did withhold payments to the government. But that offense was expected and minor. His refusal to co-operate in el Plan made our work more difficult, the work became impossible," said Fuenmayor.

"What is la Alianza?" asked Fitzjames.

"It is a cooperative alliance between Russia, Iran, and Venezuela to develop synthetically altered drugs and export them to the United States.

"For what ultimate purpose?" interjected Fitzjames.

"Biological devastation. Economic ruin would follow."

"How does the Alianza function? Where is the work done to create the drugs?"

"The science is completed in Iran and the research results are delivered to Venezuela by Iranian scientists who come to Venezuela in the disguise of businessmen. Russia provides the protection and the banking services for Iran. The testing and production are accomplished in Venezuela. However, the facility, I learned this evening, has been severely damaged by fires and explosions that occurred earlier today," responded Fuenmayor.

"Who is responsible for the program in Venezuela?" asked Fitzjames. "I want names and positions."

"Only four individuals: the president, vice president, the chief of the Ministry of Justice and Internal Affairs, and I. Just senior members of government. Only four," said Fuenmayor.

"How do you communicate and coordinate operations? How is secrecy preserved?" asked Fitzjames, moving closer to Fuenmayor and leaning forward to nearly eye level with the prisoner, while posing the question.

"Between officials, there is no written communication and only limited computer contact," responded Fuenmayor after taking a deep breath and panting thereafter. "Please, I believe I may be suffering cardiac dysfunction."

"How is communication effected? How do you coordinate the activities?" asked Fitzjames. He ignored the complaint about a potential heart attack.

"Orders and operational details are passed between us by a courier."

"Who is the courier? Who?" shouted Fitzjames.

"Estrella Jimenez," replied Fuenmayor breathlessly. "She is shared by all of us; we selected her because she is trustworthy and intelligent."

"She is shared? In what way?"

"She is our collective mistress. We pass her between ourselves. As we do so, she carries operational guidelines and instructions for the functioning of the Alianza. Most are carried by memory and thus unwritten."

"And what of your Russian contacts?"

"The Russians provide security and banking for the Iranians, as I have told you."

"Names. I want names!" again shouted Fitzjames.

"One was killed, the senior man, who organized the other. He was killed in the last few days. We do not know who killed him. He was called Pavel Morozov. The other is Nikolai Lebedev."

"Do they report to you?"

"In Venezuela, yes."

"To you exclusively? To you only?" asked Fitzjames more calmly.

"Yes," replied Fuenmayor.

"What are the names of the Iranians currently in Venezuela?"

"Ali Abbas Yazdi and Ahmad Rezvani."

"Do they coordinate their operations with you?"

"Yes."

"Scientists?"

"Yes. Yazdi is a geneticist. Rezvani is an immunologist."

"Where are they now? Where can I find them?" asked Fitzjames.

"They are in a safehouse," responded Fuenmayor.

"Where is the safehouse?" questioned Fitzjames in a louder tone.

"I do not know," said Fuenmayor.

Fitzjames looked at Torres, who in turn made a head gesture to his subordinate. The man instantly and viciously clutched and pulled Fuenmayor's hair. Fuenmayor gasped and the repeated his answer to the question.

"Who would know?"

"Ruben Moreno and Estrella. The safety of the Iranians was left to them," said Fuenmayor, as he struggled to speak.

"Release him," ordered Fitzjames and then in Spanish, "*Dejale.*"

Torres' lieutenant complied, without the requirement of a duplicate order from Torres. The man, however, remained positioned to grab the hair of the prisoner again in the event he was directed to do so.

"Where is the testing of the drug compounds conducted?" inquired Fitzjames.

"I do not understand," said Fuenmayor.

"After the manufacturing process of the drugs has been completed, where are they tested? Where are the experiments performed?"

"All experiments are conducted in Venezuela."

"Where?" shouted Fitzjames.

"In Caracas, at the facilities of the Ministry of Health," returned Fuenmayor.

"On humans? Human subjects?"

"Yes."

"Addicts in Caracas?"

"Yes, in part."

"What do you mean, in part?" asked Fitzjames.

"The poor and homeless are likewise the subjects."

"The poor?" asked Fitzjames incredulously.

"My task is to rid the streets of the poor, primarily women and children. They are enticed to participate in the experiments. We give them food and water and a little money. They are happy to volunteer," offered Fuenmayor with an air of indifference.

"Your ministry tests your synthetic drugs on poor women and children," mumbled Fitzjames under his breath. But the notion so disturbed him that he did not hear the affirmation and confirmation from Fuenmayor, who presumed that Fitzjames had posed another question.

"You see, my friend, these men are bastards. Pigs and sons of whores," said Torres to Fitzjames, as Fitzjames turned his back and walked away from the prisoner.

Torres followed him. Fuenmayor said nothing but watched as the two men moved toward the door to the outer room.

When Fitzjames reached the door, he opened it. He swung his head and over his right shoulder spoke to Torres.

"I don't care what you do to him but do it in no more than five minutes."

The door closed behind Fitzjames. He walked briskly through the retail shop and through the front door and to the sidewalk outside. He gave Torres ten minutes.

Twenty-Eight

"*Necesito cinco horas de sueno, solamente,*" said Fitzjames to Mariana Lurdes, as she gripped the steering wheel in route toward the destination. "*No mas.*"

"*Me entiendo,*" she said in acknowledgment.

She drove on and took note of the time on the clock in the Suzuki. Because it was half-past-one in the morning and because she anticipated only a few more minutes of driving to reach her home, she calculated that he would want her to wake him at half-past-six. The silence resumed. The only words that he spoke to her were the instructions about the number of hours of sleep that he required. He continued to stare out of the car window and only occasionally glanced through the windshield at the roadway on which they traveled. She was familiar with taciturnity. But the American's silence was deeper and troubling. In her experience, Americans inclined toward loquacity, even about matters that would otherwise appear to demand a muted response. Yet he was different. He was, she concluded, an intellectual, who was of a divided mind about the nature of his work and its obligations. She suspected that he disliked violence, if not hated it, and forced himself, against his aesthetic, philosophical bent to accept it. Fitzjames would have been disarmed by the accuracy of her evaluation had he known her thoughts.

"*Aqui estamos,*" she said as she pulled into a parking space in front of a colorless group of buildings that could have appeared on any Latin American street, from Monterrey, Mexico, to Santiago, Chile.

Fitzjames threw open the door, stepped out onto a rough sidewalk of uneven stone, closed the door behind him, and opened the passenger door. He removed his backpack and suitcase. He followed Mariana Lurdes along the roadside for twenty yards. At a gate, she removed a key from a small purse, which Fitzjames had not previously noticed, and applied the key to a lock. The gate was thick and heavy and was positioned between two high concrete block walls. Although dark, enough light from inside the sealed courtyard reflected that shards of glass from broken bottles had been cemented into the top of the walls for additional security. Mariana Lurdes passed inside the courtyard, and Fitzjames followed. She locked the gate behind her. They passed through the shallow courtyard, thick with vegetation, and to a door. Mariana Lurdes unlocked the door with a different key and held the door open for Fitzjames to enter. He shook his head and held out his left hand to her to enter before him. She did so.

The interior was comfortable but only lightly furnished with two old sofas, three wooden chairs, two small tables each with lamps, and a recliner. In the recliner, a young woman slept. A small child also slept by her side, on her arm, which embraced him. Fitzjames could not suppress a smile upon seeing them.

"*Mi hija y nieto,*" whispered Mariana Lurdes.

"*Claro,*" responded Fitzjames.

Mariana Lurdes approached her daughter and touched her on the shoulder. She started. "*Lo siento, Mama. Tenia sueno y fue muy tarde,*" said the daughter apologetically.

"*Esta bien nina,*" replied the mother.

The young woman observed Fitzjames and started a second time. Mariana Lurdes explained that he was an American who needed a place to sleep and that she had agreed to keep him. She told her daughter that she would need to give up her room to accommodate him. She agreed, but Fitzjames objected. He advised Mariana Lurdes that he would be comfortable in a chair and did not need to eject her daughter from her room.

After a brief exchange, Mariana Lurdes yielded. The daughter rose, collected her sleeping son, thanked Fitzjames affably for his kindness, and left the room. Fitzjames turned his wrist to confirm the time. He reminded Mariana Lurdes of the five-hour limit, and she tipped her head in acknowledgment and also left the room. He sat on the older of the two sofas. Within minutes and while still in a seated position, he fell asleep.

Five hours later to the minute, Mariana Lurdes' daughter woke Fitzjames by calling out his surname, preceded by *señor*, in ever-increasing volume until he was roused. He was not lying on the sofa but leaning against the armrest. Upon waking, he sat up and then got to his feet. The rapid movement from sleep, to sitting, to standing left him a bit unstable on his feet. Within a few seconds, his equilibrium returned, and he thanked the young woman for being so prompt. He inquired of her, in Spanish, if her mother were still asleep.

"Oh, no," she replied in Spanish. "She woke one hour ago and has returned to her work."

"Really? I expected to return with her to the offices this morning," said Fitzjames, surprised by the absence of Mariana Lurdes.

"No, sir. She must report to work very early each morning. A car will be sent 'round to pick you up in one hour. My mother made arrangements last night for the car because she recognized that she would not be available. I was told to wake you at the time that you specified, after five hours of rest, and to prepare a breakfast for you. My mother expressed concern that you had not, to her knowledge, eaten well since your arrival in Venezuela. She told me that I was to prepare any meal that you wished," she said with a pleasant, hospitable smile.

"That is not necessary. I would like some coffee," he suggested.

"The coffee has been prepared in the kitchen. But my mother told me that you would likely object to a breakfast. I was also told to overcome any objections from you with kindness, insistence, and the promise of excellent food," she said equally warmly.

"But certainly you have your son to care for. A full breakfast takes too much time."

"He is sleeping and will continue to sleep for another few hours. It is no problem and would be my pleasure. Please recall that my mother offered to you my bedroom to sleep and you refused. That was very courteous. I was prepared to sleep with my son to accommodate you. Now, I feel an obligation to prepare breakfast for you."

"You should feel no obligation. The sofa was very comfortable. I did not require a bed, only a chair and some quiet. I received a sofa and peace, more than I had expected. Thank you," he said.

"Very well. Now, we must eat. I will prepare an omelet and some bread for you. Is that sufficient?" she asked.

"Yes. Perfect. And, I would enjoy a coffee and a glass of water," said Fitzjames.

"Certainly. If you wish to shower, you may use my bathroom, as well. Come with me, please," she said.

Fitzjames followed the woman deeper into the interior of the house, down a short, narrow corridor beyond the kitchen and three small bedrooms to a tightly constructed bathroom. She removed a bath towel from a fragile, inexpensive and bright yellow plastic set of shelves outside the bathroom and presented it to him.

"A towel for your use," she said.

"Thank you. I must collect my toilet things from my suitcase," he replied.

"Yes, please. I moved your suitcase to my bedroom. It is here," she said, opening the door to the room just opposite the bathroom.

Fitzjames observed that the suitcase had been positioned next to a small chest of drawers and across from an old brass bed with a flat, heavily worn mattress. The double bed had been neatly made. Fitzjames smiled. The room had been prepared for him and he had not used it. He now considered that his choice to sleep on the sofa was less gallant than the offense he had committed by not sleeping in his hostess' daughter's bed.

Twenty-Nine

"What are your instructions?" asked Fitzjames of the driver.

"I am to deliver you to Mariana Lurdes, who is awaiting your arrival at the Ministry of Justice and Internal Affairs," replied the driver.

"Very well," said Fitzjames.

Fitzjames, who held the jacket in his lap, removed a fresh magazine and inserted it in the Ruger. He held the gun between his legs, with the barrel pointed at the car's floorboard, and examined it. He confirmed that it was in good order and that the silencing device was properly affixed and sealed. He returned the weapon to the shoulder holster. He did not speak with the driver. The driver observed his movements but made no comment and offered not conversation.

Their journey together was brief. Within fifteen minutes, the driver slowed the vehicle and turned off the main roadway and down a side street and then turned again into a narrow alley. The driver stopped and spoke to Fitzjames.

"You must exit here. Walk up the alley thirty meters and turn to your left. You will be met at that point."

"Thank you. I presume that you have instructions, as well, as to my suitcase and backpack."

"Yes, sir. Mr. Torres is to receive them directly and hold them for you until your return to the offices," responded the driver.

"Excellent."

Fitzjames opened the car door, stepped out, put on the jacket, and closed the door. The driver threw the small vehicle into reverse, backed into an open parking space along the alley, swung around despite the restricted space, and dashed off in the reverse direction. Fitzjames paid no attention to the driver's departure but focused on the short walk up the alley. Thirty meters was a short distance. The alley was quiet. Fitzjames saw no pedestrians and heard no voices, nor did any cars, trucks, or motorcycles enter the alley. The only sound was his footfall.

After Fitzjames had taken thirty or so paces, a man emerged from behind a large door and stood in front of Fitzjames. He held an open hand outward to his right to signal to Fitzjames to turn to his left and enter. Fitzjames followed the directions. Once inside, the door closed mechanically, and Mariana Lurdes greeted him.

"Good morning, Captain," she said in Spanish.

"Good morning," he returned, also in Spanish.

"My daughter was to have made a breakfast for you; did she do so?" she inquired.

"Yes. Thank you. She was very kind. The food was excellent. Thank you for the hospitality."

"You are welcome."

"Where are we, then?" he asked, thereby moving off the subject of Mariana Lurdes' daughter and on to the business at hand.

"Throughout the night, we tracked the activities and movements of Estrella Jimenez. She is expected to arrive at the ministry office within twenty minutes. She arranged a meeting with Ruben Moreno after two o'clock this morning. Moreno's practice is to send a car for her and deliver here to the ministry. We anticipate that that very protocol will be employed this morning. It is unlikely that Mrs. Jimenez would drive her own automobile. A driver is more secure and decorous," said Mariana Lurdes.

"Will we be certain of her arrival?"

"Yes, sir. We have people posted here and outside who are watching the entire building. If we do not see her arrive from this vantage point, then we will certainly see her from another. If you would like a coffee, we can have a cup made for you while we wait."

"Fine. Excellent. Yes."

"I will get it for you," she said.

She walked to the opposite side of the room. She prepared a cup of espresso coffee at a machine designed for that purpose. She completed the task as if she were at home and nothing else existed to distract her. After she poured the coffee into a small cup, she collected the sugar container to spoon out sweetener. Fitzjames stopped her.

"No, thank you. Without sugar, please," he said, while holding up his hand for emphasis.

"No sugar?" she asked in disbelief.

"Without sugar, please," he repeated.

"Very well," she said and returned the sugar container to its perch to the right of the coffeemaker.

She placed the cup on a saucer and delivered the coffee to him, as he approached her. She smiled and walked toward another member of the team and began a conversation in muted tones. He drank the coffee slowly. It was hot, perhaps too hot. But the flavor was superb. When he finished it, he tipped the cup in order to drain off the foam.

"Would you like another?" she asked after seeing him place the saucer and empty cup on the table on which the machine rested.

"No. No, thank you."

A mobile telephone rang. Mariana Lurdes picked it up and answered the call. She spoke to the caller for only an instant, then ended the call. She placed the telephone into the left-back pocket of her True Religion bootcut denim blue jeans. She addressed Fitzjames.

"She has arrived. We must hurry," she said.

Fitzjames followed Mariana Lurdes out the door that he had entered. She began to run up the alley and around the corner of the building to the corner opposite the ministry. Fitzjames ran behind her and stopped when she stopped, coolly, with the entrance of the government facility in view. Both could see

Estrella Jimenez ascending the eight stairs to double doors leading to the building's interior. A man followed her. He appeared to be a bodyguard and appeared, too, to be on friendly terms with the two soldiers standing on either side of the doorway.

"After she moves inside, we will move forward," said Mariana Lurdes.

She placed a telephone call and mumbled a set of instructions to the recipient. In less than a minute, a small van pulled into the driveway in front of the ministry. Estrella Jimenez and her companion entered the building and the door closed behind them.

"Now. We must hurry," said Mariana Lurdes.

As she darted toward the ministry entrance, she removed the pistol she carried and while running snapped a magazine into the weapon. Fitzjames ran by her side, matching her speed. He also extracted his gun from the shoulder holster.

In route and calibrated precisely with their dash for the entrance, Fitzjames and Mariana Lurdes observed a man with complete head covering to shield his identity from both onlookers and video cameras emerging from the front passenger side of the van. Both soldiers immediately reverted to an alert and cautionary status and readied their machine guns. They were too late, and their earlier jocularity with Estrella Jimenez' bodyguard proved fatal. The disguised passenger from the van aimed a heavy pistol with a long barrel and silencer at the guard to the left of the doorway and shot him in the cheek below the right eye. Before he struck the ground and before his colleague could respond to the attack, the second soldier too took a bullet to the face below the nose. The second soldier collapsed. The shooter advanced quickly toward the men up the stairs and fired two more shots into the bodies. He slipped away and returned to the van. The driver pressed the accelerator to the floorboard and the van disappeared.

Mariana Lurdes and Fitzjames thus entered the ministry without opposition. Immediately in front of them at a distance of ten yards was Estrella Jimenez, along with the bodyguard. They stood waiting for the elevator door to open. They had not observed the entrance of Mariana Lurdes and Fitzjames.

However, they heard the footfall on the uncarpeted white ceramic-tiled floor. The bodyguard did not turn 'round but glanced over his left shoulder. As he did so, Mariana Lurdes shot three times. Estrella gasped but did not scream. Mariana Lurdes commanded her to remain quiet or she would be killed. Estrella complied.

Fitzjames examined the bodyguard. His dead body was a mass of flesh at the door of the elevator. Fitzjames crouched, checked the man's carotid artery for life, clutched his wrist to confirm the absence of a pulse, dropped the limp arm, and pushed him out of the way. The elevator door opened. Mariana Lurdes signaled to Estrella to enter and Fitzjames followed the two women into the elevator. The door closed, but the elevator remained stationary.

"We expect that you will take us to Ruben Moreno," said Mariana Lurdes, coolly, in Spanish.

"Why would I do so?" responded Estrella in a haughty, highbrow fashion.

"Because if you do not do so, we will find him without you, and you will be dead," said Marina Lurdes. "Or, you will be seriously injured by me only to be killed later when the government concludes that you were an accessary to our work. You may choose. I do not have the patience to argue the matter."

"I will be killed, even if you do not kill me," said Estrella.

"We can provide protection for you," replied Marian Lurdes.

"Who can do this?" asked Estrella.

"Our organization," said Mariana Lurdes.

"What is your organization?" continued Estrella.

"The identity is of no relevance. Quickly, take us to Moreno," said Mariana Lurdes.

"Who is this man? Is he an American? His appearance is that of an American," said Estrella.

"I am an American, and I have a job to complete here in Caracas. I am the leader of this operation. I want Moreno. Take us to him, now, or I will give the order to dispose of you," interjected Fitzjames in an aggressive tone and in rapidly spoken Spanish.

Mariana Lurdes reopened the elevator door, pointed her pistol at Estrella's chest, and flicked the weapon in such a manner as to convey to Estrella to step outside. Estrella did not move; instead, Estrella touched the button on the console and closed the elevator door. She then pressed the button to the seventh floor, and the elevator began its ascent.

Fitzjames pressed the emergency stop button immediately prior to the elevator reaching the seventh floor. Estrella fell against the side of the elevator and nearly lost her balance. Mariana Lurdes was unaffected and stood with her legs well apart. As Estrella recovered and adjusted her tightly fitted royal blue dress and string of pearls, Fitzjames addressed her again in Spanish.

"Where is Moreno's office on the seventh floor and is it near the elevator or stairs?"

"The office is at the end of the corridor and some distance from the elevator. An emergency fire escape with stairs is adjacent to Mr. Moreno's office," said Estrella, discomfited.

"Is the seventh floor busy with office personnel or is it typically quiet? Tell me, instantly," said Fitzjames.

"It is not so busy," replied Estrella, her anxiety growing. "A receptionist is seated at the desk and the floor is made up of offices, many of which are unoccupied and unused."

"Armed guards or soldiers?" inquired Fitzjames.

"None that I have seen. But I have visited this office only two times," said Estrella.

"Does Moreno carry a gun?" asked Fitzjames.

"Yes, he does have a gun and, I believe, keeps it readied, even in his offices," said Estrella.

"Very well. We will exit the elevator and together, as a group, proceed directly to the office of Moreno. Do not speak to anyone. If I have doubts, at any point, about your cooperation, I will give my companion instructions to kill you. Do you understand?" said Fitzjames, threatening. He moved closer to Estrella and stood over her.

"Yes, I understand," mumbled Estrella, clearly overawed by Fitzjames and unaccustomed to the sensation. She was more familiar with deploying her beauty in such a way that cowed a man.

"Are you certain that you understand?" Fitzjames returned.

"Yes, yes. I am certain," said Estrella, looking up at Fitzjames and feigning confidence.

"Do you understand?" asked Fitzjames of Mariana Lurdes.

"Quite clearly. I will be ready to do what I must," said Mariana Lurdes coldly, while studying the face of Estrella. She replaced the magazine in the pistol by way of emphasis.

Fitzjames released the elevator, and it completed its rise to the seventh floor. Fitzjames tapped the lapel of his jacket in order to feel the Ruger in the shoulder holster. The elevator door opened, and a young woman in her early twenties, smartly dressed, greeted the party.

"Good morning, Mrs. Jimenez," said the receptionist.

"Good morning," responded Estrella.

"Mr. Moreno is expecting you. He has two guests with him and is in the conference room near his office."

"Thank you," said Estrella and smiled falsely at the young woman.

To Fitzjames' way of thinking, any awkwardness in Estrella's manner would likely be interpreted by the staff as evidence of a pampered lifestyle with its accompanying elitist attitude and thus be ignored. Fitzjames watched the receptionist, in order to assure that she made no telephone calls, as the three walked down the corridor toward Moreno's office.

Mariana Lurdes insisted that Estrella lead the party in order to be seen first. As they approached the end of the corridor, Estrella slowed at a large glass window that stretched from ceiling to floor. On the other side of the glass was the conference room. Loud chatter could be heard in the hallway from within the conference room. Fitzjames placed his left hand on Mariana Lurdes' shoulder to signal to her to stop. Estrella proceeded and walked beyond the window, through which she was observed by Moreno, and continued to the closed door of the room.

"Mi nina y carina," said Moreno affectionately, as he rose from his chair to greet Estrella. He wore a large, toothy smile that forced upward and outward his large black mustache. He bore an ugly resemblance to the aged Francisco "Poncho" Villa. *"Estos son mis amigos de Irán; hombres importantes y críticos de los programas del gobierno."*

Estrella gave no reply but permitted Moreno to kiss her on both cheeks, while placing a hand low on her right hip, such that the fingers traced over the buttocks. She remained silent and unmoved. Fitzjames, meanwhile, had overheard the reference to the Iranians. He placed his hand on Mariana Lurdes' shoulder a second time and forced her behind him. He lunged beyond the glass window to the doorway. The Iranians, who had been distracted both by the arrival of Estrella and her appearance, now recognized the threat posed by Fitzjames. Both reached for pistols that they had concealed in their jackets. Fitzjames lowered the Ruger and shot them in their seats in succession, the silencer on the gun efficiently doing its work. They fell back in the chairs on their backs when the bullets hit them. Startled, Moreno turned to confront Fitzjames, while reaching for a gun. Mariana Lurdes shot him before he could remove his hand from inside the coat of this three-piece suit.

Estrella stood aside and said nothing. As a precaution, Fitzjames fired two more bullets into the chests of the Iranian scientists. They had been killed by the initial wounds, but he could take no risks in connection with their survival. He also shot Moreno a second time. He had to be certain that all were dead.

"I am not a part of this work," said Estrella, breaking her silence. Her English was excellent.

"A part of what?" asked Fitzjames.

"The drugs, the altering of the drugs, and the shipments to the Unites States. I am not a part of the work," said Estrella.

"Didn't you transmit messages between Fuenmayor and Moreno?" asked Fitzjames.

"Yes. But I know nothing of what they were doing," she continued.

"Let's go. *Vamos, ahora, apurate,"* said Fitzjames and left the room and ran back up the hallway to the elevator.

Mariana Lurdes and Estrella Jimenez followed him. The three entered the elevator. The receptionist mumbled a goodbye, clearly confused by their hasty, awkward departure. But she did not stir from her seat. The three descended to the ground floor. Nothing was said in the elevator.

When the elevator door opened, Fitzjames instinctively dropped to the ground. Mariana Lurdes fell against the side of the elevator in reaction to Fitzjames' movements. Estrella stood erect and was killed instantly when the government's two soldiers fired their weapons into the elevator. They had taken positions after the killings at the entrance to the facility. Fitzjames returned fire and hit the soldier to the left. He tumbled over and dropped a machine gun. The fall of his colleague distracted the second man, and Mariana Lurdes put a bullet in his chest before he could discharge another round.

Fitzjames got to his knees and paused to evaluate Estrella's condition. He placed the fingers of his left hand on her neck. He felt no pulse. He shook his head.

"*Esta muerta. Debemos salir,*" said Mariana Lurdes mechanically.

"*Estoy de acuerdo,*" responded Fitzjames under his breath.

"*Vamos,*" she urged.

Fitzjames followed Mariana Lurdes out of the elevator, out of the building, and to a waiting automobile. Torres emerged and from the car and opened the passenger door for Fitzjames to enter. Fitzjames dived into the vehicle. Torres took his seat after Mariana Lurdes joined Fitzjames.

"*Nos vamos,*" said Torres to the driver.

The driver slammed the accelerator to the floor of the vehicle and raced off toward Torres' office.

Thirty

"We have made arrangements to get you out of Venezuela," mumbled Torres to Fitzjames, as the driver slowed the vehicle in which the four were traveling.

"Excellent," responded Fitzjames from the back seat.

"Once inside, I will explain," said Torres, who lit a cigarette coolly.

The driver navigated the automobile into a public parking space some four blocks from Torres' office. The driver turned the key in the ignition toward him, thereby killing the engine, and opened the door to exit. Silently, Torres and Mariana Lourdes exited through the car doors adjacent to them, and Fitzjames did likewise. Without conversation, the four walked briskly toward Torres' office. After crossing a busy intersection, the driver removed a mobile telephone from the pocket of his trouser and pressed a code on the keypad of the telephone. Seconds later, an explosion rocked the neighborhood. A bomb in the vehicle by which they had arrived had been detonated.

"The government will spend significant time addressing the burning car," said Torres with a contemptuous smile. "Certainly, the explosion will be ascribed to anarchists or fascists. The government's investigators will dither over another piece of nonsense. Here we are."

They had arrived at Torres' office. They entered the building, and Fitzjames followed Torres and Mariana Lurdes into the stairwell. The driver departed from them and entered a room on the ground floor and closed the door behind him. The remaining three of the party ascended the stairs to the floor on which the CIA's operations were conducted.

"I will check the progress of the work being completed by Ramos and Beltran. Please, take a seat in my office," said Torres to Fitzjames.

"Thank you."

"I will also explain the departure arrangements," added Torres, who extinguished the cigarette in an ashtray and instantly lighted another.

"Very good," responded Fitzjames, taking a chair.

Fitzjames waited ten minutes for Torres to return. When he did, the butt of a dead cigarette hung from his mouth. He carried two sheets of paper and presented them to Fitzjames.

"That is a summary of the findings of Ramos and Beltran," noted Torres when delivering the papers to Fitzjames.

Torres dropped the cigarette butt into the ashtray. He waited for Fitzjames to complete the reading of the summary. Fitzjames review required little time.

"I am certain that the findings are not as full as a more detailed analysis would produce," offered Torres.

"Perhaps. But this is good work, presuming that it's accurate," said Fitzjames. "It's also damning. Mathematical and chemical formulas that produce substances that can be manufactured and then, apparently and hypothetically, appended to organic and synthetic drugs. Those substances likely have chemical properties consistent with or similar to known viruses that infect a populace and result in epidemics. Thus, there're a useful vehicle for exporting biological terror."

"Yes. Extraordinary. But I believe you have put an end to it. My assumption is that your assignment was the elimination of the actors here in Venezuela," commented Torres. He lit another Belmont and blew an enormous smoke cloud toward the ceiling. It split into two halves and then settled into the room.

"You do enjoy your cigarettes," said Fitzjames with a smile. He ignored Torres' assumption.

"They will kill me; I realize this. But the pleasure is too great to give them up."

"May I keep these papers?" asked Fitzjames.

"Of course. They are for you," replied Torres.

"I'll presume that instructions will come to you to take additional steps to destroy any known manufacturing or research facilities in Caracas or elsewhere in Venezuela. I don't have the authority to give you those orders. But, they'll come, no doubt," said Fitzjames.

"Yes. I am expecting this order also and have thus begun advance preparation," said Torres. "We have identified both known and suspected sites."

"Now, tell me about the exit strategy," said Fitzjames in a manner that left no uncertainty that he did not wish to engage in any discussion about the contours of his assignment.

"Your return on a commercial flight is, of course, out of the question," remarked Torres.

"Of course."

"Every policeman in this country knows your face, and I presume most of the army. The airport would be awash in police and soldiers. I have made arrangements to have you transported quietly by speedboat. The departure point is east of Puerto Carayaca on the coast. Do you know Puerto Carayaca?" inquired Torres.

"I know of it. I know its general location. It's not far west of Caracas on the ocean," said Fitzjames.

"Yes. The flight will travel to Aruba. You will be delivered to De Palm Island on Aruba and, by boat, pass to the mainland. A car will then transport you to Reina Beatrix International Airport on Aruba. A reservation has been made for you on an American Airlines flight this evening, the last flight off the island this date, to Miami," said Torres.

"And then from Miami?" asked Fitzjames.

"I cannot do more than assure your arrangements to Miami. Your superiors must organize your travel thereafter," responded Torres impatiently.

"No problem. I was simply unsure to what extent your office could sort out the travel after my return to the U.S.," said Fitzjames, somewhat apologetically. "I'd like a have a disk with a download of as much data as possible off of the Iranians' computers."

"Fushimi has, on a flash drive, placed the computer files that were the basis of the summary that I delivered to you prepared by Beltran and Ramos. We are prepared to hold the hardware in this office until we receive additional orders. Once again, I presumed that you would require the data but would not travel with the computers," offered Torres.

"Excellent work," said Fitzjames.

"This is the scan disk," said Torres, offering to Fitzjames the two-inch-long rectangular mechanism, a PNY 32-gigabyte high-speed flash drive. He accepted it with a nod of his head.

Torres continued.

"The driver who assisted this morning, Antonio Marco, will provide transport. He is waiting for you below. Your luggage is with him. He also has the further details for you for passing through Aruba to Miami, including the travel documents. I will take you to him now."

Torres led Fitzjames out of his office through the accumulated cigarette smoke. When they reached the elevator, Mariana Lurdes approached. She carried a file that she presented to Torres. He received it and paused. He recognized that she wished to speak to Fitzjames.

"Bien hecho, señor, y mucho gusto," she said.

"Gracias a ti, para todos," Fitzjames replied.

"Buena suerte," she added embarrassingly. Her fondness for Fitzjames was apparent and awkward.

"Gracias por su calida hospitalidad y la misma a tu hija y nieto," continued Fitzjames warmly.

"De nada, señor," she said and receded.

Fitzjames and Torres descended in the elevator to the ground floor. After the elevator door opened and they stepped off, Antonio Marco greeted them with a quiet hello. Fitzjames acknowledged the greeting. Torres was silent but turned, placed the cigarette that he held between the first and second fingers of his right hand into his mouth in order to free that hand, and offered the hand to Fitzjames. Fitzjames accepted the offer, and the two men shook hands.

"We will hope that another visit to Venezuela for you will not be necessary," suggested Torres with the cigarette dangling from his lips. He smiled.

"Only for vacation, if they'll ever allow me to pass through security," responded Fitzjames cynically. He too smiled faintly.

"Both our countries have been improved by your mission here. Recall, I am a patriot, like my father," offered Torres, dragging on the Belmont and then removing the cigarette from his mouth and exhaling the smoke. "We, the patriots, will change Venezuela. I am their leader. Give me five years, and America will see a change in this country."

"I'm certain of that. Good luck and thanks," said Fitzjames.

The two parted, and Fitzjames followed Antonio Marco to the car. Once inside, Antonio Marco presented a bundle of documents to Fitzjames. As they began the short journey to Puerto Carayaca, Fitzjames reviewed the materials, in particular the entry documents to pass into Aruba, which included a mock Venezuelan passport with his photograph and a fictitious identity, Diego Hidalgo, and the details for the American Airlines flight out of Aruba.

Antonio Marco drove at a reasonable speed, unlike his countrymen, and they arrived at the destination without incident and without interference. Antonio Marco pulled the vehicle off of the *Carrera Principal La Salinas* into the seaside brush approximately one mile eastward of Puerto Carayaca's entrance. The avenue, which is known by various names, parallels the northern coastline of Venezuela out of Caracas toward Colombia to the west.

The two men stepped out of the automobile, and Antonio Marco opened the trunk and extracted Fitzjames' suitcase and backpack. Fitzjames took the backpack from the driver and put it over his left shoulder. But Antonio Marco insisted upon carrying the suitcase, like a valet, to beach. They walked through the brush and onto the beach. Fitzjames observed a Sea Ray 270 SLX speedboat floating in the surf fifteen yards from the shoreline. Antonio Marco waded into the ocean, suitcase held above his head, and placed the suitcase on board. He had kept it dry. Fitzjames adjusted the backpack and followed, and of course his trousers were soaked. Although offered assistance by one of the two men on the vessel, he refused it and hoisted himself over the side and onto the deck, with the backpack, now hanging from both shoulders, strapped to this back.

The captain engaged the engine, turned the boat abruptly, and directed the craft north and westward and out to the open sea. After reaching a point two miles off the coast of Venezuela, the captain increased the speed of the Sea Ray to its full capacity. Within a space of time much shorter than Fitzjames expected, the deckhand advised him that they were nearing Aruba. Fitzjames got to his feet and observed, over the bow of the boat, land in the distance.

Fitzjames opened the suitcase and extracted a dry pair of pants, socks, and shoes, along with two plastic bags. He slipped to the back of the vessel, removed his black Oxfords, which the saltwater had likely destroyed, along with the socks, and placed them in one of the bags. He unfastened the belt around his waist and peeled off the wet trousers. His underwear was dryer than he had expected and not uncomfortable, a condition for which he was grateful. He folded the trousers into a tight bundle and dropped them into the second bag. He pulled on a dry pair of Wrangler blue jeans, Drymax white ankle-cut athletic socks, and Asics GT-2170 running shoes. He threaded the belt through the loops of the jeans and buckled it. He positioned the two plastic bags into segregated pockets at the bottom of the suitcase and closed and locked the case.

The captain approached De Palm Island on Aruba from the southeast and brought the boat around the southern tip of the island. In the sea to the west off of De Palm Island at its southern extremity, the Sea Ray came alongside another vessel, a Wellcraft 210 Sportsman. A man of clearly mixed African and native Caribbean ancestry sat at the controls and did not respond to the approach of the Sea Ray until the two boats were side by side.

Fitzjames put the backpack over his shoulder and clutched the suitcase. Although again the deckhand offered assistance, Fitzjames refused it and thanked him for the transport, as he moved from the larger boat to the smaller. Once on board and before Fitzjames could take a seat, the operator of the Wellcraft had engaged the Mercury outboard motor and was in route the short distance to the Aruba Nautical Club. At the club and near the De Palm Island Ferry Terminal, the operator docked the Wellcraft and in good Spanish but colored with a Germanic accent, he advised Fitzjames that Fitzjames was to disembark and that after he passed through customs inside the terminal he would be greeted by name by his driver.

"*Por mi nombre?*" inquired Fitzjames incredulously.

"*Sí, señor, Hidalgo, por su nombre,*" he replied.

"*Muy bien, gracias,*" said Fitzjames.

Fitzjames entered the terminal building and approached a desk behind which sat an official in uniform and with a pistol on his hip. While nothing indicated that he was a customs official and while no signage directed Fitzjames to him, Fitzjames presumed that the seated officer could serve no other function. Once before the man, Fitzjames presented to him the mock Venezuelan passport. He glanced at Fitzjames, opened the passport to the photograph, flipped to a clean page of the back of the little book, and stamped it. He returned the passport to Fitzjames and thanked him in Spanish, with the same Germanic intonation as the Wellcraft boat captain.

Fitzjames passed through the terminal and then outside. After a few seconds, a very short, older man with a newspaper in his hand walked toward Fitzjames. He addressed Fitzjames warmly.

"*Señor Hidalgo, buenas dias,*" said the man.

"*Buenas dias,*" returned Fitzjames.

"*Vamos al carro, señor,*" said the man.

Consistent with the plan detailed by Torres, the man drove Fitzjames from the entrepot to the Reina Beatrix International Airport and delivered him to the gates for American Airlines. He pleasantly, in Spanish, wished Mr. Hidalgo a good, safe journey and suggested that he call on him in the event that Mr. Hidalgo were ever again in Aruba. With an obsequious smile, he presented a business card to Fitzjames. Mr. Ruud Vlaar offered private transport and extended tours of Aruba. Fitzjames expressed his gratitude and exited the vehicle and entered the airport.

Unremarkably, he checked in for the flight as Diego Hidalgo, the Venezuelan national, passed through security, and waited the remaining two hours for boarding and departure. After a flight of two hours and forty-five minutes, the Boeing jet touched down at Miami International Airport.

Thirty-One

"Welcome to the United States, Mr. Hidalgo," said the U.S. Customs and Immigration officer to Fitzjames, after Fitzjames had waited the ninety seconds for the officer, duly equipped with a sidearm, to examine and stamp the Venezuelan passport. The officer returned the passport to Fitzjames.

"Thank you, sir," said Fitzjames with a feigned Spanish accent over his English reply. Fitzjames had discovered years earlier that his capacity to imitate the English spoken by a native speaker of Spanish was broad; the skill came from his capacity to speak Spanish without an accent, although a native English speaker.

He passed through three short corridors and thereafter to the luggage carrousel. He identified and collected his suitcase and passed down a fourth corridor beyond another customs officer, who held a black Labrador retriever on a short metal leash. The dog applied its keen sense of smell to each piece of luggage in order to root out drugs. Fitzjames proceeded through this final passenger survey without, of course, incident. Once outside the international transit area and among the general public, Fitzjames extracted the mobile telephone from the backpack. He placed a call.

"Are you in Miami?" replied the call's recipient, in lieu of a greeting or other acknowledgment. The voice was cold.

"Yes, sir. I arrived about a half-hour ago. Passed through customs without incident on a Venezuelan passport," said Fitzjames. "I came in via Aruba."

"Excellent. I understand through our CIA contacts that you've got a flash drive that contains data connected with the Venezuelan operations," said Fuller.

"Yes, sir."

"Well, we need that data delivered to Pittsburgh and to the research team there, where you made initial contact. That team has nearly broken through the coding sequences to beat this thing, and there's agreement that the data on that flash drive may just push them over the edge to success. You're to fly to Pittsburgh immediately," said Fuller.

"Would it not make sense, sir, with all due respect, for me to get to the local FBI office, download the contents of the disk there, and have it transmitted to the scientific team in Pittsburgh," offered Fitzjames diffidently.

"Thank you, Captain. No. The decision has been made here that the data is more secure in your personal possession and with your personal delivery of it," responded Fuller. "Am I clear?"

"Certainly, sir," answered Fitzjames.

"You're to go to the Southwest Airlines ticket counter. A ticket has been pre-purchased for you under your name. They'll have it for you. You'll need to move along. By my calculation, Captain, you've got less than one hour to the flight's departure," said Fuller.

"Very well, sir. Are there any additional orders?" inquired Fitzjames.

"None. Contact me upon your arrival in Pittsburgh. It's irrelevant what time of night it is. You'll get additional instructions then," said Fuller.

"Thank you, Major," said Fitzjames by way of goodbye.

Fitzjames placed the telephone in the back pocket of the blue jeans and studied the airport's signage in order to locate the Southwest Airlines ticket counter. Despite the time of night, the terminal was crowded with passengers and visitors, all of whom were speaking languages as varied as Arabic and Chinese, along with English, Spanish, German, and French. Within five minutes, Fitzjames had found the airline counter and stood before a friendly young woman in a Southwest Airlines purple polo shirt and khaki Bermuda shorts.

"How may I assist you?" she asked, while smiling broadly.

"My name is Fitzjames. I believe there's a ticket for me to Pittsburgh being held at the counter."

"One moment, sir," she said and studied the computer monitor. "Yes, sir, we have it. May I see some identification, please?"

"Yes, certainly. Of course. Sorry, I'm a bit tired and flat. Long day of traveling," said Fitzjames, as he searched the backpack for his wallet and driver's license. His preference was, in this circumstance, to use the license rather than the passport. A passport might inadvertently convey more detail than he wished to disclose. He continued, "Here we are."

"Thank you, Mr. Fitzjames. We can also check your bag here, too. Just put it here on the scale next to the counter," she said.

He positioned the suitcase on the metal plate, as instructed, and waited for her to print a boarding pass and a luggage tag. She applied the tag to the handle of the suitcase.

"Here you are," she said, as she presented to him a boarding pass and duplicate luggage tag. She also returned the license to him. "You'll need to hurry and get through TSA security. The gate number is noted on the boarding pass. Just go down the hall and turn right. You'll see the signs for the gates and security."

"Thanks," he said.

"Oh, you're welcome," she replied, again with a sincere smile that revealed a perfect set of white teeth. "Have a good night and a good flight."

"Thanks," he repeated and turned to begin negotiating through the mass of people to the entrance to the gate.

Fitzjames, in part, retraced his steps of only moments earlier. He found the signage overhead that directed him to the very gate he sought. He moved through security and body scanning without delay and without pointless interference. He was grateful that unlike the elderly woman in front of him in the line through security, he was not singled out for an arbitrary pat-down by the TSA officers. He, by appearance and demeanor, was clearly more of a threat to the safety of an airline than an octogenarian female who limped and may have been affected by osteoporosis. But the TSA had other profiling standards. He shook his head, as he sat down to tie his shoes, in contemplation of the real risks the TSA was simply too inept to identify. Certainly, the shoulder harness that had concealed the Ruger that he had used in Venezuela and left behind in Torres' office before departing for Aruba, which was folded and stored in his backpack, might have attracted some TSA officer's attention when the backpack passed under x-ray examination.

Fitzjames migrated, with the other passengers, to the gate and arrived as the first set of travelers in the A-1 through A-30 boarding group filed down the jetway and to the plane. Shortly thereafter, in the C boarding group, Fitzjames too boarded. Three hours later and just prior to midnight, the flight landed in Pittsburgh. Despite the heavy rain and thick clouds, the pilots had had little difficulty bringing down safely the Boeing 737.

Fitzjames duplicated this arrival in the Pittsburgh International Airport with his arrival to the same locale days earlier. He secured his suitcase in baggage claim and took a taxi to the same hotel. To his surprise and mild embarrassment, Cindy Polanski was on the night shift.

"Trey, you're back and so soon after your last visit," she said with such familiarity and excitement that Fitzjames felt compelled to suppress a laugh.

"Thanks, Cindy. I appreciate the enthusiasm. But I've traveled all day, it's late, and I don't have a reservation. Can you find something for me, please?" he asked. Then, he added, "Quickly."

"Sure, of course," she replied in a friendly but moderated attitude. She had received the signal.

"Thank you," he followed.

"We have 108, just down the hall, this floor. Do you need two double beds? That's what it has," she said.

"Doesn't matter. I'll take it. Here's my credit card," he responded.

He placed the plastic card on the desktop, and Cindy accepted it with a subtle display to Fitzjames of her latest manicure and of the rings on her fingers. He ignored it.

"Please sign here and you'll be all set," she said while at the same time presenting to him an occupancy agreement on a single sheet of paper.

He signed the paper and waited an additional thirty seconds for her to program two plastic keys. Upon receipt of the keys and the return of the credit card, he thanked her and walked intently to Room 108. He entered the room, dropped the backpack and suitcase on the first bed, and pulled out the mobile telephone.

"Evening, sir," he said.

"Evening? It's early morning, Captain," replied Fuller.

"Yes, sir."

"In Pittsburgh?" asked Fuller.

"Yes, sir, at the hotel. Same one. Near the hospital."

"Good. Contact Owen Hughes of the FBI. Same protocol. He'll sort out your meeting tomorrow morning with Dr. Reimer's team. You'll remember her name from your initial visit to Pittsburgh," said Fuller.

"Yes, sir, of course," said Fitzjames.

"I'm uncertain whether you'll meet with Dr. Reimer or with some other member of her team, but Hughes will sort out the details," said Fuller.

"Yes, sir."

"Goodnight, Captain. I'll look forward to your report tomorrow," said Fuller.

"Goodnight, sir," said Fitzjames. He did not await a response, perhaps somewhat disrespectfully. He was tired and did not have the patience for more dialog in a monotone. He also presumed that Fuller had ended the call before he had, and if he had not, Fuller very probably did not sense any disregard by Fitzjames of the usual deference he showed to his superior.

Fitzjames opened the suitcase, removed the kit containing toiletries, and got out of his clothes. He showered and brushed his teeth. He pulled on the pants from a set of pajamas and a white Hanes t-shirt and turned back the spread and bedsheets. He set the alarm feature of the Breitling, extinguished the lamp light on the small table next to the bed, and instantly fell asleep.

At 5:30 A.M., the wristwatch alarm awoke him. After turning on the lamp light anew, he changed out of the pajama pants and put on running socks and running shoes and athletic shorts and left the hotel room for the fitness center. He completed a forty-minute tempo run on the treadmill, which renewed him, inasmuch as he had not had the opportunity to exercise over the preceding few days. The assignments exhausted him psychologically and often physically. Yet the labor was not the equivalent of a deliberate run. After stepping from the treadmill, he took a clean towel from among the shelves of towels in the fitness center, wiped his face and neck; drenched in his own perspiration, he returned to the hotel room.

After a cold shower, he dressed and contacted Owen Hughes. It was 6:45. Hughes answered the call after the fifth ring. Fitzjames was concerned that his memory of Hughes' number had failed him because of his delay in answering. Fitzjames was wrong.

"Good morning, Trey," said Hughes.

"Morning, Owen. Nice to speak to you again," replied Fitzjames.

"Likewise."

"I'm ready to meet you, if you're ready."

"I can be ready in less than a half-hour. I'll meet you at the hospital, say 7:15 to 7:30. Okay?"

"Fine. Good. I'll see you there," said Fitzjames.

Fitzjames put on a blazer and gathered his wallet, room key, and the flash drive and, with his mobile telephone already in hand, glanced at his appearance in the mirror and left the hotel room. He poured a cup of coffee at the station for guests in the hotel lobby. As he passed the front desk, Cindy Polanski was engaged in a desk clerk shift change with her fellow employee, the nighttime C shift yielding to the morning A shift. She was undeterred.

"Good morning, Trey. Sleep well?" she inquired in an eager, genuinely interested tone.

"Yes, Cindy, I did. Thanks. Off duty now?" he asked.

"Yeah. I've got to get to class in a few minutes. Otherwise, I'd suggest that we go to Panera for breakfast."

"Class—after being up all night? That won't be easy. Good university lecture is certain to put you to sleep," suggested Fitzjames. He grinned.

"It'll be okay. I'll have two cups of strong coffee. Keep awake for another few hours. Oh, well, I'll see ya tonight, perhaps, when I come back in to work."

"Perhaps so. Have a good day, then," he offered and walked out of the sliding double doors of the hotel into the frigid morning air. Rain was falling in a light mist.

Fitzjames finished the coffee, dropped the empty cup in a trashcan, and ran slowly through the inclement weather to the hospital. He had no umbrella. Once inside, the receptionist greeted him and suggested that he could find a towel inside the men's restroom if he were wet. He thanked the receptionist, entered the bathroom, found a clean and laundered towel, and dried his face and touched the towel lightly to the blazer to collect the water. Because the rain had not been heavy, his clothes were not drenched. He concluded that the remaining fifteen minutes before Hughes would arrive would be adequate for him and his clothes to dry. The hospital's heating system, which was in use, would also contribute. He was correct. When Hughes did arrive, at 7:30, he showed no remaining signs of having been caught outside in the rain unprotected.

"Hello, Trey. Welcome back to Pittsburgh," said Hughes, offering his right hand.

"Thank you. Pleasure to be back," said Fitzjames, shaking Hughes' hand firmly.

"Let's go upstairs. I've already phoned Bruce Greenbaum and advised him of our visit and your return," said Hughes.

Hughes greeted the receptionist and led Fitzjames beyond her station to the elevator. They ascended and met Greenbaum as they stepped off the elevator. He was waiting for them. The receptionist had called to alert him.

"Good morning, gentlemen, Agent Hughes. Nice to see you again, Captain Fitzjames. Let's go together to the lab. I'll take you down."

The three men entered the elevator and descended to the level on which the laboratory was housed. They exited the elevator and were greeted by a young man in a white lab coat. In cursive script on the left breast of the coat, Fitzjames read the name of the scientist, Paul Grassa. Fitzjames found his surname humorous, as *grassa* was Italian for fat. Dr. Grassa was very thin.

"Good morning, Dr. Grassa," said Greenbaum.

"Good morning, Mr. Greenbaum," responded the scientist, formally and stiffly.

"I believe Mr. Fitzjames here has some data for you. This is Mr. Fitzjames. And, this is Mr. Hughes," said Greenbaum.

"Good morning. Mr. Fitzjames, we understood that you were coming in. Dr. Reimer will be along in a moment to greet you. She told me that she would like to see you. Do you have the data?" asked Grassa.

"Yes. It's on this jump drive," said Fitzjames, presenting the scan disk to Grassa. "I hope it helps you. A lot of effort went in to procuring it."

"Thank you. Let's see," said Grassa.

He accepted the flash drive and returned to the area at which the other scientists were at work. At the very instant that Fitzjames was prepared to suggest that Hughes, Greenbaum, and he find some comfortable place to sit and wait for the team to do its work, Stacy Reimer emerged from an office beyond the research area. She was pale, thin, and slow in her movements. But, to Fitzjames, she was as impeccably dressed and groomed, and as lovely as the first time that he saw her. She spoke first to him.

"Hello, Captain Fitzjames. It's so nice to see you again."

Thirty-Two

"Would you, Bruce, mind if I spoke to Captain Fitzjames alone for a moment?" asked Stacy with a certainty of purpose that did not suggest that she would tolerate any objection.

"Uhh…why, certainly, Stacy. Why, I've got some research updates for Agent Hughes that I could share with him in my office. I thought Captain Fitzjames would want to see them as well," said Greenbaum.

"I'm certain there'll be plenty of time for him to see them too. I won't take more than a few minutes. Do you mind?" she continued.

"Not at all, not at all," said Greenbaum awkwardly. "Owen, let's go back to my office and leave Dr. Reimer with the captain."

"Fine. Happy to accommodate," offered Hughes with a slight snigger.

Greenbaum and Hughes returned to the elevator. They did not speak; they simply complied with the physician's request. Neither perceived that resistance would have served any purpose. Dr. Reimer was accustomed to compliance. When they had entered the elevator, Fitzjames spoke to her.

"I feel very special. You dismissed the two of them with great expertise and skill," said Fitzjames with a broad grin.

"I can be very determined," responded Stacy, returning the smile. "I had to be direct. Sometimes with Bruce, he's a little slow in picking up your intentions if you don't paint the picture for him or if you mince words. I'm not really, typically, so aggressive or direct."

"Really?" he inquired.

"Yes, really. Although I may be becoming so," she suggested.

"Well, then I'll prepare for myself."

"You should," she said, again smiling. "Let's walk down the hall and we can talk."

Fitzjames and Stacy began the walk together along a long, broad, cold hospital corridor. It was quiet, and Stacy walked slowly. Fitzjames noted her dress. She wore her lab coat over a white silk blouse and herringbone skirt. A thin black leather belt around her waist matched the black Sarah Flint black pumps on her feet. The gold necklace around her neck was the duplicate of the bracelet on her right wrist. As she had been when they first met, Fitzjames found her beautiful and alluring. Her strength of character amplified her attractiveness. She was a striking woman.

"Have you made a full recovery?" he asked.

"I'm sorry?" she replied.

"Have you fully recovered?" he inquired.

"You knew I was ill?" she asked, surprised.

"Yes. I had called and learned that you had gotten sick. Are you okay, now?"

"Yes, I suppose. You could probably see that I've lost some weight. This skirt I'm wearing today even feels a bit big on me," she responded with a giggle.

"I could see it. But you look lovely; you are lovely," he said, surprising himself with his directness.

"That's rather forward, Captain, and I'm not feeling particularly attractive because of the weight loss," she said.

"You look great. Are you okay? You didn't answer that question," he said, as they continued their walk along the corridor.

"Again, very forward, Captain—pressing questions on me, commenting about my appearance. I don't know what to make of this," she responded with a light laugh and looking at his face.

"Look, I'm worried about your health," he said.

"Does it really matter?"

"Of course it does. It's critical."

"Critical to whom? The government? Your bosses? Are they afraid of losing their lead scientist? Will they have to find another? How much time will be lost? How much more money will have to be spent? How many more deaths will occur?" she asked sardonically.

"Stacy, my question is personal and not disingenuous. I'm not making a professional inquiry. I'm worried about your health," he said gravely.

"A genuine personal interest, then?" she inquired, returning to the tone of familiarity.

"Completely."

"Fine. I'm still recovering. But I'll be fine."

"Yet you're back at work?"

"This science is important, and I do lead this team. I'm in the business of saving lives. Do you realize that hundreds of people have died? In Pittsburgh and Kansas City alone, we've had four hundred and forty deaths. I don't have time to be ill," she said, her voice slipping back to gravity.

"I respect your commitment. It's commendable," he returned.

"It's necessary. I don't want any praise or any special commendation. I don't want one of your superior's medals."

"I get that. That's two quips directed at the U.S. Government, by my count. I can also appreciate that you're probably exhausted by its regular pressing of you for reports," he offered.

"The government is oppressive and unreasonable and slow to cut a check to pay for the services it expects to be completed at record speed with certain, defect-free results. I'm tired of it and its minions. I'm doing this job to save lives and help people, not for any political cause. I'd be much happier if a private organization had sponsored our work," she said.

"I understand. I'm no minion, and my interests at this stage are wholly genuine and wholly personal. I've completed my assignment. When I delivered that flash drive, my assignment, for all intents and purposes, ended. Now my focus can return to personal matters and personal interests. I even thought about my law practice this morning as I walked to the hospital. I haven't thought about practicing law since the assignment began. I'm returning to normal. And, among my personal interests that have bubbled to the top of my mental list are Stacy Reimer and her health. That may be too forward. You may not care one wit for me or have any interest in me. But I'm very comfortable in admitting to you that I do care for you, and I care about you. My self-respect and stature are not diluted or threatened by my telling you so. I find you beautiful, intelligent, interesting, and engaging. So there it is," he said.

"That's quite a speech, Trey Fitzjames. Very impressive. You sounded like an advocate."

"It was advocacy. And the fool that I am as my own client, I hope, made his point. I'd like to take you to supper tonight, if you can get away."

"My social calendar, of late, has been pretty light," she said.

"We could go back to Cruet, if you like. That's a great place and reasonably safe," he suggested.

"That would be nice. But how'd you like to have dinner at my apartment? I could fix something that I think you'd enjoy. How about at seven tonight?" she asked.

"I don't want you to have to cook," he objected.

"It's no problem. I'll do something simple, and it'll be fun to do it. I'm a good cook," she responded.

"I'm certain you are," he said.

"Seven o'clock, my apartment. When we walk back to my research station, I'll scribble down the address for you. We should probably go back."

"That's great, provided you're being required to cook isn't too much."

"It's not. Again, it'll be relaxing and fun. I need that," she said, as she swung 'round to return to the research station and back down the corridor.

They said little more until they returned to the area near the elevator, where Hughes and Greenbaum were waiting. Stacy excused herself and reappeared a moment later with a small sheet of notepaper that had been folded in half. She presented the paper to Fitzjames, without comment. He accepted it, without comment. Stacy spoke to Hughes and Greenbaum.

"Bruce, I completed a short report last night that I can turn over, as completed, to you and to Agent Hughes. Of course, it'll likely be stale by the end of the day, if the data furnished by Captain Fitzjames proves valuable."

"I understand. That'll be great," replied Greenbaum.

"Follow me to my office and I'll print off a couple of copies," she said.

"Very good," said Hughes.

"I won't need to participate. I'll leave this stage to you, Owen. I'll contact you later, as needed. My folks may ask me to get with you again. I leave town tomorrow. I'll head back to the hotel. If for some reason you need me, just call me," said Fitzjames.

"Fine, fine," said Hughes.

Fitzjames wished them all a good day and stepped away toward the elevator. He watched the three stroll down the same corridor. He caught himself inadvertently studying Stacy's figure as she walked. He could discern, even through the cover of the lab coat, an athletic, tightly proportioned body. He collected himself, shook his head, and turned and faced the closed door of the elevator. An instant later, that same door opened, and he entered.

Fitzjames left the hospital and returned to the hotel and the hotel room. He extracted the laptop computer from the backpack, connected the power cord to the device and to the outlet on the wall above the desk, turned on the computer, and waited until it invited him to apply a passcode. Once logged in, he navigated to a secure site that required a second passcode, which he hammered on the keypad. After access was granted and his identity confirmed, he typed a brief memorandum recounting the events in Venezuela, describing the number of dead by his estimation, and providing the identities of the individuals he eliminated in connection with the completion of the assignment. He reviewed the contents of the memorandum, made two additions and three corrections, was satisfied, and then forwarded the memorandum to Major Fuller.

After shutting down the computer and returning it to the backpack, he left the room and at the front door of the hotel haled a taxi. He had much of the day ahead of him and no obligations or commitments until the evening. He spent the late morning and early afternoon walking the campuses of the University of Pittsburgh and of Carnegie Mellon University. Despite the cold and light rain, he visited the William Pitt Union, the Cathedral of Learning, and the Carnegie Museum and Library at the University of Pittsburgh. Later, he walked up and long Forbes Venue to Carnegie Mellon University and entered the Miller Gallery and then the Parnell Center for the Arts. He concluded the stop with a slow walk around The Cut. He had arranged with the cab driver to be picked up at the corner of Forbes and Morewood Avenues at 2:00. The remaining time before 2:00 he spent in the University Center at a café, where he purchased a cup of coffee, a bottled water, a fruit yogurt, and a mixed green salad. He sat, ate the food, drank the coffee and water, and left to meet the taxi.

Fitzjames asked the driver for suggestions for sites in Pittsburgh and explained that he had three hours of time to devote to the city. He further indicated that he would willingly pay the driver to serve as a guide, if they could agree upon a price. The driver contacted the dispatch, described the situation to the supervisor, and received his blessing. The driver and Fitzjames concluded an understanding for a fee of $125.00.

Until 5:00, the driver drove through the streets of Pittsburgh and enthusiastically identified and colorfully described the buildings, the churches, the homes, the parks, and other landmarks, including Polish Hill, Heinz Stadium, and the National Aviary. The driver insisted that Fitzjames visit the John Heinz History Center and waited patiently in the taxi, while Fitzjames spent sixty minutes inside the museum.

At 4:45, the driver delivered Fitzjames to the hotel. Fitzjames paid the negotiated fee, and the driver attempted to return $20.00 to Fitzjames because the tour had ended under the three-hour timetable. Fitzjames refused the money and pointed out to the driver that, from outside the taxi, the real fare, given the scope of the tour and the depth of the driver's local knowledge, warranted a fee of twice what had been asked.

Fitzjames returned to the hotel room, took off his damp clothes, put on the running shorts, fresh t-shirt, socks, and running shoes, and returned to the fitness room for a second run. He spent twenty-five minutes on the treadmill at a relaxed pace. After the run, he lifted dumbbells for an additional thirty minutes. The bench presses, shoulder presses, lateral raises, and curls took him to near exhaustion, which was his goal.

After the exercise, Fitzjames shaved and showered and dressed himself in the few pieces of quality causal clothing that he had, none of which had been worn in Venezuela. The trousers were Armani charcoal textured dress pants; the shirt was a Robert Talbot blizzard blue cotton front-button sport shirt with a cutaway collar, and the shoes were Ermenegildo Zegna dark khaki lace-up blucher style. He felt well groomed and well dressed. He had applied only a small amount of *Gucci Guilty Pour Homme eau de toilette* and thus did not sense that the fragrance was too strong. He surveyed himself in the long mirror across from the bathroom and was not dissatisfied. He draped the jacket over his left forearm and left the room. As he had earlier in the day just outside the hotel lobby, he signaled to a waiting taxi. He entered the back seat of the cab and presented to the driver the note on which Stacy had written her address.

"Hmm, not far," grumbled the driver, disappointed at the lack of distance.

"They'll be additional travel involved. I need a bottle of wine. I need for you to run by a liquor store that has a wine selection so I can grab something. Is there one nearby?" asked Fitzjames.

"Uh, hmm, let's see. Yes, sir, I believe there's a liquor store just beyond the complex where this apartment is located. I'll run you by there and then I'll double back with ya," said the driver in a typical local accent.

The taxi negotiated the traffic, which was light, and pulled into the parking lot of a large store with a neon sign indicating its status as a wine cellar. Fitzjames purchased a bottle of Cloudy Bay Sauvignon Blanc from New Zealand and a bottle of Spanish Vina Herminia Rioja. The white wine was uninteresting but the red, being from Spain, did attract his attention.

Fitzjames returned to the cab, and the driver pulled out of the lot and onto the roadway slowly and drove even more slowly to Stacy Reimer's apartment. Notwithstanding the pace, the taxi did, ultimately, arrive at the destination. Fitzjames paid the fare, included a reasonable but not extravagant tip, and expressed his gratitude to the driver. Once he had the money, the driver mumbled his thanks and then shot out of the apartment complex with a newly discovered gear in the taxi. Fitzjames entered the building after greeting the bellman and took the stairs to the second floor and apartment 2E. He rang the doorbell and waited, both hands holding bottles of wine. No one answered. He rang the bell a second time. Finally, as he prepared to ring the bell again, the door opened.

"Come in, Trey," said Stacy with a smile.

Thirty-Three

Apartment 2E, like the building in which it was located, was luxurious. The floorplan was open and spacious and was furnished with fine wooden pieces from manufacturers, such as Baker's from its *Milling Road* collection and also McGuire. A number of items struck Fitzjames as being European imports. The accessories, including the wall hangings, were of the highest quality. Original art, including oils and watercolors, and black-and-white framed photographs were dispersed over the walls of the foyer and living room.

"Do you like it?" asked Stacy, when she observed that Fitzjames was studying the apartment after entering and being led from the entrance to the living room.

"It's very, very nice. I particularly like your furniture choices," said Fitzjames.

"Do you? Do you know something about furniture?"

"Well, a bit. I just know what I like in terms of style and design. Thereafter, it's all about price and getting to the style and design that you like within your budget."

"You seem to know a little bit about a lot of things, Captain Fitzjames," she said with a light laugh. "Would you like me to take those two bottles of wine; they look heavy."

"Sure. It'd be best to put them in the refrigerator for a few minutes. I didn't know what you were serving for supper. So, I got a red and a white."

He presented the bottles to her. She took them, and he followed her to the kitchen. She had changed out of her professional clothes and was wearing a Kay Unger printed chiffon wrap dress, which had a mix of animal prints in browns, black, and white. The dress was a cocktail style, cut low in the front and falling to a point two inches above the knees. Her shoes were black patent leather sandals from Jimmy Choo with a three-inch covered heel. Her hair had been reworked and curled slightly below the shoulders. She was beautiful, and the dress suited her, given her recent illness and loss of weight.

"I'm glad you like the apartment," she offered, when opening the door to the refrigerator.

"I do. It's really nice. The kitchen is as impressive. Granite countertops and something like Electrolux stainless-steel appliances," said Fitzjames.

"Actually, Bosch appliances," she responded.

"Very nice," he repeated.

"The food's a bit behind schedule. It's in the oven now," she said.

"I can smell it. Smells great."

"It's simple. A beef casserole. It's a German thing. I hope you'll like it. I've also got a tossed salad in the refrigerator," she said.

"That's terrific. The wine is optional. It's yours if you just want to hold on to it, or we can open it. The red is a Rioja from Spain and will probably work well with a beef casserole. I'm also in no rush to eat. A delay is no big deal," he said.

"It'll probably take another half-hour or so, maybe a bit less. I have to check it periodically. I was delayed getting home from the hospital."

"Really? Is that good or bad?" he asked.

"Good. I mean outstanding. The data you furnished, from wherever it was that you went, had the organic chemistry codes that we've been trying to tease out of the data we've collected. With that information, we can very certainly work up a remedy, either in an oral form or in a vaccine, to unravel this thing. You've probably saved thousands of lives. I hope your people give medals for work like that," she said with a confidence and satisfaction that he had not heard her express.

"That's great news," he said, somewhat despondently, and then continued. "And, no, they don't give medals to me and my sort until we're dead. At our funerals they say nice things and cover us in decorations, including an American flag draped over the coffin. Small comfort and consolation at that point. But hearing that the effort was successful is good news. I'm still a bit wound up, and that sort of report helps me unwind," said Fitzjames.

"Can you talk about what you do?" she inquired.

"No," he replied with a shake of his head. "And, you wouldn't like it or necessarily, I imagine, approve of it. I'm sorry that I haven't mentioned to you yet how lovely you look."

"Thank you, but you're changing the subject. You, too, I'll say, look very nice. You're a handsome man, Captain Fitzjames."

"Call me Trey, and if you must use my surname, *Mister* Fitzjames will do," he said, smiling.

"Mr. Fitzjames, the lawyer, right?" she asked, returning the smile.

"Yes. The lawyer. The lawyer who hasn't attended to his practice in some time and will likely pay a high price for being away."

"Why don't we stop talking in here in the kitchen and sit in the living room?"

"Fine," he agreed.

Fitzjames and Stacy sat together on a couch that was more appealing as a piece of art than as a place to sit. They talked about her medical practice and his day in Pittsburgh and later moved to a dining room table and continued the conversation over the casserole, salad, and red wine. No breaks or awkward pauses broke the flow of the discourse. The more that they talked, the more deeply Fitzjames found himself losing himself in Stacy Reimer. At the end of the meal, she stood and asked him to give to her his plate take to the kitchen.

"Are you going to take my plate, while I just sit here like the lord of the manor?" he asked.

"Well, you're my guest, after all. I'm also a traditionalist."

"That may be true, on both counts. But I'll clean my own mess and save you the trouble," he said and also stood and collected the plate and silverware and again followed her into the kitchen.

As he put the items in the sink over her left shoulder, she leaned into his chest. He could smell her hair and her perfume, which was a light floral fragrance. He kissed her lips and then kissed her neck below the left ear at the hairline. With her left hand on his hip and her right hand in his hair at the back of his head, she kissed him deeply and lovingly. They returned to the living room and an hour later moved, at Stacy's insistence, to the bedroom.

At 5:30 the following morning, while still dark outside, Fitzjames kissed Stacy Reimer, told her that he would call her later in the day from the airport, and left the apartment over her objections that he stay and allow her to prepare breakfast for him.

Rather than calling a taxi, he chose to walk through the cold to the hotel. The weather had cleared, the rain no longer fell, and the temperature had dropped. The distance to the hotel from the apartment was something more than a mile. But the weather made the walk easy, and he needed the time to sort out the previous evening and night. He shrugged off feeling irresponsible in having stayed with Stacy; the larger concern was the depth of emotion. Falling in love with women was the weakness in his armor. He struggled with the notion that he would be unable to do his job, when called upon, if he had to consider the effect of his death on a woman. He had ended untold numbers of relationships for that reason. This situation with Stacy was similar to others like it. Yet, something more was present here. He shook his head, recalled that he was getting older, and recognized that no woman could or should suffer the loss of a man, whom she loved, mysteriously and without explanation. Receiving a note after his death advising that he had died in the service of his country was small comfort.

At the hotel, as he expected, Cindy Polanski was on duty. She was energetic, despite having been on duty since 11:00 the previous night. She was inquisitive. Returning to the hotel at 6:00 in the morning before the sunrise, fully clothed, raises questions. He was friendly but also a bit frosty and told her he had to hurry because of a plane flight home. She released him with reluctance and not before asking him if he had enjoyed Pittsburgh's nightlife.

Once in his room, he undressed, shaved and showered, and then put on clean clothes, including Lee blue jeans and an Izod long-sleeved tennis shirt with a white t-shirt below it to keep him warm. He re-ordered the contents of his suitcase and closed it. He threw the backpack over his left shoulder and with the suitcase in his right hand left the room. In short order and, again, irrespective of Cindy's efforts to chat with him, he checked out of the hotel. A taxi took him to the airport.

Because he arrived three hours before his departure time on Southwest Airlines, once through security he purchased two local newspapers and *The Economist* magazine to spend the wait in reading. At 10:30, he pressed in Stacy's telephone number on the keypad of his mobile telephone. She did not answer and voicemail system engaged. He did not leave a message. He tried the cellular number that he had for her. She did not answer that call, and it too rolled to voicemail. He was unmoved. He repeated the exercise at 11:30 and was likewise unsuccessful. At 1:00, immediately prior to boarding the airplane, he called both numbers a third time. No response. He paused, considered that he may have misread the situation, and focused on dismissing it by concentrating his mind on the legal work he knew awaited him at his office.

Fitzjames took a seat on the airplane as a member of the last boarding group. He arrived in Orlando at 3:45. As he had no transportation, he considered the most efficient means of getting home. He elected to rent a car from Hertz. The process of procuring the vehicle was simple. Within an hour, he was in route to his home in a simple car, a Hyundai Accent. The automobile was unappealing, but he doubted that he would receive any objection to the cost of the rental when he submitted the reimbursement voucher.

The road trip to his home required ninety minutes. Upon turning into the driveway of the house, he examined its exterior. It was unchanged since his departure. His hometown had clearly received rain prior to his return; the Resurrection fern that grew wild in the oak trees was verdant and thick. The fern added color to the oak canopy that shaded the structure. The lawn man had also only just mowed the grass in the yard and edged the driveway, front walkway, and street line. The yard was also a deep green, thus reflecting rainfall. Subtropical regions of Florida disclosed by clues the weather patterns.

He shut off the engine of the rental car and climbed out and stretched his legs. He was stiff from sitting on the airplane and in the automobile. He removed the suitcase and backpack from the back seat. He locked the car doors, walked up the driveway and then along the walkway, unlocked and opened the front door, and entered the residence. The interior was warm and dark and had an odor of having been sealed for some extended period of time without human habitation. He turned on the light at the switch, after placing the suitcase on the red Mexican tile floor just inside the front entrance, and immediately lowered the temperature on the thermostat to seventy degrees in order to circulate air and reduce the temperature. He also switched on the ceiling fans.

He left the piece of luggage at the door and moved to the sofa and dropped the backpack. He unzipped the outermost pocket, found the mobile telephone, powered it on, and checked for voicemail messages. None had been left. He considered another call to Stacy but, upon rethinking the notion, chose not to do so. He left the telephone on the table adjacent to the sofa and walked through the living room to the kitchen. He opened a cabinet, removed a drinking glass, and filled the glass with water from the tap. The telephone chimed, as he finished drinking the water. He returned to the living room and, with some excitement, answered the call without reviewing the caller identification.

"Hello," said Fitzjames.

"Hello, Captain. I received your report," said Major Fuller.

"Yes, hello, sir," responded Fitzjames.

"You don't sound particularly satisfied with yourself after having done excellent work."

"I'm sorry, sir. I had not expected the call to be from you, with all due respect."

"Well, sorry to disappoint you," said Fuller coolly.

"No, sir, not at all, sir. I've only just returned home and am a bit worn out from the travel and labor. My apologies. I'm also a bit preoccupied with unattended legal work at my office. I did leave unexpectedly on the assignment, which always causes clients frustration," said Fitzjames diffidently.

"Understood. Okay. We'll see if we can do without you for a time. Let you get your civilian life back in order," said Fuller.

"Thank you, sir."

"You also need a rest."

"Yes, sir."

"Trey, this job was completed with a high level of expertise and success. I've looked good through this thing, and I thank you for that," offered Fuller.

"You're welcome, sir. I got a general report before I left Pittsburgh that the data on the jump disk that I delivered was what the scientists were looking for," said Fitzjames.

"That's wholly accurate. I received that confirmation mid-afternoon today."

"Good. Any other issues, sir?" asked Fitzjames.

"We're getting the usual and expected blowback from the Venezuelan government. Their embassy people are screaming. They also know your face. But they don't have any real, useful information. The local CIA affiliates disposed of the two Iranian scientists and they're claiming that you did that and that an international incident has occurred. All nonsense. We'll give the Venezuelans some bits and pieces to mollify them, maybe give them some names, and then they'll back down. They know how much oil we buy from them. They need the hard currency from the oil sales and can't jeopardize that lifeline. I don't care how much they squawk that China can be swapped out for the U.S. Also, they've got too many domestic political troubles to tarry over this matter for too long. They'll soon be distracted. You may also have, in the end, done the governing clique down there some real favors by removing some dangerous and ugly characters. They should be grateful," said Fuller with cynicism.

"Understood, sir."

"So, get back to being an attorney and doing whatever it is you do," suggested Fuller.

"I will, sir. Thank you."

"And get some sleep. You sound exhausted. I'll be in touch."

"Yes, sir. Goodnight, sir," said Fitzjames.

He ended the conversation and felt disquiet. Again, he was of two minds about whether to call Stacy. After a few seconds of contemplation, he tossed the telephone toward the backpack. The device bounced off the face of the backpack and came to rest on the sofa. He locked the front door, turned off the light, and went to bed.

During the following three days, Fitzjames' life returned to its normal order. He completed early morning runs, got into his office at 8:30, and did his job. Much of the labor was recovery work and assuaging clients' anxieties. Being out of the office, irrespective of the cause, creates challenges. Fitzjames worked through those challenges diligently. In the late afternoon on the third day after his return, he received a call at his office. The receptionist advised him that an Owen Hughes from Pittsburgh was on the line. Fitzjames picked up the receiver.

"Owen, how are you? I didn't expect to hear from you," said Fitzjames.

"Hello, Trey. Hope I'm not disturbing you," said Hughes.

"No, not at all. What can I do for you?" inquired Fitzjames.

"Trey, I just wanted to tell you how much our office appreciated your efforts. We really appreciated it. I also wanted to pass along some bad news, which you may not know," said Hughes somberly.

"What's that, Owen?"

"Trey, you may have been aware that Stacy Reimer had been sick, caused by some event related to the research she was doing. She had improved and was back at work. Well, she had a relapse and died two nights ago."

Closing

One week after learning of her death, Fitzjames attended the funeral in Pittsburgh of Stacy Reimer. During the service, he sat in the back of the sanctuary of a large Roman Catholic church. The ornate structure resembled a cathedral designed on a European model. Only many of the parishioners who attended the funeral wore Pittsburgh Steelers jackets, a distinctly American touch. The sanctuary was filled to capacity, and most of those in attendance, including many of the men, were moved by the priest's very personal homily. Most were crying.

Fitzjames avoided the few people whom he recognized and slipped out the door as quickly as he could at the conclusion of the service. He was in no mood, or condition, to talk with anyone. He procured a taxi as rapidly as possible, got to the airport, and was back in Florida by the evening.

After a poor night's sleep and an even worse morning run, Fitzjames arrived at the office. He felt haggard and disconcerted. But he went to work on a project of drafting an agreement between his client, the seller, and the purchase of a commercial complex. He found the labor and the required concentration therapeutic. As he neared the end of the crafting of an addendum to the contract, the firm's receptionist channeled in to the telephone in his office.

"Mr. Fitzjames?" she asked over the speaker.

"Yes. What is it?" he responded slightly impatiently. He disliked having his train of thought derailed.

"Mr. Fitzjames, two men have arrived who have asked to see you. They say that it's urgent," said the receptionist.

"Who are they? Did they give you their names? I'm not expecting anyone this morning," he responded. His tone was more tetchy than he had intended.

"They didn't give me their names. They look official. It's mysterious," whispered the receptionist.

"Okay. I'll be right out," he said.

Fitzjames completed the sentence that he had started and that had been interrupted by the receptionist's page. He put down the ink pen, stood, and walked briskly to the front desk. He was in no mood for nonsense and began framing, mentally, potential responses to the disruption. He opened the French door separating the interior of the office from the lobby and discovered two men whom he had never met. Both were heavily built, muscular, and wore the same crewcut hairstyle. Both were also badly dressed in pants and sport coats that appeared to come from discount stores or charity shops.

"I'm Trey Fitzjames. How can I help you?" he inquired. He studied both men, who stood together, shoulder to shoulder like a pillar.

"Mr. R. P. Fitzjames?" asked the taller of the two men.

"Yes. I'm R. P. Fitzjames," he replied.

"Sir, my name is Lars Lundquist, Deputy U.S. Marshal. This is Deputy U.S. Marshal McKay. Sir, we're under instruction to take you into custody, sir. Will you cooperate with us?" he asked mechanically.

"What? Taken into custody? On what charge?"

"Sir, we have a warrant for your arrest through the Venezuelan embassy," responded Lundquist.

"The U.S. Marshal's office is acting on behalf of a foreign embassy?" Fitzjames asked incredulously.

"Sir, will you come with us peacefully? We have our orders," interjected McKay.

"What's the charge?" demanded Fitzjames.

"Murder," mumbled Lundquist.

Fitzjames considered for a moment, said nothing, and turned around to be handcuffed. As he was led out of the office, he asked the receptionist to tell his partner, Mr. Peterson, what had transpired.